Praise for *Wolfbreed*

"Lilly lives in a w... wolves have to fight ... rooting for her from the very start. Before long, I was falling for her, too! *Wolfbreed* is a thrilling yet deeply moving journey that I never wanted to end."

—ROBERT MASELLO, author of *Blood and Ice*

"A mesmerizing story that entertained me thoroughly and moved me deeply. *Wolfbreed* is an exciting nonstop action-adventure involving the supernatural. More than that, though, it demonstrates how the human spirit, even when in a not-entirely-human body, can be transformed and redeemed by the power of love. I adored this book."

—MARY BALOGH, *New York Times* bestselling author of *First Comes Love*

"S.A. Swann has written a spellbinding fantasy of the Teutonic knights and the great Northern Crusade, set in a little-known period of history amidst the gloomy forests of Prussia and Lithuania. Vivid and visceral, dark and delicious, this one kept me turning pages from start to finish."

—GEORGE R.R. MARTIN, *New York Times* bestselling author of *A Feast for Crows*

Wolfbreed

S. A. Swann

BALLANTINE BOOKS
NEW YORK

A Spectra Trade Paperback Original

Copyright © 2009 by Steven Swiniarski

Published in the United States by Spectra, an imprint of
The Random House Publishing Group, a division of Random House, Inc., New York.

SPECTRA and the portrayal of a boxed "s" are trademarks of Random House, Inc.

Library of Congress Cataloging-in-Publication Data

Swann, S. Andrew
Wolfbreed / S.A. Swann.
p.   cm.
ISBN 978-0-553-80738-7 (pbk.)—ISBN 978-0-553-90688-2
(ebook)   1. Werewolves—Fiction.   I. Title.
PS3569.W555L56 2009
813'.54—dc22   2009003070

Printed in the United States of America

www.ballantinebooks.com

2 4 6 8 9 7 5 3 1

Text design by Diane Hobbing of Snap-Haus Graphics

This book is dedicated
to my wife, Michelle, for putting up
with me and this book.

ACKNOWLEDGMENTS

Lots of research goes into a book like this, and while I can't note every source, I would like to mention *The Northern Crusades*, by Eric Christiansen, which is probably the best English-language reference on this time that I had access to. I would also like to mention the Web site The ORB: On-line Reference Book for Medieval Studies (http://the-orb.net), which provided a number of translated primary sources, including the rules and statutes of the Teutonic Knights. Google Books was also a major help with finding various out-of-print resources from the nineteenth and early twentieth centuries, including *The History of Prussia* (vols. 1 and 2), by Captain W. J. Wyatt, and *Die altpreußischen Personennamen*, by Reinhold Trautmann. I would also like to thank my critique group, the Cajun Sushi Hamsters, whose members read parts of this before it had a real setting. I would like to thank my agent, Eleanor, for representing this and giving me a bunch of good suggestions, and my editor, Anne, for buying this and giving a bunch more good suggestions.

Last, and most important, I want to give credit to Lynn Okamoto, author of the manga and anime *Elfen Lied*, which provided the initial inspiration for this novel.

Wolfbreed

Prelude

Anno Domini 1221

In the darkest woods in Burzenland, south of the Carpathian Mountains, a knight of the Order of the Hospital of St. Mary of the Germans in Jerusalem, Brother Semyon von Kassel, ran as if he were in pursuit of the devil himself.

Mud smeared his mail, leaves and stray twigs poked out from tangles in his hair and beard, soot darkened his skin, and crusted blood smeared his face. His lips cracked and bled as he whispered a Pater Noster over and over. The scabbard for his longsword dangled empty at his hip, and in his hand he clutched a shiny dagger too ornate for one of his order.

He stared out at the dark woods with eyes wide, shiny, and hard.

Drag marks in the loam of the forest floor marked the trail he followed. Occasionally, tarlike smears of old blood marked a tree or an errant part of someone's armor. He had passed half a dozen remnants of his brother knights; helmets, gauntlets, boots, all marred by their knights' blood and occasional shreds of flesh or hair.

Half a dozen signs of his dead brethren Semyon had passed since he had burned a respect for the Lord God into the pagan priest who had bequeathed him the dagger in his hand. Semyon prayed that in the excruciation of the pagan's punishment, the man's lips had been compelled to speak the truth.

The beast he followed showed no impulse to hide its trail. Why would it? What fool would brave these woods against it? To confront a creature that hunted men the way a man would hunt a hare?

Eleven men it had killed. Eleven men armed with sword, shield, and the grace of God; eleven that would have been twelve if the master of his priory had not sent Semyon away alone to meditate on his sins.

Semyon's late master had chastised him for showing an impulse toward cruelty. Now Brother Semyon knew that the hand of God moved with him, because by meditating on his own cruelty he had been spared the cruel fate of his brothers.

He had left his decimated camp and hunted down the priest of the false pagan religion that infected this region. That priest had perished in his own sacred fire, but not before telling Semyon of the beast that had taken his brother knights.

Again, Semyon prayed that the pagan's last agonized breaths had whispered truth.

He followed the trail over a deadfall. Bone-gray branches clawed at him, tearing at his armor and his uncovered skin as he climbed past. On the other side he faced a clearing about fifty paces wide.

Past the clearing, opposite the deadfall, a dark hole sat at the base of a rocky mound projecting from the forest floor. The ground in front had been swept clean by travel in and out of the den. Semyon saw a human skull, cast aside a few paces away and half buried in a pile of dead leaves.

He clutched the dagger so tightly that his knuckles ached.

A growl resonated through the clearing, and every bird in the trees around him took flight at once, the beating of a thousand wings overpowering the beast's growl. Semyon braced himself and stared into the abyss of the burrow. A pair of eyes glinted back at him—

A nightmare of black fur and muscle erupted from the burrow. The monster was shaped in broad outline like a wolf, but a wolf that had aspirations to become a man. Even in the flashes as it attacked, Semyon saw perverse echoes of the human form in the way its head was attached to the torso, in the way its forelimbs ended in something like deformed hands, and in the way it was almost upright as it leapt at him. Its fangs glistened in its lupine muzzle and its near-human eyes burned with hate.

Semyon felt God's hand move his own as he brought the priest's ceremonial dagger up. The silver blade sank into the creature's throat, and Semyon pulled it across, tearing open windpipe, tendons, and arteries. Its muzzle snapped shut short of Semyon's own throat as hot blood gushed over his arm and face.

For a few moments, they stared at each other, the brother knight and the demon wolf. In its too-human eyes, Semyon thought he saw surprise. It shuddered, breath frothing from the wound in its neck.

Then it fell to the side, still.

Brother Semyon von Kassel, last survivor of his convent, had survived again. In Brother Semyon's mind, there was now no question of God's providence.

Not even when he heard the cry of a human infant coming from the dark hole of the dead creature's burrow.

Lauds

Anno Domini 1239

Os iusti meditabitur sapientiam,
et lingua eius loquetur iudicium.

The mouth of the righteous speaketh wisdom,
and his tongue talketh of judgment.

—Psalms 37:30

i

"Please?"

Manfried Hartmann did his best to ignore the voice that came from behind the heavy oak door. He stood at attention, on the opposite end of the corridor, shivering slightly. Even with his mail shirt and the padding underneath, he was still chilled by the damp, mildew-thick air.

But maybe chilled even more by the pathetic *weakness* of the woman's voice coming from the cell he was guarding.

It was hard not to see this guard duty as anything more than a punishment detail. Perhaps, in a more charitable moment, he could think of it as a form of mortification, his Teutonic masters seeing to it that his soul was purified through labor and obedience. Still, despite what the sergeant might say about "prisoners of a certain status," there was little about this that Manfried could see as particularly elevating. He certainly didn't feel any closer to God in this hole.

If he brought up the subject with one of the priests, or—Lord help him—one of the knights of the Order, Manfried knew from long and onerous experience that the answer he would get would involve prayer, penitence, and probably a long meditation on their Lord's suffering on the cross.

But, by God, if he wanted to say that many Pater Nosters he would have stayed in Lübeck and joined a monastery.

This wasn't to say that he hadn't spent five nights down here as a heathen, his back to God. But expecting a soldier to spend the entire night from Compline to Prime in silent contemplation of Christ was expecting a bit much.

A bit much, especially with a young woman's voice pleading with him. And thanks to this woman's keeper—province commander of the Teutonic Order, Landkomtur Erhard von Stendal—and his commandments not to talk to, or even look at, the prisoner, the boredom was maddening.

"Sir? Just a word? Some water?"

Perhaps the knights of the Order thought their soldiers would fear Hell more if they allowed them a foretaste.

This was not why Manfried had made the trek north. As the third son of a minor landgrave—very minor—he had only martial skills to trade upon. He had come to the wilds of Prûsa as a soldier of Christendom, to defend the church and win new lands and peoples to the way of Christ.

He told his mother that he would bring home honor for his family name, and possibly gain his own estate in the newly Christian lands of Prûsa. He had not thought his crusade might end in this dank corridor, breathing niter and mold, listening to the echoed pleas of some pagan prisoner. However, by the grace of God, here he was, standing in the bowels of a keep in a town that had honored the cross for eight years now, guarding a woman who barely had the energy to speak.

He wondered at what point he had annoyed God so much as to deserve this fate.

"Sir?" Her voice was weaker this time.

Even though he had been left here, grating under the command of the Prûsan converts left to man this keep, Manfried did know enough to remain obedient. While he had not taken the oaths of a religious order, and was absolved—by law if not by circumstance—from the binds of chastity and poverty, he was still bound by the tenet of obedience. Fealty was expected of all in service to the Order; priest and knight, serf and slave, religious and secular.

He was not to converse with the prisoner or approach the door.

Why this was so was none of his concern. He knew nothing of the prisoner other than rumors. All he really *knew* of her was her voice. He was never present to see anyone else approach the cell door to see that the prisoner was fed, or exercised, or questioned. He simply changed places with one man at Compline and with another upon leaving at Prime.

Her voice was quite young, just barely a woman's. It was also painfully dry, cracked, and becoming weaker with each passing day.

Manfried thought of his own sister, barely two years his junior.

The prisoner is probably her age . . .

Just the thought—comparing the unknown, unnamed woman to his younger sister—made him feel a sickness in his soul as black as the mold growing on the stone floor.

What has she done to place her here? Someone's sister? Someone's daughter?

This seemed unnecessary, even for a pagan. If the woman did not accept baptism, she should be granted death, or sold to some estate where she might be put to useful work. Abandoning her here seemed cruel and pointless.

There were the rumors, of course. Even though the Order frowned on gossip, some sins were just too minor to expend the effort to expunge.

Manfried had heard from several men who claimed to have talked to members of Landkomtur Erhard's retinue. The provincial commander had been en route northeast, toward Balga, pausing here in the fortified town of Johannisburg to leave this woman in

the care of this garrison. Everyone agreed that this was not originally Erhard's intent, as he was supposedly joining forces that were
massing for a spring assault in the wilds north of Warmia.

The general belief was that Landkomtur Erhard had been called
back to Marienwerder to meet with the Landmeister of Prûsa.

As to the girl he had left, theories abounded. Many thought
that she was some barbarian princess, taken as hostage to assure
that some pagan duke or captain took his baptism seriously. Others thought that she was being taken as some bribe to encourage
one tribe against another—since, unlike the Infidel in the Holy
Land, the pagan tribes inflicted wars as savage on each other as
they did upon the lands of Christendom. Yet others thought that
she was a reward for some great landed knight who had donated
land or men to the Order's mission.

Erhard's command not to speak to or approach the girl inspired
other rumors: she was such a beauty that any man who viewed
her would be instantly seduced and forced to free her; she was so
hideous that she might strike a man dead with a look; perhaps she
was rich enough to offer bribes or other favors.

The last one, Manfried thought, would be high on Landkomtur Erhard's list of concerns. The knights of the Order were as
concerned for the virtue of their servants as they were for their
own. And while they did not force secular soldiers to emulate their
brothers and sleep in common rooms that were perpetually lit to
prevent the concealment of sin, they did pay close attention to
their conduct.

Many of the men left in this garrison were converts, only a few
years Christian, and probably more than likely to accept, or simply
take by force, such inappropriate favors.

Such men did not take boredom well.

After a moment, Manfried reproached himself for feeling such
concerns. This woman was some unchristian pagan, serf or slave,
unbaptized and unworthy of such worries.

Also, these thoughts only served to increase his sense of unease. Developing sympathy for his prisoner was akin to showing mercy on the battlefield. He was a soldier. He had a duty. He had come here to serve God and the Order.

But down here, he didn't feel very close to God at all. He could be righteous facing a pagan army that slaughtered priests and burned churches—but a single girl?

He whispered a Pater Noster for strength of spirit.

When he finished, the words *sed libera nos a Malo* died in the still, fetid air, leaving silence behind.

The silence continued.

"What?" he whispered, instead of "Amen."

There was no answer; not even a whimper from behind the banded oak door that he was not permitted to approach.

His unease deepened. No one had told him what crimes this prisoner may have committed, or why she was so important. Only that, according to Landkomtur Erhard and Manfried's Prûsan sergeant, this was the most important post he would ever fill.

Still, she did not speak.

For four nights, her voice had been his constant companion down here, echoing off the damp gray stone; asking for water, asking his name, sometimes singing in a low voice he could barely hear. Sometimes in Prûsan, sometimes in German, never answered, but always talking.

Always.

It crossed his mind that if she died down here, his awful, tedious job would come to an end and they would have to find him something else to do. That thought, and the brief flash of cruel optimism it brought, made the sick feeling in his soul even blacker.

How horrible to die down here.

Several long minutes of silence passed, perhaps as long as a quarter hour, before he violated his first order.

"Hello?" he called out in Prûsan. He didn't know that language beyond a few words, so he asked in German, "Are you well in there?"

What a preposterous thing to ask, he thought as his query went unanswered. *He* wasn't well down here, and he was the guard.

But what if there was something wrong with the prisoner? If she was so important, shouldn't he do something?

He was within reach of the alarm cord, which would ring the bells for the watch. That's what he should do. He should sound the alarm.

But what if she's just sleeping?

Manfried was already looked down on by his barbarous comrades, his German blood a liability in the midst of the near-pagan community of this garrison. His duty here was intolerable as it was. Giving them an actual *reason* to look down on him? That would be positively excruciating.

And calling an alarm in error wouldn't only be embarrassing, it might result in a reprimand. Such a mistake might not concern his soul, but the Order was a military organization as well, possibly the best in Christendom, and they did not get to be so by tolerating such error, however well intentioned. He could lose the chance to serve as a proper soldier, and be trapped the whole season as a glorified prison guard.

But if something *was* wrong, that could just as easily result in the same fate. He knew enough of the world to know that when inconvenient things happened to important people, saying you had followed orders would not excuse you of being held responsible, no matter how unearned the responsibility.

Deep in the shadows he heard water drip with a sound barely louder than his own breathing. The quiet made the air feel that much heavier, the damp pulling the warmth from the skin on his face and hands.

He needed to know what was happening in the cell.

So he broke his second order.

The door was at the end of the corridor opposite Manfried's post, lurking in the shadows of a narrow vault where the flickering glow of the lanterns barely reached. The door was heavy oak, banded with iron. In the whole keep, only the main siege door was stronger.

Two lanterns kept his guard post lit. Manfried took one lantern from its brass hook and walked down the vaulted corridor, toward the door. It was heavy, the iron bands ocher with rust, studded with egg-sized rivets. A small iron hatch covered a window set at eye level. The flat slab of metal resisted his pulls, grinding with a metallic screech that set Manfried's teeth on edge. Flecks of corrosion fell from the little-used mechanism, dusting the backs of his hands and giving the appearance of some swamp-borne plague.

Does no one use this at all?

He looked through a square barred window that was barely two hands' breadths wide. Beyond, the cell was dark as a well.

"Hello?" he called into the dark, first in Prûsan, then in German.

"Please, help." Her voice spoke barely audible German.

Manfried lifted the lantern, opened its shutter as wide as he could, and held it up to the portal, shining light into the cell beyond.

He stared in for a long while before he finally whispered, "Jesus wept."

Sprawled facedown in filth that was unfit for a slaughterhouse was the young woman he had imagined. She was naked, her smooth white skin blemished by the filth she was forced to wallow in, her head hidden by a halo of hair that might once have been long and flowing, but was now defined by ragged layers of encrusted mats.

Seventeen, Manfried thought her age, perhaps eighteen at most. The same as his sister.

In response to the light, she stirred, raising her face from the floor to look at him.

"Please, some water."

Under the dirt, the face that looked up at him was smooth, unscarred by time or labor.

She had to be of noble birth. It was the only explanation for such unmarked hands, face, and skin. Even his sister, who had married well, had hands that were hard from maintaining a small house that wasn't landed enough to afford servants.

"Do they provide you with nothing?" Manfried muttered more to himself than to the prisoner. She appeared beyond hearing him. Her eyes were unfocused, their unusually deep green hue reflecting into a void that was invisible to him.

Her left leg trailed behind her, and that ankle was caked with blood and rust where a gray-black metal manacle had rubbed it raw. The blood was awful, and the stench worse, the foot swollen with infection and turned at a nasty angle. At some point she had broken the bone, and it looked as if she had collapsed in an attempt to walk toward the door.

The sight was so appalling that he never once considered the fact that he had never heard her cry out in pain.

"By Christ," he cursed, "is the Order not the Hospital of St. Mary?" Even an unrepentant pagan should not have her wounds fester without succor.

The manacle was connected to an iron chain that seemed more of a weight to anchor a drawbridge or lower a portcullis than something meant to restrain a girl half Manfried's size. Despite its weight, the chain was taut, leading back to a massive staple in the cell floor. Just tripping with that weight could have broken her ankle. As mortified as the flesh was, and how weak she appeared now, it could have happened days ago.

Manfried considered himself a hard man. He had never been one to wince at pain or blood. Pitched battle held no terror for him. But this?

This was not how women were treated.

They were Christians here; they were supposed to be better than the idolaters, better than those who sacrificed their women and infants to their demonic gods, better than those who preyed on the weak, pagan and Christian alike, only to aggrandize themselves.

But he wasn't looking upon the acts of a Christian.

He had no name for this kind of obscenity, but he was certain that it was at the hands of these half-pagan Prûsan brutes. His disdain for them flared into full-blooded hatred.

"Hold on, I'll get you some water."

Manfried forgot his orders. He might be a soldier serving the Teutonic Order, but he was also a human being.

ii

Sergeant-at-arms for the garrison of the Hospital of St. Mary of the Germans in Jerusalem at Johannisburg, Günter Sejod, awoke to a bell ringing. It took a moment for him to realize what it was.

The prisoner!

The other soldiers in the barracks were already stirring as Günter erupted from his bed and ran, dodging the other beds. In his head, he simultaneously prayed to Jesus Christ and to the old god Perkûnas. He pleaded to both that it was not the cell door, that it was some mechanical failure. Perhaps a rat gnawing the bell cord or maybe it was accidentally pulled by a weak-bladdered subordinate unable to hold his water until Prime.

"*No,*" Günter whispered as he stepped out the doorway.

Across the hall from the barracks, a niche was set in the wall with a series of bell ropes. This one for the general alarm, this one to call Compline, and this one to sound the opening of the cell door in the lowest levels of the keep.

The latter rope still moved, jerking up and down, causing an asynchronous clanging above him.

This was no accident, no animal gnawing the fibers.

Someone had broken Landkomtur Erhard's silver seals and had started opening the door. Günter grabbed the rope that signaled the main alarm.

Lord Christ, Father Perkûnas, have mercy on us all . . .

Günter had the feeling that he prayed, as always, to deaf gods.

The door was almost more than one man could open by himself. Manfried had to lean his whole body back to get it to move. It took several minutes just to open it wide enough to walk through and let some light in from outside.

He set his lantern down just beyond the threshold. He knew better than to bring a canister of flaming oil within reach of a prisoner, no matter how weak. With the same logic, he had already set aside his sword, his keys, and the ornate silver dagger that the sergeant had presented to him on Landkomtur Erhard's behalf.

The dagger was distressingly worldly, despite being engraved with Latin from the psalms. He knew that other men here, probationary brothers who wished to emulate the warrior monks of the Order, were distressed at being given such an ornate weapon, despite their vows to obey the dictates of their superiors in the Order.

Manfried didn't care a fig for its ornateness, or the precious metal. What bothered him was that silver made for an inferior weapon. He might have cared enough to raise the issue with the sergeant if he had expected to see battle. However, that seemed so unlikely that they could have armed him with a sausage, for all the difference it would make.

No lamp, no dagger, no sword—the only thing he was going to bring into the cell was a tin cup of water.

With the door open enough, he reached down and picked up

the water. Bending over, he saw what made the door such an effort to move. Something had caught between the flagstone and the lower edge of the door. It had scraped across the stone, leaving gray-white markings. Some sort of soft metal, lead perhaps. He stared, wondering what to make of it—

"Please?"

The voice had regained some of its strength. And it appeared that she could focus on him now. She gazed at him with shining green eyes, and he could see that she was actually quite a lovely creature under the filth. Tears had washed tracks of pure white on her cheeks, and as she pushed herself up, she folded her arms across her naked breasts.

Seeing that, Manfried thought that she might be afraid of him. She might think he was here to abuse her.

"No." He shook his head and held out the cup. "I brought you some water. See?"

She sniffed, as if he might have put something evil in the water. But then she smiled. Her teeth were small, white, and even—a sure sign of noble birth.

"Thank you," she whispered, holding out her hand for the cup.

He had to take a few steps forward, because the chain on her leg wouldn't let her reach that far. In fact, when she shifted her leg, the broken foot remained stationary. He winced, even though she showed no sign of pain.

When he reached her, she took his hand in hers. The joy he saw in her smile was absolutely glorious.

"Manfried! By all that is sacred, get out of that room!"

Hearing Sergeant Günter's voice filled Manfried with a barely containable rage. He spun around, arm still held by the young girl. "You pathetic, heathen bastard, treating a woman—"

The rage lapsed into confusion as he saw six soldiers in the hall, beyond the door, all clad in full mail and helmets, weapons bared. The soldiers milled about, looking confused, as if they weren't sure about why they were present. But in the sergeant's face he saw something he didn't expect.

Fear.

Her grip tightened on his arm, above the wrist. He dropped the cup and looked down. She pulled him toward her, as if she wanted to say something. She placed her other hand on his chest and smiled up at him.

"Manfried, get out of there n—"

The hand on his chest pushed him away, and Manfried felt a sudden shocking pain that took the air out of his lungs. He grabbed his shoulder as he fell to his knees . . .

But all he felt was an empty mail sleeve.

Next to him, the woman stood, tossing aside Manfried's naked right arm.

Manfried felt his life spill out of his wounded shoulder. He dimly heard Günter screaming at his men, followed by men grunting and metal screeching.

He stared up at the prisoner, uncomprehending.

Muscles rippled under her pale flesh, tensing like cables as the flesh itself twisted and turned dark. Her hands twisted and bones stretched as fingernails became claws. Her face twisted and her pretty white-toothed smile grew into a red-furred muzzle.

But the lupine demon still looked at him with the same green eyes.

He choked out, "I was only—"

Her forearm shot out, stealing his voice, his consciousness, and what little remained of his life's blood.

"Seal the door!" Günter screamed again. "Seal this damned door!"

Three men were already trying to push the banded door shut. A fourth joined them as the metal screeched against the silver seals wedged at its base. It moved a finger's breadth. Then another.

Beyond it, the creature turned toward them and it almost seemed that its monstrous face was grinning at them. The red-furred thing stood in the center of the cell, hunched behind where Manfried's body had fallen.

"Don't panic!" Günter yelled in a voice that was near panic itself. "That chain is too strong for it to break. It can't reach us." He spoke more from hope than from knowledge. The manacle on the creature's leg was banded in pure silver, it was supposed to prevent her from becoming this . . . thing.

Half human. Half wolf. Its limbs were long and muscular, and even with the stooped, downcast posture it stood upright, as tall as a man. The arms were nearly human, ending in large inhuman hands that flexed fingers ending in curving black claws. Its head was that of a monstrous she-wolf, with jaws that could snap a man's neck in half.

It panted as it stared at him, tongue lolling from its muzzle.

Not waiting for his subordinates, Günter threw his considerable weight into the door. It moved slightly.

Even without the silver seals intact, just getting the barrier closed would be enough to hold the thing. Like the chain, it was much too heavy, even for the strength of . . .

"Sergeant!" one of his men screamed.

"Are you children? I told you! The chain—"

Out of the corner of his eye, he saw the creature take a limping step forward, over Manfried's body.

Impossible! The manacle is pure silver. The chain is too heavy, too strong. It couldn't break—

It hadn't.

Now that the creature had moved forward, Günter could see something he had missed before. On the floor, connected to the wall by the heaviest chain that the German blacksmiths could forge, wrapped in a silver manacle banded with iron, rested the rotting foot of a seventeen-year-old girl, dismembered above the ankle.

The door slammed open, blowing free from the seal wedged between it and the floor. The door threw Günter backward, and one of his men screamed as the door pinned the man's arm against the wall.

The beast stood in the doorway, its hunched posture uneven because one red-furred leg terminated in a bloody stump. Even as Günter watched, the leg seemed to lengthen, growing toward where the amputated limb should have been.

"Silver!" he yelled at his men. "Use the silver weapons!"

Jacob led a trio of men, jumping over Günter to reach the beast. All three were young, in training to become knights of the Order. They all had the fire in their belly, and Günter expected they would storm the gates of Hell itself.

The way they screamed out to God and Heaven now, it was possible that they believed that was exactly what they were doing.

Jacob reached the beast first and, even in the narrow confines of the corridor, the young man's form was perfect, bringing his sword up and under the beast's reach, cleaving into the torso under the beast's left forearm. The force in the blow would have taken an armored opponent to his knees, cracking the ribs of anyone wearing less than a solid breastplate. Against the naked red-furred torso, the edge cut deep into the side of the chest and should have cleaved a lung at the very least.

But the blade was not silver.

"Damn Erhard," Günter spat. "Damn him to Hell for this."

No one heard his cursing in the midst of the shouts and prayers that echoed through the stony halls.

Landkomtur Erhard von Stendal had bequeathed this monster to them. He had told Günter that there was no true danger. He had said that the silver manacle and the silver seals safely bound the creature. He had said that the daggers he gifted the garrison, and the bolts locked upstairs in the armory, were mere precautions.

There was no reason to burden the men, especially those who were recently baptized, with knowledge of the prisoner's nature. Silver-clad swords and axes would raise too many questions, beyond the questions of unseemly extravagance.

Jacob laughed at the beast, obviously convinced he had delivered it a mortal blow. Blood flowed down the blade, foaming at the wound when the thing panted.

"Your dagger," Günter ordered, even as he realized that Jacob wasn't wearing it. Jacob couldn't accept such unseemly wealth on his belt, the pious idiot.

Günter scrambled to his feet, drawing his own silver weapon from his belt. He charged to save the fool, who didn't even realize he was in mortal danger.

Jacob turned to him with a bemused expression. "Sergeant? I have it—" Jacob's gloating was cut short. His blow should have driven any creature into shock, but not this one. This beast was only given a moment's pause by the sword piercing its side, and when it moved, it showed no sign of pain.

It tore the sword from Jacob's grip, pulling it out of its side, and rammed it, hilt-first, into Jacob's face.

The blow was strong enough to be instantly mortal, and the force of it sent Jacob's lifeless body through the line of advancing men, onto Günter.

Günter fell to the ground, his helmet bouncing off the stone floor hard enough to stun him.

Around him he heard the sounds of screams, and prayers, and tearing flesh. His stomach tightened at the smell of blood as he spent a short eternity pushing Jacob's corpse off of him. His hands slid in blood as he tried to regain his feet.

Günter shuddered and took a step back, raising his dagger.

The only other man left alive down here was a softly weeping soldier, one of Günter's fellow Prûsans, who still had his broken arm trapped between the heavy door and the wall. The corpses of five other men sprawled on the floor between Günter and the creature, some in several pieces.

The creature panted, limping down the center of the hallway toward Günter, its forearms and muzzle smeared with blood that glistened black in the lamplight. Günter thought he could see remnants of human flesh caught in its claws.

The beast regarded Günter with pitiless green eyes.

Günter backed up to the wall, holding the tiny silver blade between himself and the creature, praying to Christ, and Perkûnas, that he would at least die well.

Again, the gods refused to pay any attention to Günter Sejod. The beast snarled at him and bared its teeth—or maybe it smiled at the impotent blade shaking between them. Then it hunched over and loped past him on three legs, faster than Günter would expect a man to run.

It ran toward the stairs.

iii

Oytim scrambled down the narrow spiral staircase toward the keep's granary. He carried three crossbows and a canvas bag of, of all things, silver-tipped bolts. The weapons had been in a special locked case in the armory. No one had ever mentioned the case or its contents to him—not until the alarm bells woke him from sleep and Sergeant Günter had grabbed him, handed him the key, and ordered him to retrieve the contents.

As Oytim had rushed toward the armory, Sergeant Günter had led every other soldier barracked in the keep down toward the lower storerooms where the prisoner was kept.

After Oytim retrieved the weapons, the bells had stopped ringing. Oytim ran as fast as he could down the stairway, slowed by his field boots and cumbersome burden. His thoughts swung wildly between two questions:

The first question was, what happened? It couldn't just be the prisoner escaping; there was only the one woman.

The second . . .

Silver bolts?

The bolts frightened him. While they were silver, they were

nothing like the ornate daggers they had been given by the Land-komtur, Erhard von Stendal. There was nothing fancy or ceremo-nial about them. The shafts were purely utilitarian, except for the precious metal forming the tip.

But why? Silver was a soft metal, and might have difficulty piercing even light armor. There was no point in making a real weapon from such material, unless . . .

Oytim came from a small village deep in the Prûsan country-side, on the fringes of a wilderness where even the knights of the Order were wary to tread. He had listened to the stories of his grandparents, telling about the things that lived in the wilderness, still guarding the sacred groves; things that preyed on men who had walked away from honoring the old gods. Things that could only be bound or injured by the purest of metals.

No, those were only stories. Just fragments of a false faith he had discarded. He was baptized Christian, and he knew that the spirits of the forest were falsehoods, deceptions by Satan that had no power over those with a true faith in Christ.

Besides, they were nowhere near those woods here. Even if the creatures from his grandmother's stories did haunt the shadows of that dark place, they wouldn't be *here,* in *this* keep, in the heart of Christian Prûsa.

At the end of the curving windowless stairwell, Oytim burst through the vaulted archway into the granary. The large stone room was filled with ranks of wooden bins holding wheat, rye, and barley against the winter. It was the highest of the storehouse lev-els, and with the winter just fading, it was the only level now being used as such.

Beyond the ranks of storage bins, a heavy wooden door barred the way to a set of curving stone stairs that descended several levels un-derground, where there was space to store supplies for all of Johannis-burg in the unlikely event the town was threatened with siege.

A dozen soldiers stood, weapons drawn, facing the door. More than half the garrison was here. Sergeant Günter and most of the German soldiers were nowhere to be seen.

One of the soldiers, a man named Tulne, turned to Oytim.

"Where in hell have you been?"

"The sergeant ordered me to get these." He handed Tulne one of the crossbows.

Tulne sheathed his sword and took the weapon. "What is he thinking? Crossbows?" He looked around the granary. "Does this look like an open field?"

Oytim shook his head and pulled three quarrels out of the canvas bag.

"I'm wondering about our sergeant, Oytim. If a battle comes up here, it will be over before a second shot's nocked." He held up a bolt. "What's this tipped with?"

"Silver."

Tulne snorted. He set the front of the crossbow on the ground, placing a boot in the stirrup and bending over to pull the tension. "That's nonsense. No one would put a silver tip on a crossbow bolt. Get those others loaded. We might have three shots before the fun's over."

Oytim bent and loaded the second crossbow. "Where is the sergeant?"

Tulne tilted his head at the door as he hefted the loaded crossbow. "He took the Germans down there and told us to bar the door until he came back." Tulne yawned. "Don't look so nervous, Oytim. Don't you think six soldiers can handle a single prisoner?"

Oytim looked around and saw none of his tension reflected in the dozen other guards facing the door. Everyone had weapons drawn, but they were at ease, talking softly to each other.

Tulne laughed and slapped him on the back. "A *woman*, Oytim. A single woman against six battle-hardened soldiers? Or perhaps you doubt the Germans' mettle? No worries then. We have thirteen Prûsan warriors up here."

A few others overheard and glanced at Oytim, sharing Tulne's amusement. Oytim had allowed pagan superstitions to cloud his thinking.

He laughed at himself. "You're right, of course—"

Something heavy slammed into the door. The thud of the impact echoed across the stone vaults, leaving the assembled soldiers in sudden silence.

"No," Tulne whispered.

A second impact, louder than the first. The massive oak bar holding the door shut vibrated, and stone dust puffed from behind the iron braces supporting it.

Oytim was abruptly aware of a flaw in the keep's design. The door they faced, while it was barred, was not intended to keep an enemy at bay. The defensive doors were all placed at choke points, to give the defenders the advantage—but those doors were all placed assuming the attacker came from outside, from the single entrance. The enemy they faced now came from the opposite direction. This door was one of few that could be barred from the "wrong" direction.

Even the bar that sealed it was an afterthought, as it was rare that the lower levels were used as a prison.

It was never meant to withstand a heavy attack. It was too large, formed of a single layer of oak planks, and lacked even the metal studs to interfere with a chopping weapon.

The space of one heartbeat passed, then the door shook again. The sound of groaning wood filled the storeroom. Half the soldiers ran to the door to hold it in place, leaning their shoulders against the bar holding the door closed.

One of the soldiers next to Oytim, a barrel of a man, grabbed the third crossbow and took a step back so that he, Oytim, and Tulne formed a row blocking the exit of the granary.

"An army," Tulne muttered.

"No," Oytim said. "Silver bolts." He knelt and braced the loaded crossbow on his raised thigh. He sighted at the door, which was visibly moving forward with each impact, the gaps between the oak planks widening as its surface slammed against the bar. The force of each blow pushed the soldiers on the door backward.

"Superstitious nonsense," Tulne said.

Oytim wasn't listening anymore.

He steadied his breathing. There was only going to be one shot, and he needed to be ready. Whatever came through that door, he couldn't flinch, couldn't hesitate.

The next impact was accompanied by a distinct metallic snap. One of the iron brackets holding the bar broke free of the wall. The men holding the door scrambled to keep the bar from shifting. The three remaining brackets still held.

The pounding stopped.

Tulne lowered his crossbow. "What? Did they just give up?"

"No," Oytim whispered.

Not meant to take this kind of punishment, the wrecked door sagged. The third plank, near the center, creaked and tilted out a hand's breadth at the top of the doorway, pivoting on the oak bar. One of the men, Cawald, reached up to push it back into place.

Cawald suddenly fell to his knee, screaming, his right leg disappearing into the gap the tilting board had made in the bottom of the door. His neighbors reached for him as he thrashed to the ground.

He screamed and kicked at the door with his left leg, his right one vanishing through the door, all the way to his hip. His comrades grabbed him under the arms, braced their feet against the wreckage of the door, and strained to pull him back.

The two men fell backward as Cawald disappeared through the gap. His piercing scream came to an abrupt stop and the tilted plank slowly rocked back the way it had come.

Then it kept going, falling into the chamber beyond the doorway, leaving a dead column of darkness in the body of the door.

Oytim took aim at the gap, certain he would see something move in the darkness, a glint of tooth or eye—

"No, you idiots!" Oytim screamed at the men by the door. Two had closed on the breach from either side. Using the remains of the door for cover, they bared their swords to strike at anything that might reach from the gap. But they blocked any shot Oytim had at the chamber beyond.

Something moved in the darkness and the soldier to the right of the gap lunged at it. His sword arm lost itself in the darkness, and then his body froze, as if his blade had just hit a stone wall. A look of almost comical surprise crossed his face. Then his body lurched forward, as something pulled his sword arm and slammed his torso against the door. He turned toward the man next to him, as if about to call for help. Then his whole body twisted sideways, his feet leaving the ground as his body was yanked completely through the breach.

"Gods preserve us," Tulne said, voice cracking.

The other men were closing in on the door, but of the original six men who had been holding the door, there were now only two. And one of them was staring at the darkness that had swallowed his comrade rather than holding the door.

Something slammed the door again, and the brackets holding the oak bar in place gave way with a scream of twisted metal and a cloud of masonry dust. The heavy oak bar fell as the remaining splintered planks of the door collapsed outward.

❖

Günter ran after the creature, armed only with the silver dagger. It was suicidal, but the carnage had pushed him beyond reason. He did not want to survive to see his men slaughtered.

Dagger in one hand, lantern in the other, he ran up the five dark levels toward the main door. The stairway was close, and turned tightly, so that any step might bring him face-to-face with the creature. The stone steps were slick and uneven, and he nearly twisted his ankle several times in his haste.

There were doors at each level of the stores, though only the uppermost one had been barred. Even so, the creature had thrown open each one with enough force to crack the timbers and wrench iron hinges from stone. One door had been so damaged it took several minutes to pull it open enough to allow him through.

Once Günter was past it, his gaze fell on a bloody handprint marring the stone wall. No human hand had made it. The palm was padded, like a wolf's paw, and the fingers were longer and thicker than a man's. Above the print, the creature's claws had been strong enough to leave four parallel scratches on the worked face of the stone.

Somewhere above him he heard a powerful impact. He looked up, and a fine dust filtered through the cracks in the stonework above him, stinging his eyes.

She's reached the main door . . .

He shouldn't have felt the fear as deeply as he did. Even if she could force open the oak bar on the door—something that should require a battering ram—beyond it were thirteen Prûsan warriors, and he had ensured that they would at least have the silver bolts to use on the creature. Thirteen trained battle-hardened men, armed with silver.

It should be enough.

He feared it wasn't.

Redoubling his efforts, he ran. But he wasn't surprised when the screaming began.

He shuttered the lantern and cast it aside, hoping that if he came up behind the monster, he might have a clear attack on its back. He ascended the darkened stairway, listening to screams, the sounds of sword against stone, and a low growling that tried to turn his guts to water.

He took the last turn in the stairway to face a corridor filled with light that shouldn't have been there. The light spilled in from the granary beyond the now-open doorway. Shadowed against the light of the granary, he saw a chaos of bodies moving in the hallway. The air was thick with the sound of Prûsan cursing and the smell of blood. Even if he could make no sense of the chaos in front of him, he saw enough to understand that they fought more than a bloodthirsty monster.

It was a beast that knew enough of tactics to fall back into the corridor after smashing the door. The greater part of the Prûsan guards had fallen in after it, into a space too enclosed and dark to fight effectively against even a normal enemy.

Günter gripped the useless dagger, ordering his men to fall back into the granary, where the open floor might give them a chance. But his shouts were nearly inaudible for the sound of clashing metal and screaming men.

From beyond the melee, a crossbow bolt struck the stone near Günter's head, striking sparks.

No, wait until you see a target.

A man fell near Günter, anonymous in the dark. The man groaned briefly before he stopped moving. Günter reached for him, to drag him to the safety of the stairwell, but as he grabbed the man's shoulder and pulled, he had the sickening realization that the weight only amounted to half a body.

He fought his gorge and stepped out of the stairwell, past the dead man, toward the rapidly disintegrating melee. He saw the silhouettes of two more bodies strike the walls to either side of the corridor, and he saw the clear, hunched form of the monster standing unobstructed in front of the doorway.

Günter charged, too late, at the creature's back. As he moved forward, he heard a crossbow fire and a howl filled the chamber unlike any sound Günter had heard from the throat of man or beast. The wolf-thing in front of him charged out of the doorway just as Günter struck. The blow that should have sunk the silver dagger into a vital part of its neck instead had Günter tearing at the air, losing his balance, and tumbling onto the splintered wreckage of the door.

He looked up and saw the lupine demon clearly in the light of the granary; rippling muscle, blood-red fur, claws, and gore-drenched muzzle all closing on the two men still standing, Oytim and Tulne. Both were at the far side of the granary, holding crossbows. Oytim still had a bolt nocked. It had been Tulne who had fired the bolt buried in the beast's shoulder, and he was desperately trying to reload the crossbow as the creature charged.

As Günter scrambled to his feet, the creature descended on Tulne. The massive red-furred back hid Tulne from Günter's view, but the man's scream was cut short before he hit the ground.

Günter ran, jumping over broken timbers and broken bodies while, in front of him, the beast turned its snarling, gory muzzle toward Oytim.

Oytim fired the crossbow up, into the creature's face. Less than two paces away, the bolt tore into the creature's head. The beast screamed as it clutched its face, the howl torn free from the throat of Hell.

Günter was halfway to them when the creature grabbed Oytim by the throat with its free hand and tossed the man aside like a rag doll. He hit the side of one of the grain bins with enough force to crack the wood. He fell to the ground and did not move.

Günter stopped because the creature was whipping around wildly and howling, one hand clutching the side of its face, the other thrashing blindly around. It was frenzied, lashing out with a reach half again as long as Günter's.

All he had was a single silver dagger.

He stood just out of reach, praying that Oytim's shot was true and had pierced its eye, putting a killing shot into its brain.

But Günter's gods were deaf.

The creature slowly stopped howling, and stopped its wild thrashing. To Günter's horror, the creature lowered its hand and looked at him with *two* green eyes. Oytim's shot had been too high, too far to the right, and at too steep an angle. The shot had cracked the bone, but had been deflected by the curve of the monster's skull and didn't penetrate. Blood streamed down the creature's face from the gory wound, but it was neither dead nor dying.

It stared at Günter, an evil snarl on its lips. Hopeless, Günter raised his dagger, closed his eyes, and prepared to die.

After several moments, when the attack didn't happen, he opened his eyes again.

The beast was gone.

Uldolf wasn't having a good morning.

He had already checked five of his snares, and he hadn't caught anything. One would think that if he was going to risk his freedom trapping game on the Order's land, he might, just once, capture *something*. However, it had been a hard winter, and it seemed that the game had been picked thin even on the land directly under the Germans' keep.

So when, in the early dawn hours, he approached his sixth snare, hidden in the underbrush by a lightning-uprooted hemlock, and saw a hint of fur, he almost cried out in triumph, despite the risk of being caught.

Instead, he just allowed himself a smile.

His breath came out in a puff of fog as he knelt down next to the snare. He had a hare—a thin beast with patchy fur, but still a hare. His sister was recovering from a fever. She needed the meat and Uldolf wasn't about to be choosy.

He glanced around the woods on the off chance someone else might be around. This was the most dangerous part of his crime. Even if he was found on this land with a hare in his bag, he could probably protest effectively that it came from elsewhere. Unlike elk or bear or any other large animal, there wouldn't be the automatic assumption that he was stealing from the Order. At least, as long as no one saw him setting these snares in the woods below the Johannisburg castle wall.

Uldolf didn't see anyone, but that was unlikely in the sliver of time before sunrise and Prime. The maze of thickets, steep hills, and ravines that rolled out from the eastern edge of Johannisburg was not inviting to casual foot traffic. It was thick and treacherous enough to be part of the town defenses from the time before the town had a Christian name or a stone keep lording over it. If he wished, he could have easily come within a hundred paces of the castle itself without being observed—all the way to the narrow frontier where the woods were cleared before the lower wall.

Because of the steep character of the land there, there was no village between the east side of the castle and the lower wall—just the mound of earth shrugging up from the hillside to support the smooth gray walls of the castle. The town itself unfolded west of the castle, where the slope of the land was more gentle and even.

Few people came down here, and fewer still now that the old modes of worship were suppressed and the groves sacred to Perkûnas were destroyed, ignored, or forgotten. Uldolf remembered, though. Not because he honored the old gods—he was a baptized Christian like every free man in the Order's domain—but because it was one of the few parts of his childhood he could remember without feeling pain or loss. He had known these woods since before the injury that had claimed his right arm. He knew it better than the German, Dutch, and Polish tradesmen, clergy, and farmers the Order had brought in to swell the ranks of Christian Johannisburg.

Once he was certain he was unobserved by any immigrant Christians, he bent to retrieve his bony prize.

Long practice allowed him to quickly retrieve the hare and reset the snare faster than many people with two arms might have been able to do. The dead rodent found a home in a leather pouch that Uldolf wore around his shoulder.

The pouch had enjoyed a prior life as a set of plain saddlebags that had once belonged to one of the knights of the Teutonic Order, until they'd seen ruin in battle. The man who had taken possession of them had known better than to try and sell his looted prize openly in the Johannisburg market, and Uldolf had been able to buy the remnants in one of the secret Prûsan-only markets for a pittance, back when he had pittances to spare.

He had used it to help perfect his leather-working skills. He had disassembled the original, retrimmed the pieces, and created a satchel that he could probably trade in Johannisburg's open market for a few months' worth of venison—if his mother would let him.

Uldolf, she had told him, *what then would you have to show people your skills?*

Even with it, Uldolf had not found many people who believed that a one-armed peasant could be a competent leather worker. Certainly not the foreign tradesmen in Johannisburg, who saw everyone of Prûsan blood—baptized or not—as little more than heathen savages. At times, Uldolf thought they were surprised he could speak.

Instead, Uldolf bartered his services to the Prûsan farmers around the area—people who'd known his adoptive parents since before Johannisburg was a province of Christendom. Uldolf suspected it all had started as a sympathetic gesture to his parents, who had the ill luck to have half a son and a sickly daughter. Or maybe it was out of respect for Uldolf's heritage. His first father had been the last chieftain of Mejdân, before the village fell to the Christians.

He felt a small measure of pride in the fact that what might have started as sympathy had, over the past two years, evolved into an appreciation of his skill. There wasn't a farm within a day's walk that didn't now have a saddle, or a bridle, or a harness that bore his mark somewhere on it.

But his skills couldn't make the winters easier. Those who traded happily for his workmanship suffered the same hardships his own family did when the cold fell, and what was in the larder had to last through the first fruit of spring.

So he was happy for the hare he had managed to catch. With it, and some barley, his mother would be able to make a stew that would last a week. Harsh as the winter had been, the last snows were mostly melted except for the deepest parts of the forest, and by midday the ground would stop crunching with frost under his feet. They would be able to start planting soon, and afterward he could peddle his services again. Maybe this year he could find a merchant to apprentice with and be able to work year-round.

"And maybe this year my arm will grow back," he muttered to scold himself. He reached over to his shoulder and rubbed it, although he couldn't touch the ache he felt in the long-absent limb.

Even if he had two arms, he was too old for an apprenticeship now. The years he could have spent learning a trade he had stayed with his parents, working hard to keep the farm going.

In the distance, he heard the church bell in Johannisburg sounding for Prime. He stood and looked up. The dawn glow had lightened to full daylight, and above him the sky was sharp cloudless blue. He shouldered his pack and tried not to think of what he felt in the arm he didn't have.

He had some meat, and it was time to return home.

His route through the woods was an extended loop that avoided obvious game trails and the few established paths. He followed the bottoms of ravines that gave him cover from anyone who had more legitimate business traveling through the Order's land. He had now reached the point where he was as close as he ever wished to come to the castle and the Johannisburg city wall.

Uldolf was glad to be out of sight of the keep as he followed the creek bed at the bottom of this ravine. Not just because it helped him remain unobserved, but because he always found the sight disturbing. Something about the outline of the man-made hill it rested on, the way the fortifications squatted on top like an evil stone toad on a pile of refuse. Just thinking about it made his absent arm ache worse.

Something in him was thankful for the fever that had stolen the memory of the injury and most of the year preceding it. As painful as it was when he thought of his childhood with his parents, now eight years dead, it would be intolerably worse if he remembered their deaths.

He stood quietly for a moment, uncomfortable with where his thoughts were going. He forced himself to think of his present family: Gedim, the man who was father to him now; Burthe, his mother; and his baby sister, Hilde. Thinking of Hilde finally brought a smile to his lips. How could he be morose when his sister's fever had finally broken during the night?

Past is past, he thought as he resumed walking.

Soon, ahead of him, he saw the moss-covered trunk of the great oak he used to mark his turning point—as close as he would come to Johannisburg. It grew where the ravine ended, the sides gently falling away into mere hills. At the point where the oak grew, the creek he followed forked into two streams—one turning deeper into the forest, the other filling a deep pool ahead of him.

Between a steep shale cliff and the massive crown of the oak tree hovering over it, the pool was invisible from the village. Even naked, the oak's black limbs seemed to reach out and claim the pool for itself. In high summer, this area would take on the character of a verdant cave.

Uldolf smiled every time he saw this place, especially at the boulder next to the roots of the oak. The white rock was about a head shorter than he was now, but had seemed gigantic when he was young. Even so, there were rewards for the child who climbed its smooth surface all the way to the top. It placed the lowest limbs of the oak just within reach.

In the years before . . . before he lived with Gedim, he had spent endless spring and summer afternoons here, jumping from the limbs of the oak into the pool. It had always been his secret place. He had never shown it to anyone.

If it wasn't so late in the morning, he might have climbed that rock again. Not to climb the oak, but just to sit and look at this place. It calmed him, especially when he was troubled by thoughts and dreams of the past. And for some reason, the past felt very close to him right now.

He reached the fork, and was about to follow the stream away from the pool, deeper into the forest, when something about his oak tree made him stop.

Some animal had mercilessly clawed at the trunk. Fresh white scars glistened in the dawn light, dangling shreds of bark and moss. Some of the claw marks reached higher than his head. The sight filled him with a sick unease, as if something had attacked the one good childhood memory he had managed to hang onto.

What kind of animal?

Something moved at the foot of the boulder by the creek bed. He froze for a moment, not quite comprehending what he saw. Several seconds passed before the flashes of hair and skin resolved into something concrete.

In the water, curled against the white side of the boulder, her back to him, was a naked woman.

Her skin was so pale that at first Uldolf thought her a corpse. But, after a moment, he could see her breathing. He ran to the boulder, boots splashing, abandoning all pretense of stealth.

"Hello? Are you all right?" He placed a hand on her shoulder.

At his touch, the woman whipped around and uttered a scream of such pure terror that Uldolf lost his balance and fell backward into the creek.

The woman scrambled away from him. She panted, breaths coming in great sobs. Uldolf could see now that she was badly injured. There was a nasty wound in her right shoulder, barely clotted, trailing blood down her arm. The right half of her face was covered in blood from a massive gash that cut from her temple to up under her hairline. She kept pushing with her legs, away from him, until she backed into the oak. When she hit it, her eyes widened and she shuddered, crying out and grasping the wound on her shoulder.

"Please," Uldolf said, grabbing the boulder and pulling himself upright. "I want to help you."

She shook her head.

Not only was she covered with blood from her wounds, she was coated in filth from her knotted red hair down. The only part of her that was remotely clean was her left foot, which was spotless. *Must have trailed in the water awhile,* Uldolf thought.

"What happened to you?"

She drew her knees up to her chest and hugged them with her good arm. She shook, obviously cold and terrified. Uldolf took a few steps toward her, but she flinched and tried to pull herself into more of a ball, burying her face in her knees.

Uldolf stopped approaching and crouched so he wouldn't loom over her. With their heads roughly on the same level, he said, "I don't want to hurt you."

After a moment, she raised her head slightly. A pair of green eyes stared at him through strings of wet, blood-clotted hair.

"My name's Uldolf. I live on a farm near here." He gestured toward the other fork in the creek.

She peered at him over her knees, attempting to hug herself tighter, as if that was possible.

"What's your name?"

She sucked in a deep breath, but didn't say anything.

"Do you understand anything I'm asking?" Uldolf wished he

had made more of an effort to learn German, or Polish, or any of the other languages that the Christians had imported into Prûsa. He tried one of the few German words that he knew, pointing at himself. "Friend."

She only stared at him. She still shook, but at least it now seemed to be more from cold than from fear.

Dozens of possibilities were flying through his head. The most likely one was that she was the victim of vicious outlaws. A blow like that to the head, and someone with murder on his mind would most likely be satisfied to leave her to die. Even uninjured, throwing someone naked into the wilderness was a death sentence. She couldn't have been here much longer than half an hour, or the cold or some wild animal would have killed her.

Uldolf glanced up at the scarred skin of the oak tree and shuddered. What that animal could have done to human flesh did not bear thinking about.

He took a step back and looked about. Fortunately, he saw no sign of man nor beast. Listening, he heard no additional breathing, no footsteps.

He looked down at the woman. Her shivering was painful to watch.

"We have to cover you up," he said, reaching for her.

She raised her head toward his hand and bit him. He yanked his hand away and shook it.

"You can't do that!"

She stared at him.

"Don't you understand? *I only have the one!*" He waved his hand in front of her face, the meat between thumb and forefinger bright red. He balled it up into a fist. "Do you want me to leave you here? Is that what you want?"

She cowered and started crying.

Uldolf looked at his fist and suddenly felt wretched. It wasn't her fault, but one of his greatest fears was having some injury happen to his remaining arm. He had had eight years to adjust to his loss. It was hard, but he managed as well as anyone. But if anything happened to the arm he had left . . .

But she hadn't even broken the skin.

He crouched again, rubbing the inflamed part of his hand against his leg. "I'm sorry, I shouldn't yell at you. But that hurt."

Now that he was within arm's reach of her, he could see the wound on her head better. The flesh was torn around it, and in the center he thought he could see bone glisten. "Still, you must hurt worse."

She sniffed, and turned her face to look at him again.

"You don't understand a word I'm saying, do you?"

At least she had stopped crying.

"I just startled you, didn't I?" He sighed and took his leather satchel off his shoulder. "I'm going to do this slowly, and we're going to have no more biting. Do you understand?"

He took off his cloak. It was dark brown and had a sheepskin lining he had tailored himself. It was very warm, and it had comforted him through the worst of three winters so far. Very cautiously, he reached around and draped it over her. Still, the motion startled her, and she actually tried to duck out from under it before it settled across her shoulders.

Uldolf backed away, stood, and let her watch him. He held up his arm. "See, I'm not trying to do anything."

She looked at him, then at the cloak that was half draped over her back. She grabbed at the edge of the cloak and pulled it around herself. She was a fair bit smaller than he was, and in a moment she was completely covered except for her head. She looked up at him, and for once her green eyes didn't show fear, just confusion.

Uldolf shook his head. "I'm afraid that blow to your head may have rattled your brain a bit. We should have my mother look at it. She was a midwife."

She hugged the cloak around herself, rubbing her cheek against the sheepskin around the collar. Then she smiled—and Uldolf was struck that someone so ill used could muster such a joyful expression.

He reached down and retrieved his satchel, shouldering it. "So, will you trust me to help now?"

He held out his hand.

She looked down at his hand and, for a brief moment, Uldolf thought she was going to snap and bite him again.

"Can you stand? It would be awkward for me to carry you home."

It seemed a long time that he stood with his hand outstretched. Uldolf was convinced, at this point, that she understood what he wanted. He felt, somehow, that she was deciding if that was what *she* wanted.

After a few minutes lost in thought, she reached up with her good hand and grabbed his. Her skin was cold and clammy from the water, but her grip was much firmer than he expected. He didn't have a chance to help her up; she pulled herself up using him as leverage. He might as well have been the tree.

Unfortunately, she had not clasped his cloak, and it slid off as she stood. Even though she was still injured and filthy, her nakedness was much more distracting now than it had been when she was helpless, huddled on the ground. She was a striking beauty, with the kind of curves and proportions that Uldolf had never seen exposed before.

She let go of his arm and reached up, frowning, realizing that the cloak had slid off. Her lack of modesty made her nakedness even more distracting.

Uldolf stepped around her and retrieved the cloak from the ground, shook out some leaves, and tried to replace it on her shoulders. However, now that she was standing, it was more difficult than it looked. He placed it on one shoulder, and as he moved his arm around to place it over her other shoulder, the cloak's weight would make it slide off. He did it twice before he stopped, realizing that it wasn't working.

He tried to never become frustrated over his missing arm. Like his past, it was a fact that would never go away. Cursing it, obsessing over it, led to places he didn't want to go. But he couldn't help the futile rage that built up inside him now. What kind of rescuer was he? He couldn't even properly drape a cloak around a woman's shoulders.

She looked over her naked shoulder at him, and Uldolf felt his face burn as he tried to keep his hand from shaking. He forced a smile he didn't feel and said, "I'm sorry. I just need to think about this for a moment."

She cocked her head at him, and he saw her hand reaching around, over her wounded shoulder.

He stared at her hand a moment before realizing what she wanted. "Thank you," he said with mixed gratitude and embarrassment. He handed her one end of the cloak. While she held that end, he draped the other around her good shoulder.

He walked around her so he could show her the clasp. Holding it up so she could see, he threaded the long carved bone through the hole in the opposite side. "See? That's how it stays on."

She looked up, and he felt embarrassment again.

"Forgive me if I'm treating you like a child, but you don't seem to understand me."

She reached up and fumbled with the bone. She frowned. It had probably looked a bit easier to do one-handed when Uldolf had done it.

"Look, if you do that—"

Before he had finished talking, she had the cloak undone and it fell off her right shoulder again, exposing her wound, the fullness of her right breast, and most of a smooth muscular thigh.

Uldolf swallowed and stepped forward to grab the edge of the cloak again, but he had to stop when she held up her right hand between them. The hand trembled slightly, and Uldolf thought of how painful that arm must be to move, even a little bit.

"You shouldn't strain . . ."

He trailed off, because even if she did understand him, she wasn't listening. She had taken a step back and had pulled the cloak completely off. Holding it before her, she stared at it, then changed her grip and deftly pulled it up over her own shoulders. With both hands, she closed the cloak herself, refastening it.

She looked down at the cloak with an expression of satisfaction, then looked up at Uldolf and smiled.

"I understand." Uldolf smiled back. "You aren't helpless."

She took a step forward, and Uldolf saw the strength go out of her legs a moment before she realized it. Just as she swung her good arm out for some sort of support, Uldolf grabbed her. She fell into him, wrapping her arm and half the cloak around his chest. He found himself with his arm under the cloak, holding her to him. He felt his face flush for reasons completely apart from frustration at his missing arm.

She sucked in a sob, and looked up at him. He looked into her face and saw something there trying to push back the tears and the frustration.

He patted her on the back, careful to avoid her right shoulder. "I know how you feel. But I think if we are going to get anywhere, you'll have to lean on me."

She sniffed and nodded, as if she might be able to understand him.

M other? What's that sound?"

Burthe looked over at her suddenly wakeful daughter. Hilde had sat up in bed, her nightshirt hanging loosely on her too-thin frame. Burthe set down the trousers she was mending and hurried over to Hilde's bed. She felt the side of Hilde's face for signs of fever, and was gratified to find that it hadn't come back since breaking during the night. Still, she put her hand on Hilde's shoulder to keep her from sitting up any farther.

"Be still, child. You've been too ill to be jumping around."

"It's Ulfie, Mama. Don't you hear him?"

Burthe grunted. Her daughter had always had keener ears than she did. Age, and an infection that had savaged her after Hilde was born, had left her half deaf.

"Do you think he brought something for me?" She tried to toss her blanket aside, and swayed a little. "Oh . . ."

Burthe put her hands on Hilde's shoulders and firmly guided her back into bed. "If your brother's home, he'll be here soon enough. The more you rest, the sooner you'll be able to get up." It took all of Burthe's considerable will to keep the heaviness she felt out of her voice. Over the last month, she had exhausted what herbal lore she knew trying to break Hilde's infection. She had not told Uldolf or her husband, but she had begun to doubt that Hilde would get better.

Because of that fear, she found it hard to give into the same relief Uldolf had shown this morning. She held onto the worry, perhaps fearing that to let it go too soon would be to invite the evil back into her child's body.

So even though part of her wanted to encourage her to jump on the bed like any other six-year-old, she only gave Hilde a stern stare as she drew the blanket up to her chin. "You rest, child."

"I've been resting *forever.*"

She bent down and kissed her forehead, thinking, *I mustn't cry.* "Don't talk like that. You have not been resting forever, and you know it."

"I'm sorry, Mama."

The words echoed in Burthe's head. *Resting forever.* Hilde had two siblings the child had never known about. They would have been ten and eight, had either lived. Her older brother, Masnyke, had died of a fever before he was one year old. Hilde's sister had never had a chance to have a name, as the Christians had come when Burthe had been five months with child. She had fallen in the panicked rush to city gates ahead of the invaders. The fall had torn something inside her, and she had lost the child during the too-short siege that followed.

After the city fell, she and her husband, Gedim, had taken in the orphaned Uldolf. They thought she had been left barren and he would be their only child. And after so many losses, he was a blessing.

But two years later she had Hilde. And as difficult as the pregnancy was, as painful the birth, her daughter was a miracle. Like the adopted brother she worshiped, Hilde had reserves of strength that left Burthe humbled and a little bit in awe. As a midwife, she saw boys years older succumb to illnesses not half as vicious as those she'd seen grip Hilde.

Yet now she was smiling, had a good color, and was chatting away as if she'd just woken up from a nap. "Mama, Ulfie sounds like he needs help."

Burthe kissed her again, then stood up and listened. Muffled, outside, she heard someone calling, "Mother!"

It *was* Uldolf.

She stepped toward the door, casting a warning glance at Hilde. "You stay there, understand?"

"Yes, Mama."

Burthe pushed the door to the cottage open and stepped out into the front field—the one that largely went to grow the taxes and the tithes that allowed their family to remain here unmolested. The week's thaw had stripped the black earth naked, but when she stepped outside, her footsteps crunched; the ground was still stiff with frost.

The field between the cottage and the road was framed by a rough stone wall that testified to the rocky nature of the soil. Every stone had been clawed out of the mud years ago by Uldolf and her husband. Similar walls marked off the other fields they tilled and the pasture where they kept the livestock, when they had livestock. Since midwinter, the pasture only served their one horse, which was absent at the moment, having taken Gedim and the wagon to Johannisburg.

Uldolf was just now walking along the outermost wall, by the road. He stopped at the waist-high gate that led in to the field.

From inside the cottage, Burthe heard Hilde ask, "Did he bring something?"

That he had.

Uldolf saw her and called, "Mother, help!"

It took a moment for Burthe to respond to her son's plea, because she was unable immediately to make sense of what she saw.

Uldolf cradled his cloak in his arm, half draped across his shoulder like a sack of grain.

"Oh, by the gods!" She ran across the field, realizing that Uldolf was doing his best to carry a human body one-handed. As she reached him, she amended the thought.

A woman's body.

Burthe could see the bloody temple and scalp resting against her son's shoulder. She didn't bother to open the waist-high gate. She just extended her arms over it. "Hand her to me."

With a grunt and an audible sigh of relief, Uldolf unloaded his burden into her arms. The woman was small, but dead weight, completely unconscious. Even though Uldolf was wearing just a linen shirt in air that fogged the breath, he was coated with sweat and deeply flushed.

"How. Is. She?" He was so out of breath he could barely speak.

Burthe looked at the woman.

Not a woman, she thought. *Only a girl.*

The girl in her arms was taking breaths that were even and deep, and her skin was of good color. "Despite the wound, she looks better than you." She stepped back so Uldolf could open the gate and come in. "How far did you carry her?"

"Not far. I found her in the woods by Johannisburg's eastern wall, I think bandits—"

"By Johannisburg? That's five miles at least."

"She was able to walk herself, at first."

Burthe looked back at the girl's head. The damage was awful, and were it not for the fact that this girl was flush and breathing, she might have thought it mortal.

"And how far did she walk, with such a grievous injury?"

"A quarter mile, maybe."

Burthe shook her head. "No wonder you're late."

✦

"Mama, who's that?" Despite Burthe's instructions, Hilde was sitting up on the edge of her narrow little bed.

"A guest," Burthe told her. "And she's hurt, so don't you be bothering her."

She laid the girl down in Uldolf's bed. The girl sighed slightly and seemed to relax, but she didn't regain consciousness. The bottom of Uldolf's cloak slid open, revealing a filthy naked leg.

Uldolf stepped next to Burthe. "She's got a bad wound on her shoulder, too."

"Draw me some fresh water, and bring some clean linens." Uldolf nodded and went outside to the well. The ground here might be hard and rocky, but at least they had good water. Their Christian masters might have taken most everything, but they hadn't taken that.

Burthe undid the cloak and unwrapped the girl so she could get a good look at her.

"Oh, you poor child."

"Mama?"

"Shh, Hilde, Mama's working."

The shoulder wound was awful, as well—a ragged crater in the middle of shreds of torn flesh, larger than the head wound. It was incredible that the girl hadn't bled to death. Incredible enough that Burthe checked her breathing again, and felt for her heartbeat.

"You're strong," Burthe whispered. "That's good."

Strong like her own children, maybe strong enough to fight off the fever that would inevitably come after such an injury.

"Young, too. That will help." Burthe went to a small chest she stored on a shelf next to the hearth. She walked back to see Uldolf standing over the girl's bedside holding a large bucket of water, the linens draped over his shoulder.

Burthe glanced at her son's expression, then down at the girl, lying uncovered in her son's bed.

"Uldolf!"

He tore his gaze away from the injured girl's nakedness to look at her.

"Set those things down, and maybe allow our guest a little modesty?"

Uldolf's face turned bright red and he set down the bucket. He started walking away, but Burthe cleared her throat. "Those as well."

For a moment, her son looked confused. Burthe sighed, reached up, and took the linens off his shoulder. "Go on, then. Don't you have game you can dress?"

He nodded and headed out the door, closing it behind him.

Burthe turned back to her guest. The girl was her son's age, maybe a little younger. There was no denying that she was attractive, even in her distressed state. She really couldn't blame Uldolf for staring.

"Can I help, Mama?"

Burthe sighed and looked at her daughter. Hilde was still on her bed, but only just. She was up on her knees and straining about as far forward as she could without falling off. Burthe's annoyance was tempered by the fact that Hilde's excitement seemed to have renewed her strength.

Better to placate Hilde's curiosity before it got her into trouble. "Only if you can be very quiet and still. Can you do that?"

Hilde's face lit up. "Yes, Mama!"

"Then pick up that stool and come sit over here."

Hilde scrambled out of bed and brought the stool over, sitting at the head of Uldolf's bed. When she sat, Burthe handed her the chest. "Now, when I ask you for something, you hand it to me."

"Yes, Mama." Hilde nodded vigorously, a very serious expression on her face.

"Good."

Burthe took one of the linens and dipped it in the water. First things first; she needed to clean those wounds.

I t was a long, laborious process, and Burthe was grateful the girl was unconscious. Even though the wounds were remarkably clean, without pus to drain or dead flesh to cut away, they were deep and ragged. After cleaning the dirt, she cut the hair from around the girl's head wound.

Cleaned and exposed, Burthe saw that there were two wounds, as if something had impaled the poor girl's flesh, cracking but not quite breaking the skull underneath. A surgeon would more than likely take a drill to the skull there, releasing the vapors and evil humors that would gather at the injury.

"It isn't sunken," she told herself. "She's not in obvious distress."

"Mama?"

"Shh, my child."

If there had been tremors, or chills, or cold white skin, she might have tried to open the skull, despite not having the proper skills or equipment. But with the girl merely unconscious, the risks did not seem worth it.

As to what had impaled her at such an angle, Burthe had no clue. "Perhaps she fell on a branch."

Though that wasn't a satisfactory answer, since she couldn't conceive of what kind of force that would require, or imagine the kind of tree that grew branches this thin that could pierce flesh without splintering.

Regardless of how she had come by her injury, Burthe knew well how much pain this wound could cause, even after it healed. She'd been a young girl once. She took great care in sewing the raw edges of the wound.

"What are you doing, Mama?"

"If someone is hurt this badly, Hilde, the skin won't heal together all by itself."

"It won't?"

"No. The edges of the wound need to touch to mend properly."

"Does that mean she's going to have a seam in her head, like my dolly?"

Burthe smiled and knotted the thread on the third stitch. She was tying them as small and close as she could. That, and some salve, would help to minimize the scar. "Just for a little while. When the skin heals back together, I'll remove the thread."

As she worked her way up the scalp, her patient remained blissfully unconscious.

"Does that hurt?" Hilde asked her.

"Not as badly as it did when she injured her head."

"I don't think I could sleep through that."

After she had stitched and bound the girl's head, Burthe started working on the shoulder.

Once the wounds were taken care of, Burthe turned her attention to cleaning off the mud, blood, and filth. It was an exercise that took almost as long as tending to the girl's injuries. As she cleaned the girl off, Burthe did notice one other strange thing. Filth and blood covered her entire body, except for her left foot. That, for some reason, had remained untarnished by whatever had befallen the unconscious girl. It was even clean under the toenails.

As inexplicable as that was, Burthe didn't think any more of it once she was done.

❖

She awakened, naked, in a strange bed, as if she had been asleep for a very long time. As if she barely remembered ever being awake.

She remembered dreams—dreams of being someone else, being some*thing* else. She remembered being someone cold, unfeeling, angry, and very cruel. The nightmares she remembered frightened her, even though they were all mixed up in her head in a confusing muddle.

It felt as if she had been dreaming for years.

She tried to move, and winced, pain shooting through her shoulder and her skull. Something that was half memory and half dream told her that there were men who wanted to hurt her. She wanted to think that was just the dream; it wasn't real.

But the pain was very real.

She wondered where she was, who she was, and how she had come to be in such a place. She thought she knew, but as she reached for the thought, something inside her flinched, as if it didn't want to know.

She remembered, vaguely, the man who had pulled her from the stream. He had given her his cloak and had kept talking to her. The words should have made sense, but she couldn't understand. It had frustrated her so much that when the man reached for her, she had bit at him.

He had yelled, making her cower. But after a few moments, he had lowered his fist and had started speaking lower, more softly. That's when she had realized he only had one arm. She had realized then, because he hadn't struck her, that he couldn't be one of the bad men.

The thought of bad men brought a painful flash of memory—of blood, of men screaming, of flesh tearing; too vivid to be a dream, too horrible to be anything else.

She swallowed and pushed the evil thought away.

Those weren't the people here. She was somewhere else now, away from the bad men.

Maybe here she would be safe.

Interlude

Anno Domini 1229

Ten years before the bloodbath at Johannisburg Keep, before the keep existed and before the town bore the name of Johannisburg, Erhard von Stendal, a knight of the Order of the Hospital of St. Mary of the Germans in Jerusalem, had been elevated to the title of Landkomtur, province commander of the Teutonic Order. Before then, he had been serving in the Holy Land as a simple knight of the Order.

His elevation had been no common event. Normally, a brother arrived at a position of authority in the Teutonic Order by a consultation of his peers. It would be the collective wisdom of the Kommende—the house where the knight served—that would raise him to commander. Likewise it would be the collective wisdom of a province's commanders that would raise such a Komtur to the level of Landkomtur, province commander. Until he'd been granted the title himself, Erhard had no idea that a brother might achieve that rank in any other way.

However, only a few weeks after the Holy Roman Emperor

Frederick II was crowned king of Jerusalem in the church of the Holy Sepulcher, the grand master of the Order himself, Hermann von Salza, had informed Erhard of his new duties. Erhard was to leave his own house and travel to the frontier of Prûsa. No brothers had consulted to elevate him because, as far as Erhard could tell, there were no brothers in the province he commanded. Nor, in fact, did there seem to be an actual province.

Erhard accepted these orders without question, even though he had little idea why the grand master would call him from his brothers in Jerusalem, or why he was elevated in rank in such an unusual manner. He was certain that any adventures to Christianize Prûsa would create more houses and provinces for the Order, though he had never heard of creating leadership for such beforehand.

When he rode into Kulmerland on the southwest edge of the Prûsan wilderness, he still believed that his destiny would be to lead a force of men into battle against heathen, infidel, and pagan. He expected to use the point of his sword to protect those who preached the glory of God, and those who had accepted the words of Christ. He had never thought that following the Lord's will would be the easy path, but he still believed he knew where it led.

On this summer day, that path led him to a monastery east of the city of Torun, along the River Drweca.

Thanks to a rare episode of agreement between the Holy Roman Emperor Frederick II and Pope Gregory IX—an agreement brokered by Grand Master Hermann von Salza himself—the lands just to the north of Erhard had been jointly granted to the Teutonic Order. By virtue of papal and imperial authority, the Teutonic knights held sovereignty over the whole of Prûsa.

Currently, it was a fief in name only, as Prûsa was still untamed, stretching through bog and dense woods to the north and east along the Baltic. The pagans who made those woods home had a reputation as fierce as any Saracen.

The Prûsan appetite for Christian blood had troubled all their neighbors: Danes, Saxons, and Poles. The Poles' failure to contain the continual pagan raids across their northern border led the duke of Mazovia to beg for the intervention of the Teutonic Order in the first place.

The monastery Erhard now approached was a testament to that Prûsan barbarism. The walls were scarred by fire and partway collapsed, crosses had been defaced, and a statue of Mary that had once filled a niche near the entrance had been toppled, the head removed. Yet Erhard knew that the building did not suffer the worst. The brothers serving this mission who hadn't been killed outright had been taken as slaves by their Prûsan attackers. It was only one in a long line of offenses against the body of Christ: slaughtered bishops, destroyed churches, and enslaved converts.

However, this patch of Christendom had since been reclaimed, as shown by the Teutonic standard flying above the remains of the bell tower. The black cross whipping in the summer breeze lifted Erhard's spirit. It showed that no defeat of the righteous was permanent.

It did trouble him somewhat that there was little sign of anyone reclaiming the mission here. He saw no monks as he approached, only armed men bearing various tabards over their armor, all quite serious in their bearing. Erhard could tell by their dress and the varied ways they wore their hair and trimmed their beards that these men were all secular.

At least this house of God is well defended.

He rode up and one of the guardsmen took the reins of his horse as Erhard dismounted.

"You must be our new Landkomtur," came a voice out of the entry.

Erhard turned to face the voice. "Brother Erhard von Stendal," he said, squinting. The intense sunlight rendered the shadows in the recessed entry near impenetrable, and his host's approach had been masked by the fact that he wore black, from tunic to trousers to worn leather boots.

The man stepped into the sunlight to meet him. "I am Brother Semyon von Kassel."

Brother Semyon held out a hand, and Erhard noted that he even wore black gloves. Erhard took his hand and said, "Hochmeister Hermann von Salza sends his greetings."

Brother Semyon smiled. "But more important, he sends you."

There was nothing particularly unusual about the man, other than his choice of black clothing in the summer heat. Brother Semyon was about Erhard's height, if more slightly built. His face was lined by approaching age, but his hair still held most of its color, white only invading at the fringes of his temples and around his neatly trimmed beard. His eyes were gray as a stone.

The face was unremarkable, but the smile . . .

There was something in Brother Semyon's smile that made Erhard uneasy. There was knowledge there—knowledge that probably was best not shared.

"I am here," Erhard said. "But I've not yet been told why."

"Why? To serve God, and the pope." Brother Semyon chuckled and let go of Erhard's hand. "Come, I have much to show you, and we have much to discuss."

Brother Semyon and one of the secular guards led him down a corridor black with shadow. It was a relief to be out of the sun, but the dimness rendered the brother little more than a darker shadow beside him. Erhard had the uncanny sensation that the darkness here was more than the absence of light.

"You've been given quite the honor. To be first to lead one of our special 'provinces' is a unique duty, and one that the Hochmeister only trusted to the most disciplined and discreet knight of the Order. Your command will be exclusive. You will have no peers."

"I assume you're going to tell me what this command is?"

"All things in their proper order." They stopped in front of a massive door. "Do you know why you were chosen?"

"I have not been enlightened."

"The reasons are manifold. In the Holy Land, you proved adept at the more subtle arts of warfare—attacking the heathen in the mind and the soul as well as the body. You are adept with spies, subversion, and assassination."

"I serve the Lord, my God."

"And you do so with an admirable lack of sentimentality."

Brother Semyon's guardsman opened the door. It swung inside silently on well-oiled hinges. It revealed a corridor beyond, lined with several long cages. The cages were new, the black iron bars showing no rust, the stones forming the floor flat, even, and closely fitted together. The cages were tall and narrow, along the single outside wall, and lit only by vent holes in the upper wall no larger than Erhard's fist.

Even so, after the darkened corridor, his eyes were adjusted well enough to see the cages in their entirety. They were barely wide enough for a man to spread his arms inside, and about twice that long. The occupants were uniformly naked, each chained by one leg to a heavy staple set in the center of their cell.

Children.

Six of them, male and female, all about eight years old. All of them were quiet, looking down at the floor as Brother Semyon led Erhard and the guardsman down the aisle in front of the cages.

Erhard said a quick prayer for his own soul then turned on Brother Semyon. "What *is* this? Are these children baptized? What are they being punished for?"

Semyon laughed at him. "No, my good knight, you would no more baptize these children than you would your horse."

Erhard felt the first prickings of horror. "Why would you deny them Christ? Absolution of their sins?"

"Sir, sin is the province of humanity. These you are calling 'children' are far from human."

Erhard couldn't credit those words.

He looked at the prisoners and saw nothing to distinguish them from children anywhere. Except, perhaps, one thing—

They were unnaturally silent.

These children did not babble, did not fidget, did not respond to his presence at all. The only indication Erhard received that these creatures were even aware of their surroundings was when he caught one girl's steel-blue eye furtively watching him from behind the ragged strings of her blond hair.

"I am deeply troubled, Brother. You say these children are not human. How can I accept those words when I see this?" He waved at the cages.

"You will see more," Brother Semyon said.

"Why do they say nothing? Are they mute?"

"No. They are merely well trained." Brother Semyon shifted his speech to the barbarian tongue of the Prûsans. Fortunately, the grand master had sent Erhard north with some Prûsan slaves to be guides and to tutor him in the language. "Only speak when spoken to. Isn't that right, Rose?"

"Yes, Brother Semyon," whispered the naked little girl with the stringy blond hair. She didn't straighten up and, despite answering, didn't raise her head or turn to look at him. The one eye that Erhard could see through the tangled hair remained fixed on him.

"Staring is impolite, Rose," Semyon continued in Prûsan.

At the brother's words, the eye blinked and the girl's head shifted. Now her face was completely hidden.

"Who are these children?" Erhard turned to look at Brother Semyon. "What are you doing here?"

The brother smiled at Erhard and resumed speaking in German.

"I am doing things you could not have conceived of when you spoke your vows in Jerusalem. However, before I explain, I must show you something."

He turned to the guard, who until now had silently stood by next to the wall. "Please ready yourself," he told the man.

The guard walked to a rack on the wall that held a number of iron rods and polearms. The guard selected a long spear that had a broad leaflike blade that shone silver in the dim light.

But that wouldn't actually be silver, would it?

Erhard turned back toward Rose's cage. Brother Semyon had already slipped inside, closing the barred door behind him. He crossed the floor, bent by the little girl, and unlocked the manacle binding her ankle. Erhard thought he might have seen a glint of silver in the manacle as well.

Brother Semyon returned to the front of the cell, opposite Erhard. He commanded, in Prûsan, "Rose, come here."

Reluctantly it seemed, the girl walked forward, next to Brother Semyon. The other children, Erhard noticed, had finally turned their attention toward them.

"Give me your right hand, Rose."

The girl held out her arm, hand open, trembling slightly. Semyon grabbed her wrist with his left hand. His grasp nearly pulled the girl off-balance.

"Very good, Rose."

Still holding her like that, Brother Semyon turned toward Erhard and resumed speaking German. "Would you be kind enough to lend me your dagger for the purpose of a small demonstration?" He held his right hand through the bars.

The girl's detachment started to crumble. She made small sobbing noises, and those steel eyes pleaded openly with Erhard. But she didn't struggle.

Erhard whispered a Pater Noster to himself.

"Please? I cannot hold her here forever."

Erhard had always been a decisive man, not disposed to debate things with himself. His service had never been one he doubted. But seeing this girl held by Brother Semyon was causing some of that certainty to crumble.

"*Landkomtur Erhard!* Should I remind you who sent you here, or whom you serve?"

Erhard's vows were more important than any momentary doubts. He drew his dagger from the sheath on his belt. This was not the time or place to question his vocation.

Erhard placed the hilt in Brother Semyon's right hand. The blade shone dully, reflecting the small amount of sunlight that filtered in from the vent holes. The girl—Rose—became very still, only moving her eyes to follow the motion of the blade.

The chamber was so silent that Erhard was aware of the sound of his own breathing.

Brother Semyon deliberately slid the blade across the meat of Rose's palm. Even though he was almost expecting the casual brutality of the act, Erhard's breath caught as if it had been his own flesh that had been violated.

Rose shut her eyes and gasped, but she didn't cry out as the blade crossed her palm. Blood welled up and began to drip from between her fingers. When Brother Semyon was done, he lowered the dagger and turned her wounded palm toward Erhard.

Christ help me, Erhard thought. He couldn't help but think of the nail wounds on the hands of his Lord. "What exactly are you demonstrating?"

"Watch her, not me."

Erhard looked back at Rose's hand, the obscene wound spilling blood on the floor. But the blood was thick now, almost black. *No, the cut is too deep. Without pressure, it cannot begin clotting so soon.*

From his experience on the battlefield, even minor wounds like this might bleed forever if not quickly bound. But the blood still turned dark and slowed its flow.

And then the impossible happened. The edges of the wound knit themselves together. Almost, it seemed, the flesh melted and flowed together, like two streams joining. Erhard watched as the wound shortened, the edges traveling down the girl's palm until it disappeared, leaving the girl's hand bloodstained, but intact.

When Brother Semyon let go of Rose's wrist, she half stumbled, half ran to the center of the cell and curled into a ball, facing away from them. Her head trembled and, for a moment, Erhard thought she might be weeping.

But she was licking the blood off her hand.

Semyon walked up next to her, saying in Prûsan, "Very good, Rose. Your master is pleased." He reached down and replaced the silver manacle on her leg. He spoke to Erhard in German. "They may feel pain like men, but for them most injury is transitory. Fingers, limbs, organs, all regenerate without even a scar in most cases."

Erhard stared at the creature in the cell. Part of him, the worldly part, still thought of Rose as a child. The spiritual part, the part of him that served God and the Order, saw her as something else, something alien and threatening.

"Are they immortal?" he asked as the guard lowered his spear and let Semyon out of Rose's cage.

"By no means. They may be the spawn of some pagan demon, but they're as mortal as you or I. They age, of course, and they can be killed."

"How, if they heal like that?"

"Destroy or remove the brain or heart and they will not survive. Bound by silver they will not heal better than a man. Likewise, if they're wounded by an edge made of silver"—he gestured toward the spear that the guard was replacing on the rack—"they recover only slightly faster than a human being."

Erhard felt his stomach tighten when he realized that Brother Semyon spoke from his own experience. How many of these "children" did he start with to gain this knowledge? How many brains and hearts did he remove to demonstrate their mortality? Erhard tried to steady his voice as he asked, "What *are* they? Where did they come from?"

"There are too many names for what they are. Their kind dwells within the darkest primeval wilderness, preying on man. Few who witness their true nature survive. Those who do only contribute to the legends."

"But what are—"

"Come, you must see what you will be commanding in bringing this heathen land to God. I've arranged for Lilly to have a training session today."

"Training?"

"Oh, yes."

Brother Semyon returned Erhard's dagger. The blood on the edge was still bright red and liquid.

◈

Brother Semyon brought him to a balcony that overlooked what had been the main courtyard of the monastery. Erhard could see that since the monastery had been reoccupied, all entrances into the courtyard had been mounted with heavy iron-banded doors. The courtyard had been completely closed off. Inside, all ornament, all plant life, even stone walkways, had been removed, leaving a bare earthen floor and nothing else.

"What is this?" Erhard asked.

"You will see."

Below them, one set of doors opened. A pair of mail-clad guardsmen escorted a naked girl into the courtyard. Her red hair was long, reaching down past her shoulders and hiding her down-turned face from view. The guards reached down and freed her legs from a set of silver shackles.

"Brother Semyon—"

"Please, watch. Questions later."

The girl, whom Semyon had called Lilly, couldn't have been much more than seven or eight years old, the same age as the others. She stood at one end of the courtyard, motionless, as if she wasn't quite aware of where she was. The wind shifted, and Erhard thought he heard something.

Is she singing?

If she was, it was too quiet for Erhard to hear exactly what at this distance. All he made out was the barest hint of a tune, three or four notes in a young girl's voice.

Lilly's guards retreated out the doors they had entered, and once they had done so, doors at the other end of the courtyard, closest to Erhard and Brother Semyon, opened. Six men walked out—three guards, and three men in chains.

The men were obviously Prûsan prisoners. They still wore the rough leather skins that were their armor, and the largest one still had remnants of blue war paint striping his face. The guardsmen set a trio of swords on the ground before the pagans. Then, as two guardsmen leveled crossbows at them, the last guard released their chains.

The pagans still wore expressions of confusion as the guards retreated back beyond the door they had entered.

Four people were left in the courtyard—Lilly and the trio of Prûsan warriors.

"What in hell is this?" shouted one of the Prûsans in a dialect Erhard could barely decipher. He was a heavy brute with a full black beard and the face paint. "Are you Christ-kissing bastards playing games with us?"

Lilly finally looked up. Her face was blank, except for her eyes, which smoldered green with something that might be hatred.

"No games," she said.

All three turned around to look at her. Next to the heavy one was a thin man with braided hair. He stared at Lilly. "What is happening here?"

"They want me to fight you," Lilly said quietly.

The bearded man laughed. "This is a joke." He turned around and looked at the balcony, directly at Erhard and Brother Semyon. "Is this how you German scum entertain yourselves? You wish us to slaughter a child for you?"

Lilly shook her head and spoke quietly. "No. They wish me to slaughter *you*."

The third man was bald and smaller than the other two. He made a fist and stomped across the courtyard. "Child or not, the brat needs to learn some respect."

When he reached Lilly, he backhanded her across the face. The force should have knocked the girl over, but she remained standing. The bald man turned around to face his two comrades. "Now what kind of ridic—"

His words were cut short by a liquid gasp. He stumbled forward, and Erhard saw Lilly clinging to his back, hands buried in the sides of the man's neck. Her limbs seemed to have grown and her face was strangely distorted.

The man fell to his knees, trying to reach behind him, to dislodge the girl on his back.

Only it wasn't a girl anymore. It was something else, long-limbed and red-furred, with a long canine muzzle whose snarl revealed long, nasty teeth. The man still struggled underneath it, until the thing pulled its forearms up and out, at which point the man stopped moving.

The surviving two men snapped out of their shock and grabbed for the swords before them.

The creature had barely stepped from the back of the corpse when the bearded man ran forward, bringing his sword down on the creature's neck. The thing that had been Lilly didn't flinch, and didn't duck. It turned its muzzle toward the blow, and caught the man's wrist in its slavering mouth. The man's eyes went wide and the sword tumbled out of his grip as the thing shook its head back and forth before letting go.

The man stumbled back, cradling his ruined arm and screaming Prûsan obscenities. The other man brought his weapon up and managed to run it through the creature's unprotected belly.

"There," he said triumphantly, "it's done."

The paws at the end of the creature's forearms still had enough of the aspect of human hands to grab the attacker's sword arm. The thing turned its face toward him and spoke. "No. It isn't."

Hearing human language come from that inhuman throat was even more monstrous than seeing the girl transform. It was still a girl's voice, but bestial, and very angry.

The man belatedly tried to pull his arm free, but he only pulled the monster toward him. The creature continued pulling him forward, driving the sword deeper through its body, until the hilt was flush against its gut, and the man's throat was in reach.

Erhard had seen endless battles, and had seen countless men die, many at the end of his own sword, but he turned his eyes away as the man tried to scream.

This was no battle. This was little different from the pagan Romans throwing Christian martyrs to wild animals to be torn apart for the sport of it. The fact these men were armed made little difference.

He looked across at Brother Semyon, who watched the slaughter with a dire intensity. Erhard had to remind himself that he was in the company of a servant of God, a man who had taken the same vows as Erhard had. He was not in a position to judge a man's heart, and Erhard was never more grateful for the fact that judgment was in God's hands alone.

"Do not turn away, Brother Erhard," Brother Semyon said quietly.

Erhard reluctantly turned back to the scene on the field. Two men were dead from grievous wounds to the neck. The last surviving pagan had backed into a corner, clumsily wielding his sword one-handed, the ruin of his wounded right arm shoved under his armpit.

Lilly stood upright to face him. Blood covered her, glistening on her muzzle, matting the fur on her legs and torso.

The wounded man did his best to keep the shaking sword point between him and Lilly. "D-don't come any closer . . ."

Lilly slowly walked toward him.

"No. I will—"

Lilly stopped a single step from the tip of the threatening blade.

"I won't let you—"

She grabbed the blade in her half-paw, half-hand. She easily tore it free from the man's grip. Her paw bled where she had grasped the sword, but only for a moment. The massive wound in her belly had already sealed itself.

The bearded man shook his head, weeping, as Lilly stared at him with pitiless green eyes.

"By the gods," he said. "Mercy."

"Why?"

She descended upon him, giving him little chance to scream.

◈

Wolfbreed, Brother Semyon called them. Beasts that could cloak themselves in a human skin at will. Things that lurked in the nightmares of every rural village and hamlet. Anywhere that bordered a wilderness could harbor such unholy things.

Lilly stood in the courtyard, in the form of a human child. The only sign now of her bestial nature was the blood staining her naked skin. She faced the two of them, staring up at Erhard. The bottom half of her face was black with gore, and her eyes glinted green behind the clotted strings of her hair.

"Where did she—" Erhard began. "Where did *it* come from?"

"A wild version of what you saw—a wolf of human size and posture—slaughtered a convent of brethren of the Order nearly eight years ago."

Brother Semyon stared down at Lilly. He had never once turned away from the carnage she had wrought, but now, to Erhard he seemed to be looking through her.

"I never heard of this," Erhard prompted.

"It was never made widely known. It was when we still defended the crown of Hungary against the Cumans, three years before that troublesome man expelled us for asking the respect due us . . ." Brother Semyon smiled. "But you don't care for the politics of the matter, do you?"

"Such a creature attacked the Order?"

Semyon nodded. "My convent. My brothers. We were crossing the frontier. The beast struck first at our horses while we slept. We did not know at the time what we faced, and thought ourselves bedeviled by some human villain." He finally turned to face Erhard. "Now, in that Transylvanian wilderness, the old pagan modes of worship still abound. A nearby village had a reputation for not fully embracing Christ, and we went there to find satisfaction for our losses."

"What did you find there?"

"At first? Protests of innocence. But I was persuasive. I uncovered the priest of their false god, and the site of their sacred groves, and tales of their vengeful spirits and the things that lived in the woods."

"The wolfbreed?"

"My name, not theirs. I will not pollute my tongue with the names of the pagan gods by which these were called . . ."

"What happened?"

"My Komtur was a righteous man, but prone to err on the side of mercy when doing the Lord's work. He did not approve of the aggressiveness of my questioning, or the cost in blood for my answers. He took the priest in chains, and sent me to meditate on our Lord's mercy. But the beast came for them that night, and when I returned from my meditation, I found only their blood." Semyon turned away from Erhard to stare again at Lilly. "But it left me the priest."

"Lord have mercy."

Semyon nodded. "I did not. And I learned from the priest, before he died."

An animal, Semyon told Erhard, a beast fed upon the sacrifices of the village. The priest believed that he had called its wrath down upon the Christians. From the priest, Semyon heard of its ability to change its shape at will, its ability to heal from most any wound and, most important, its weakness.

"We had confiscated from the priest a dagger of silver. After his death, I took that weapon and followed the beast to its lair. The monster was beyond anything you've seen today, and it was only by the grace of God that I landed a mortal blow before it tore out my throat."

"But these children?"

"That creature was feeding its young, Brother Erhard. Our horses, my brothers, all meat for its larder. I walked into its lair and found bones and half-eaten corpses, and ten of her whelps. Two months old, if that."

"Rose? Lilly?"

"Birthed of that creature, and weaned on human flesh."

Erhard prayed to himself.

After a long pause, he finally found the strength to speak. "Surely this is the hand of evil itself. How can the Order give succor to such things?"

"As you must realize," Brother Semyon said, "there has been much debate upon this matter. Come, and I will enlighten you." Semyon led him away from the balcony as a trio of guards came to place silver shackles on an unresisting Lilly.

❖

In the twisted idolatry of the pagan tribes, these beasts were a personification of their brutal gods, red in tooth and claw.

Of course, Semyon said, that was a satanic deception meant to veil pagan hearts and minds from the glory of God, and lead them away from salvation.

When divine providence led Brother Semyon to find a litter of these creatures, the debate had been over exactly what *kind* of deception they were.

There were three possibilities.

The first possibility was that these creatures were members of the legion of Hell itself—demons sent to Earth to harass mankind. Three facts argued against that. The creatures were formed of earthly matter—blood, flesh, and bone like any other animal. They were also mortal, difficult but not impossible to kill. Last, evidence of the infant creatures showed that they gave birth, aged, and would eventually die.

The second possibility was that they were children of men, witches and warlocks possessed of demonic forces that gave them the monstrous ability to transform. However, it was argued that the creatures' ability to heal was not a false miracle. As such, it could only be granted by God. And were they possessed by the forces of Hell, those forces would be vulnerable to the rites of exorcism. But the words of Christ showed no power to compel them begone, or halt their changes.

The last possibility, given that they seemed neither demon nor men possessed, was that they were some order of earthly beast heretofore unknown within Christendom. No more a demon than the creature that had swallowed Jonah. Just a beast. One that could be trained, like a dog, or a horse, or a slave.

In the end, Brother Semyon had explained how fitting it was that the forces of Christendom could forcefully rend the veil of falsehood from the eyes of pagans by turning their own brute gods against them.

As Brother Semyon told Erhard this, Erhard couldn't help remembering the courtyard, and Lilly facing the Prûsan brute.

Could such a thing be an instrument of God?

But was it any crueler than what he had seen, and done, in the Holy Land? If this was the path God had set before him, Erhard would have to follow it.

"Brother Semyon," he asked, "you said that you found ten of these creatures. I saw only six."

In response, Semyon nodded. "Their training has been hard," he explained.

Prime

Anno Domini 1239

Nolite fieri sicut equus et mulus,
quibus non est intellectus.
In camo et freno maxillas eorum constringe,
qui non approximant ad te.

Be ye not as the horse, or as the mule,
which have no understanding:
whose mouth must be held in with bit and bridle,
lest they come near unto thee.

—Psalms 32:9

vi

Ten years after first setting foot in Brother Semyon's half-ruined monastery east of the city of Torun, by the River Drweca, Landkomtur Erhard von Stendal had left Lilly in the care of the keep at Johannisburg. He originally had no plans to visit that outpost again. He had been on the way to Balga and the spring campaigns to the east, as he had every spring for nearly a decade.

And then a courier arrived with a summons for him—a plain piece of parchment that had borne the seal of the Hochmeister of the Order. It had read, "Your audience is required at our houses in Marienwerder, no later than this Easter."

It was signed "Hochmeister Conrad of Thuringia."

Conrad's predecessor, Hermann von Salza, had elevated Erhard to Landkomtur in Jerusalem. Conrad had only borne the title of Hochmeister for a few weeks. Now, abruptly, he was in Prûsa, commanding an audience.

Erhard had briefly contemplated taking Lilly, but despite her training and her human appearance, she was still a grave secret. A convent of knights accompanied by a maiden bound by a silver chain would raise questions that would be unwelcome to Erhard, his Order, and his mission.

Fortunately, Johannisburg was small and now had a keep equipped to keep Lilly safe and unobserved while Erhard met with the new Hochmeister. Erhard was unconcerned about the limited springtime garrison at the keep. In a decade of service, no one but Erhard had ever had to lay a hand on Lilly. Of all her siblings, she had always been the most obedient, the most intelligent, and the most accepting of the missions given to her. She was the one ultimate expression of Brother Semyon's plans for the wolfbreed, and trained so, Lilly was only a threat to enemies of God and the Order.

When he had taken Lilly to Johannisburg, she had walked meekly into her cell to await her master's return.

That was almost a week ago.

Landkomtur Erhard von Stendal now rode the streets of Marienwerder, his mount slogging through a mixture of mud, slush, and manure that stank despite the cold.

The buildings leaned over the streets, crowding between the city walls and the shoulders of the castle. The bishopric here had been founded less than a decade ago, yet the gates Erhard had just ridden through led into the most important city in Christian Prûsa—a city as populous and diverse as any in northern Christendom. Around him, Erhard heard German, French, and Italian, and even the broad-nosed men of Prûsan heritage were speaking some more civilized tongue.

The castle here was three times the size of the keep at Johannisburg, and was a hive of activity, almost more crowded than the city below it. Grooms took their horses, and servants led them to a barracks that could easily hold twoscore knights.

Erhard and his men took the evening meal with the resident brothers, more than two dozen men, enough for two full convents of brethren. They ate in silence as scripture was read, and after the clerks read the concluding prayers and the servants took the remaining bread for alms, one of the lay brothers came to Erhard and said, "They will see you now."

⬦

"They" were several of the highest-ranking members of the Teutonic Order in Prûsa. It included the Landmeister of all Prûsa as well as the new Hochmeister, Conrad of Thuringia himself. To Conrad's right sat an unfamiliar man in a bishop's robes. The brothers of the Order were all plainly dressed in white or somber-hued linens decorated only by the black cross of their Order. The only departures from the ascetic dress of the knights were the rings worn by Hochmeister Conrad as a token of his rank.

In contrast, the bishop was as out of place as a peacock within a murder of crows. The man's hands glittered with rings, and his cloak had obscenely voluminous velvet sleeves trimmed in fur. He wore a heavy gold cross on a chain. The bishop was heavy as well, and the chain for his cross disappeared into the folds around his neck, which were nearly as full as the folds in his robe.

To Erhard's surprise, the bishop was the first to speak.

"You are Landkomtur Erhard von Stendal?" The bishop's German was heavily accented.

"Yes, Your Grace."

The bishop nodded. "You have the title of province commander, but you have no province. Can you tell me how you came by this title?"

Erhard narrowed his eyes and looked at Hochmeister Conrad. The grand master's expression was grave. "Please do well to answer Bishop Cecilio's question."

"It was granted to me by Hochmeister Hermann von Salza when I served in Jerusalem."

The bishop grunted something in Italian. Erhard didn't know the language well enough to understand much of what the man said, but what he did hear sounded something like, "*stupid diversion of resources.*"

Erhard stood a little straighter, steeling himself against the unchristian resentment building in his breast. He knew that there was no shortage of men in the Church who questioned the priorities of the Order's mission in the north. There were those who believed that any and all forces of Christendom should be directed to supporting and defending the Holy Land. To them, the fact that the Baltic was home to tribes of heathen barbarians was almost irrelevant.

Such men were also concerned with how quickly the Order had grown here, and how many more secular crusaders were being recruited for the campaigns in Prûsa than for the support of the Church's tenuous hold against the Infidel in Jerusalem. Men like the bishop didn't account for the fact that the crusaders to Prûsa had a much shorter and easier journey, and could travel home at the end of a campaign in a matter of a month. To men like the bishop, every sword in Prûsa was one less sword in the Holy Land.

Erhard thanked God that it wasn't his place to make that argument here. He waited for the bishop to continue his questioning. Instead, the bishop addressed Hochmeister Conrad in a tone that Erhard thought bordered on disrespect. "Is this kind of elevation a common practice in the German Order?"

Who is this odious man? Erhard thought.

Hochmeister Conrad educated the bishop on the normal course of affairs in the Order as far as the brethren rising in ranks. Erhard watched the bishop gesture as he spoke with the grand master. In the flashes of glittering jewels on the bishop's fingers, Erhard saw an explanation, and it was a grave one.

In the midst of the jewelry was a papal signet.

The bishop was a representative of the pope, and one that seemed hostile to the Order. That wasn't a good sign. The Teutonic Order had prospered in the last decade because of the dual patronage of both Frederick II of the Holy Roman Empire and Pope Gregory IX. Both rulers, spiritual and secular, had granted the Teutonic Order domain over Prûsa. Support for the Order was one of few spots of common ground ever found between the two. The hostility between Gregory and Frederick was epic and long-lived, escalating to the point where the pope had actually invaded the emperor's lands when the emperor had gone to the Holy Land to fulfill his vows in a crusade.

Relative peace had reigned between the two for the past decade mainly because of the diplomatic intercession of Hochmeister Hermann von Salza, who had maintained close and friendly relations with both. His abilities had not only helped to secure peace between the Papal States and the Empire, but had managed to increase the Order's temporal power to the point where it was a near autonomous force in the north of Europe. Within the confines of Prûsa, the Teutonic Order was legally answerable only to the pope, but in effect, answerable only to God.

Since the recent death of Hermann von Salza, however, Erhard had heard that the tenuous peace between pope and emperor was crumbling. Now it seemed the unquestioned favor granted to the Order was beginning to crumble as well.

When Hochmeister Conrad completed his explanation of the normal process of ascension in the ranks of the Order, Bishop Cecilio shifted his massive bulk forward to peer at Erhard from deep-set eyes. "This is not your story, is it?"

"No, Your Grace, it isn't." Erhard looked back at the bishop's face, and he could tell that this was a man for whom simple respect was not satisfactory. Bishop Cecilio was a man who was accustomed to command through fear. The sense of entitlement Erhard felt from the man was in stark contrast to Hochmeister Conrad,

who had several years ago abrogated a noble birth and title to join
the Order as a simple knight.

"Perhaps you can explain your position and how you came by
it."

Erhard did not like the sound of where this was going. What
he did for the Order was a secret of monumental significance. He
looked directly to Hochmeister Conrad for guidance. "With my
master's leave, Your Grace."

"Do not try my patience, Brother Erhard. I come here with full
papal authority to review this matter."

Erhard nodded to the bishop. "To whom I owe fealty and obedience. I serve at the pleasure of His Holiness first of all." He turned
back to Hochmeister Conrad. "But of those present in this room,
after God, my duty is to my master."

"Such insolence," the bishop muttered. Erhard was prepared
for more of an outburst, but it didn't happen. Bishop Cecilio
seemed to defer ever so slightly to Conrad. It seemed the Order
still reigned here, although the balance was more precarious than
Erhard would have liked.

Hochmeister Conrad steepled his fingers. "There are no secrets in
this room. Speak freely and enlighten Bishop Cecilio on how it is you
have served God, the Church, and our Order these past ten years."

Erhard nodded and silently prayed for strength. Then he raised
his head and spoke. "In the year of our Lord twelve hundred and
twenty-nine, in Jerusalem, I was called to an audience before
Hochmeister Hermann von Salza . . . ."

Erhard told the bishop of the young wolfbreed children trained
by Brother Semyon in his half-ruined monastery. He told him of
the first use of the trained beasts, to spread superstitious panic
and confusion in the villages harboring bands of tribesmen that
troubled the movements of Christian soldiers and tradesmen. He
told them that, based on those successes in the first year, they were
able to use one wolfbreed child to break a siege of a Prûsan fort
that had been resisting for nearly a year.

He told him of the greatest success, when they used the monsters' human appearance to slip them into villages before a siege began. One creature alone could decimate the leadership, shatter morale, and panic the population in the space of a night or two. Once the Order had adopted the tactic, it wasn't unusual to have the villagers open the city gates to the invaders. They believed that their old gods had come to punish them, and the Order was happy to bring the power of Christ to their rescue.

"Because of these animals," Erhard said, "we have grown the borders of Christendom farther into Prûsa than anyone before us, with fewer men lost and many more converts gained." Erhard didn't mention the losses among the wolfbreed themselves. Most hadn't been as adept as Lilly at learning the basics of tactics, and had fallen to wounds too great to heal from.

The bishop nodded, leaning back in his chair. "I see. Do you have any more to say?"

"Only that it was the providence of our Lord God that brought us possession of these remarkable creatures, and it is His continued providence that allows for our continued successes in this heathen land."

The bishop nodded and brought his sausagelike fingers up to rub the bridge of his nose. Lamplight glistened off the skin of his face, which was oily with sweat. Erhard had thought it chilly in the stone halls here, but then he was not covered in heavy robes, or grotesquely obese.

"This is obscene," the bishop said finally.

"Your Grace—" Erhard began.

"No," the bishop snapped, "your statement is complete. It is clear from your own testimony that you have engaged in offenses against God and Nature that are nearly beyond credibility. You walk into my presence and have the temerity to speak of the providence of our Lord."

Erhard stepped back and shook his head. He cast a pleading glance at Conrad. "But—"

The bishop cast an accusing jeweled finger at Erhard. "Silence, or I will have you silenced."

When Conrad didn't intervene, Erhard stood mute.

"I have had leave to investigate what has transpired under the auspices of the Order, and what has occurred at your hands, and at the hands of Brother Semyon von Kassel. I have heard testimony in regard to the monstrous wretches in your care, and of their fates. Three supposedly died at the hands of the pagan tribes they were set upon." He cocked his head and his next words dripped with derision. "Surely a sign of our Lord's providence."

Erhard strained against the impulse to speak out, to explain, but to do so now would only worsen his case—a case he now feared had been lost long before he ever set foot in Marienwerder.

The bishop slammed his hand on the table, his rings clattering against the wood. "You have given succor to agents of Satan. Worse, you have given these demons human flesh to feed on, and have used them to aggrandize yourself on the battlefield. You have been so deeply and vilely deceived by the Father of Lies that I almost doubt the possibility of your redemption. It is fortunate that there are men who speak highly of your righteousness, and you have not been given to deception in your own testimony. I leave it to your Order to decide by what means you will show proper repentance."

"As His Holiness would wish," Conrad finally spoke. "If Brother Erhard has done evil, it was not from evil intent. He is a faithful servant of God and the Church. If he has gone astray, it is as much our Order's responsibility as it is his."

"Yes," said Bishop Cecilio. "And His Holiness will expect proper repentance of the Order as well."

"You will return to Rome with tribute that His Holiness should find more than sufficient."

"That, of course, is not for me to decide." The bishop turned to Erhard. "But I make one demand on behalf of the pontiff that comes before all else. Use of this abomination shall immediately cease, and the remaining creature shall be destroyed by fire."

He must have seen Erhard's disquiet on his face, because the bishop allowed himself a small smile. "Yes, you need not concern yourself with Brother Semyon, or the creature that remained in his care. They have both been dealt with, and the site of his abominations has been burned and purified by exorcism."

The bishop made a dismissive gesture with his hand. "You may go."

As Erhard left, he heard the bishop say, "I will pray for your soul." His tone indicated he would do no such thing.

❖

Erhard left the disastrous meeting in stunned silence. He had never once considered the possibility . . .

He closed his fist and leaned heavily against the stone wall of the corridor. No, it wasn't because the pope didn't know of what Erhard was doing in the name of God and the Order. The pope himself had approved the reasoning that Brother Semyon had explained to him so long ago.

For nearly eighteen years these creatures had been of earthly nature by papal decree.

The situation has changed, Erhard thought.

It was not pleasant to concede the fact that the Church made moral decisions based on politics, but the pope was as much a temporal leader as he was a spiritual one. And all worldly rulers soon enough erred between what was right and what was profitable.

His Holiness Gregory IX had decided that it was no longer in the interest of his own power that a monastic order so close to his rival the emperor might have access to such a devastating weapon.

Brother Semyon's wolfbreed children had been too successful.

Landkomtur Erhard von Stendal knew this, but he also knew that the knowledge did not change his duty to God, the Order, or the Church. He had taken an oath of obedience. He would have to return to Johannisburg, take Lilly, and set her to fire.

For some reason, he remembered a time shortly after he had taken charge of Semyon's wolfbreed children. He had been scourging Lilly for some infraction; what it had been, Erhard didn't remember. When he had finished, and her back was healing, she looked up at him and said, "Master?"

His first impulse had been to whip her again, for speaking out of turn, but something—perhaps mercy—made him ask what she wanted.

She asked, "Do you have a master?"

"My master is my Lord and Savior, Jesus Christ."

She looked at him very strangely for a moment, and then she asked, "Does your Lord Jesus whip you when you disobey Him?"

Erhard stared at her childlike visage, but he saw the beast within her. "My Lord does something far worse, should I disobey Him. He turns his back upon me and leaves my presence."

She had nodded, apparently understanding.

"Please do not turn your back on me," she had told him.

The words echoed in his memory, as running steps echoed through the corridor, growing louder. Erhard turned to see one of his young knights in an unseemly scramble, running toward him. Erhard would have reprimanded him but for the distress evident in the young knight's face.

"What is it?"

"Johannisburg," the knight gasped in a voice ragged and out of breath. "A messenger fresh from Johannisburg."

Erhard grabbed the knight's shoulder and asked, "What news?"

As the knight told him, Erhard felt the road God had laid for him over the past ten years crumble completely, leaving only the Abyss under his feet.

vii

Gedim rode home from Johannisburg in a foul mood. It was bad enough to scrape an existence together for his family through a harsher than average winter. Now he had to deal with the arcane rules of trade established by the Order. He had gone to Johannisburg with a pathetic collection of skins harvested from all the meat they'd had to trap to supplement their food supply. He had hoped, now that it was spring and people were coming north again, that he would be able to barter for some iron tools: a hoe or axe head, or—in his more grandiose dreams—a plow to replace the wooden blade he was constantly repairing.

Of course, his skins were nowhere near enough for a new plow, especially when the guard at the city gate insisted on taking a quarter of his goods in tithe and taxes.

He had almost spat in the guard's face and said, "I bow to your God. How many more indignities do you want to heap upon us?" He hadn't, because the man taking his skins was as Prûsan as he was. Gedim probably knew the man's father. Like Hilde, the guard had been baptized into a new world—though he had been Uldolf's age, so he probably remembered a time before the cross had laid its shadow on this town.

So, instead of carrying a new plow, or new tools, the wagon rode empty except for a box of salted herring. The smell of fish on the bumpy ride home did little for Gedim's mood.

I do what I can.

He had also purchased a vial of medicine for Hilde, which was certain to cause his wife to scold him. What did he know about caring for the sick? Burthe would probably tell him that the mixture was useless for her fever, and that he had wasted his money. However, he was more comfortable with having that argument than he was with doing nothing at all.

Besides, they now had herring.

His cart rounded the last curve in the dirt track before his farm and he came in sight of his cottage. *Home.* Seeing the thatch roof and rough log walls raised his spirits.

Uldolf was sitting on a bench in front of the cottage, working with a knife. Even at this distance, Gedim could see him scraping shreds of meat away from the skin of some small animal. Uldolf had one leg bent up on the bench to hold the skin flat, and Gedim could see a patch of gray-white fur curling up from the edge.

Still poaching . . .

Gedim pulled the cart around to a barn formed by three timber walls surrounding a pair of currently empty stalls. As Gedim took his time unhitching the horse, he wondered if he should reprimand Uldolf or not. They both knew that the small area a free man was allowed to hunt had been scoured of game two months into winter. Just to get the hare whose skin he was cleaning, Uldolf would have had to go nearly to the walls of Johannisburg itself.

Then again, Gedim had just returned from trading on his son's trapping ability.

Gedim let the horse into their small excuse for a pasture and walked around to the cottage, carrying his box of fish. While he could never quite approve of what Uldolf was doing, he usually decided to pretend he didn't realize where the game came from.

."Father," Uldolf called to him.

Gedim smiled and waved as he walked across the muddy field. No sense bringing his frustration into the house. "How is Hilde?"

"Her fever broke in the night. She was bright-eyed and chattering away, last I looked."

It was hard not to stumble with relief. He would personally thank Christ himself if it turned out that the medicine in his pouch was a true waste of money. "That's good."

He walked past his son and toward the door. Hilde had been asleep when he had left for Johannisburg four days ago. It would be nice to see her awake.

"Father." Uldolf had set down his knife and grabbed Gedim's arm.

Gedim stopped in his tracks and turned around. "What?"

Uldolf looked downcast and slightly embarrassed as he muttered, "We have a guest."

◈

Gedim managed to pull the entire story out of Uldolf, despite the boy's tendency to omit details.

He wasn't quite sure if the boy was embarrassed, modest, or afraid Gedim might be angry at him. But Uldolf insisted on telling his tale in a circular pattern, going back and elaborating when Gedim prodded him.

The day after you left for Johannisburg, I found her in the woods and brought her here. You see, she was hurt, I think by bandits. I was out trapping game and following the creek bed. She didn't understand me at first, I think because of the head wound. And she had a bad injury to her head and her shoulder . . .

It went back and forth like that, until Gedim had the whole story. At least, he hoped it was the whole story. It wasn't until the fourth time around that he got the details that the injured woman had been naked in the creek when Uldolf had found her, and that he had ended up carrying her nearly all the way home.

During the story, Gedim caught himself hoping that no harm had come to Uldolf's cloak. They didn't have the resources to replace something like that right now.

But the thought shamed him.

There had been a time when that kind of thing didn't matter so much. Gedim had once been part of the warrior clan that ruled the village of Mejdân, the younger brother of Radwen Seigson, and heir to a wealth of land, slaves, and cattle. When Mejdân fell, he had been one of the few baptized that the Teutonic Order, in their strange Christian logic, had considered of "noble" blood. So, the Order had allowed him to retire with his farm, his cattle, and a few of his slaves.

Over the past eight years, the Germans had ended up with the great part of the wealth he had been allowed to keep—if not through taxes and tithes, then simply in barter so he could keep his family fed through winter.

His last ox had died during the past winter, and Gedim was loath to admit that it was the meat from its carcass, and the grain they would have fed it, that had helped keep his family fed through this winter.

He didn't want to think about next winter.

Just when Uldolf finished recounting the details about his difficulties with his cloak, Gedim's wife came out to call them in for dinner.

They followed Burthe into the cottage, which was filled with the smell of barley stew. Gedim thought he could smell the remnants of the former occupant of the skin Uldolf had been cleaning.

Hilde was up and smiling, the first time Gedim had seen her out of bed since a week before he'd left for Johannisburg. She sat on a stool by the hearth, where a stew pot hung over the coals on an iron hook. Hilde had a look of intense concentration as she stirred the pot with a long-handled wooden spoon.

The newcomer sat at the table. Burthe had managed to clothe

her in a threadbare surcoat and a ragged chemise that had been destined to be recut for Hilde to wear. Through the loose neck, Gedim could see the edge of the bandages on her shoulder. More bandages wrapped her head, so he couldn't see the damage Uldolf had told him about. Her hair was long and red. The way the girl smiled at Uldolf gave no sign how close she had been to death.

Gedim shook his head at his new houseguest.

"So, what's your name, child?"

She looked at Gedim and frowned.

"I don't think she can understand you," Uldolf said.

"No? You've been speaking Prûsan, I take it?"

He looked at the girl and repeated in German, "What is your name?"

She didn't respond any better.

"That is inconvenient." He eased himself into the chair at the table opposite the girl and studied her. "Where did you come from?" he asked. The girl might have been all of seventeen, but the frustrated expression on her face made her look younger. "How are we going to get you back home?"

She opened her mouth as if to say something, but it only came out as a grunt. She shook her head, and looked down at the table. She seemed close to tears.

"You see—" Uldolf started to say.

Gedim held up his hand and said, "Shh, son."

When he had been a warrior, before this end of Prûsa had become a province of Christendom, he had seen men suffer from head wounds, and those who survived were never unchanged. The evil effects of such a blow could damage a man in ways more profound than simply losing an eye or a limb.

"Child, you do understand me, don't you?"

She looked at him with piercing green eyes. She tried to speak again, but her lip trembled and she appeared on the verge of tears.

"Don't try and talk," he told her. "It's the blow, I think."

Uldolf sat down and looked at her. "She's mute, then?"

"I've seen head blows on the battlefield steal more than speech from a man." He turned to the girl. "I wonder if you know how lucky you actually are. Not just that you survived those wounds, but that my son found you."

She looked at him with her head cocked as if she might be trying to understand him.

"What do we do with you?" Gedim said. "You cannot tell us who you are, or where you belong—"

"She belongs here!" Hilde pronounced, walking around the table and proudly placing a steaming bowl of stew on the table. "She's our guest. Mama said so."

Burthe slid a spoon in front of him, and Gedim gave his wife a look that asked, rhetorically, Who exactly is the head of this household?

She smiled back with an expression that said, We both know the answer to that question. Now eat your supper.

Gedim pulled his spoon toward him and said, "Well, if that's what Mama said."

The girl sniffed the bowl, then looked at the four of them as Hilde set spoons down in front of her and Uldolf.

"Go ahead," Uldolf said. "The guest breaks bread first."

She licked her lips, looked at her spoon, then looked down into the large common bowl again.

"It's all right," Uldolf told her.

After looking back and forth between Uldolf and the bowl, she finally reached down and shoved her hand into the stew.

"Ew!" Hilde said.

Even Burthe seemed taken aback as the otherwise attractive girl shoveled handfuls of the stew into her mouth.

Uldolf looked mortified.

For his own part, it took a supreme effort of self-control for Gedim to keep from erupting in laughter.

"I guess she was hungry," Uldolf finally said.

She certainly was. When she looked up from the bowl it was with a quizzical expression, as if she was wondering why no one else was eating. Burthe took the opportunity to reach over with a rag and wipe off her face.

The girl glared at Burthe, which made Gedim want to laugh all the more. "Prûsan," he muttered, chuckling. "Red hair aside, the girl is pure Prûsan."

"What are you saying, Gedim?" Burthe gave him a harsh look.

"I'm saying she just needs to see an example of proper manners," Gedim said, raising his spoon.

◈

Gedim walked out of the cottage and found Uldolf standing out in the field, staring up at nothing. The sky was cloudless, and stars coated the moonless sky like a layer of frost. The last claws of winter bit at his skin as he walked up next to his son.

"You should come to bed."

"I know."

"You did good."

Uldolf shook his head. "No, I didn't. I was a coward. I was a few minutes' walk from the town gate. But I carried that woman five miles rather than try and get help there, just because I didn't want to get caught for poaching a damned hare."

Gedim reached out and placed a hand on Uldolf's shoulder.

"She could have died because of that," Uldolf said.

"Son, has it occurred to you that she might have been a victim of the soldiers in the garrison there?"

Uldolf turned and looked at him, frowning. "You think so?"

"If someone was going to just abandon a woman to die in the shadow of Johannisburg Castle, who is the most likely culprit? Some random brigand, who can safely ply his trade an hour's ride away from any law at all, or the only men in the area who have little to fear from Christian law?"

"You think they could?"

"Son, I've seen war. I've also seen the men that the Order uses. They hire anyone willing to buy their God's favor with blood, gold, or a few mealy words. The Prûsans they employ— A Prûsan in the service of the Order is little better than those brigands you're concerned about."

"But—"

"A man who looks for his own flaws will always find them," Gedim said. "I know you. You are not a coward. If you really believed you could trust the soldiers in Johannisburg, I know you wouldn't have hesitated a moment to go there, whatever you might have been accused of. Now come back. Hilde needs her sleep, and I don't want you waking her by crawling into bed at some ungodly hour."

"Father?"

Gedim turned around, hoping that the boy was done belittling himself.

"How bad do you think it is?"

"Her head?"

Uldolf nodded.

"I don't know, son."

"You said you had seen men injured like that."

Gedim sighed. He didn't talk much about his years as a warrior. Not just because he had little use for the glory that men tried to ascribe to the brutish business, but it showed how he had fallen in his own eyes. When he should have fought, in the end he had capitulated and accepted baptism. Though, looking at the man Uldolf had become, he couldn't come to regret the decision.

"Most died quickly," he told his son. "But I saw two men survive. One was struck blind even though his eyes were undamaged and still reacted to light. The other could speak, and knew his life up until the blow fell, but he lost the ability to remember anything after. He would greet everyone by saying, 'Well met, I have not seen you in ages,' even those he broke bread with that morning. Months after, you would talk to him and he would be convinced that he had just woken up from being struck down in battle."

"What about her? I thought at first she spoke some other language."

"I don't think she speaks any, at the moment."

"So she lost her memory, like the man you remember?"

"Not like him. He would talk to you, and remember who you were, if he had known you before the injury. She hasn't lost her ability to remember. From her looks, she remembers *you* quite clearly."

Uldolf turned so Gedim couldn't see his face. "Like a child, an infant, then."

"If so, she is a quick one. I've not yet seen a baby that could learn the use of a spoon that quickly."

"Maybe she'll learn to speak again."

"Maybe." Gedim took Uldolf's shoulder and led him back toward the cottage. "Now Hilde needs her sleep. We can talk about this later."

viii

Eight days after the carnage at Johannisburg Castle, Sergeant Günter Sejod had the dubious honor of greeting a full company of fresh soldiers, secular knights, squires, turcopoles, and various men-at-arms—all led by seven armored men bearing white mantles over their shoulders, displaying the black cross of the Order of the Hospital of St. Mary of the Germans in Jerusalem.

Günter had expected the Landkomtur to return with some dramatic gesture on behalf of the Order. Christian charity aside, he couldn't help but picture it involving his head parting company with his shoulders.

He had *not* expected Landkomtur Erhard von Stendal to return with nearly fivescore men. When the Landkomtur had left his monstrous prisoner in Günter's inadequate care a fortnight ago, he had originally been heading for campaigns east with only six other knights, a few retainers, and the redheaded woman.

The redheaded monster.

The mass of men rode inside the castle walls and made camp in the bailey, in the shadow of the stone keep where so many had recently died.

Riding at the fore was Landkomtur Erhard himself. He rode his mount across the bailey and drew the animal up within a few paces of Günter. One of Günter's surviving men, arm still splinted from when the cell door crushed it, reached up to hold the horse for the Landkomtur to dismount.

Günter walked up and held himself at attention. He watched as the Landkomtur surveyed the half-dozen men who remained. Erhard's frown was ominous.

"Sergeant?" The man addressed him in flawless Prûsan.

"Yes, sir."

"By my count you've lost fourteen men."

"Yes, sir."

Erhard shook his head. "God have mercy. Christ have mercy." The knight stared up at the keep, whose gray-white walls were turning scarlet in the setting sun. The reflected light gave a bloody tinge to the white of his mantle. "I am afraid we are to be sorely tested."

"Sir, may I ask why——"

Erhard held up his hand. "Please, not here. Tell me first, did she trouble the townsfolk?"

"No." He added, "Praise be to God," making a conscious effort to use the singular in front of Erhard. "The creature made its escape to the east."

"What is in that direction?"

"There is a road and some farms when the land flattens again."

"Did you find any signs of what became of her?"

You mean, did I send out my four remaining able-bodied men after that thing, armed with silver daggers? No I did not, you addle-brained monk. Some of us are not quite as eager to meet God as you are.

"After tending to the dead and injured we did search the woods below the eastern wall. We found nothing of substance. A footprint in mud, bloody fur caught in a thicket, a tree freshly clawed."

Erhard nodded. He whispered something in Latin then reverted to the Prûsan tongue. "Show me the scene of the disaster."

✦

After the removal of the soldiers' remains for proper burial, the lowest levels of the keep's storerooms had been left as they had been after the monster's escape. Günter led Erhard alone. None of Günter's men wanted to retrace these steps, and Erhard took none of his own.

They each carried a lantern, and the pair carved long fingers of shadow across the damp walls—shadows that mirrored the ribbons of ruddy black where blood had dried. It smelled of rotten meat and death down here.

Erhard paused briefly by the short table where Manfried's sword and dagger still rested. Then he walked down the corridor to the banded door and checked its edges.

"I told you," Günter said. "Manfried opened the door on his own." He wanted to make it clear that this was no Prûsan's doing.

Erhard nodded. "I see that." He examined a long gouge on the floor that traced an arc from the doorway halfway to where the door now hung open. Unrecognizable fragments of silver rested on the ground where the gouge terminated. "He didn't know enough to remove my seals before opening the door. The lower one was wedged under it."

He picked another silver remnant from the edge of the door-frame and shook his head. "This was the second line of defense. How did she escape the shackle? You cannot tell me that Manfried removed her chains as well?"

"No." Günter waved inside the cell. "The creature amputated its own foot."

There was a long pause before Erhard said, "She did what?"

"You can see for yourself, if you don't smell it already."

It seemed to dawn on Erhard that the stench was coming from inside the cell itself. He turned and shone his light inside, muttered "Christus," and crossed himself.

"The state of this cell . . ." He turned to look at Günter with an expression that was half accusing, half shock. "Was this your doing?"

Günter shook his head. "We followed your strictures. Food and water, no other contact." He gestured at the feces- and urine-soaked straw. "She had a clean bucket for refuse, which she chose not to use."

Erhard looked down at the filthy straw mats, his face white-skinned. He walked in and knelt next to the manacle that still held a woman's foot, now black with rot. In the lamplight, the slightly glistening skin undulated with an infection of maggots.

"She couldn't break the silver?" Günter asked.

Erhard nodded, looking at the cell. He shone the light around, until it settled on a corner of the room where a small pile of clothing rested on top of an upturned bucket.

"She shed her clothes and befouled this cell. She tore her own foot off to free herself from touching the silver binding her—so she could change herself. This was long in the planning." Erhard straightened. "Manfried was a young man, wasn't he?"

"Yes."

"Romantic, perhaps?"

"Sir?"

"She is more of a monster than I knew. She seduced a man with his own pity. God have mercy on his soul."

It *was* appalling to Günter, the lengths this thing had gone to, to delude poor Manfried. However, at the moment, there were other aspects of the monstrosity that concerned him more.

"Sir, I tried to ask you before, silver is supposed to kill it. Why is it still alive?"

"What do you mean?"

"One of my men fired a silver-tipped crossbow bolt into the creature's head."

Erhard straightened up. "He did? Are you certain?"

"Yes, I witnessed it myself. Just before it slaughtered him." Günter shuddered at the memory, but for some inexplicable reason, Erhard was taking Günter's news very well. In fact, it seemed to brighten his mood considerably. Günter didn't understand the reaction. "Don't you understand what I'm saying? You told me that silver was the only thing that could kill it! But it *didn't!*"

"Silver isn't poison to this creature, Sergeant. All a silver weapon does is give it a normal wound. A cut from a steel sword will seal up as soon as you withdraw the blade. This foot had probably regrown within an hour. But your man's crossbow bolt—that would injure her as well, as it would have injured you, had he fired it into your skull."

"But it didn't kill—"

"Men have stumbled off the field with similar wounds, most to die very shortly after." Erhard clasped him on the shoulder. "If you'd pray for something, pray for that."

When Erhard let go of him, Günter heard him add in German, *"And pray that I find her body."*

ix

At night now, Hilde had to share her bed with Ulfie. Hilde liked being close to her brother, even though Ulfie snored like her father did, and sometimes he moaned and had nightmares. But when he was quiet, she liked to rest her head against his chest and listen to his insides gurgle, and she liked the way her brother smelled after the day was over. Earthy, like the field after a hard rain, or like their horse when he wasn't working and got so full of himself that he rolled in the pasture.

She was probably too old to sleep with her brother—he was almost too big for her bed, feet hanging off the end—but their guest was sick from the nasty wounds that Mama had sewn up. Mama said that fevers almost always came after someone was hurt that bad, and as bad as it seemed, Mama said she thought that their guest was doing well. Better than Mama expected her to.

Hilde was still scared for her. She didn't know if Mama really thought she was doing well, or if Mama just didn't want Hilde to worry. Sometimes Mama and Papa would avoid saying things, afraid that Hilde might not understand what was happening.

However, Hilde understood what a fever was, and how awful it could be. Sometimes it seemed that she had spent most of her life fighting to wake from a fever, and it made her wish she could make their guest feel better.

But there was also some selfishness with the sympathy. Hilde loved Ulfie, yet there were times she wanted a big sister.

It was very late. The sun had been down for hours, and Hilde thought she was the only one in the house awake right now. Ulfie was snoring as badly as Papa was, and Hilde wondered how Mama could sleep through all the racket. However, even without the noise, Hilde didn't feel tired. She supposed that she'd had so much sleep when she'd been sick that she didn't need as much now.

She spent her time in the dark wondering about their guest— who she was, where she had come from. She was so pretty that Hilde imagined she must be a lost princess, or a fairy, from some far-off place where people didn't talk like normal folks. Maybe that's why she didn't speak—

Hilde heard something odd in the cabin and held her breath. In her mind she had made their guest a fairy princess who had escaped from a tribe of evil ogres. The sudden odd sound made her think that the ogres might have come for her . . .

But that wasn't what she heard.

Very quietly, she thought she heard a girl's voice say, "No."

Hilde sat up. Ulfie didn't stir; he slept like a stone. A very loud stone.

She looked across the cabin and saw their guest stirring. She was speaking, but low, and her voice sounded like a girl's. Not much older than Hilde even though she was nearly Ulfie's age. Hilde thought she heard her say, "No," again.

Hilde carefully slid out from between her brother and the wall, off the foot of her short bed. The light in the cabin was dim, cast by strips of moonlight filtering through the shutters, but Hilde could see enough to keep from stumbling as she walked to Ulfie's bed.

She stopped at the head of the bed. A strip of moonlight had fallen diagonally across the woman's face, lighting part of the bandage on her head, a strand of hair, a slice of her damp brow, and a single eye, half-lidded, looking at Hilde.

Hilde touched her shoulder. "Are you all right?"

She grabbed Hilde's hand so quickly that Hilde gasped and tried to pull away. But the grip was much stronger than Hilde was. The woman's eyes opened as she looked at Hilde, though she didn't seem to quite see her.

"Rose?" the woman whispered. "Is that you?"

"You're talking!" Papa had said that she couldn't talk because of the wound to her head, but if she talked now, it meant that Mama was right; their guest was getting better. Hilde smiled. "Let me wake Mama."

"No!" The woman's grip tightened. "Don't get the guards. He's their master, too."

"You're hurting me," Hilde whispered.

Her grip loosened. "How did you get through the bars, Rose?"

"What bars?"

"You can't escape, Rose. They won't let you."

"Why are you calling me that?"

Her hand let go, and she reached up and touched Hilde's face. "Don't leave me again. I don't know if I can face him alone."

Her breathing became heavy. Hilde looked at her and thought of how her own fever had made her dream of things that weren't really there. She didn't remember much of those times, but she did remember when she had talked to Mama thinking Mama was their horse. She had kept asking how he had gotten through the people door, and why he had started talking in Mama's voice.

Hilde touched the woman's brow, under the bandages, and it still burned with fever. The woman didn't know what she was saying. Hilde saw the tears on her cheek and decided if she wanted to call her Rose it was fine. "I won't leave."

"Thank you." Her hand lowered to the blanket.

"If I am Rose, who are you?"

"Don't you know me? I'm Lilly, your sister."

⬦

In the morning, after Ulfie and Papa had gone out to work in the field, Lilly began waking up. Mama went to fetch a bowl to feed her and Hilde grabbed her sleeve.

"Mama?"

Mamma looked down at her. "Yes?"

"Can I feed Lilly?"

"Lilly?"

Hilde suddenly felt a little nervous. Lilly had been so scared last night that Hilde might tell someone something. But she had been so feverish that Hilde hadn't been sure whom, or what. Still, Lilly had trusted her.

But Hilde certainly could tell Mama, right?

"Uh, I spoke to her last night." Hilde glanced over at Lilly, and Lilly looked back at her, a little groggy.

"She spoke?"

"Yes. She didn't make much sense, though. But she said her name was Lilly and that she was my big sister."

Mama smiled and turned away for a moment, covering her mouth.

Is Mama laughing?

She turned around, still smiling, and said, "Of course you can feed . . . Lilly?"

"That's her name."

"It's a pretty name," Mama said. She bent over and kissed Hilde on the forehead and whispered, "You have such sweet dreams."

Mama handed her a bowl of barley porridge and went to do other chores without asking Hilde any more about her conversation with Lilly. Hilde looked at Lilly and frowned. "I don't think she believes me."

❖

Uldolf worked in the front field, by the tree line. They had the third frost-free morning in a row now, and it was time to start the first tilling. His father had already begun, taking a loaf of bread baked with last year's grain and plowing it into the field. Since they were Christian, it was less an offering than a gesture of respect for the old god Patrimpas.

His father had already begun at the rear of the farm, working back and forth behind their horse, guiding the wooden plow, churning up the soft black earth. Up here, by the road, the earth was paler, the sign of too much clay. It always seemed to Uldolf that this sad patch of ground experienced different seasons than the rest of the farm—as if on this small acre, winter lasted longer, and days were shorter.

It certainly had the most problems.

On the second frost-free morning, one of the massive oak trees that bordered their land had toppled over. There was no storm to account for it, and it wasn't apparent what had happened until Uldolf and his father had walked out to look at the damage.

One of the small creeks around their farm had been fat with snowmelt and had been washing into some animal's winter burrow under the tree's roots, undermining the land between the tree and the wall bordering their field. It had probably been going on all winter, accelerating now with the combination of snowmelt off of the high ground and the softening earth.

The tree had crashed through its lesser brethren, knocking them aside, covering the cleared area between the field's wall and the woods with the splintered remnants of four or five fallen companions. Only the oak itself reached past the wall, its crown reaching ten paces into the field beyond. The wall underneath had been broken apart, its large stones scattered beneath a trunk that, on the ground, was better than waist high on him.

Naked branches clawed the sky two and three times Uldolf's

height. Massive limbs, as thick as his waist, stabbed into the ground.

Even if they hadn't lost the oxen this winter, it was still more than any team of animals would be able to clear. And since his father had to begin planting—with some urgency now that there was an additional mouth to feed—it fell to Uldolf to chop the tree into manageable pieces.

This was his second day at it, and it was still hard for him to tell if he had made any progress. He had to scramble into the branches with his axe hanging off a leather strap around his chest, chopping the branches free while precariously holding onto the main trunk with his thighs. By midmorning, his legs ached as if he'd been riding at a gallop, and his arm felt like lead.

He watched his latest small victory, an upward reaching limb the thickness of his thigh, crack under its own weight and slowly topple to the ground beneath him. He set down his axe and wiped the sweat out of his eyes with the palm of his hand, the only part of his arm not coated with wood chips. As he blinked his eyes clear, he saw the knight.

Because he was up in the tree, he could see the knight and his company approaching while they were still several minutes' walk down the road. Over his armor, the knight's plain white surcoat glared in the sunlight, the black cross upon it stark and unmistakable. He rode in the lead, followed by a half dozen other men, all on horseback.

It was not a common sight. The road here was not a major route. It didn't lead to any other towns or villages. It was just a rutted dirt track that led from Johannisburg to a number of more far-flung farms, then returned to Johannisburg. A good day's leisurely ride would return you to where you started.

These men were riding from the short route to Johannisburg, and they rode slowly, and all eyed the woods, as if looking for something.

Uldolf lowered his arm when he realized what they might be searching for. His father's words echoed in his ears.

If someone was going to just abandon a woman to die there, in the shadow of Johannisburg Keep, who is the most likely culprit?

Uldolf untangled himself from the branches of the fallen oak and slid to the ground. He had the unfortunate sensation of great urgency combined with the panicked realization that he didn't know what to do. Their stranger was in bed, recovering from the fever brought on by her wounds. There was no way to move her or any place to hide her. And, if he ran there, he would only draw attention to the cottage and his own unease.

He didn't have much time to consider what to do, because the knight had already come within sight of the farm. His party came up even with the wall, and for a moment Uldolf had a brief hope that they might just keep going.

Then the knight raised his arm as he brought his mount to a stop, and yelled, "Hold!"

Uldolf turned and saw his father stop tilling and look around.

Someone said, "A word, my son?"

Uldolf turned around to face the knight, who was leaning down in his saddle to talk to Uldolf. "Who works this land?"

"Gedim, sir." Uldolf pointed across the field. "My father," he added. He made sure his head was lowered, both to show proper respect, as well as to hide his unease.

"Fair land, here," the knight said. "You are freemen? Christian?"

"Yes, sir."

"Has your farm been troubled lately, lad?"

"Troubled?"

"By strange beasts? Men or animals killed or injured?"

Uldolf furrowed his brow. "No, nothing like that. We lost some animals during winter."

"I am sorry for your losses." The knight waved one of the other men forward to hold his bridle as he dismounted. Uldolf heard the man address the knight in German, but all he understood was the knight's name, Gregor.

Once on the ground, Gregor turned to face Uldolf. "I also need to ask you, have you seen any strangers in the past week, possibly injured?"

Uldolf's stomach burned and his heart raced, because he felt certain that any lie would be visible on his face. Instead he asked, "Who are you looking for? What do they look like?"

"Then you have seen someone?"

"Only travelers down this road." Uldolf hoped that the flush on his face and the catch in his breath sounded more like exertion than falsehood.

If the knight suspected him, he hid it. "A woman, about your age, with red hair and green eyes, wounded in the head and in the shoulder. She is a witch and a murderess."

"I see," Uldolf said.

"Now, we need to look in your house and the barn there. Just to see if she's hiding anywhere."

Uldolf looked at the knight and the still-mounted soldiers, and realized that there was absolutely nothing he could do at this point.

"Yes, sir," he told the knight, in as even a tone as he could manage. "Of course."

Uldolf walked along one side of the wall while the knight followed on the other. He saw his father walking across the field toward them, but he wasn't going to reach them before they got to the cottage, and he must have had Uldolf's realization that if he ran, he would draw undue attention to the situation.

We should have come up with some common story. Something in case people asked questions. The girl isn't going to be in bed forever. People are going to see her . . .

They reached the gate and Uldolf opened it. The knight, Gregor, stepped through while the others rode up and stopped on the road next to the gate.

Uldolf's mind raced with a hundred scenarios, none of which had a remote shred of plausibility.

Uldolf had the knight halfway to the door of the cottage, and his father was just reaching the wall that bordered the front field and the area around the cottage, when Uldolf's mother burst through the front door, hair tied severely up behind her head, her expression pure venom.

"What is the meaning of this?"

"My lady, we are looking—" the knight began.

She didn't let him finish. She stormed up to Uldolf and poked him in the chest with her finger. "I've told you that your sister needs rest. Hilde is very sick, and we can't have you bringing—"

"Pardon me," the knight said.

She turned on the man with a glare that Uldolf thought would make anyone wither. Gregor took a step back, but apparently knights of the Teutonic Order were trained to withstand a mother's wrath. It spoke well for the Order's discipline, since Uldolf would himself prefer to face all the knight's company in combat before he'd willingly face Burthe's anger.

"We are looking for a fugitive, a murderess."

Burthe folded her arms and tried to stare the man down. It didn't work.

"My lady," the knight said, "this woman is evil, a threat to your family and your immortal soul."

Uldolf's mother sighed and stepped aside.

"Thank you," the knight said, walking to the door of the cottage.

"But don't you *dare* wake Hilde." When she turned after him, Uldolf saw the back of her head, where her hair was braided and wrapped in a tight bun. Only there was something oddly ragged about it now.

"I only need to look inside."

"Quietly," Burthe insisted.

Uldolf swallowed. His heart raced as he followed Gregor and Burthe into the cottage. He had no idea how his mother could have hidden their guest.

He stepped inside, and saw that she hadn't.

Hilde wasn't asleep. She was up and wiping a cloth across the face of their unconscious guest. She turned as the knight entered and said, "Shh."

A damp towel covered their guest's brow, completely obscuring the bandages on her head. Uldolf didn't understand how, at first, but the hair curling from under the towel was blond, not red.

Then he realized that the hair was exactly the same shade as his mother's.

Gregor turned to Burthe after looking around the cottage's single large room and said quietly, "Thank you. I will say prayers for your daughter's recovery."

X

"What do we do with her?" Gedim asked.

The knight and his men were long gone, and Burthe was using a tin mirror and a knife to even out the violence she had done to her hair. A third of her long blond tresses were now in a pile by the head of Uldolf's bed.

Gedim admired her quick thinking, and appreciated her distrust of the Germans, but couldn't help but wonder if concealing their guest was the best decision.

That guest was awake right now, and Hilde was doing her best to spoon the last of the stew into the girl's mouth.

That was the other thing. They were running out of food.

"What do you mean, do with her?" Uldolf responded.

"Did you see how many men they had looking for her? They're not going to just go away. And the extra mouth to feed, especially with her appetite . . ."

"Husband," Burthe said sharply, "you are *not* suggesting we put out an injured guest?"

Gedim looked at the wounded girl and Hilde. The two of them had made the feeding a game. Hilde would hover the spoon near the girl's mouth, and the girl would appear to ignore it for several moments, and then she would try to snap up the spoon before Hilde jerked it away. He would have scolded Hilde for the food that was splattering on the covers, but it had been too long a winter without seeing his daughter smile.

"No, I am concerned about when she heals." He turned to Burthe. "She *will* heal?"

"The wounds, yes." She put down the mirror and the knife and looked over at the girl and Hilde. There was an odd expression on her face.

"What is it?" Uldolf asked her.

"It's just . . . I've never seen anyone heal so well before."

"Well, that's good." Uldolf paused. "Isn't it?"

"She's a strange girl," Burthe responded.

"When do you think she'll be well enough to move?" Gedim asked.

"The fever's broken. She could be moved now, but—"

"Please," Hilde interrupted, "can't Lilly stay?"

"Lilly?" Gedim and Uldolf said simultaneously.

"Hilde named our guest," Burthe said.

Hilde looked up at Burthe. "She *told* me her name."

Uldolf looked across at him and Gedim shrugged. He had a very imaginative daughter. Gedim asked her, "And when did Lilly tell you her name?"

"At night, she talks. Sometimes she sings." Then, in a very tender gesture, Hilde took her sleeve and wiped the food off the girl's—off Lilly's—face. "I think she's lonely."

Burthe gave Gedim a look that dared him to talk about moving their guest in front of their daughter.

◈

Later on, Gedim took Burthe outside to talk in private. The sky was purple with twilight, and the air vibrated with the sounds of all the chirping insects and the birds returning to feed on them. Gedim sat on the stone wall closest to the house.

He sighed. "While I see our daughter is attached to her, our guest has become a serious problem."

"I know."

"The Germans will be back. Even if they aren't, someone will eventually come by and see her. Even if they don't tell the Order or their servants about her. A new member of the household? A new, young, attractive, female member of the household? The rumors will sweep every family in the area."

Burthe ran her fingers through her newly shortened hair. "You think I haven't been dwelling on this since that man rode up the road? And I've been keeping an eye on our supplies. I don't know how we're going to eat." Her shoulders were shaking. "But . . ."

"We can't abandon her."

"No."

They both were silent for a long time.

"So, she's doing better than you expected?"

"Better than anyone has a right to expect. She had a fever, but it was shorter and shallower than anything I've seen after such a bad injury, much less two of them. There's barely any inflammation or drainage from either wound. The flesh is knitting together so well that I'll be able to take the stitches out in a couple of days. Even her hair's growing back faster than normal."

"She has the gods' favor."

"At the very least."

Gedim sighed. "She certainly eats like one of the saga heroes."

"What do we do?"

Gedim stood up and put his arm around Burthe's shoulder. "I don't know."

❖

hilde hated it when her parents decided to talk around her, as if she was the chair or the table, as if she didn't know what was going on. She hated it worse when they *did* realize she was there, and decided to go talk about their adult things in private. It was so *hard* to listen, with all the crickets and the birds.

Hilde sat by Lilly and listened anyway. She heard a lot about how Lilly was sick, but she felt a lot better because Mama was still saying that Lilly was doing well. Hilde knew that if Mama didn't realize Hilde was listening, what she said about someone's health was much closer to the truth.

She leaned close to Lilly and spoke in a conspiratorial whisper. "Mama says you're going to get all better. She may take the seam out of your head tomorrow."

Hilde was happy about that. But the other things her parents said weren't as happy. They were running out of food, because Lilly ate too much. Ulfie might have to go out and find something big—and that would be very dangerous. The Germans might find Ulfie then, and take him away like they tried to take Lilly away. That frightened Hilde.

Hilde looked down at Lilly. Her pretty green eyes were half closed and looking at the ceiling, past Hilde's head. Hilde remembered how she had felt when she was sick. It was no fun, only being awake enough to know you weren't quite sleeping.

Hilde now had news, about their food, that she *should* tell Lilly. But that would certainly upset her, and she was sick. Hilde didn't want to make Lilly upset, or sad, or guilty. Hilde liked her.

But Hilde knew that she hated it when her parents tried to hide those things from her. Lilly was her friend, and as much as Hilde wanted to be nice to her and make sure she was happy, she decided it would be wrong to keep things from her.

Quietly, Hilde told Lilly about the things she had heard her parents say.

Hilde kept herself awake that night, hoping that Lilly might wake up and talk to her again. She liked talking to Lilly, even if she never quite knew who Hilde was. Sometimes Lilly called her Rose, sometimes other names.

But as the fever got better, it had been happening less and less. Hilde didn't know if that was good or bad. Lilly still didn't speak during the day, but it seemed that she understood everyone more.

Tonight, Lilly didn't speak to her, though she still muttered things in her sleep. Most were too quiet to make out, but she smiled when she heard Lilly's voice change tone between Ulfie's snores.

Lilly was singing again. When she thought Hilde was Rose, she had sung it to her, and once she knew the words, Hilde had sung it with her.

Now Hilde sung the words inside her head:

Fear not the road before you,
The broken stones, the empty trees,
Mother will protect her child,
Wherever that road leads.
Fear not the bear, the troll, the wolf,
Or other evil things,
Mother will protect her child,
No matter what the darkness brings.
Fear not the cloak of slumber,
When the sky has lost its sun,
Mother will protect her child,
Should any nightmares come . . .

Hilde fell asleep, her head on Uldolf's chest, and no nightmares came.

In the half-sleep of her fading fever, Lilly sang to herself.

The words were the only comfort against the dreams.

Against the things Lilly *needed* to be dreams.

But they weren't dreams. She had gone away so long ago *because* they weren't dreams. She had gone and left the cold one in her place—the one who didn't care about the pain, or the blood, or the hurt. The one who could endure all the vile things that Lilly tried not to remember.

In her head, her wounded memory sucked her down like—

—like a muffled roar as the water sucks us into a frigid embrace that turns our skin into ice—

She pleaded with the cold voice digging into her brain. She didn't need her anymore.

—we gasp and suck in a mouthful of water. Our body wants air, and we have no idea where the surface is—

"Stop," she moaned. "Don't want to remember."

We must.

"No. Happy. Don't need you."

You need me more than ever.

"Please don't."

I have to. Go to sleep, child.

So, Lilly slept . . .

. . . and woke.

Interlude

Anno Domini 1229

Master often had the guards take them, one at a time, to be trained, or to be punished. Lilly never knew who they would take, except at night. If the guards came to take someone at night, they always took Rose.

It was never very long, and most times Lilly was awakened when they brought her back. This time wasn't different. Lilly woke up hearing the boots of the guards and the creak of the door opening. She squeezed her eyes shut even as she sensed the light of their lanterns falling across her eyelids. She froze in place, barely allowing herself to breathe. Always, the best way to avoid punishment was to avoid being noticed in the first place.

She smelled them next; the sour sweat of the guards; the blood, piss, and fear from Rose; and the sour, musky smell that Lilly associated with her master.

She heard the door to Rose's cell creak open, and she heard the rattle of chains. She could hear Rose quietly crying, and Lilly winced. With tears came beatings. They all needed to accept whatever master gave them. They were the animals, and if they couldn't serve men properly, they were no use for man or God.

And when their master decided that one of them was useless, he removed them. Lilly's sister Dahlia had tried to run away, and master had cut her with silver, many times, and the wounds did not heal. It took a very long time before she had stopped moving. Worse was her brother Ash, who one day simply stopped talking or moving. Master beat him, but Ash didn't move or react. Eventually, master just had the guards take Ash away.

From listening to the guards, and the bits of their language she could understand, she knew that she had once had two other siblings she didn't even remember. It was one of the few things she allowed herself to feel sad about. She couldn't contradict her master, even in her mind, but she could feel regret at forgetting an unknown brother or sister.

She didn't want to lose another sister. She tried to will Rose to stop crying. *Please, not in front of the guards.*

She risked cracking an eye open, and saw one of the guards standing in front of Rose's cell, watching her cry. At first Lilly's heart sank, until the guard knelt down and she recognized him.

Lilly felt the tension ease, because of all the men who kept them at the mercy of their master, there was one who took no joy in correcting them. One who offered them, especially Rose, some small comfort.

Once he was alone with them, he started singing to Rose.

❖

The first week he was at Brother Semyon's monastery, Erhard von Stendal, province commander without a province, still nursed doubts. He had never once questioned his vocation, but what he had seen here had brought him too close to that point.

Even after seeing the charter for his new mission, bearing the seals of the pope and the Hochmeister, it was difficult for him to see these creatures as the work of God . . .

In the end, though, it was not for him to say. Duty, fealty, and obedience demanded he follow the path set before him. His reservations amounted to nothing. His actions were constrained by vows more powerful than any unease he might have felt.

The church had declared Semyon's wolfbreed monstrosities of earthly origin. Fallen, like all terrestrial matter, but—as Brother Semyon had said—no different than Erhard's horse.

However, my horse cannot speak, and my horse cannot change into a slavering monster and dismember a group of armed men.

Earthly they might be, but the half-lupine creatures Semyon had imprisoned here were surely born of some primeval wood on the borders of Hell itself.

Only a few hours ago he had seen, for the third time, an eight-year-old child turn into a twisted demonic wolf and kill full-grown, armed Prûsan warriors.

The last demonstration was only with two Prûsans, and it made Erhard wonder if it was due to the relative skill the last child had at killing, or if it was because Brother Semyon only had a limited number of Prûsans on hand.

I must stop thinking of them as children. They are not human.

"You speak of using these creatures against the pagans," Erhard asked him. "How, exactly? These creatures must be caged under guard, bound by silver manacles. You train them to show their prowess in combat, but how can we be sure that prowess is not used against us?"

Brother Semyon paused. He had been leading Erhard on a path through a series of gardens to the abbot's house where Erhard had been taking his residence, having yet no proper convent to attend to.

The house stood near the crumbling monastery where the guards lived, along with the false children they guarded. The house stood on a bluff overlooking the River Drweca, and seemed to have avoided the violence inflicted on the monastery. Or, more likely, it had been more carefully rebuilt.

The path to the house wound through exotic flowering plants. The perfume of the flowers was as thick as syrup, forcing Erhard's stomach into slow, uneasy rolls.

Brother Semyon turned to Erhard, his expression showing an unseemly joy at such a brutish business. He tapped his forehead. "With any wild animal, Brother Erhard, the most important restraints are the ones that cannot be seen."

"Wild animals with the wits of men?" Erhard asked.

"Is breaking a man any different than breaking an animal?" Brother Semyon walked up to one twisted bush that grew in an unnatural spiral. "Or breaking one of these creatures?" He traced the outline of the topiary with a black-gloved hand. "Especially if you begin with an immature specimen."

He reached up and touched a budding flower that rose out of the surface of the twisted bush. "You bend it where you want it to grow." He pinched the bud between his fingers, crushing it and releasing a small trail of fluid, red in the glow from the setting sun. "And cut away the things that you don't need."

"But those things kill."

Brother Semyon broke off the crushed flower. "So do men. So do well-trained dogs."

"Those things are not dogs."

Brother Semyon turned to face the crimson sunset. "It is simple, my brother; punishment and reward, dominance and submission. If every small sin is punished with an iron fist, they will no longer even conceive of large ones." He tossed the crushed flower into the wind. It fragmented, the wind tearing the immature petals apart as they drifted down toward the river. "Their masters dominate their every waking thought. They obey us not to avoid pain, but because our approval is the only light and pleasure they are allowed in this world."

"Brother . . ."

"They exist to serve us," Brother Semyon said. "That is all. They serve, or they die."

◈

The guard who sang to Rose treated them all with something like kindness. The few months he had been here marked the first time Lilly knew that humans could share anything but cruel discipline. He seemed to care for Rose most of all, especially when he brought her back from their master in the deep of the night.

His attention seemed to make Rose stronger. She didn't cry as much. And when the guard sang to her, Lilly didn't need to pretend to be asleep. Sometimes she would even quietly sing along.

But, in time, their master found out.

He burst in, radiating such fury that the sharp smell of fresh piss came from several cells at once. The fear was suffocating. However, this time the rage was not focused on Lilly, or Rose, or Holly, or Timothy, or Sage, or Ivy—

For the first time Lilly saw her master's rage focused on another human being. He shouted fast, and loud, and in the other language the humans spoke among themselves, not the pagan language they used to speak to her. Even so, the syllables burned into her ears so deeply that she remembered them long enough for the sense to follow.

"How dare you interfere with the Order's work here!"

The guard spoke slower, and was easier for Lilly to understand. "Interfere? I thought Christ called on us to show compassion."

"Do not presume to speak to me of our Lord. These are animals. Your service here is at an end."

"Isn't that for the new Landkomtur to say, Brother Semyon?"

"I am your superior. Do *not* test me!"

The guard nodded and started walking to the door. Lilly held her breath, because she knew her master's expression, and

posture, and the smell of his anger. He would not leave until someone was corrected.

Severely corrected.

At first, Lilly thought it would be her or her siblings who would
suffer. But then the guard said, "Does your master know how you
correct the blond one? Or do animals fall outside your vows of
chastity?"

Lilly's master stood mute as the guard laughed and turned
to go.

She saw her master grab an iron rod from a rack on the wall, a
rod he used many times to discipline his charges. He turned and
struck the guard across the back. Lilly could hear Rose gasp in the
cage next to her.

Her master brought the bar down on the guard five times.

Lilly had quickly healed from receiving twice as many blows.
But she wasn't human.

The guard was.

❖

Rose cried herself to sleep that night, and wouldn't stop, no
matter how many times Lilly sang to her.

❖

Two days later, they took Rose away in the night, and she
didn't come back. The following morning, her master had a
fresh scar on his face, and beat all of them more severely than Lilly
could ever remember. His heaviest blows were reserved for Lilly
and her sisters.

Rose never returned, and a week later, the guards came and
took Lilly away to see her master in the middle of the night. In a
dark room, he bound her with silver chains and showed her what
he did to make Rose cry.

❖

Lilly kept herself from crying, mostly by pretending to be some-one else when she needed to be. It was easier to sing to comfort someone else than it was to comfort herself. Though the other person Lilly made for herself was stronger, and colder, and didn't need to be comforted.

It was after being with her master one night, when she was talking to her other self in her head, that she understood how she could leave this place.

You know your master has his own master. If you work to please him, above all others, then maybe he will take you for himself.

❖

It took nearly a year before Erhard finally chose one of Semyon's wolfbreed to use in battle. He had followed the brother's path of disciplining the creatures, teaching them to view him as much their master as Semyon. At times—especially when Semyon had Rose destroyed for attacking him—Erhard had thought his duties here would come to naught. That despite Semyon's assertions, the creatures were untrainable.

However, over time, he decided that one of the five remaining wolfbreed *was* trainable. Lilly seemed more intelligent, easier to instruct, than the others. It had been several months since he had taken over her discipline completely from Brother Semyon, and now, if anything, she showed him more deference than she had to her original master.

Her keepers had washed her, dressed her in a simple peasant smock, and placed a silver shackle on her left ankle. They led her outside and she blinked in the daylight.

"You will come with me now," Erhard told her.

She looked down so he couldn't see her face under her hair.

"Do you understand?"

"Yes."

"Look at me."

Lilly looked up into his face. He searched for something in those burning green eyes, but he saw nothing, no emotion at all. "You will obey me."

"Yes."

"I will tell you to wait, and you will wait. When you wait, you shall do nothing. Do you understand?"

"I understand."

"I will tell you the time at which you will stop waiting. You will kill only then—*only* then. Understand?"

"I understand."

He looked for understanding in her face, and saw only blankness. He wondered if this creature understood death. What was he speaking to, the child or the animal?

Did it matter?

"Master?"

"Yes?"

"Will it make you happy if many die?"

"At the place I will take you? Yes, it will."

"Then I will kill everyone I find there." She smiled at him, and even under the beating sun, he could feel the depths of his gut turn icy.

Terce

Anno Domini 1239

Si occideris, Deus, peccatores,
viri sanguinum, declinate a me.

Surely thou wilt slay the wicked, O God:
depart from me therefore, ye bloody men.

—Psalms 139:19

xi

Dawn came and Uldolf blinked the sleep from his eyes. He was still acclimating to waking up in the full glare of daylight. The nights had only recently become warm enough to leave the shutters open. Hilde's bed was away from any windows and the drafts they let in, but that meant they were directly across from the southeast window that let in the full ruddy glare of sunrise.

Hilde was snuggled against his right side, between him and the wall. He always put her there, because if she slept on the left, where his arm was, he was more likely to knock her out of bed. She would also use his arm as a pillow and the pins and needles of his arm going to sleep would wake him up halfway through the night. Last, it just made it simpler to get in and out of bed without waking her.

He edged away from Hilde and sat up, stretching.

Uldolf jumped to his feet, knocking his head against a low-hanging rafter. He didn't notice the pain even as he half stumbled into the middle of the cottage. "Mother? Father?" He bent over his empty bed. "Wake up, she's gone!"

The covers had been thrown aside, and on the pillow were the scraps of a bandage, clotted with blood and strands of red hair. Uldolf grabbed the pillow, heart racing. It was cold.

"Mother?"

Hilde sat up in her bed. "Ulfie? What's wrong? What's happening?"

"She—" Uldolf spun around. "Lilly. She's gone."

Hilde looked at him wide-eyed. "No, she wouldn't go." Tears welled up in her eyes. "She *wouldn't!*"

Uldolf shook his head. Lilly—he thought of her using Hilde's name now—wasn't in her right senses. She could have walked off anywhere during the night.

"Father?" he called.

Worry started to slip into panic as he realized his parents' bed was also empty.

"Mother? *Father?*"

Then he heard his father from outside. "Out here, son."

"Ulfie?" Hilde's face was streaked with tears. "Ulfie, she's not mad at me, is she?"

Uldolf walked over and hugged his sister. "No, little chipmunk. She's just confused."

Hilde nodded into Uldolf's shoulder and sniffed. She muttered, "I shouldn't have told her."

"Told her what?"

"Son." Burthe's voice came from outside. "I think you need to come out here."

❖

Uldolf walked out of the cottage and hugged himself against the sharp morning air. His breath fogged a little as he followed his parents' voices around to the back, where the main field was. He rounded the corner and saw both of them standing by one of the low stone walls that separated the front field from the back.

They were both staring into the field.

Uldolf walked up next to them. "What's going on? Lilly's gone . . ." He trailed off.

"She's right there," his father said, unnecessarily.

About twenty yards away from them, standing ankle deep in the black fresh-turned earth, stood Lilly. Her borrowed bedclothes were torn and dirty, flapping in the early morning breeze. The bandage was gone from her head, and her red hair hung down past her shoulders. Where Burthe had cut it—above the red scar of her wound—her hair had grown back a stark white. The wound on her temple was bleeding, and she held her bloody hands in front of her face, as if she wasn't sure where the blood had come from. She stared at the blood a long time.

"Thank the gods she didn't go far. Is she . . ." Uldolf didn't finish the question. He had just looked down to see the other thing out there in the middle of the field.

The carcass of a young bull elk—antlers barely sprouted for the spring—was sprawled another ten yards from Lilly. The elk had been in full health, standing nearly as tall as Uldolf at the shoulders and probably close to a hundred stone in weight.

And the elk had been savaged. Claw marks had cut deep grooves in the side of its chest, and ragged bite marks had torn across large sections of its neck. The elk's head was turned at an unnatural angle and stared at Uldolf with dead black eyes, the hide on its brow glistening with the morning dew.

"Did you see what killed it?" Uldolf asked.

"No," his father said. "But I think she saw whatever it was."

"Lilly?" Uldolf called out trying to get her attention. "*Lilly?*"

All she could see was the blood.

She could try to hide, to close her eyes, to forget.

It would always be there.

What did we do?

A voice, colder, older, answered her, *We did what had to be done.*

I don't want this anymore.

You never wanted it. That is why I am here.

I don't want you!

She clutched her hands, shaking, remembering—

Ulfie's voice.

She turned her head, away from the blood, and saw him standing by the low wall around the field. He stood there unscathed, next to his parents, staring at her.

Lilly thought her heart would burst from relief.

◈

Lilly turned around, and when she saw Uldolf, her eyes widened.

"*Ulfie!*" she cried.

For a few moments, Uldolf was too stunned to react.

She started running toward him, waving her arm as if she was trying to get his attention. "Ulfie! Ulfie! Ulfie!"

Oh, no . . .

Uldolf vaulted over the wall because what was about to happen was painfully obvious. "Lilly, no! Don't run."

But his warning was too late. She only ran a few steps before her foot bogged down in the soft ground and she tumbled, face first, into a pile of newly turned earth. She pushed herself up on her hands and knees, sputtering, coated with dirt from her brow down.

She started sobbing.

Uldolf reached her and bent down to extend his arm to help her up. Instead of grabbing his arm, she threw her arms around him in a hug that knocked him enough off-balance that he almost went facedown in the dirt on top of her.

"*Ulfie.*" She sobbed into his shoulder.

Uldolf felt his face redden. He wrapped his arm around her and helped Lilly to her feet. She was shaking so hard that he could hear her teeth chatter.

"She's terrified," he whispered.

His parents had walked into the field after him, using the gate. Burthe stepped in front of him with a little "harrumph" that made Uldolf's face burn a little hotter. "Let me see her head."

Uldolf nodded and tried to turn Lilly toward his mother. Lilly wouldn't cooperate, refusing to let go of him. Burthe watched him struggle for a few futile moments, then sighed, walked over behind Uldolf, and lifted Lilly's chin off of Uldolf's shoulder so she could look into her face.

"How is she?" he asked.

"Filthy."

"Her head, she was bleeding . . ."

Burthe tsked a few times and moved Lilly's hair around. Lilly winced, yanking away and burying her face in Uldolf's neck.

"I guess she likes you," Burthe said finally.

Uldolf patted the back of Lilly's head. "But is she all right?"

"She's fine. Some stitches opened up and bled a little, but the scar's holding together. I don't think I'll need to put new ones in." Burthe walked around in front of Uldolf, watching Gedim as he examined the elk. "She is certainly touched by the gods if the animal that killed that beast didn't turn its attention to her."

"You think it was here when she came outside?"

"Look at her, Uldolf. You said yourself, she's terrified. Besides, no predator would abandon a fresh kill unless it was scared off." Burthe's voice lowered. "Take her inside. Whatever killed it may still be out here somewhere."

Uldolf remembered the words of the knight from yesterday. *Has*

*your farm been troubled lately . . . by strange beasts? Men or animals
killed or injured?*

Could this have something to do with Lilly?

Uldolf let the nonsensical thought go. "Come on, Lilly. We'll get
you cleaned up."

As he led her back to the cottage, he tried to cheer her up. "So
Hilde taught you my name, huh? Did she tell you that I find that
nickname really irritating?"

"Ulfie," she whispered.

"No, I guess she didn't."

She grabbed his arm and hugged it, stopping him. He looked
down at her. She squeezed her eyes shut, and nearly shook with
the effort of speaking. "I . . . I . . ."

After seeing her mute for so long, he was amazed that she was
speaking, but he was also scared at the effort he saw in her face. It
was almost as if trying to speak was painful for her. "It's all right,
Lilly. Don't force it."

She shook her head violently. "I . . . I . . . I never h-h-hurt
Ulfie."

"What?"

"I will never hurt you, Ulfie."

Uldolf thought of how panicked he must have looked, running
outside. "You just scared me, running off like that."

She buried her head in his shoulder and whispered, "Ulfie."

"Just don't do it again."

She didn't say anything more as he walked her back to the cottage. Apparently, the one sentence had taken a lot out of her.

❖

"What killed it?" Burthe asked.

Gedim looked up from the carcass and shook his head. "I
don't really know. The tracks here look like a wolf, but they're too

big, and there aren't enough of them. You'd need a whole pack to take on a bull this size—but a pack would pick on an animal that's already sick or injured, or a calf."

"A mountain cat?"

"Maybe." Gedim stood up and looked around.

"You think it's still here?"

"No," Gedim said. "I think we would have heard it, whatever it was. I'm surprised we didn't hear it make the kill in the first place."

"I'm not, the way you snore." Burthe turned to look at Uldolf leading the girl back to the cottage. "And it appears that Lilly heard it."

"Um."

"Well," Burthe went on, "this should certainly stock the larder for a while. It seems that the gods have favored more than our guest, this time."

"Uh-huh." Gedim stared off toward the woods.

"What is the matter, husband?"

Gedim shook his head. "Nothing. It's obvious what happened. Some animal attacked this elk off in the woods somewhere, and this bull was strong enough to stumble out here, and our guest managed to scare the animal off . . ."

"It seems her name's Lilly."

Gedim looked at her a moment. "Oh, yes. *Lilly* scared the animal off."

"Are you sure nothing's wrong?"

Gedim shook his head. "Yes. And you're right. This is a stroke of luck—as long as we butcher it before some Germans walk by and decide we're poaching. This meat needs to be dressed and stored today. Have Uldolf bring the wheelbarrow and some knives out here."

◈

As the day progressed, the dressing and disposition of the carcass took all of Gedim's attention, so much so that he completely forgot the unease he had felt earlier. As he had said, it was obvious what had happened. The elk had stumbled into their field and collapsed from its wounds.

Despite the marks he saw, leading back into the woods . . .

The elk was nearly sixteen hundred pounds. There wasn't any predator Gedim knew of that could have *dragged* it here.

XII

By midafternoon the next day, despite Uldolf's best efforts, about half the tree was still there. Gedim had done his best to work around the obstruction, but it was now at the point where the fallen tree was holding up the plowing. So now, with the sun halfway down in the sky, both Gedim and Uldolf were working to clear it.

They worked in silence, removing the last few branches from the tree's crown. After nearly an hour Gedim said to his son, "You've been awfully quiet lately."

Uldolf looked up from the limb he was chopping. He shrugged and looked back down at his work. When it appeared that Uldolf had nothing to say, Gedim went back to the limb he was working on.

He was finding it both frustrating and a source of pride that his one-armed son was disassembling the tree almost twice as fast as Gedim himself was. Almost to the point that it might actually go faster if Gedim wasn't in the way.

They worked in silence for a few more minutes before Uldolf asked him, "That elk. That was a good stroke of luck, wasn't it?"

"The best we've had in quite a while."

Uldolf nodded, chopping harder. He was shirtless, and his upper body was coated with sweat. "If it hadn't . . ."

Gedim lowered his axe. "Son, 'might haves' are pointless."

Uldolf kept at the limb. It was nearly twice as thick as his thigh, and Uldolf was halfway through it. Each blow of the blade threw up splinters and wood chips. They adhered to Uldolf's sweaty arm, making it look as if he had sprouted a thick coat of blond fur below the elbow.

"What would we have done with her?" Uldolf asked, breathing the words between blows of the axe. "We were nearly out of food."

"Not 'nearly.' "

Uldolf shook his head and stopped chopping. After a moment, he asked, "Did you ever talk about giving me up?"

"Don't be ridiculous."

"Am I?" Uldolf shrugged his right shoulder. Only a slight hollow marked where an arm had been. "A crippled child? That had to be a huge burden."

Gedim sighed. "You've been our son since we took you in."

Uldolf started attacking the branch again.

"Now, hold on." Gedim walked up so only the trunk of the tree was between them. "Stop!"

The axe stopped moving, but Uldolf didn't look up.

"I *should* toss you out of the house just for talking such nonsense." Gedim folded his arms. "If you so much as hint to my wife that she doesn't love you as much as the woman who bore you, I will personally beat you within a hair's breadth of living."

Uldolf nodded.

"We took you in because we loved your first family, and we loved you— Look at me, you self-pitying brat." Uldolf raised his head, and Gedim could see tears. The sight filled him with anger, frustration, and an aching sadness. "Damn it, son, are you going to doubt me now?"

"No, Father."

Gedim stood there while Uldolf resumed chopping the branch. He was dumbfounded about what to do next. He thought those wounds were long healed. He had long ago dropped the "adopted" when he thought of Uldolf. Uldolf was as much his son as if he'd been born of his own flesh.

Uldolf had certainly come into their house with the requisite blood and tears. The memory was seared in Gedim's brain; he could still taste the smoke, smell the blood.

He could still see his uncle's chambers as he had found them. He remembered stepping over the eviscerated corpse of his five-year-old niece Jawgede, Uldolf's little sister. He remembered the blood streaking the walls, the tapestries hanging in rags. He remembered the small tearing sounds as the soles of his boots adhered to the blood on the floor.

He remembered a woman's hand, bejeweled and manicured, discarded in a soldier's empty helmet; a boot holding a leg from the knee down, somehow standing by itself; the head belonging to the chieftain of Mejdân, Radwen Seigson, staring at him from beneath half a table.

And he remembered finding his ten-year-old nephew, Radwen's son Uldolf, bleeding to death from his shoulder.

Gedim didn't remember exactly how he had gotten the boy out of that hell, but he remembered the boy's delirious pleas. The same two words, over and over again.

"P-please, stop."

Uldolf never described what had happened in that room, and Gedim had never asked. Uldolf had said more than once that the fever from the wound had stolen much of his memory. Though sometimes Gedim heard his son cry out in his sleep, and wondered if Uldolf simply didn't *want* to remember.

✦

Uldolf felt something snap under his axe, and he took a jump backward as the weight of the limb tore it free of the small amount of wood holding it upright. It fell next to him with a satisfying crunch.

He stared at it for a few moments, trying to think of something to say that wouldn't anger his father more than he'd been angered already. His father's words still stung him, but probably not quite as much as Uldolf's words had stung his father. He couldn't question the faithfulness of his parents, and certainly couldn't compare them to his first mother and father.

Both of them had proved themselves beyond any accident of birth. They had chosen him, crippled, half dead, and fevered . . .

"Father," Uldolf said finally.

"What?" Gedim looked up from gathering stray branches from under the fallen tree.

"You're right, I *am* a self-pitying brat. I'm sorry."

"Forget it, son."

No, Uldolf thought, *I shouldn't.* How many parents out there would just give up on half a child, even one that *was* their own flesh and blood?

I should have it carved on the back of the arm I still have: "Be grateful for what the gods have given you."

"Ulfie!"

Uldolf looked up from his wood-chip-covered arm to see his mother with her arm around the shoulders of a briefly unfamiliar woman. The new person had long midnight-black hair that glistened in the fading afternoon light.

Then Uldolf saw the vivid green eyes, the cock of her head, and the smile. The confusion must have been visible on his face because she repeated, slower, "Ulfie?"

Uldolf looked at his mother. "What did you do?"

"I took some oak gall and prepared a dye. It seemed that blaze of red hair would attract attention."

Lilly held up a full bucket of water toward Uldolf.

"And she's gotten to the point where she's well enough to get into trouble if we don't give her something to do. You men looked thirsty."

Gedim came around the tree, shaking his head. "Thank you, my lady." He gave Lilly a small bow before pulling the ladle out of the bucket.

Uldolf frowned. "Her shoulder. Should she be carrying that?"

"Don't worry," Burthe said. "She's stronger than she looks. And I took out the last stitches this morning."

When Gedim was done, Lilly walked over to Uldolf, still holding out the bucket. "You can put that down if you want," Uldolf told her.

"I'm going to leave her to watch over you two." Burthe turned to go.

Uldolf took a step toward his mother, but he walked into a bucket that swung into his path at chest level. Water splashed his chest and ran down his arm.

His father laughed. "I do believe you should take a drink from the young woman."

Lilly nodded at him. "Ulfie," she said.

Uldolf sighed, grabbed the ladle, and took a drink.

❖

Lilly stayed, watching them for the rest of the afternoon. She sat on the wall about three yards from where the trunk had crashed through. Every time Uldolf glanced in her direction, she would smile at him. Uldolf would respond by turning away and chopping harder.

It didn't keep him from imagining her sitting there, rocking her legs back and forth.

He would have imagined that dyeing her hair such a dark color would have made her less attractive. However, all the black hair did was make Uldolf realize how much her original fiery mane had distracted from the rest of her features. Even with the angry red gash above her right eye, her face was something that men more talented than he wrote lyric poems about.

And he shouldn't be thinking that way about her. The more she recovered, the more he saw that there had to be a family somewhere, agonized about losing her. Such a beauty would almost certainly be betrothed to someone, if not married already. As delicate and unmarked as her skin was, Uldolf strongly doubted that that family, or her absent husband, worked the land like him.

Yesterday, after she had blurted out a complete sentence, he had tried to ask her about her family, but she had only responded by shaking her head and saying, "No," or "Ulfie." When he had asked her where she lived, she had said, "Here," and smiled at him.

Uldolf still didn't know if she didn't understand his questions, couldn't yet form an answer, or was having fun at his expense.

Still, she *was* starting to speak again. And eventually they'd be able to have her tell them where her people were. *Then I'll take her home,* Uldolf told himself.

And if she was of noble birth, it was near certain that there would be a reward for the man who brought her safely home. That might give his family the resources to make it through another winter. He hoped that would make taking her home easier.

Besides, betrothed or not, a woman with such a generous, happy spirit deserved more than half a man.

By the time the sun reached the tops of the trees on the western edge of the field, the fallen oak was finally so much cordwood. Lilly surprised him, again, by announcing, "I help!"

She joined him and his father as they moved the segmented logs off of the field. At first she would lift one and Uldolf would take it from her, but then she'd just smile and grab another, larger log. He worried about her shoulder; he could vividly remember her right hand shaking as she fastened his cloak around herself.

However, from all appearances, the wound no longer bothered her. And, whatever her family history might have been, she showed no aversion to working.

Once they had removed all the branches from the main trunk, they chopped the trunk itself into four segments. When Gedim came back with the horse and a harness, they had to push the large sections so the horse could drag them out of the divots the tree had dug in the soft earth.

Uldolf and Lilly rocked the sections as his father drove the horse forward. Lilly had placed herself shoulder to shoulder with Uldolf so that her arm touched his side. As the sweaty skin of her forearm slid against him, he could feel her muscles flex and tense.

Like his mother had said, she was stronger than she looked.

And not just physically, Uldolf thought.

The tree was gone before the sun.

XIII

Now that she was well, Lilly's words "I help" became a familiar phrase around the household. Initially, because of her communication difficulties, and her apparent lack of any practical knowledge of how to do anything, Uldolf's parents met that phrase with some trepidation. But like her strength, she had reserves of intelligence that simply weren't apparent on the surface. Just by watching Burthe prepare one meal, she was able to cook a passable stew on her own. And after a few minutes with Gedim, she was able to hitch up the plow as if she had been working the farm all her life.

It made Uldolf feel better about bringing her into the house. The more tasks she did, the more she made up for the extra food she ate. It was something that Lilly seemed to understand, and Uldolf suspected that it drove her statements of "I help."

In a strange way, he was proud of her. Not just the intelligence and the strength, both of which he suspected she was born to and was just reclaiming as she healed. What most gratified him was her selflessness, her desire to help everyone.

But clearly her preference was to help Uldolf.

And right now, that meant sowing, scattering barley seed evenly across the new-turned earth.

The two of them worked down the furrows, Lilly ahead of him with a basket of barley, scattering the seed. Behind her, Uldolf harrowed the row by hand with a wooden rake. They had a horse-drawn harrow, but his father was still turning earth in some of the more reluctant parts of the field.

Hilde was watching them from on top of one of the stone walls closest to the cottage. While she spoke quietly to her dolly at the moment, she had her own job that would occupy her for much of the spring. She scattered the birds that would come to try and pick at the new-sown seed. Every once in a while, Uldolf heard her calling, "Shoo bird, shoo bird," accompanied by the fluttering of wings.

It was good that Lilly was here. Even before their ox had died, the sowing often came late simply because they had too few people to work the farm. And sowing was a two-person job, at least. Because of the birds, they couldn't leave a sown field unharrowed with the seed exposed for very long. With the crop uncovered, a flock of crows could strip an acre bare in an hour, and a farm this small didn't have enough days or bushels of seed to undo that kind of damage.

Even with Lilly's help, Uldolf mourned their ox. Dragging the heavy rake across the earth, breaking clods of dirt and covering the barley seed would be exhausting with two arms. The day was two-thirds over, and they should have an acre sown at least, but they had barely finished half an acre. It was frustrating, because Uldolf knew it was his work that was slowing them down. Even with the deliberately self-conscious way that Lilly was scattering the seed, she could have easily covered two acres by now if she hadn't needed to wait for him to catch up every few minutes.

Worse, the sky was darkening with rolling clouds, and he felt a few cold drops hit the back of his neck.

They might not even get a full day's work done.

Uldolf reached his arm out, bending and extending the rake to pull another foot or so of barley under a blanket of earth.

"*Damn.*" Uldolf cursed as a spasm went down the length of his back. As the muscles tensed up along the length of his body, he thought, *Blasted idiot. So you worked slower than you wanted. When was the last rest you took?*

Uldolf called himself a fool three times as the rake fell from his hand. He tried to straighten up, reaching for the knot in his back, and gasped, losing his balance. By the time he was windmilling his arm and falling into the freshly seeded loam, the embarrassment hurt worse than his back.

"*Ulfie!*"

"Oh, no," he muttered, spitting dirt and barley out of his mouth.

Lilly was on her knees, pulling him out of the furrow. He hoped to all the gods that his father and his sister weren't watching him being pulled out of the muck by a woman half his size.

"I'm all right," Uldolf protested.

Lilly clutched him to her chest, embracing him so hard it fired the pain in his back again.

"Please," Uldolf gasped.

She buried her face in his neck.

"I'm fine, Lilly. Really, it was just a knotted muscle."

She mumbled something into his shoulder. It sounded like, "N-no hurt."

"What?"

She let him go and leaned back so he could see her face. Her eyes were red and puffy, and there was a black streak on her cheek where her tears had washed some of the dye from her hair. She grabbed his shoulders, and with a very serious expression, said, "No hurt, Ulfie. No hurt!"

"I told you, I'm fine."

She shook him. "No hurt!"

"Lilly, I'm fine." He was beginning to wonder if she actually heard him. She looked into his face, but he didn't know if she was actually seeing him. He tried to sound reassuring. "Stop this, before my family sees us. It's embarrassing."

She stopped shaking him, hands on his shoulders. Her lip was quivering, and he reached up and wiped one of the tears away.

"There's nothing wrong. I don't even feel it anymore." He leaned forward, caressing her cheek. "So, *please* stop."

Lilly closed her eyes, and abruptly pushed him away with all her might. Uldolf flew backward into the neighboring furrow. "What?"

"*No!*" Lilly screamed. She stood up, hands balled into fists. "*No!*"

"Lilly?" Uldolf tried to get upright, but his hand slid in the dirt, refusing to give him purchase.

She shook her head violently, her hair flying into a disordered cloud around her face. She struck her legs with her fists, still screaming, but if there were words in it, Uldolf couldn't make them out.

"What's wrong?" Uldolf heard the first trace of fear in his own voice.

✦

The same two words ran over and over through Lilly's mind. *Ulfie's hurt. Ulfie's hurt.*

She ran to him, terror clutching at her heart, her stomach sick with every bloody memory she'd tried to forget. She clutched at him as if she could pull him out of the mud like he pulled her out of the frigid water.

No hurt. No hurt. No hurt.

Everything became mixed up in her head. Her master, her sister Rose, Hilde, Ulfie, Uldolf . . .

She pulled Ulfie up off the ground. He was the only thing left that made sense. The only thing in the maelstrom that was her world that she was sure of. She shook him, trying to tell him.

No hurt.

Then she heard him say, "Please, stop."

Her thoughts froze. She couldn't think, couldn't speak. All she could do was feel.

In her head she saw the blood. Smelled it.

She heard the screams.

And she knew what she had let the other one do, in the name of her master's god. And it terrified her.

✦

Gedim was rocking the plow back, trying to dislodge it from a stubborn patch of clayey earth, when he heard Lilly scream.

He whipped around at the sound, instantly convinced that something had happened to Uldolf. Looking across the field, he didn't see his son at first. Gedim's pulse raced and his tongue became heavy with the copper taste of fear. Lilly was hunched over, screaming, shaking her head back and forth.

Below her, he finally saw his son sprawled in the fresh soil.

"*Uldolf!*" Gedim didn't know what had happened, but he started running toward them.

✦

Mama!" Hilde cried, **jumping down** from her place on the wall overlooking the rear field.

Burthe had been planting herbs in the small garden by the side of the cottage. For once, she heard the problem at the same time as her daughter. Lilly sounded terrified, in agony, like every mother's worst fear compressed into a single hysterical wail.

Burthe dropped the spade she'd been using and turned around toward the field. She saw Gedim already running from the other field and she saw Lilly wailing, but her heart froze when she saw no sign of her son.

⬦

Uldolf backed up, pushing himself along the furrow with his legs. "Lilly, you're scaring me."

At the sound of his voice, she turned around and glared. Tears still streaked her cheeks, but her eyes were wide, and her lip was curled in something that was almost a snarl.

What had come over her?

"It's me, Uldolf. Don't you recognize me anymore?" The snarling expression receded a fraction, replaced by confusion.

"Please, stop it."

She shook her head violently.

"Uldolf?" She blinked as if she was suddenly surprised to see him. Her expression had changed, too, the terror and the inexplicable snarl replaced by something else.

Sadness.

She spoke again, and her voice carried none of her earlier hesitancy. "I am so sorry."

Lilly looked down at him, and he saw the same deep sadness in her eyes. She no longer cried, as if what she felt had passed beyond tears.

"I am so sorry," she repeated, the depth in her eyes now reflected in her voice. "I can't—"

Her voice broke, and she turned and ran for the far wall.

"What?" Uldolf finally got his arm purchase to help him get to his feet. "Lilly!" He called after her. "Wait!"

She ran in a headlong sprint for the edge of the field. When she reached the stone wall around it, she vaulted it without slowing. He ran after her, but by the time he reached the wall, she had vanished into the woods.

Uldolf leaned against the wall, staring uncomprehending as the clouds began to unleash their rain in earnest.

Gedim reached his side, panting. "What happened there?"

Uldolf shook his head. He didn't have an answer. "I have to go after her."

"There's a storm coming."

He turned and grabbed his father's shirt. "I have to go after her!"

xiv

Sir Karl Lindberg rode his horse through driving rain. He was cold and damp, and wanted to be somewhere else. Drinking by a campfire, bedding a woman, setting fire to some pagan village—anything but this pointless search for nothing.

Perhaps he should have killed his brother. If his father only had one heir, the old fat wretch might not have been so free vowing his family's service to the Church. The old man was not quite as free to promise the service of his firstborn—but number two, Karl, let's send him to the Holy Land. And if that is not enough, let's send him to the pagan wastes north.

Perhaps Karl should have killed his brother *and* the old man.

Instead, he killed dark-skinned infidels and light-skinned pagans. And while that was not quite as satisfactory as roasting his treacherous family on a pyre, it did allow him a few moments of pleasure in the midst of long months of excruciating boredom.

Boredom like he suffered now, under the command of the Teutonic Order.

One of the few things Karl regularly thanked God for was the fact that his father's political ambitions, and his need for the

Church's favor, had not yet forced his second son into taking religious vows. Karl would sooner slit his own throat than be forced
into the privations of a monastic order.

Men were not meant to live like that. To love God so much as
to give up all worldly pleasures? Better to dive into battle, sword
swinging. You would meet Him soon enough.

It seemed that this year Karl would be denied even that much.
He was trapped in the midst of Christendom, where it would be unseemly to raise his voice to the peasantry, much less his weapon.

When this had all begun, and Landkomtur Erhard von Stendal
had told Karl and his fellows what it was they hunted, Karl had felt
a measure of excitement. Here was something exotic, something
more interesting than a simple squad of rough swordsmen. Something that might put up more of a fight. Anything that could take
on nearly a score of soldiers, Prûsan brutes or not, was something
to be respected.

It was excitement that quickly waned.

It was clear that had this creature the sense of a senile mule,
it would have long since escaped to the remote wilderness miles
from here. Every day spent retracing their steps was another day
for the creature to get farther away.

Karl sneezed and his mount's ears twitched.

Eight years late, he thought. If he had been here before this place
had become part of Christendom, this would be all different. None
of this deferential treatment to these barbarian "Christians." He
would walk where he wanted, go in as he wished, and Christ would
weep for whoever got in his way.

He thought back to earlier today, before the rain began, on
a farm they must have searched for the third time. There was a
blond woman shepherding five children. If this place wasn't under
the rule of the Order . . .

He smiled when he thought of what he could do with her, had
he leave and some time.

"*Sir!*" called out one of the foot soldiers accompanying him.

"Hold!" Karl called out, so the half-dozen men with him might wait for the current interruption. *What now?* Karl wondered. *Another miserable little farm? Some kid cutting trees in the Order's woodland? One of his men found a burrow with his boot and broke an ankle?*

Karl looked around. If it was another farm, it wasn't visible from the muddy gash in the woods that passed for a road. Trees pressed close on both sides, leaning in over them. The soldier who had called to him came up to hold the bridle of his horse.

"Rutger found something," he told Karl.

Karl dismounted. His boots splashed in the brown river the rain had carved down the center of the track they followed. He called out "Wait" to let everyone know that they would be stopped for a while. Those who needed to had time to piss.

He reached into one of his saddlebags and removed the silver collar that the Landkomtur had given him along with the admonition, *Only use this if she is completely subdued. While I wish to question her, she is to be put to death. So if there is any doubt about your own safety, kill her.*

If Karl had been optimistic enough to think he had a chance of finding their quarry, he might have found the time to wish that the Order had more silver weapons to distribute. But of course that wasn't going to happen. The beast had been long gone before Karl ever arrived, and he was slogging through the rain and mud now for no good purpose.

❖

Rutger heard the distant call behind him.

"Hold."

Then, moments later, "Wait."

The woman still hadn't noticed his presence. Possibly the rattle of the rain through the branches above him covered his call for help, though she may have been sobbing too hard to hear him. She was still a good twenty yards away, huddled against the trunk of a massive fallen tree, whose gnarled roots towered over the saplings that sprouted in the clearing its collapse had made. Her clothes were so mud-spattered and wet that he had little idea what their original color might have been. She hugged her knees to her chest, and he could see her long black hair shaking as she cried, face buried in her knees.

Lost, Rutger thought. *Wandered into the woods and lost herself in the storm.*

As if in response to his thought, the sky opened up with a flash of lightning, punctuated almost immediately by a chest-aching echo of thunder. The woman looked up at the sound with an expression of grief on her face. She stared up into the rain, either asking pity from God, or cursing Him.

Rutger walked forward.

The woman didn't even look in his direction. She stared open-eyed into the descending rain, sucking in shuddering breaths.

"Need? Help?" he asked in broken Prûsan.

She looked down at him with striking green eyes. Rutger sucked in a breath, but the woman they were looking for had red hair.

"No worry," he said. "We help."

The woman shook her head. He didn't know if she was contradicting him, or if she just couldn't understand his accent. With her back to the trunk of the fallen tree, she pushed herself upright with her legs. Her eyes widened as she looked at him.

Rutger had never thought he was particularly intimidating, even in full mail. He was small, and had a face ten years younger than it should be. But this woman shook and stared at him as if he were some wild animal.

Rutger undid the strap to his helmet and removed it. He hoped that looking into his unobstructed face might reassure her. The rain was cold against his close-cropped scalp. He kept smiling, and took another step forward.

"Your name?"

The woman ran.

Rutger dropped his helmet and ran after her. Fortunately, he didn't need to run far. She had run back toward the road and straight into the arms of his knight, Karl Lindberg.

Karl grabbed the fleeing woman and turned to face Rutger. "What do we have here?"

"She was lost, crying." Rutger was relieved to be speaking German again, but he suddenly realized he'd dropped his helmet back by the clearing. He swallowed, knowing that that would mean several very long nights. Karl was far from forgiving to his men. A small lapse in discipline meant days of hard labor.

Large lapses . . .

The woman tried to squirm out of Karl's arms. "She's a wild one." Karl chuckled, almost as if he was enjoying the struggle. "Do you know who she belongs to?"

"No, sir. She hasn't spoken to me. She just ran away."

"God's teeth, you can't catch one fleeing woman?"

Rutger felt better. Karl was in sudden good humor, and either hadn't noticed Rutger's lapse with the helmet, or had decided he didn't care. "Sir," he said, "I was chasing her *toward* the road."

Karl laughed. "Aren't you selfless? Forcing this handful into the hands of your fellow squires."

The woman still struggled, pounding on Karl's chest, shaking her head. It was all Karl could do to hang onto her. He looked down at her and started to speak in Prûsan much better than Rutger's. "Calm down and—"

In the woman's struggles, one of her hands managed to strike under Karl's helmet and bloody his lip. From Rutger's vantage it looked like a panicked accident, but he felt his gut tighten as Karl's expression turned into a red-tinted snarl.

"*Bitch!*"

Karl balled a fist and struck the woman across the face. She sprawled at Karl's feet, barely moving.

"Sir . . ." The expression of fury on Karl's face kept Rutger from completing the objection.

Karl rubbed his face, smearing the blood from his lip. "You useless bitch!" he shouted in German she probably couldn't understand. "If we weren't in Christian Prûsa, I'd teach you a proper lesson. If you weren't . . ." He trailed off, staring at his hand.

"Sir?"

A cruel red smile cut into Karl's face. He spat a gobbet of blood and phlegm on the woman's skirt then he bent down and twisted his hand in her hair, pulling the dazed woman's head up out of the mud. Rutger saw now an angry red scar, barely healed, on the woman's temple.

Karl's hand was turning black.

"The bitch dyed her hair."

Karl pulled a silver torc from his belt and slapped it around the woman's neck.

Rutger stammered, "S-she's the—"

"Ha. And you're the hero who found her." He knotted his hand tighter in her hair, and her eyes opened. She gasped, reaching for the silver collar now encircling her neck. "Quick, her wrists."

Rutger grabbed what little rope he had and ran up, seizing the woman's wrists. She cried, kicked, and screamed, but Karl struck her again, knocking her senseless enough for Rutger to bind her wrists together.

Rutger looked into her half-dazed eyes and she muttered something that sounded something like, "No, Ulfie."

Now, this close, Rutger could see that the rain rolling down from her forehead had turned a dirty gray. Red highlights were just visible where the black was washing away.

"It *is* her." Rutger backed away. "She killed how many . . ."

"Relax," Karl told him. "I've collared the murderous bitch. She's helpless now."

"Why didn't she attack us?"

Karl spat another gobbet of blood on the ground. "She dyed

her hair, obviously in the hope of avoiding our notice. She knew full well that if she did anything, everyone in these woods would descend on her."

Rutger wondered at that. There were six of them, and this monster had supposedly killed easily twice that many. And he had come upon her sobbing . . .

He was glad that it was not his duty to deal with her.

"Let's get her back to the Landkomtur, quickly." Rutger turned to shout to the others.

"Rutger!" Karl yelled at him. "Did I order you to do anything?"

Rutger turned around. "No. I thought—"

"Please refrain from thinking for a few minutes." Karl grabbed the woman's wrists and dragged her back toward a nearby stand of trees.

"The road—" Rutger pointed. "It's in the other direction."

"What did I say about thinking, Rutger? Stay there and shut up." Karl reached one of the trees, where a thick branch had broken off just within arm's reach. He lifted the woman and looped her wrists about the branch so she hung there, the balls of her feet barely touching the ground.

"What are you doing?"

"I'm teaching this bitch a lesson." Karl drew out his dagger. Rutger watched the blade shine in another flash of lightning and had no idea what he should do.

❖

Thankfully, the runt Rutger shut up when Karl took out his dagger.

He spat again. His lip still burned where she had struck him. The pain only served to intensify his anger—anger at the rain sliding down the back of his neck, anger at being pulled from his proper duty to search barns for some pagan nightmare, and most of all, anger at the bitch hanging on the tree in front of him.

"You've caused me much grief, monster," he whispered.

Her eyes fluttered, and he slapped her.

"I want you awake for this." He spoke German, not caring if she understood him or not.

Her green eyes snapped open, staring at him.

"Good." He touched the blade of his dagger against her cheek. "Feel that? It's silver. The blade's shit for much else, other than cutting you."

"No," she sobbed in Prûsan.

He laughed. "A little scar to remember me by?" He drew the blade down her face. She pulled away, a fine thread of blood on her cheek, little more than a scratch.

"N-no hurt."

He kept talking, not caring that his German words were lost in her Prûsan ears. "Different, isn't it, with that collar? No monster coming to save you, little girl." He jerked the blade down, catching the collar of her surcoat and tearing down. Her muddy clothes hung in open rags now. A few more flicks of the wrist, and he had her exposed from neck to knees.

"My, aren't we an attractive monster?"

He held the dagger up under her jawline, above the silver torc around her neck. With the other hand, he loosened his belt. He whispered into her ear. "It's sad. The Landkomtur is going to have to kill you anyway."

Lilly struggled against the man pressing her to the tree. She shook her head, eyes shut, tears mixing with the rain as the man forced her legs apart with his knee.

"No," she said.

Like her first master, this man didn't listen.

"No!" she shouted.

The man brutally thrust himself forward, slamming her back into the tree. Her head jerked back with a gasp and a cry, and her entire body went limp as Lilly curled up inside herself.

Help me, she cried into the darkness inside her.

A cold, angry voice answered.

Karl lowered the dagger as he felt damp warmth spreading down his naked thighs. He reached down, and his hand came away covered in blood, the bright red turning pink in the rainfall.

"I'll be damned." Karl laughed. "The monster is a virgin."

From far away, Karl heard a voice call out, "Sir!"

"Shut up, Rutger!"

The monster in front of him stirred, muttering something.

"Fool . . ."

"What did you say?"

Karl started bringing the dagger back up to her neck, but before he could, he felt her naked legs wrap around him above his waist and pull him forward so violently that he lost his grip on the weapon. His face was a finger's width away from hers. He could feel her breath on his cheek as he felt her thighs squeezing his lower ribs. It was hard to breathe and he tried to push himself away from her.

The green eyes didn't cry, didn't show terror. All Karl saw was a horrible emptiness as she smiled. Her head snapped forward, and he felt her lips on his.

Then he felt her teeth.

Rutger had stared at the rape with sickening fascination. Unable to turn away, he watched his knight brutalize the woman as he kept telling himself that this was a murderess, a monster. But that didn't change the terror in her face. The expression he saw there was so deep, so wrenching, that he knew the instant it changed.

Karl was laughing at something in his hands, and the woman's eyes opened. What he saw there made Rutger gasp, "Sir!"

"Shut up, Rutger!"

The woman stared at Karl with a cold disregard, the way Karl might look at a dog. The way a wolf might look at a pile of dung.

He drew his sword as she brought her legs up around him, and he was running for her as Karl fell back, clutching his face with blood-drenched hands.

Sprawled on the ground, Karl shouted something that sounded like, "Kill her!"

The neck, Rutger thought. *Even without a silver blade, separate the head from the body and it will die.*

Rutger swung, but she pulled herself up, impossibly quick, over his stroke. He gasped as his blade embedded itself in the tree with an arm-numbing impact.

He looked up. The woman crouched on the limb above him, snarling, face covered in gore. She pulled her arms apart, snapping the cords that bound them. He tried to pull his sword free, but it was stuck fast.

She leapt down onto his unprotected head.

⬥

At the base of the tree, Karl scrambled, clutching his ribs, searching for the dagger.

He found it, sticking upright out of a tree root. He grabbed the hilt—

And a naked foot stomped down on his wrist, grinding it into the ground. He rolled onto his back and she loomed above him, naked, blood trailing ribbons down her chin, her neck, curving across her breasts, her thighs. She looked down on him with those empty green eyes and spoke in perfect German. "Maybe a little scar to remember me by?"

"Bitch!" he spat at her.

She reached down and pulled the dagger free from the tree root. "They'll—" Karl sputtered, trying to pull his arm free. "Kill you."

She stood, holding the silver dagger. Karl noticed that she still had a hairline cut down the side of her cheek.

"Do you like virgins?"

Karl stared at her.

"My first master, Brother Semyon, liked virgins."

He grabbed for her ankle, but she dropped to one knee on his chest. Pain shot through him from ribs that were cracked or bruised or broken.

"He liked us because we heal."

She reached down and grabbed his penis, shrunken and still covered in her maidenhead's blood.

"You see, these are not made of silver."

She slashed with the dagger, and Karl screamed.

XV

Rain soaked Uldolf to the skin, and chilled him with an ache that hurt worst in his absent arm. The gray clouds above didn't let him know if the sun had set or not.

"*Lilly,*" he called out.

His only answer was a peal of thunder.

The wind tore through the tops of the trees, and the rain pounded his exposed skin as if someone was pelting him with wet gravel. He barely heard his own voice above it all.

"*Lilly!*" he called again. His voice was hoarse. It was getting too dark to see properly, and he knew that continuing at this point was more than foolhardy, but he kept going. He knew these woods better than anyone, even in darkness.

He couldn't go back without her. He didn't understand it, but she was out here because of him, because of something he had done. And that was something he couldn't bear.

Did I insult her? With her language as broken as it was, what did she think I was saying?

He had just wanted her to stop crying.

His foot caught something in the underbrush, and he fell to his knees before he could grab anything for support. His hand sank into the soggy floor of pine needles and rotting leaves, brown water squeezing up through his fingers.

He had to turn and sit down at the foot of the pine next to him to get his foot untangled. At first, he thought the thing stuck on his boot was a discarded bucket. But it was lighter, metallic . . .

A helmet?

Free from his boot, Uldolf held up the offending article. No question. It was a German helmet. Not some relic from an over-grown battlefield, either. The metal still glinted, despite the soil and pine needles adhering to the smooth surface.

A flash of lightning illuminated the woods, and Uldolf saw movement through the trees, little more than twenty yards from where he sat—a pair of soldiers. And while he was still dazzled from the lightning, Uldolf thought they might have had their weapons drawn.

He set the helmet down quietly, even though the volume of the storm and the pounding rain was more than enough to cover the sound of anything short of a scream. He scrambled around to the other side of the tree before another lightning flash lit the woods.

It didn't seem as if they'd seen him.

"Now what?" he whispered to himself, the words nonexistent under the sound of pounding rain.

He glanced around the tree and saw another three soldiers approaching at a dead run through the woods. Uldolf grimaced. The road was that way, and who knew how many more soldiers. He'd have to retrace his steps to avoid all of them.

Then, in a flash of lightning, he saw something that froze him down to his soul. One of the soldiers, who was shouting inaudibly to the other men, held up the remains of a surcoat. It had been torn down the front.

It was the one Lilly had been wearing.

No! I'll kill all you German bastards.

Hand gripping his hunting knife, he crouched low and began creeping up on the soldiers. He was less than a dozen yards away, barely hidden by trees and underbrush, when another lightning flash showed him the scene around the Germans. The sight was chaos in his mind for a few moments, and he froze.

What am I doing? he thought as the thunder shook the ground under his knees. His knuckles were white on the handle of the knife, and tears of rage burned his eyes.

He couldn't do this. It was worse than suicidal. It was brutal and selfish. He was about to salve his own pain by throwing himself on the swords of these men, and in that he would be guilty of those men's cruelty three times over. What right had he to take himself away from his parents and Hilde?

Slowly he sheathed his knife.

Lightning showed him again the scene by the guardsmen. Now it made sense. Two men were sprawled on the ground. From the brief glimpse, the one farther away looked as if he'd been savaged by an animal. The skin was gone from the lower part of his face, and he was drenched in blood from the waist down.

Uldolf backed away.

He saw no sign of Lilly other than her clothes. What if they had found her, and some animal had attacked? Uldolf's gorge rose at the thought of some wild beast dragging away Lilly's body.

He crawled backward through the underbrush, out of sight from the soldiers. He spared them a couple of glances as he retreated. They were slowly moving deeper into the woods, keeping a tight formation.

Were they looking for a wild animal, or Lilly?

Or Lilly's body?

He backed over a rise that put him fully out of sight of the soldiers. At that point he should have stood up and run home. Instead, he put his back to a blasted stump and stared up at the forest canopy. Rain beat his face so intensely that he could pretend he really wasn't crying.

Chasing after her, Uldolf had realized how quickly and how deeply Lilly had become part of his family. Even though he knew that her presence was temporary, until they knew where she really belonged, the thought of her absence left a hole in his family—in *him*. It was an absence that ached worse than his missing arm.

He could endure that if she was going home, to *her* parents, *her* family. But, losing her like this?

I have to go home. I'm doing no good here.

He stood, and it occurred to him that the soldiers were moving slowly in one direction. That suggested that they knew what direction the animal went.

Uldolf might not be a soldier, but he was a hunter. He slid his knife out again. He would have the blood of Lilly's murderer, human or not. And if it *was* too large for him to take alone, he would bring the soldiers to it and see that they finished it off.

Uldolf quickly moved around in a large circle that would take him in front of the soldiers.

Uldolf was able to keep ahead of the Germans, weaving a zig-zag pattern in front of them, looking for signs of Lilly or that animal the soldiers were following. It wasn't long before he found one . . .

On the banks of a muddy creek that was overflowing with rain-water, Uldolf saw fresh human footprints. Bare feet, about half the size of his own.

She's alive.

Uldolf couldn't imagine what had happened, but that was of very little importance to him now. He ran along the swelling creek, boots slogging in the mud, chasing her trail.

Branches whipped across his face, and the mud tried to suck his feet under. His cloak dragged on him, the wet material pulling down on his shoulders. His breath burned in his throat, and pain dug into his side, cutting up toward his empty arm socket. When the trail turned to cross the stream, he followed, the knee-deep icy storm water trying to pull his legs under.

On the other side, he stumbled away from the muddy edge of the creek into the woods, where the tracks were lost in the dark, the underbrush, and the springy mulch that formed the forest floor.

"No." The word burned his throat.

Darkness had come fully to the woods around him. The sun had set, and what moon there was wasn't enough to penetrate the clouds. The only illumination came from the intermittent lightning tearing through the trees. He didn't know exactly where he was anymore. He had run after her without fully getting his bearings. The creek snaked through these woods with dozens of branches. He didn't know where the road was from here, where the soldiers were, and with the storm-covered sky, he couldn't even figure north from south.

He felt very cold.

"Where are you?" Uldolf whispered into the storm.

He leaned against a tree and wiped his face with the back of his hand. Now that he had lost his bearings, going back was no longer an option. He was lost until the storm broke or morning gave him the light to discover where he was, or at least where north was.

Lightning arced above him, close enough that the thunder was immediate, resonating down into his bones, even in his phantom right arm. In the flash, he saw something through the trees—a flash of white against the brown, black, and gray of the starkly lit tree trunks.

Uldolf walked toward it, wondering if the flash had dazzled him into seeing a mirage. The thunder still echoed as another flash lit up the woods around him with an apocalyptic blast.

"Lilly!" Uldolf called out.

The white-skinned figure turned toward him. She was naked, hair drenched and plastered to her skin, hiding most of her face. Enough of the black had washed out that Uldolf could see the white streak in her hair that had grown from the scar in her temple. She breathed hard, and trails of blood mixed with the rain rolling down her breasts.

She raised a shaking hand between them, and Uldolf saw the flash of a dagger. The blade was bloody, and her hand was streaked with diluted blood as well.

"What happened?"

She took a step toward him, raising the blade. Uldolf took a step back, when another lightning flash showed him her neck streaked with blood, slashed with multiple cuts—

"You're hurt."

She lowered the blade, staring at him through the wet strings of her hair. "Uldolf?"

Given the enormity of the scene, it barely registered that she called him by his full name.

Uldolf sheathed his hunting knife and walked over to brush the hair out of her face and away from around her neck. "What happened?" he repeated.

"Y-you came?" Her voice sounded low, husky, almost as if she was talking to someone else.

Maybe she's hoarse from crying.

Uldolf lifted her chin to look at the wounds on her neck. There was something else, too, smeared with blood, some sort of metal collar. It was in two parts, and appeared locked in place. He saw rings that might have fit a chain. He hadn't seen anything like it before, but it was obviously some sort of restraint.

Uldolf felt sick when he realized that she had done all this damage to herself. He saw the scratches in the metal, in line with the cuts in her flesh. He looked down at the dagger in her hand. Obviously from one of the guardsmen, it wasn't a tool for this kind of work. It was thin, long, and double-edged—not much use aside from putting a hole in someone.

"Let me have that," he said, reaching down. "You'll cut your own head off before you get that collar off with this."

"I . . ."

He took the bloody weapon from her hand.

She stepped back and hugged herself. She shook her head. "This isn't right."

"Lilly?" He looked at her, and felt something odd about her manner, her expression. She was talking without difficulty, but the person speaking felt different. "What isn't right?"

She lowered her head and turned away from him. "I can't."

He reached over and placed a hand on her shoulder. Her skin was cold and damp, and she trembled. "Don't worry, I'll get that off."

"I . . . I . . ." He couldn't make out all of what she was saying through the rain. After a moment, she turned around and buried her face in his chest.

"Whatever happened back there," he said, "I found you. That's what's important."

She looked back up at him, her green eyes wide and lost. "I'm sorry, Ulfie." It might have been his nickname, but Uldolf thought he heard her voice regain the tone it had when she had first called to him across his father's field.

He stroked her hair and told her, "I forgive you."

"Ulfie!" She embraced him in a rib-bruising hug.

❖

Uldolf led them along the creek, into a ravine. He stopped at the first reasonable shelter he saw—a long shelf of rock projecting over both them and the bottom of the ravine. Several trees had fallen from the wall of the ravine to pile against the rock, providing better cover from the storm than he had a right to expect.

Lilly shivered in his cloak while he crawled under the projection and checked to make sure it was safe. The big rock above seemed stable, even supporting the weight of several dead trees. The ground was clean dry slate that seemed high enough not to be flooded. There was the stale musk from an old animal den, but Uldolf heard nothing moving back here. The prior occupants seemed long gone.

Uldolf backed out of the dark and looked up at Lilly. She was smiling at him, despite the angry red scratches on her neck. At least she seemed to have stopped bleeding.

He waved her under the rock with him. "Come on, we can wait out the storm in here."

She crawled in after him, and he backed up as far as he could into the cavern to give her a dry place to sit. She crept forward, little more than a silhouette against the gray storm outside. Even the lightning flashes didn't seem to reach in here.

She fumbled blindly for a moment until he felt her hand on his leg. Once she found where he was, she crawled up and huddled against him.

She shivered, and he placed his arm around her shoulders. "We just have to get through the night."

Lilly huddled closer and rested her cheek on his chest. She reached up and stroked his cheek.

"Lilly?" He took her hand down. "Why did you stop talking to me?"

"Ulfie?"

Uldolf sighed in frustration. "You were almost speaking in full sentences back there. Why won't you talk to me now?"

He felt her pull away. "Y—You don't like me?"

What the hell? "Of course I like you. But why are you having trouble talking now?"

"H-hard remembering."

Uldolf cursed himself for being too hard on her. She was still recovering from the head wound. The blow had taken something away from her, even if it wasn't as obvious as his missing arm. Even now, he still had to deal with the frustrations his own injury had caused, and those didn't even compare to how it was when the memory of having both arms was fresh in his mind. The pain of losing his arm had only started with the injury—

"Ulfie?"

The concern in her voice made him realize how tense he had suddenly become. He was breathing hard, his heart was racing, and he could barely feel why. *Hard remembering* . . .

"I'm sorry, Lilly. It isn't your fault you have trouble speaking."

"I— I try," she whispered.

"I know you do. But don't force yourself on my account." Uldolf shook his head. They were too tired, cold, and wet to work out her language problems anyway. He opened his pack and hoped his tinder was still dry.

He felt her hand on his wrist. He looked up at her, barely a darker shadow in the darkness. "I— I—"

"Lilly, it's really all right—"

"I like you, too."

◈

He found some dry wood wedged in the back of the cavern, enough to get a small fire going. He worried a little about the soldiers, but they were far away in the storm, hunting in unfamiliar woods. There was a good chance the Germans had more sense than he did, calling off their search once the dark and the storm became dangerously impenetrable.

All in all, a far more immediate threat was the cold and wet— especially for Lilly.

By the time Uldolf had a small fire going, she was asleep. She had unfolded the cloak underneath her and had curled herself up into a little ball on top of the sheepskin lining. There was no way he could cover her up with the cloak without waking her, so he removed his shirt, which had mostly dried out, and draped it over her.

"This is becoming a habit," he muttered, shivering.

He kept watch for soldiers, expecting them to find their little shelter at any moment. When he didn't worry about the Germans, he worried about his family. He hoped they had enough confidence in him not to worry.

Outside, the storm picked up, lightning and thunder rolling on top of each other in a near-continuous rumbling. The rain eventually became so heavy that someone would have to be right in front of their shelter even to see Uldolf's small fire.

"What happened to you back there?" he whispered to Lilly.

He pulled the dagger out of his belt. It was certainly German, not only from the design, but from the script engraved upon it. He recognized the style, if not the words. The blade itself glinted whiter than steel, and Uldolf frowned at it.

Silver?

"This isn't a weapon. It's a piece of jewelry." Despite the heft and the wicked edge, it wasn't a very good blade. He could see several scratches and dents in the edge where Lilly had tried to pry her collar loose.

There had been two dead soldiers on the ground back there . . .

He looked at Lilly sleeping peacefully next to him. He tried to picture her hurting someone, killing someone, even in self-defense. He couldn't—especially with this excuse for a dagger.

He looked down at the bloodstained metal collar still wrapping her neck. There was no question that the Germans had taken her captive, though. She had one of their daggers, and they had stripped her clothes. They had her, and meant to rape her—or worse.

So how did it end with two dead soldiers, and Lilly deep in the woods chopping at her neck with an ornamental dagger?

"That man was savaged by some sort of beast," Uldolf muttered into the fire. "Wolf, wildcat, maybe even a bear." He nodded and slid the silver weapon back into his belt. "They would have been distracted by the attack. You could have grabbed the dagger and escaped."

He brushed the hair away from her cheek, and saw another wound, a very thin cut down the length of her cheek. "Father is right," he whispered. "Those bastards are the ones responsible for hurting you. I'm sorry I didn't find you sooner."

She mumbled, sighing, and pulled his shirt tighter around her shoulders.

"Sleep." He pulled his hand away. "When I have better light, I'll see if I can get that thing off of your neck."

⬦

Uldolf dreamed in fragments, single images, torn from a larger, more painful whole. Each image—Radwen Seigson laughing, his mother smiling, his sister Jawgede running through the halls of the stronghold—every one was outlined in blood and faded into a dark abyss.

He couldn't see through the darkness, but he smelled the blood, and felt the flesh being torn from his body.

⬦

Uldolf woke, sucking in breaths, feeling his heart race, and feeling the black tendrils of nightmare fade in his memory. Morning light streamed under the rocky ledge, and Uldolf had to blink a few times before he even realized he had fallen asleep.

Sweat coated his skin as if he had just spent the night working the field. He felt Lilly hug him tighter.

Lilly!

Uldolf was abruptly awake enough to realize that during the night Lilly had curled up against his naked chest. Her breasts pressed against his stomach and one naked thigh was resting on his leg. She hugged him again.

"Please," she whispered, "d-don't be afraid."

It was heartbreaking to hear that from this girl—this woman— who had been so abused, so injured, so close to death. She worried about him when she was the one who had reason to fear. Those who wished her ill were real, out there, and had already done things that Uldolf didn't want to contemplate.

What was *he* afraid of? Ghosts? Memories?

He stroked her hair with his hand and said, "Only bad dreams. That's all."

"You have—" She squeezed him harder as she fumbled for the words, pushing the breath out of him. "You have g-good dreams. P-please?"

"I'll try." The way she was pressing herself into him, he could certainly imagine better dreams he could be having. Embarrassingly, his body was starting to agree.

Does she know what she's doing?

She gently kissed his chest and Uldolf decided that if she didn't know, she had a pretty good idea.

What was she thinking?

What was *he* thinking?

He had come out here to save her, not to ravish her like some warlord collecting his spoils. Even if she was willing—if he took it like some entitlement, as if being Radwen Seigson's son still meant something, it would make him little better than the German brutes who abused her.

"Lilly, get up."

She lifted her face from his chest and looked at him. She smiled, though the smile receded as she looked at his expression. "Ulfie?"

He placed a hand on her naked shoulder and sat up, forcing her to do likewise. When he was free of her embrace, he bent over and grabbed his shirt from where it laid, on the other side of the burnt-out campfire. He held it out.

For a moment she stared at him, fully naked in the light of day, for once not covered by filth, or blood, or darkness. She was the most beautiful thing he had ever seen, so much that it ached to look at her.

He was grateful when she took his shirt and put it on.

She smiled at him and cocked her head. When she did, she grimaced, reaching up to tug at the collar around her neck.

"Can you tell me what happened to you?"

"Ulfie?"

He reached out and touched the collar. "Can you try? I want to help you."

She shook her head. "No."

"No?"

She looked at him very seriously and said in a firm clear voice, "It's bad to remember."

Something in the way she said it made him feel as if she was talking about more than last night. He knew about bad memories. Even after eight years he still couldn't—

A memory—less than a memory—tore through the back of his mind, making him shudder.

"Ulfie?" She reached out and touched his face. "No cry."

Uldolf blinked and the half-felt horror sank back into the dark place it had come from, unseen and forgotten. He shook his head and said, "I'm not crying."

"Ulfie?"

"I'm fine." He worked to steady his breathing. "Let's take a look at that collar."

He took her hands away from the collar, one at a time, setting them in her lap. Then he concentrated on the damage she had done to the collar and her neck. Fortunately, all the cuts appeared superficial. His mother would have a more expert opinion, but the fact that none seemed deep, inflamed, or weeping was a good sign as far as Uldolf was concerned.

He looked around the circumference of the collar, and found the latch in front. It needed a key to open, if it still could open; Lilly had already done considerable damage to the lock. That part of the collar bore the most extensive damage from her attack with the dagger.

Unfortunately, the damage to the collar was as superficial as the damage she had done to herself. Uldolf looked around, brushing her hair out of the way, to look at the back of her neck.

"If there's a weakness to this . . ." He found the hinge. The two halves were wrapped around a thick pin, which was held in place by two small tongues of metal—one on top, one on the bottom—that had been bent over and hammered in place.

If the collar had been iron, he would have had no hope of removing it. But now that he had light, he could see that it, like the dagger, was made of silver.

"Why?"

He suddenly revised his thoughts about where she had come from. Beautiful and untouched, she could be a noblewoman, someone's betrothed. But she could also be someone's slave. Not all slaves were for heavy labor, and if her owner kept her for beauty or pleasure, wouldn't he want her bonds to be decorative as well?

He had a sick feeling in his stomach when he realized that Lilly might not be lost. She might have *escaped* from her real home— the home that Uldolf had been planning to return her to.

"Lilly," he whispered, "is that why you won't talk about your past?"

She turned around to look at him, wincing at the collar.

"I promise I will never give you back to anyone who would hurt you." He took out his hunting knife. "Now, you stay still. I don't want to scratch you any more than what you've already done to yourself."

He began working on the hinge.

Interlude

Anno Domini 1231

Landkomtur Erhard von Stendal, as Brother Semyon had said, was adept in the more subtle arts of warfare. Semyon might have trained his beast children to respect their Christian masters, but Erhard had taught Lilly how to fight.

She had the brain of an eight-year-old child, but even an eight-year-old could grasp some strategy. The wolfbreed were not invulnerable, but Erhard drilled into his charge simple principles that would maximize her strengths against her pagan foes.

Three were primary. First was surprise, to strike quickly and without warning when and where the enemy did not expect. Second was to choose the battlefield. Humans were most effective when they had space to move, light to see, so she should choose to fight them in confined spaces where they could not wield their weapons effectively, and meet them in darkness. Third was numbers. She needed to limit her combat to one to three men at a time.

Lilly was the first, and Erhard was not disappointed.

She learned well, and Erhard used her well. The first season he slipped her near enemy camps, and she made good on her promise to kill everyone she found there. While he treated her with the suspicion required to handle a wild animal, she never acted contrary to his direction. While he was careful to remove her shackles only when he was the sole Christian in immediate danger, she never once moved to escape or attack him. Instead, she looked at him with a devotion that was uncomfortably intense.

In the last months of that summer, he had her slip inside a village just ahead of the Order's army. She was pulled inside the walls with the other villagers fleeing before the Christian forces. It was a significant test. She had to remain out of contact for days, waiting for Erhard's signal, blasted on a hunting horn nearly a week after the siege began.

It was a successful test. Within one night, most of the armed defenders had died or attempted to flee, and the Order's army lost not one man. When they overtook the village, Lilly was waiting in the stables by the central fortress, sitting by the half-eaten carcass of an ox.

"Are you pleased with me?" she asked him.

Not the words Erhard would have chosen.

The next summer, Erhard decided to use her against the troublesome village of Mejdân.

❖

Midsummer of the year 1231, Erhard traveled to the frontier by Mejdân, a fortnight ahead of the Order's troops. He was not dressed as a knight now, and the horse and cart he led were those of a tradesman, not a warrior. The two men with him were no more than would be expected for someone attempting to transport goods across the Prûsan frontier.

Even the girl, not quite ten years old, had the appearance of a Prûsan slave, her shackles plain, painted black to obscure the precious metal with which they were constructed. The small party traveled the woods without incident. Once, a petty Prûsan warlord demanded a tribute of amber for their safe passage, but Erhard reacted as any tradesman would, paying the pagan strongman for his safety. That ensured Erhard and his party stayed no longer in the Prûsan's memory than his last meal.

A few miles from Mejdân, Erhard stopped his small procession and took Lilly off the wagon. He instructed his men to wait, then he led the shackled beast-child off into the woods, toward the eastern side of Mejdân. When he felt he had moved a safe distance from his men, he reached down and removed Lilly's restraints. She idly rubbed her wrists, but otherwise watched him, unmoving.

"Do you understand what you are to do?" he asked her.

"I am to wait, unobserved, until I hear your call."

"And when you hear my trump?"

"When I hear three long blasts, followed by two short blasts, I will enter the village. By the gate if I can find a crowd to be lost in, or if I can't, I climb the wall in darkness."

"Then?"

"When I hear the call again, I go to the big building on the hill." She looked up at him and smiled. "Everyone will die, master."

Uldolf stood in the bedchamber's doorway and called out to his sleeping parents, "Mama, Papa?"

He hugged himself, shivering, naked feet cold against the wooden floor. Papa muttered something that might be a curse. Mama sat up in bed and extended her arms. "Come over here, Uldolf."

Uldolf ran to his mother, wrapping both arms around her neck. "What's wrong, son?"

"He needs to grow a spine," Papa muttered from the other side of the bed, "and some common sense."

"You be quiet," Mama said.

"I heard her singing again," Uldolf told his mother.

Papa snorted.

"Radwen!" Mama snapped at him. She stood, taking Uldolf's hand. "Forgive your father. There are many things that worry him right now."

From under the covers, Papa mumbled, "And phantom little girls are not one of them."

Mama held Uldolf's hand all the way back to his room. "Now, what was she singing?"

"I never heard it before," Uldolf said. "It was pretty, and sad."

Mama opened the shutters on his window and looked outside. Uldolf's room was on the eastern side of the stronghold, opposite the village, so there were no streets or houses below. Below Uldolf's window was only a small patch of grass before the stronghold's inner wall, the massive timbers painted in a serpentine pattern that was bright even in the moonlight. Past the wall, the ground dropped away for a few hundred paces until it met Mejdân's dark outer wall—a much rougher structure of tree-sized logs, concealing the woods beyond.

She leaned out. "I don't see anyone now, Uldolf."

Uldolf sat on his bed. "I *heard* her."

"I'm sure you did, son." She tucked him back in, pulling the covers over him. "But on warm nights like this, sound can travel far. I do not think she was as **close as you** thought."

"She sounds so lonely."

Mama kissed his brow. "You **need** to sleep, Uldolf."

"Yes, Mama."

She stood and turned to the window.

"Mama?"

"Yes?"

"Can you leave the shutters open tonight?"

She frowned slightly, then turned to look outside. "I suppose it's warm enough." She turned away from the window and rustled his hair. "Now, you sleep. No more annoying your father."

"Yes, Mama."

Mama left him alone, closing the door, shutting out the light from the hallway. The unshuttered window let moonlight stream in. On the warm air he smelled horses, cook fires, and outhouses. He heard dogs barking, and the boots of guardsmen walking the inner wall.

And, soon, he heard her voice again. Low and sad, he knew that it was out there, whatever his mama said.

> *Fear not the cloak of slumber,*
> *When the sky has lost its sun,*
> *Mother will protect her child,*

"Should any nightmares come," Uldolf whispered back into the darkness.

Sext

Anno Domini 1239

Quia os peccatoris et os dolosi super me apertum est:
locuti sunt adversum me lingua dolosa.

For the mouth of the wicked and the mouth of the deceitful
   are opened against me:
they have spoken against me with a lying tongue.

—Psalms 109:2

XVI

Landkomtur Erhard von Stendal stood alone with the bodies the men had brought back from the woods. They had laid out the corpses in the chapel at Johannisburg Castle. The remains rested on two long tables, close to the altar. Despite the fact that these were not brothers of the Order, Erhard had told the priest to say the full office of the dead for both of them, and ordered his fellow knights to say the traditional one hundred Pater Nosters usually reserved for deceased brethren.

The dead—Karl Lindberg and one of his squires—weren't men he had known well. They were just examples of the petty lords and knights that chose to serve God for a few months in exchange for absolution and the favor of the Church.

Erhard concluded his own prayers in the presence of the corpses. He stood in the shadow of the chapel's simple cross, attempting to reconcile his twin feelings of guilt and cynicism.

It wasn't right to question a man's service to God, however that man came to serve. Such judgments were reserved for the Lord. Still, given what he did know about Karl Lindberg, Erhard certainly wouldn't characterize the man's service as joyful or without reservation.

And the way he had died did not testify to the man's righteous character.

The corpses were shrouded in preparation for burial, but Erhard had already seen the damage. At first, it appeared that it wasn't Lilly's doing. The wolfbreed killed with tooth and claw, rending their victims flesh from bone. Karl's squire bore not a mark on him other than the black bruise that encircled his neck. And while Karl Lindberg's face had been savaged, the marks in what was left of his cheek came from human teeth. Also, his manhood was taken with a bladed weapon—probably his own dagger, which was missing.

The assault was savage, but human. That meant it probably wasn't Lilly's doing, despite the missing silver collar.

However, if it was?

My hubris, Erhard thought.

Günter's men—that had been unprecedented. Before that point, none of the wolfbreed Erhard had taken to battle—not Lilly, nor any of the three siblings that followed her—had ever laid a hand on a Christian. The three others were years dead, but had all died in their service to God. Nothing, absolutely nothing, would have led Erhard to expect Lilly to turn against her masters.

So Erhard might be excused responsibility for the loss of Günter's men here.

But these two?

These deaths were upon him. He had his instructions; Lilly was to be exterminated. Was it his own moral weakness that made him order Lilly to be brought back for questioning? Was it asking too much, placing too high a price on his own doubts?

He needed to talk to her, but were his questions important enough to cost the lives of these men?

Erhard stood and walked over to the only other evidence of the debacle last night. The tattered remnants of a peasant woman's surcoat rested across one of the benches, where Erhard had left it during his devotions. Now that he had paid his respects, he picked it up and held it in his hands.

The front had been slit open, and the blood spattered upon it gave testament to Karl Lindberg's ill intentions.

Erhard had been all Lilly had; she knew nothing else, no other source of pleasure or happiness. Escape should have been inconceivable.

Could she still be here?

"Could she have gone insane?" he whispered.

Somehow, the prospect of her going mad was more ominous than the idea of her disobedience. He dismissed the thought. Not only was her mind as strong as her flesh, but her acts were not the acts of someone mad. She hadn't gone on the bloody rampage he would have expected. She had spent days planning and staging her escape. She had outmaneuvered her guards, and remained hidden.

He remembered telling her that for all her inhuman prowess, surprise was still her most potent weapon.

She had learned that lesson all too well.

He had seen what she could do when given rein to her bloodlust. Sergeant Günter thought he had seen carnage, but he was mistaken. Eight years ago, when this village was little more than a wooden stronghold held by a petty Prûsan nobleman, back when its name was Mejdân, *that* had been carnage. The wrath of God Himself had descended to this spot of ground, killing the occupants of this fortress—man, woman, and child. When the fire cleared and the Order had taken possession of the land, they counted more than fifty victims, but because the stronghold had burned, they probably never found all of them.

The slaughter had the desired effect, and the survivors accepted baptism almost to a man. In Johannisburg now, from what he had seen, the remaining Prûsan population rarely talked about the stronghold's fall. If they did, it was in hushed tones of superstitious dread. As if naming the evil might cause the demon to return.

Little did they suspect he had brought it back to them.

Perhaps that is why? Someone here spoke your name?

He would have laughed at himself, if he had any humor left. Lilly did not spontaneously abandon seventeen years of training, toss aside the will of her master, just because some ignorant villager uttered too much of what she had wrought here.

However, if her escape was so calculated, why would she stay close to Johannisburg? Her wounds were healed by now. Enough that she would have had little problem killing Karl and his squire, but also enough so she could quit Johannisburg and disappear into the countryside.

But why would Karl use the torc on a woman if he didn't believe, didn't *know?* That he did so, and ended up dead for his trouble . . .

That itself argued that it *was* Lilly. And if so, something was keeping her here.

❖

When he left the chapel, one of his brother knights was waiting for him by the doorway. The sun had set, and the bailey was deep in shadow.

"Have you been waiting for me long, Brother?"

"Not too long." He handed Erhard a sealed message. "A messenger arrived while you were in prayer."

He took the message and stepped back into the doorway where light leaked from the chapel's lanterns. Above him, bells began to ring Compline.

He hesitated before breaking the seal.

"Is there something wrong?"

Erhard shook his head. "No." What had given him pause was the presence of a bishop's miter on the seal.

He opened the message, reading it several times before he low-

ered it. He looked back into the chapel and stared at the cross for
several moments.

Your path is never easy.

"What is it, Brother Erhard?"

"We must make preparations for a guest."

"Who?"

"A personal representative of the pope, Bishop Cecilio."

xvii

"I s this a good idea, son?" Uldolf's father leaned against the door
frame and shook his head.

Inside the cottage Lilly stood by Burthe, chopping vegetables
and humming to herself. Her hair shone black from a fresh attempt to color it. The scratches on her neck had faded to a few
red lines. She showed no other sign of the ordeal she had been
through four days ago.

Uldolf spoke low, because there was little question that Lilly understood their speech as well as anyone, even if she still had some
difficulty talking. "I think we need to know more about what's
going on with Lilly, don't you?" Uldolf looked away from Lilly, to
his father. "We're actually ahead on planting because of her help.
One field's sown, and you've got the horse done plowing so you
can pull out the big harrow. You can spare me for a few days."

Gedim grunted. "Ahead?" He lowered his voice to a whisper.
"By my count we lost two days because you had to run after her."

"I know."

"I'm not saying it's your fault, son," Gedim said. "Or hers even.
This is just a bad time."

"The Germans will be back."

"You're sure they . . ." Gedim glanced over at Lilly. If Lilly heard their conversation, she showed no sign of it.

Uldolf still shook his head. It wasn't something they should talk about in her presence. Instead he told his father, "There will be rumors. Some word of where she came from, why they're searching for her."

"You're right. I just wish she'd tell us herself where she belongs." The way Gedim said it made Uldolf think that Gedim had begun to have the same suspicions that Uldolf had. The thought that Lilly had escaped from something too painful for her to dwell upon.

I suppose we both know about that sort of thing.

"I'll find out," Uldolf said.

"Perhaps I should be the one to go."

"No." He whispered it loud enough that he heard Lilly stop chopping.

Gedim narrowed his eyes at Uldolf.

"No." Uldolf lowered his voice. "Better I go. Then the farm's only losing one arm, not two. And, it's better that the head of the house is here, if the soldiers come back."

His father frowned. "I suppose . . ."

Uldolf could see that his father suspected that he had another motive. Uldolf just hoped that he wouldn't press him about it. He told them of the soldiers, and what they must have done to Lilly, and he told them of the animal attack that must have given Lilly the chance to escape. But he hadn't told his parents everything, specifically omitting the presence of the dagger, or the silver collar.

He hid those because he knew that his parents would think it too dangerous to try to sell them. Yes, he wanted to find out where Lilly came from, but if a satchel he had made from some old saddlebags could give them a week's worth of venison, the silver in those two items could feed them through next winter. There were markets frequented only by Prûsans, and Uldolf was sure he could sell both outside the notice of any Germans.

Perhaps more important, it would mean that his family could get along without him for a while. That was going to be important, if it turned out that Lilly needed to be taken somewhere far away—either toward her household, or, the way things were starting to look, *away* from it.

Either way, keeping her on the farm couldn't last, not with all the soldiers searching for her. Wherever she needed to go, it was almost certain that Uldolf would have to take her there, soon.

◆

The next morning, Uldolf set out on the walk to Johannisburg. A brisk pace would put him there somewhere after midday. In addition to the dagger and the collar, he brought a sack of hare and rabbit skins that should help pay his way. He would have liked to take the elk hide, but it might raise the question at the gate how he had come by it.

He had barely stepped out onto the road when he heard a voice from behind him. "Ulfie!"

He sighed and turned around. "Lil—"

She ran up and threw her arms around his chest, knocking the breath out of him and almost toppling him over. He gasped and patted her on the back. "It's fine. I'm just going to town. I'll be back soon."

"Stay," she murmured into his chest.

He stroked her hair. "I have to go."

She looked up at him. "I— I—" She frowned, lip trembling. "Stay!"

"It's only a few days. I'll be back." He smiled and touched her cheek. "Don't you want us to find out who you are, where your family is?"

She shook her head. "No."

Uldolf took a step back out of her embrace. He smiled and tried to look reassuring. "I'll be back. I promise."

He turned to take a step down the road. Lilly grabbed his shoulder and spun him around.

She stared into his eyes. Her gaze was sad, lonely, and questioning. A flush had come to her cheeks, and for a moment it seemed she had stopped breathing. He brushed a loose strand of black-dyed hair from her cheek. *I'm not abandoning you. Whatever demons haunt your past, whoever you really are, I won't abandon you. You know that, don't you?*

"Lilly?" he whispered. "I—"

Before he could get another word out, she leaned forward and kissed him. Her lips and tongue melted into his so quickly that she was pulling away before he realized what she had done. But she left behind a heat that felt as if it burned all the way to the core of his body.

He glanced up and saw his parents standing by the wall, watching him. *Great . . .*

Lilly grabbed his shirt in her fist and pounded on his chest. "Come back."

He looked back at her.

"You come back," she repeated. "I want you to come back."

He reached up and untangled her hand from his shirt. "I told you I would. Why wouldn't I come back?"

She took a step back and shook her head. "It's bad to remember."

He sighed and decided to ignore his parents watching them. He reached down and cupped her chin, lowered his face, and kissed her back. He saw her eyes wide with surprise as he pulled back, and felt a selfish pleasure in surprising her exactly the same way she had surprised him.

"I don't care about your past," he whispered. "I just care about you."

She threw her arms around him in a crushing hug. She whispered something into his chest that sounded like "I don't want to lose you again."

Again?

He took a moment to disengage himself and said, "I have to go."

Lilly nodded.

"Don't give my parents any trouble," Uldolf said. "And be nice to Hilde."

She looked down at the road with a posture so dejected that Uldolf's heart ached. It almost made him reconsider.

"Please, Lilly, don't run away again."

She looked up at him.

"Please? Promise?"

Lilly nodded, and said, "I— I promise."

❖

The day was warm—the fifth sunny day since the thunderstorm—but the center of the road was still a semiliquid mess of mud and manure. Uldolf walked as close to the edge as he could. For a road that only led to the local farms and a few good hunting spots, there had been a lot more mounted traffic than usual.

Could it all be for Lilly? It didn't make any sense, even with accusations of witchcraft and murder. There were plenty of murderers in the woods outside Johannisburg's protection—and plenty of witches for that matter, that being the term the Christians used for anyone who actively practiced the old religion.

None of that had ever aroused such attention before.

However, the closer he got to Johannisburg, the more trampled and muddy the road became. He had to walk almost in the woods just to keep his boots on his feet.

"Has your farm been troubled lately, lad?" the knight Gregor had said.

"Troubled?"

"By strange beasts? Men or animals killed or injured?"

Strange beasts? Like the one that had killed the elk?

He kept an eye on the woods as he walked. He had a sick feeling that he had seen signs of it, in the woods with those soldiers who had attacked Lilly. The one man had been savaged by something.

Thinking of such an animal, claws, teeth, fetid breath hot on his face . . .

Uldolf stumbled into the road, heart racing, remembering . . .

⬥

Make way, you fool!"

Uldolf turned around and saw a line of horsemen bearing down on him.

"Make way for the representative of His Holiness!"

The horses took up the entire road, and showed no sign of slowing down. Uldolf had to dive into the woods to avoid being trampled. Even so, a brown rain splattered him as a series of cantering hooves kicked up the soup of mud and horse shit that was the main road into Johannisburg.

Main road?

Uldolf rubbed his head and walked out after the horsemen had passed. He *was* on the main road, and he didn't remember how he had gotten here. He looked up at the sky, and by the position of the sun it was close to midday—which made sense, since the road from his family farm only fed into the main road, about a quarter mile from the gate to Johannisburg. He'd been walking for three or four hours.

Lilly's words echoed in his head: *"It's bad to remember."*

"I don't remember!" Uldolf shouted at the receding horsemen. "I don't remember, and I don't want to!"

He rubbed his right shoulder, vainly trying to make the ache in his missing arm go away. *Why now?*

Why would it be troubling him now? He was no longer a child suffering feverish dreams. All of this was eight years gone. He had thought he had been safely through all this years ago. Now, suddenly, it was getting worse. It was no longer the occasional nightmare, it was happening nightly. The moments when he had to stop and catch his breath were almost a daily occurrence now.

Now he had lost part of a day. Nothing like that had happened since . . .

"Please," he pleaded with whatever demon guarded the gate to his past, "I don't want to remember." It took an effort of will to push it away, as what had happened to him felt as close upon him now as it had eight years ago.

Think of something else, anything else.

And he thought of Lilly.

He thought of holding her, kissing her. The good memory helped push out the bad. He allowed himself the daydream, that she would heal completely, and that he would take her away somewhere. Somewhere safe from both their pasts.

He shouldered his bag, wiped the shit off his face, and started walking to Johannisburg.

❖

Uldolf walked up to the gates of the village. Beyond the walls, Johannisburg was a crowded hive of activity, timber houses crowding each other over the narrow muddy streets. Above it all was the mound on which Johannisburg Keep squatted like a lumpy gray toad. The air was thick with the smell of too many people and animals in too cramped a space.

A bored guardsman walked up to him from his station by the edge of the gate. "Greetings, good man. You approach the Christian city of Johannisburg. In the name of the Hospital of St. Mary of the Germans in Jerusalem I must ask your name, where from you hail, and your purpose in coming here."

Uldolf recognized him. "Lankut?"

The man blinked a moment, looked Uldolf up and down, and laughed. "Apologies, I didn't recognize you with all the shit on your clothes."

"You can thank the 'personal representative of His Holiness' who just galloped through here."

Lankut snorted. "The bishop? Lord forgive me, but I thought the knights of the Order were arrogant pricks—then I met him. I think he's convinced that Prûsans all secretly worship Satan, or rape the livestock, or piss in his beer . . ."

"I wonder what he's doing here."

"While you do that, you can wonder about the hundred or so soldiers and knights they have up at the castle. So how's your family?"

Uldolf spent a few moments catching up with his friend. He told Lankut about things at the farm—leaving out the parts involving Lilly—and Lankut let him know about the wave of armed Germans who had invaded Johannisburg. Germans to which were just added one Italian bishop and his attendants.

Lankut repeated the story that the knight who'd come to the farm had told him. They were looking for a redhead with green eyes, seventeen years old, a witch and a murderess. He knew that fourteen men had died up at the castle about three weeks ago, a week before all the Germans came.

Fourteen men?

As to how the men died, rumors abounded. Demons, wild beasts, and an invading war party were all possibilities. While the Order itself said that the witch they hunted had conjured a monster, Lankut was enough of a Prûsan to be skeptical whenever they brought up the term *witch*. The priests and priestesses of the old religions here were not in the habit of summoning murderous hellspawn. If they had been, this town would probably still be named Mejdân.

"So, what theory do you subscribe to?" Uldolf hoped it would be a little less disturbing than the one Lankut voiced about witches and monsters. It was a vain hope.

"The only one that makes sense is they are worried about a revolt," Lankut said. "Half of Prûsa, east of Balga, is still ruled by tribes that would love nothing more than to push the Christians back into Kulmerland. After eight years, a counterattack is inevitable."

Uldolf lowered his voice. "Lankut, you almost sound cheerful at the prospect. Aren't you a Christian?"

"I serve my Lord Jesus Christ, *not* the Germans. I don't share the opinion that a Christian Prûsa needs rule by a foreign sect of armed monks."

Uldolf shook his head. "What about the woman?"

"Isn't it obvious? What's the most fearful thing the Order faces? That the tribes of Prûsa stop fighting among themselves and unite against them. How would you do that?"

"I don't—"

Lankut slapped Uldolf's shoulder. "Marriage, you fool. You put the right families together, and instead of facing a dozen clans, the Germans face four, or three, or two . . ."

"You think she's betrothed to someone?"

"Why else would they hunt so hard for her, unless she represented that kind of political threat?"

Uldolf nodded. Lankut's argument had some merit, especially in light of how many soldiers had descended on Johannisburg. It made more sense if the Germans were expecting some sort of rebellion. "That makes sense, though I haven't heard about anything like that here before."

"No." Lankut smiled at him. "I am sure *you* haven't."

Uldolf's brow furrowed as he looked at Lankut. "What exactly are you saying?"

"Nothing of import. You still haven't stated your business in Johannisburg."

"I came to trade some skins, maybe stay a night or two."

"I am sure." Lankut hadn't stopped smiling.

They stood there looking at each other for a while. Uldolf finally asked, "Aren't you going to claim the Order's share?"

"Between us," Lankut lowered his voice, "the Order is in no need of your taxes or tithe right now."

"Pardon me?"

"Enter freely, son of Radwen." Lankut gestured into the village.

Uldolf frowned. "What are you trying to say?"

"As I said, nothing of import."

"You can't be thinking . . . Do you have any idea how wrong you are?"

"Of course, Uldolf. Everything I've told you is mere speculation. The Order doesn't deign to tell us poor heathen Prûsans what is going on." Lankut leaned forward. "But at the end of the third path to the right is an inn run by an old man with no reason to love the Germans."

"Thank you."

"All I ask is that, should you have the opportunity, please remember those who treated you fairly."

Uldolf walked into Johannisburg, pulling his mud-splattered cloak about himself to better conceal his missing arm. He prayed that no one else was under Lankut's misapprehension that being the crippled son of the last chief of Mejdân somehow placed him in the leadership of a Prûsan revolt.

XVIII

Erhard was discussing the ongoing search with his fellow knights when the great hall suddenly echoed with heavy footfalls and butchered German.

"Brother Erhard!"

Even had Erhard not been uncomfortably familiar with the voice, he would have known who it was. None of the brethren had the arrogance to raise their voices in such an unseemly manner. Bishops, on the other hand . . .

"Brother Erhard!"

He quietly dismissed his fellows and turned to face the invader, who stomped down the center of the hall toward him. A petty impulse, and one that Erhard was almost ashamed of, made him stand and wait for the corpulent bishop to walk all the way to him.

When Bishop Cecilio reached him, Erhard made a token obeisance and said, "Welcome to Johannisburg, Your Grace."

"What work of Satan has been happening here?"

"Lilly escaped."

The bishop's mouth opened, then closed, briefly making him resemble a fresh-caught herring gasping in the air. "Lilly?" he sputtered.

"That's her name."

"You named it?" The bishop shook his head. "A Christian name?"

Erhard had not named her, but it seemed pointless to explain Brother Semyon's penchant for floral appellations.

The bishop continued. "I am unsure if you are deliberately flouting God's will in this matter, are willfully ignorant, or simply incompetent."

"Your Grace, might I remind you that this is the Order's house, and not your bishopric?"

The bishop pulled a folded piece of parchment out of his voluminous robes and slapped it against Erhard's chest. "Consider your words, Brother Erhard. I was not the only one appalled at the situation here."

Erhard took the parchment and saw that it was closed with the seal of the Hochmeister.

He shook his head, knowing what he was about to read, but not wanting to believe it. He broke the seal and read the short note.

Johannisburg, for the moment at least, *was* now part of the bishopric of Bishop Cecilio.

The man doesn't even speak Prûsan. He can barely speak acceptable German . . .

Erhard knew the forces Hochmeister Conrad must be facing. With the twin patrons of the Teutonic Order, pope and emperor, again at each other's throats, could he do anything but accommodate the pope—especially in something that could be so damaging to the Order?

"Do we have an understanding?" the bishop asked him.

But does the pope's man have to be so distasteful? "Yes, Your Grace."

"Good. Then you shall enlighten me now on the evils I have inherited in your wake."

Bishop Cecilio paced while Erhard talked. He pursed his lips and fidgeted, running stubby bejeweled fingers over the fur trim on his robes. It was as if the concepts of discretion and frugality were so alien to the man that even economy of movement was beyond him.

When Erhard finally ended the history of events in Johannisburg, the bishop nodded. He wiped his sweaty palms on his robe and examined Erhard carefully.

"Brother Erhard, I see you ask the right questions. However, I believe you are still too close to these events to reason clearly. You are puzzled because you see this thing as a trained beast."

"Where do you fault my reasoning?"

"You continue to question why she would choose to escape here in Johannisburg. Then you question why she would stay here in Johannisburg. It seems probable that those two reasons are related, if not the same."

"And you have discovered the answer?"

"No, Brother Erhard, *you* have. You just haven't seen it. The death of that knight, what was his name again?"

"Karl Lindberg."

"Yes. What strikes you about that attack?"

"Aside from the vile way he was mutilated—"

"I see that Satan has done well distracting you. What about your beast? With that attack she told you all you need to know about her reasons."

After a moment, Erhard said, "Perhaps you should explain them to me."

"Your beast left here a naked animal. However, in the aftermath of Sir Lindberg's ill-fated rape, you find a set of clothing. When you combine that with the fact that you have heard no news of mutilated men or beasts, no wolf-creature terrorizing the country-side, or so much as a rumor of naked women prowling the woods here, you are left with a single conclusion."

"And what is that?"

"The creature has a protector here. Perhaps a whole coven."

"This is a Christian town."

"And who has clothed her? Fed her? You took this place eight years ago. Is that so long that you think there is no memory of when that thing was an embodiment of their own rough gods? You think none of these Prûsans have gone straight from baptism back to their wooded groves and idols and tried to scrub God off of their skins?" The bishop shook his head. "Even aside from this beast, there have been questions raised in Rome about how easily the Order here accepts professions of faith."

"There is no truth to—"

"In the few hours I have been here, I have seen a distressingly lax attitude toward these Prûsan converts. Pagan names still abound. I greatly fear what I might hear if I questioned your priest about who has received the sacrament, or has confessed their sins and who has not."

"These people have accepted Christ, Your Grace."

"Brother Erhard, the facts remain to be seen. However, it is clear to me, as it should be to you, that within this demesne, those who honor the false gods of Prûsa have given succor to your monstrosity, and their presence here led to its escape."

Erhard did not want to believe that, but the bishop's logic had a fatal inevitability to it. After all, how could it be otherwise? Someone indeed had to be sheltering her, and how could any sane household do that unless it was in service to their gods?

"I will talk to those who witnessed the escape," Bishop Cecilio told him, "and I will question the men individually. One may have set these events in motion."

"You think there may be a traitor here?"

"And, Brother Erhard, I need to question the people. I mean to discover who has housed this creature."

"I will send my knights out to question—"

"You did not listen," the bishop interrupted. "I said that *I* must question the people. We will start by bringing every Prûsan who was present for the fall of the Mejdân stronghold here."

"Your Grace, the farms are in the midst of sowing—"

"Brother, need I remind you of your vows?"

"No, Your Grace."

"The sooner these Prûsans face my inquisitor, the sooner they can get back to their labors."

◈

Sergeant Günter met Erhard in the great hall. The Landkomtur was alone, leaning against one of the rough wooden tables where the brothers prayed and took their silent meals. Erhard stared into the wood, not turning his head, and for several long moments, Günter was unsure if he knew that he had entered the hall.

Finally, Günter cleared his throat. "You wanted me, sir?"

Landkomtur Erhard nodded to the table. "How long have you been here?"

"I've been assigned—"

"I mean *living* here. You come from this village, don't you?"

Günter nodded. "That's why I was sent back here, I believe. Better for the people to see one of their own running things."

"You were living here when Mejdân was sacked?"

"I was twelve years old . . ."

"But you *were* here."

Günter frowned, wondering where this conversation was going. Was Erhard beginning to question his loyalty? "Sir, what are you asking me?"

"It's a simple enough question. You were present when the Order breached the walls and took Mejdân. Am I correct?"

Günter closed his eyes. He had a brief memory, smoke and shouting, the sound of timbers breaking . . .

"Yes, sir, I was here."

"You know then, what other Prûsans were present?"

"Do you know how few survived that bloodbath?" Günter whispered, questions about his own loyalty forgotten. Some things transcended allegiance.

"Then," Erhard spoke quietly, to the table, "it should be a small matter to assemble those few for some questioning."

"What?"

Erhard straightened up and turned to face Günter. His expression was cold, hard, and bloodless, his words slow and measured. "You and your men are going to bring me every man, woman, and child who survived."

"Sir, the spring planting has just started. Many of the farms around here need—"

"Do not question this, Sergeant!"

The look in Erhard's eyes made Günter take a step back. "Yes, sir."

Erhard turned away. "Get moving. You have three days."

XIX

During the two days after Uldolf departed, Gedim's mood oscillated between amusement and concern. Lilly came with him to finish the planting, and every time he looked at her, especially at the melancholy expression she wore, he couldn't help but think of the way she had embraced his son when he had left.

Uldolf had always been an unusual child, always finding the capabilities to do something even when fate put massive obstacles in his path. Never quite satisfied with how he was doing, he was always striving to do better.

Burthe might have despaired sometimes at her son's marriage prospects, but Gedim never did. He always knew that, somehow, Uldolf would persevere. Somehow, even though it was nothing that Gedim would have ever predicted, finding a maiden in the woods and having her fall in love with him, in retrospect, seemed very much like his son.

It was also obvious that Lilly's affection was not flowing in only one direction.

He stopped the horse at the end of another furrow and turned to lead it around to follow where Lilly was casting the seed.

Should have been casting the seed. Instead, she stared off in the direction of the road. At first, he thought she was looking for some sign of Uldolf. But something about the way her eyes narrowed and her nostrils flared made him turn to look himself. He saw a glint of sunlight through the trees—a helmet, or shield. Now that he listened, he could hear hoofbeats. They stood on the far end field, and they weren't in direct sight of the soldiers yet, but they would be in a few seconds.

He ran up to her and grabbed her basket of barley. "Hide!"

She looked up at him, eyes wide. "B-but—"

"There's no time." He dropped the basket into the furrow, seed spilling out of the upturned basket. He grabbed her shoulders and turned her toward the wall dividing the field, about five yards away. "Hide yourself, now!" He gave her a shove toward the wall.

She looked over her shoulder at him, and the panic in his face must have broken any hesitation she had. She ran toward the wall, vaulting over and ducking behind it with only a few seconds to spare.

Gedim wiped his hands on his trousers, trying to compose himself as he walked back toward his house. He prayed that none of the soldiers had seen her. He kept thinking back to his son's description of what those German bastards had done to her in the woods. He thought of the scratches on her neck and face, still fresh; the wounds in her temple and her shoulder, only just healed.

He asked the gods to grant him his son's restraint. It was going to be hard not to throttle these men who were approaching his farm.

⬥

Günter was not enjoying his day.

The first day, going through Johannisburg to "request" the cooperation of the Prûsans who had survived the sack of Mejdân eight years ago had been much better. Tradesmen weren't tied to their shops as the farmers were to the soil. Most all of them had an apprentice or a spouse to run things in their absence. Those who had to close their business at least did not suffer losing days of business that were more important than any others.

Out here, in the countryside that fed Johannisburg, asking these people to leave the farm was like asking them to give up their children. Günter faced tears and curses, and twice today had to bear men off their land in chains.

On the return loop to Johannisburg, they stopped at their tenth farm, the horse team drawing a long wagon that usually carried bales of straw and hay. Today it was half loaded with men, women, and one or two children. It would be completely full when they returned to Johannisburg tonight.

When he drew even with the gate in the stone wall encircling the small homestead, he raised his arm and called "Hold!" to the whole procession. He looked over the farm, seven or eight acres of freshly plowed earth with low stone walls snaking around and through the fields. A horse stood in the field, the square framework of an old harrow dug into the earth behind the beast.

A man walked toward them from the field. A woman opened the door to the cottage, a young girl of five or six peeking at him from behind her skirts.

This is not going to go well. Not well at all.

He knew the couple. Not personally, but he knew of them. Gedim and Burthe were the only married couple from Chief Radwen Seigson's household to have survived the fall of Mejdân whole. They even had taken in Radwen's only surviving child—

That meant that he needed to take everyone.

He dismounted and waited for Gedim to reach the cottage before he approached the gate. Gedim walked up and nodded at him without opening the gate. "Can I help you?"

Günter watched him survey the small procession. Unlike the

one that had been through this area before, their job didn't include searching for the creature. Günter could see in Gedim's expression that he understood the difference. He probably knew most of the people who peered down at him from the old hay wagon.

"I'm Sergeant Günter Sejod—"

"Hognar's son. I know, I recognize you."

Of course you do.

"I've been ordered to retrieve for questioning all people who survived the sack of Mejdân."

Gedim's eyebrow rose. "I am in the middle of planting."

Günter looked up at the wagon. "They were planting as well."

"Do you people not want Johannisburg to eat?"

"A few days at most," Günter said. "The Church requires it."

Günter watched as Gedim surveyed the six mounted soldiers who accompanied the wagon. "It seems that I have no choice but to be a good Christian." He opened the gate. "I will accompany you."

Burthe stormed out of the cottage. "What do you think you're doing?"

Günter put his hand on Gedim's shoulder. "I'm sorry. Not just you."

"You bastard," Burthe spat at him. "What gives you the right—"

"The rule of this land by the Order, and the pope, give me the right," Günter told her. Behind him, two of his men dismounted. "I need to bring back you, Gedim, your wife, and Uldolf."

"Uldolf isn't here, you spineless—"

"Burthe!" Gedim snapped at her. "Think of our girl. Calm yourself."

She looked as if she was going to spout more invective against Günter, but thought better of it. Günter looked away from her and at the cottage, where their daughter was quietly sobbing.

Günter shook his head. *This is a disaster . . .*

"Sergeant, my son has gone into town. It's only the three of us here."

"Son?" Günter looked up at him. *Oh, Lord Radwen's child.* "Uldolf, you mean? Is he due back soon?"

"He just left."

"I see . . ." Günter looked out at the field and narrowed his eyes. The horse still stood, and a basket was scattered in the furrow before it. That was a two-person job. And how likely was it that Gedim would allow even partly able-bodied help to go away to town right now? Why, in fact, would he be as agreeable as he *was* being?

"Hilde," Burthe said abruptly. "We can't leave her here, alone. And our horse is still in the field."

Günter looked at her and smiled. *We both know she wouldn't be alone, now, would she?*

"You can bring Hilde with you," Günter said. "You will not be kept away more than a few days."

Gedim and Burthe looked at each other. Then Gedim looked at him and said, "May we take care of our horse, and close up our house?"

Günter nodded.

In the end, Günter decided there was no point in making this scene even more difficult for the sake of someone who was little more than a child when the savagery of the Teutonic Order fell upon Mejdân. There was nothing that Uldolf might know that would be of any interest to Erhard or the bishop.

⬧

Lilly pressed against the stone wall, shaking, her eyes shut. She tried not to hear the men, or smell the horses. She tried to think of Ulfie, that he would come back.

He *would* come back, and everything would be all right.

"Why?" she whispered into the stones. Tears burning with the effort, she struggled with the single question. "Why?"

In her head she heard a colder voice. *You know why.*

"No."

You can't forget me . . .

"No!" She spat out the word, too loud. The men up there, by the road, would hurt her if they found her. Even worse, they might hurt Ulfie's parents.

Or Hilde.

Her fingers dug into the soil at the base of the wall, anger growing. If anyone got hurt—

On her hands and knees, she sucked in gasping breaths, eyes burning. She didn't want to be angry. With every nerve, with every bone, with every clenching muscle she did *not* want to be angry.

Listen to Ulfie's father. He said to hide. Listen to him now, how calm he's talking to the men on the road.

He smells of fear, the other one spoke in her head.

"He doesn't want th-them to hurt me," she whispered into the earth.

We can hurt them first, the other told her.

"No. Don't. Please."

We can hurt them enough that they will never hurt anyone, ever again.

Lilly buried her face in the soil and screamed into the ground, "Stop it!" Her voice was muffled, and she inhaled dirt, making her gag and cough.

She froze, thinking the men would hear her. She hugged herself, wheezing, leaning against the cold stones. She didn't even dare to peek, so she kept her eyes closed, listening.

Panic gripped her chest when she heard someone coming, walking across the earth. The horse snorted. She sucked in gasping breaths trying to be calm, be hidden.

They were coming for her.

Then she heard Ulfie's father whisper, "It's all right. Nothing to worry about."

He was whispering to the horse, but she knew the words were for her. She listened as he led the horse away. Maybe the men were going to leave?

They did leave, but they took Ulfie's parents and Hilde with them. It was a long time after she had heard them leave before Lilly risked looking over the edge of the wall.

No one, just the horse in his pasture, craning his neck to reach some grass that was just outside the gate. She brushed the dirt off her clothes and her face, spitting out pieces of soil.

She was alone.

Ulfie would come back. He would know what to do.

But she had heard them talking. The men wanted Ulfie, too. The men wanted to take *everyone* from her. She shook her head. They couldn't take Ulfie away. They couldn't.

You need me.

"No," she whispered. "I—I—I—" He voice kept catching on the word. She finished the thought in her head. *I can do this myself.*

Always, when something horrible happened, she let the other one take over, begged for her to take over. She might be frightened, but she was just as strong and smart as the other one. She *could* do it herself.

She could get help. She could find Ulfie.

You promised to stay.

No, I promised not to run away.

She wouldn't be running away, she'd be running *to* him. She stood next to the cottage and swallowed. Following Ulfie meant she would have to go in the same direction the men took his family. The men who wanted to hurt her.

The scar on her head hurt, and she absently rubbed at it.

When she caught up with them, she would just have to go through the woods, around them.

She walked to the edge of the road and walked through the gate. She looked off in the direction the men, and Ulfie, had gone. Not far. Not far at all, if she ran. She could run fast.

Lilly bent and pulled her skirts up, tying them high around her waist. Then she ran.

Lilly smelled the men before she was in sight of them. The sweat of the horses, the sour smell of tired men, the fear from the cartload of prisoners, all thick in the air above the road. She slowed, barely panting, and stepped off of the road and into the woods. There was no path here, and the underbrush caught at her legs. Branches whipped her face and tugged at her hair.

She pushed deeper, until she came across a small game trail that followed the road. She stayed on it, bending low, trying not to be heard. However, as she closed on the small caravan, she realized that the men probably couldn't hear her even if she tried to get their attention. Far out of sight to her right, through the woods, they traveled in the midst of a dissonant symphony of hoof-beats, creaking wagon wheels, and the babble of the people in the wagon.

Lilly strained and she heard Hilde's voice saying, "What about Lilly?"

Someone, Ulfie's father she thought, whispered, "Shh. Don't talk about that now."

Lilly's vision blurred, and she ran faster down the game trail, getting ahead of these men. She ran until she could no longer hear the cacophony of their progress, and their smells were just a faint memory.

Safely ahead, she cut again through the underbrush and stepped out on the road. Running on the road, where other people traveled, was dangerous. She might be seen . . .

But she had to follow Ulfie, and until she got close to him, the road was the only sure way she had to follow him. She could move much quicker on the road than she could in the woods. Besides, men were smelly and noisy, and if she paid attention she would notice someone else long before he noticed her.

XX

It seemed that every hour that passed served to show Uldolf what a bad idea coming to Johannisburg had been. The village was crawling with foreign soldiers, brother knights of the Order, secular knights, squires, bonded foot soldiers—and all were looking for Prûsans who had survived the sack of Mejdân. It was clear that Lankut was closer to the truth than Uldolf would have liked. Uldolf credited the fact that he was still a free man to his following Lankut's advice as to where to board for the night.

He had spent his first evening trading his furs, then acquiring a small narrow room from the proceeds. That night he had not slept well, waking up several times from now-constant nightmares that left him only the impression of an onrushing menace.

Upon waking and going to breakfast, he discovered that the dread he felt had more of a basis than a barely remembered dream. The gray-haired proprietor had whispered to him of the Germans who were taking all the Prûsans who had been present at the siege of Mejdân. The surviving son of Chief Radwen would obviously be of particular interest.

That day, while the soldiers went to and fro along every street in Johannisburg, Uldolf did not leave the house where he boarded. And that night, the nightmares were worse—though he still could not remember them.

The following day, the soldiers seemed to have completed their task. At least they didn't overwhelm the streets with their numbers.

Even so, he waited until early evening to slip from the house. He stuck to the narrowest alleys between houses, trying to stay out of sight without looking as if he was staying out of sight.

His winding journey stopped in the shadows next to an old timber-frame building facing the road out of Johannisburg. He could look out from the shadows, down the main road, toward the gate. He waited until he saw his friend Lankut take his post at the gate. Delaying his leave until his friend took that duty gave him one less thing to worry about as he slipped out of town.

He was freshly aware of just how conspicuous he was, a one-armed man known to nearly every Prûsan in town. Even the soldiers who didn't speak the language would be able to guess who he was. From a distance he was able to hide his missing arm under his cloak, but the moment a knight or some other soldier stopped him or tried to speak with him, his pathetic disguise would fall apart.

Worse, the Germans were no longer overwhelming the city in their search for the survivors of Mejdân. They had most likely spread their search into the countryside, and that meant it was no longer just Uldolf who was at risk.

It now meant his family.

The soldiers would come to his home and find them, and Lilly as well.

However hopeless it seemed, he *had* formed half a plan. He would slip out at dusk, just before the gates closed, and travel home under cover of night. If he beat the Germans to the farm, he could take Lilly and slip into the woods. He knew enough to survive out in the wilderness for several days at least. Enough to bypass any searches.

However, now that the sun was setting behind the gate, stretching shadows of trees and buildings toward him, he had another problem. Between him and the gate, on the main road, two German knights were talking.

If they had been knights of the Order they would soon be heading off to the keep for prayers and devotions, and whatever ascetic meals the warrior monks allowed themselves. However, this pair didn't wear the black cross of the Order. These two knights dressed in garish red and green and were under no such obligation. They showed no signs of taking their conversation elsewhere.

Uldolf huddled closer to the shadows, debating if he should move or wait for the Germans to walk away. They didn't appear to be actively searching for anything; they just stood next to the road talking to each other. But they had been talking for half an hour, and if Uldolf waited until after dusk and the gates were closed, he would draw even more attention trying to leave.

Because he held to the shadows, paying attention to the German knights, he didn't see Lilly until she was already walking through the main gate. He just glanced away from the Germans for a moment, and he saw her dyed hair blowing slightly in the breeze, skirts smeared with soil and leaves. Even at this distance, with the black that hid the white streak in her hair, he could still see the angry red scar that marred her temple.

No!

She had slipped behind a group of Dutch merchants entering the village, apparently to keep from drawing attention. The idea might have had merit, if her peasant clothing had not been completely at odds with the furs of the merchants, and if she wasn't very obviously keeping the merchants' wagon between herself and the Germans up the road.

What are you doing, Lilly? he thought.

The moment someone tried to speak with her, ask her name or her business here . . . He had to get to her before that happened.

The Germans hadn't paid her any attention, yet. The merchants had paused, debating among themselves. If they cared about the anonymous girl who entered the gate on their heels, they didn't show it. Lilly walked a few paces away, separating from their group, and looked around at the buildings, as if she was considering where to go.

By the gate, Lankut looked back in her direction, as if he realized that she wasn't part of the tradesmen he had just admitted.

No choice.

Uldolf pulled his cloak fully about himself, concealing his missing arm. He left his face uncovered, since the Germans would know him only by description. If he raised the cloak's hood in the daylight it would be even more notable than his absent arm.

He made an effort to calm his breathing and a racing heart, and began an unhurried stride down the main avenue of Johannisburg.

Lankut had decided to investigate. He left the other guards at the gate and began walking toward Lilly. The merchants settled their conversation and broke up into two smaller groups, dispersing down two separate alleys, parting like a curtain between the German knights and Lilly. The Germans were still talking to each other, neither looking toward Uldolf or Lilly.

Lankut was much closer to Lilly than Uldolf was, and Uldolf felt the copper taste of fear in his throat. He had hoped to reach Lilly before Lankut talked to her, but there was no way to close the distance in time without breaking into a sprint. Uldolf passed the two Germans, less than four yards away across the street. It took all his will to avoid looking at them as he passed.

Lankut walked up behind Lilly. She was still turning, away from him, surveying the village.

Uldolf heard Lankut say, "Excuse me, miss?"

Then Lilly saw Uldolf. The smile, wide eyes, and shout of "Ulfie!" came with such an explosive lack of subtlety that Uldolf expected the Germans to strike him dead on the spot. She ran to him, throwing her arms around his neck and kissing him with such enthusiasm that he felt faint from lack of breath.

He took a step back and Lilly followed, hanging on him, ending the kiss only to rest her cheek on his shoulder.

Expecting the quick and forceful end of her embrace, Uldolf glanced over to the Germans across the street. He had quite obviously failed in his effort to remain unnoticed. However, to his great relief, the Germans were staring at them with amusement, not with any hostile intent. They were chuckling at Lilly's public affections and Uldolf's obvious discomfort. His face burned, and they laughed harder.

"Excuse me?"

Uldolf turned and looked at Lankut, who had followed Lilly from the village gate. He was half smiling himself.

"Yes?"

"I was going to ask her business in Johannisburg, but that's apparent."

Uldolf brought his arm from under his cloak to hold Lilly, and turn her slightly so she was between him and the Germans, facing away from them and hiding the right side of Uldolf's body from observation. "She came here to meet me," Uldolf said.

"I am hoping you do not allow her to travel alone on these roads."

Uldolf never felt more his deficiencies as a liar. He looked down at Lilly and said, "I don't know—" *What to say?* "She should be with her family."

"Oh. She was coming with others?"

Uldolf kept looking down at Lilly so Lankut couldn't look into his eyes. "Maybe, when she got in sight of the town, she ran ahead."

"She was quite excited to see you."

Uldolf nodded, looking up. "And I, her."

Lankut looked off toward the Germans who had gotten bored with the spectacle and were talking again between themselves. "Are you betrothed?"

Gods, how do I answer that? "Perhaps, with her father's permission."

Lankut chuckled. "Your father would be amused at your excessive politeness."

Uldolf was about to say something, but he realized that Lankut was not referring to Gedim. He felt the tall shadow of Radwen Seigson looming over him.

"In his day, if he eyed such a beauty, he would have simply taken her. Woe to father, brother, or uncle who objected."

"Things are different now."

"Perhaps," Lankut said. Still looking at the Germans across the street, he continued softly, "Are you aware that those men would probably like to talk to you?"

"I have heard."

"Good." Lankut smiled. "As you are here, and they are here, I have done my duty."

Lankut turned and walked back toward his post at the gate, and the Germans, still talking to each other, finally made their leave.

❖

U ldolf still wanted to get out of town, but his driving urgency had been to get Lilly away from his family. It wasn't quite clear what the Germans were doing by taking so many Prûsans from Mejdân to the keep, but it *was* clear that if the Germans found Lilly with his family, there would be some dire consequences.

Now that Lilly was here, Uldolf had to rethink his plans. He couldn't take her back home. So instead he took her back to his room at the boarding house. Even if the master of the house was no friend of the Germans, Uldolf was still discreet about bringing his guest. He took her around the alley in back, between the inn and the stables.

His room's single window looked across an alley at the stable. He had fortunately left it unlatched, and was able to open the shutters from outside. He boosted her up so she could climb in.

He followed, clumsily, until she reached out and grabbed his arm. She showed her strength again as she practically lifted him into the room after her. His relief at being quickly inside, unobserved, overrode any embarrassment he might have felt.

She backed up to give him space to enter the narrow room. The air was thick with the smell of mud and horses drifting in from the open window. The light burned red with the setting sun.

Uldolf stepped around the chair and the short bed, the only furniture in the room, and reached around Lilly so he could latch the door shut. Once that was done, he breathed a sigh of relief.

Lilly was sandwiched between him and the door. She placed a hand on his chest. "Ulfie?"

"Sit down while I try and think of something to do." He backed up, taking off his cloak and laying it on the bed next to her as she sat down.

As he set down his pack, she grabbed his shoulder. "Ulfie." She opened her mouth, closed it, and frowned at him. "I— I—"

Uldolf frowned at the frustration evident on her face. He sat next to her and placed a hand on her shoulder. "Calm down, Lilly."

"I— I— I—"

He lifted his hand and placed a finger on her lips. "If you keep forcing things, if you let the frustration overwhelm you, it gets even harder. Speak slowly, one word at a time if you have to. Take a breath."

He lowered his hand and Lilly nodded. She took a breath and said "I came t-t-t—" She shook her head and took another breath.

"To you m-m-m—" She sucked in another breath and said, "My-self."

There was a hint of a smile at completing the sentence. But it didn't reach her eyes. He could tell that there was more she needed to say.

"Why, Lilly?" He shook his head. "You had to know how dangerous it was."

A single tear rolled down her cheek.

"I— I— I—" She balled her hands into fists.

"Shh. You need to calm down."

She buried her face in his chest. "L-l-let m-m-me do this."

"Let you do what?" Uldolf stroked her hair.

❖

The other was a suffocating presence in Lilly's mind. *You need me.*

I can do this. She tried to fight it. *I can!*

You can't get three words out.

No.

He needs to know now.

No!

In the end, though, it was why she had come here, and only her dark half had the words to tell Uldolf what he needed to know.

❖

"You're safe right now," Uldolf whispered. "That's what matters."

"No." She pushed herself away, fists balled on his chest. "No."

"No? What? I don't understand."

She faced away and didn't seem to hear him anymore. She shook her head, then her voice became low and deliberate. "Uldolf?"

Uldolf placed his hand on her back. "Are you all right?"

She reached up and pulled his hand away. Uldolf drew back as she unfolded from the bed, pushing herself upright. "I have to leave."

Uldolf stood and grabbed her. "What are you talking about? The Germans are hunting you, to kill you, or worse—"

"Do not concern yourself with me."

"How can you say that, after what my family's done for you? Hilde thinks of you as her big sister—"

Her shoulders sagged and he let go. "I came to tell you. The Germans came today. They took your family."

Uldolf shook his head and backed up. "They can't . . ."

"Your father hid me in the field, but the soldiers made them board a wagon with a score of others. They were on the road an hour behind me."

He sat down on the bed. What could he do now? Nothing. How could he do anything now that the Germans held his family? Why had they been taken in the first place?

Lilly walked to the door, and Uldolf reached out and took her hand. "Don't go."

She turned to look down at his hand, and then she turned away. "I can't stay here."

"Why?"

"I've done too much to you already."

"This isn't your fault. It's the Germans who're doing this."

She spun around, and the agony in her face made Uldolf shrink back. "Don't speak about fault. After what I did—" Her voice choked off in a gasp.

"Lilly?" Uldolf let go of her hand and touched her cheek.

She stared at him, confusion in her face. "Don't you remember?"

He looked into her green eyes and felt . . .

✦

Somehow he was sitting on the bed, sucking in deep breaths. Sweat coated his skin as his heart tried to pound its way through his ribcage. He clutched his empty shoulder so tightly, and the pain was so bad, that he looked at it expecting to see blood from a fresh wound. It felt as if it had just been torn from its socket.

Lilly held him in a crushing hug, shaking him. "Ulfie! Ulfie! Ulfie!"

He stared at her, not understanding the inexplicable panic he felt fading in his breast.

"Ulfie!"

"I'm fine, Lilly. Calm down."

She stopped shaking him. "D-d-did she hurt you?"

"Did who hurt me?"

She swallowed and asked, "Did I hurt you?"

"No." Uldolf shook his head. "It was me. Now, let me go."

She released him, and it was suddenly much easier to breathe.

"It wasn't anything you did, Lilly. Don't blame yourself." He looked down at his single arm, clenching and unclenching his hand. "I lost my arm a long time ago. I was a child when the Order came and destroyed my home, killed my family." It was the first time he had talked to anyone about this. For some reason, he felt that Lilly was the one person who could really understand.

"U-Ulfie . . ."

"And I can't remember. No, that's not quite right. I can remember, but every time I do, when I think too closely on what happened—" Uldolf tried to calm his breathing, which was starting to accelerate with his pulse. "It's almost like it is happening again; the fear, the pain. I can't think about it, or anything close to it, or I black out. Even if I dwell on my first parents too much . . . I suppose I'm a coward, I can't even look at my own past straight on."

"No!"

Uldolf looked over at Lilly, and she grabbed him, pulling him back into a hug.

"No! You aren't a coward. You're very brave!"

She rocked him back and forth as if she were comforting a child.

"Ulfie's brave," she repeated. "Uldolf's brave."

Interlude

Anno Domini 1231

It was a bright summer day, and a nine-year-old child named Lilly sat in the woods to the east of the pagan village of Mejdân.

True to her master, she waited.

She waited, anticipating the moment when she would be able to go into the city and punish the evil people who so troubled her master and his God. She would do well, and she would show him how all the pain and discipline was worth it. She would demonstrate that she was worthy of him, and of his God.

But first, she had to wait.

She sat on a black, moss-covered log. Occasionally she would rock her legs back and idly kick it with her heel, denting the rotten wood and scattering strange little crawling things to scurry across her legs. Sometimes she sang the lullaby she had used to sing to Rose.

Sometimes she wished her new master would sing to her.

However, even if he didn't, she knew that she was special to him simply because he took no pleasure in correcting her.

Unlike her first master who enjoyed punishing any error until the prospect of pain was an overwhelming shadow over every step she took, her new master only beat her when she did something truly wrong. More important, beating was *all* he did. He didn't use anything to cut her, or insert into her body. Compared to rape and mutilation, a heavy rod across her back was almost a pleasure.

And, because of that mercy, she would do anything. She would take the life of every person in this village if it would please him.

But first, she waited.

Dappled sunlight spread across the woods around her, and a gentle breeze rustled the leaves, tugging at the simple tunic her master had given her. Occasionally she would run her hands over the fabric. She was still unused to being allowed to wear real human clothing. If she did well, maybe her master would allow her to keep it.

Around her, insects and birds chirped, and the air was rich with smells. She could smell mud and loam, as well as horses and people from the village. And she loved the smell of the pine trees around her. Even the rotting log she sat on smelled rich and earthy—an improvement over the smells of blood, urine, straw, and stone she was used to from her life before her new master.

"Hello?"

Her eyes widened, and she spun around.

No, she was supposed to be hiding and waiting. No one was supposed to see her. If someone found her, she would fail. Her master would have to beat her or, worse, he might return her to the monastery.

She expected a huge hairy man in armor, like the pagans they made her train on. The man would draw his sword, and Lilly would have to kill him, spoiling her master's order not to kill anyone until it was time . . .

But it wasn't a hairy pagan swordsman.

It was a child, no more than a year older than she was. He stood only a few paces away, smiling. The boy was taller than her, and held a sack slung over his shoulder. He waved at her with his free hand. "Hello," he said again.

She was on her feet and backing away from him. She wasn't supposed to be seen by the village, but she wasn't supposed to kill anyone, either. Maybe she should just run away.

"My name's Uldolf. What's yours?"

"Lilly," she said reflexively. She couldn't help it. You answered a direct question or you were beaten . . .

She shouldn't be talking to this boy.

"Was that you I heard singing, last night?"

Please, no! It was her fault. Master would abandon her for sure.

"I— I don't know what you mean."

But lying was even worse. Even as she spoke the words, she could feel her old master twisting her arm until it snapped and forcing himself between her legs—

"Come on," he said. "Admit it."

"I shouldn't be talking to you."

"Why not?"

"I'm waiting . . ." Lilly trailed off, not knowing what to say. She couldn't tell him the truth. That would be worse than all her other mistakes combined.

But the boy, Uldolf, just shrugged and said, "Are you hungry?"

Lilly stopped worrying long enough to be completely confused. "What?"

"Are you hungry?" Uldolf asked again. He walked up to the log and set his pack down. "I have some cheese."

She didn't know what to do. She folded her arms and shook her head. "I shouldn't be talking to you."

Uldolf laughed. "That's fine, I shouldn't be talking to you, either. I'm supposed to be with the other kids, keeping the cows in the meadow."

"Cows?"

"Stupid things would walk off a cliff if someone wasn't there to shoo them away." Uldolf unwrapped his bundle revealing two things inside, neither of which was familiar to Lilly. One was a lumpy whitish-yellow object, whose edges crumbled like dry earth. The other was rough, round, and mostly brown. Neither object looked particularly interesting.

But the smell . . .

She sucked in deep breaths just to have more of it. The smell was sharp and warm and unlike anything she had ever smelled before. She licked her lips and closed her eyes, trying to breathe in every particle.

"So, you want some?"

Lilly's eyes snapped open. She suddenly remembered that she wasn't supposed to be talking to anyone.

The boy was alone; maybe she should kill him? The boy had sneaked away. He had said so. No one knew he was here. She could hide the body somewhere they would not find him, at least not before her master brought the army of Christ to this city.

She could kill him right now . . .

He held up a broken part of the white-yellow thing to her and she realized that part of that wonderful smell was coming from it.

Lilly didn't understand for a moment.

"Go on, take it. You look hungry."

His words cut through the confusion. She reached out and took the crumbling thing. The texture was something like rotten clay— slightly sticky, maybe a little oily. She couldn't believe that anyone might just give her something that smelled so wonderful.

She held it to her face so she could breathe it in. She enjoyed it for several moments when she realized the boy, Uldolf, was frowning at her. She lowered her hand and looked around. Was someone else here?

"Are you stupid?" the boy asked.

She didn't understand. Why would he give her such a wonderful thing, and then say she was stupid?

The other part of her whispered, *Kill him. Let us kill him now.*

"W-why would you say that?"

He frowned. "You're playing some sort of trick on me, aren't you?"

"N-no. I'm not. Please, tell me why you're saying that."

She was feeling weak, uncertain, in a way that she hadn't felt in a long time. Not since before the time she understood what her masters wanted from her. For years now, the one thing she was sure of was that she knew the rules. She knew which actions brought pain, and which did not.

You will not feel this way if he dies . . .

"Stop it!" she snapped at herself.

"Stop what?" Uldolf said.

Lilly could feel tears welling up in the corners of her eyes, and that made her feel worse. Her master did not like it when she cried. It was weak. It brought more beatings. She looked at the thing in her hand and made a fist around it.

"Why did you give this to me?" she shouted, and threw the thing back at Uldolf in frustration. It hit him in the middle of his chest, breaking apart into a shower of crumbled fragments.

His eyes were wide, and his face mirrored the confusion Lilly felt. She turned away so he couldn't see her crying.

"I'm sorry," he said.

Lilly sucked in a breath, unsure if she had heard the words correctly. She wiped her eyes. "What did you say?"

"I'm sorry I called you stupid."

Who was this boy? Lilly was the one who said sorry. She was the one who asked forgiveness. No one ever apologized to her. She shook her head. "I *am* stupid." If she wasn't stupid, she would be able to figure out what to do now.

"No, I was being mean."

She felt his hand on her shoulder and shuddered.

Change now, sink our teeth into his neck. Tear his stupid head from his stupid body.

She turned around, and Uldolf held up another piece of the wonderful-smelling cube. "Here, you can have my half."

He shoved it into her hand before she could reach out and take it. She looked down at it. Nothing made sense to her. She had just thrown his gift back at him. He should be taking a metal rod and whipping her across the back and legs, at the very least.

"It smells so wonderful," she whispered.

"It does stink, doesn't it?"

She blinked so she could focus on the object in her palm. "What is it?"

"Now I know you're tricking me!"

"No." She looked up at him. "Please, tell me."

"You say you don't know what cheese is?"

Lilly shook her head.

Uldolf frowned. "So what do *you* eat?"

Lilly didn't know what that had to do with anything, but she didn't see any harm in answering. "I eat meat."

Lilly thought of the elk calf that she had killed two nights ago. She'd hung the carcass in a tree, and even after two days it still had a good section of the haunches left. She thought of the red flesh and the rusty smell of the calf's entrails, and her mouth watered. She *was* hungry. Now she wanted to get rid of Uldolf so she could go back to her kill.

"Only meat? And I bet your father is duke of Mazovia."

"No," Lilly said. "I don't know who my father is."

"Oh."

"What else would I eat?"

"Well, cheese, of course."

She looked at her palm.

"You really haven't eaten cheese before?"

"No." She lifted the crumbling object to her lips and took a bite. It melted into her mouth with a flavor unlike anything she had ever tasted. That wonderful smell turned velvet and wrapped her tongue.

How could someone just *give* her this?

"I'd better go," he said.

Her eyes snapped open. "What? You just got here."

"Well, it took me a while to find you. They'll be expecting me home soon. It's late."

"Oh."

"I can come back if you want. You'll be here?"

"Yes." *Why did I say that? I'm supposed to stay hidden.* "Please, don't tell anyone I'm here."

"No, I don't want to get into trouble." He walked back to the log and picked up the other object. "Here, you can have the bread, too." He tossed it to her. It was all she could do to grab it before it tumbled to the ground. "You know about bread, don't you?"

"Y-yes," she lied.

He picked up the cloth that had made up his bundle and waved at her. "Good-bye."

She watched him disappear into the woods before she bit into the "bread" he had given her. At first she thought it was some sort of trick, but then she realized that it was like a thick bone she had to break to get at the spongy contents. Inside, it was almost as good as the cheese.

Lilly knew it was wrong, but throughout that night she thought more of the boy Uldolf than she did of her master's wishes.

She built up elaborate excuses for herself. Her master had told her that there was to be no killing before it was time, so she really shouldn't have killed him. Her master had also said that she wasn't to be seen by anyone in the village, but Uldolf wasn't *in* the village when he came to her.

Uldolf had been right, she *was* stupid. She should have killed him. Everything her master told her was for the purpose of keeping the village from knowing she was here.

She crouched in front of her kill, tearing large strips of flesh free from the leg of the calf, her muzzle sticky with old blood as she devoured the slick length of muscle. Around her, the moonlight-dappled woods were silent except for the sound of her own chewing. Even with the air rank with elk blood, she could tell that most of the animals had given her and her meal a wide berth.

If Uldolf came to her now, there wouldn't be a choice, would there? She had shown her real face to enough people, pagan and Christian, to smell the fear she caused. Even in her master.

Would he give you cheese now?

Lilly stopped eating, because she didn't like the way that thought made her feel. The other's voice was becoming more and more forceful lately, cold and angry. She didn't understand why, after leaving the horror of her first master. She crouched and lifted the remains of the elk, climbing up and dragging the remains after her into the tree.

She dropped to the ground, and spent a few long moments licking the blood off her fur. She needed to be as clean as possible before she retrieved her carefully folded clothes from the rock where she had placed them before she ate.

"He doesn't know, does he?" she whispered, staring at her hairy forelimb and the clawed hand she'd been cleaning.

That was it, of course. That realization was what allowed her to be true to her master. Uldolf didn't know she wasn't human. Uldolf had seen nothing of fur, fang, or claw. What could he tell the villagers in Mejdân? Only that he met a girl in the woods who knew nothing of cheese.

Even better, now that she thought about it, she really *shouldn't* kill Uldolf. After all, a dead boy would certainly be more alarming to the people of Mejdân than anything Uldolf might say. Lilly looked up at the night sky through the leaves, and smiled as much as her lupine muzzle allowed.

✦

He isn't coming.

Lilly tried to push the thought away even before she knew whose thought it was. The echo of it kept taunting her as she sat on the black, moss-covered log overlooking Mejdân. She had come here in the early dawn, after waking. She had actually run here, afraid he might come before she arrived.

And here she was, and the sun kept creeping higher in the sky.

For some reason, she remembered the man who had sung to Rose in the monastery, and how severely her old master had corrected him.

Could her old master have found Uldolf?

If you care, her other voice told her, *you only hurt yourself.*

"I don't care," she whispered, wiping her eyes.

Lilly tried to think of the pagans of Mejdân and what she would do to them. How she would bring the vengeance of God down upon them, and how pleased her master would be.

"Hello, Lilly."

She spun around. "Uldolf?"

There he was, wearing the same clothes, carrying the same bundle over his shoulder. "Were you waiting for me?"

"N-no. Not long."

He smiled. "I'm glad I found you."

Lilly stood up, brushing leaves from her clothes. Then she noticed that she had blood under her nails, so she hid her hands behind her back. "Why?"

Uldolf shrugged. "I don't have many friends. My dad's the chief, so they don't like playing with me."

Lilly didn't understand what he was saying. She knew the words *friend, chief,* and *play,* but she couldn't interpret Uldolf's sentence in any way that made sense to her. She didn't want him to call her stupid again, so she just repeated the words back at him.

"They don't like playing with you?"

"Well, my dad bosses around their dads, and they think I
want to boss them around. If I tell them I want to do something,
everyone will want to do something different. I end up alone a
lot."

The last bit Lilly understood. "I'm alone a lot, too."

"Hey, want me to show you something fun?"

Lilly hesitated a moment, then said, "Yes, show me."

✦

T hey stood in the middle of a shallow creek bed, cool water
bubbling over their ankles. The creek ran along the floor of
a ravine whose walls receded ahead, the creek branching at the
base of an ancient moss-covered oak whose limbs stretched an
emerald canopy over a hidden pool. The pool reflected shards of
blue and green so intense that it hurt her eyes. The air was alive
with the sound of rushing water, chirping frogs, and singing birds.
She smelled the earthy moss, blooming plants, and over it all the
coolness of the water.

For several moments, all Lilly could do was stare.

"You like it?" Uldolf asked.

"It's beautiful."

Uldolf walked up to the oak and leaned against a giant boulder
next to it, as tall as he was. "I love this place."

To her surprise, Uldolf set his bundle on top of the boulder,
barely within reach, then scrambled up the side of the rock. He
stood up on top of it and grabbed one of the lower branches with
both hands. Then he swung his legs and pulled himself up.

"What are you doing?"

"This tree is great for climbing," he said as he started scrambling
up, branch by branch.

Lilly thought of the tree where the elk hung.

He knows. He's taunting you.

"Come back down."

"You come up."

"What?"

"Come on up here."

Lilly balled her hands into fists. "What if I don't want to?"

"I told you I was going to show you something fun." Uldolf looked down from a dizzying height. "You aren't scared, are you?"

If you pounce and dig the claws in . . .

Lilly shook her head. Uldolf still had no idea what she was, and as long as he didn't, she wouldn't have to kill him. She looked up and said, "I'm not scared." The way her voice shook made her a liar. "But how did you get up there?"

She almost added, "Without any claws?"

"Just climb up the rock. There's a good foothold about halfway up."

As she approached the rock, Lilly tried to remember what Uldolf had done. Things like this were so much easier when she was in her real form. She had never thought of attempting anything like it in this weak little body. How could her pink clawless fingers pull her up a tree?

The first few moments were embarrassing, her feet slipping all over the base of the rock. She was tensed, ready for Uldolf to call her stupid again.

"You can do it," Uldolf called down to her. It sounded as if he actually believed it.

"Come on," she whispered. "Why should the furry one get all the fun?"

"What?" Uldolf called down.

Lilly didn't answer. She felt around until her fingers found a good grip on the bumpy top surface of the boulder. She surprised herself with how easily she could pull herself on top of the rock.

On her knees, on top of the boulder, she looked at her fleshy pink hands and said, "Maybe they're not so useless."

"That was great," Uldolf called down to her. "Now just pull yourself up on that branch."

Lilly looked up at the knobby limb reaching over her head and smiled.

She leapt at the branch as if she *was* a wolf. But, instead of trying to dig nonexistent claws into it, she wrapped her arms around it and swung her leg up over it. In a moment, she sat straddling the branch.

She exhaled and laughed. "See? I don't need claws to do it."

From above her, Uldolf called down, "That was great!"

She looked up at him, flushed, breathing heavy, suddenly afraid he would ask something uncomfortable about claws. But apparently he hadn't heard her.

"Come on up." He motioned her up to the branch where he was sitting, above the water. It suddenly didn't seem that far. She leapt up and grabbed the branch above her and swung around. Then she did it again. She was laughing louder with each jump.

All her masters, all her keepers, always talked about what the furry one could do. That was what made her special, worthy of attention. That was the part she had to hide, that was the part that could do things—awesome, bloody, violent things. No one had told her that this body, the form she shared with Christian and pagan, was capable of anything—and certainly not *this.*

She dangled from a branch, allowing her legs to sweep through empty air. Her heart raced as the trees rocked back and forth around her, the ground so far below. If she let go, it seemed that she might fall forever.

"Hey, Lilly. Down here!"

She looked down and saw Uldolf looking up at her. She had become so involved in climbing that she had crawled nearly twice again as high as he was. He grinned up at her.

She dangled and looked down at him. Maybe it wasn't a trick. Maybe he was a friend. She let go and fell to a lower limb, then jumped down twice more to get to Uldolf's branch.

"Wow, I never saw anyone climb that well!"

Lilly caught her breath and said, "Really?"

"I never had the guts to go all the way up there." He looked up at the branch where Lilly had been dangling.

"See?" Lilly said. "I'm not afraid." She was no longer lying.

"Great. Then let me show you the best part." He stood up, grabbing a higher branch for balance. After steadying himself, he let go and pulled his linen shirt off over his head. He tied it up into a ball and tossed it back down toward the boulder. He did the same thing with his shoes. Then he started taking off his breeches.

"Wait—what are you doing?" Lilly thought of carefully removing her own clothes before she changed. Could he be like her?

Uldolf tossed the rest of his clothes down so that they fell on the ground by the boulder. Naked, he said, "I don't want to get my clothes wet."

He walked carefully out along the branch. Then he jumped.

"Wahoo!" he shouted as he hit the pool below with a cataclysmic splash. Lilly stared at the rippling water until Uldolf's head poked up. He stared up at her. "Come on!"

She looked down at the pool and felt her heart racing, but she was not going to act afraid, not in front of Uldolf. It was still fresh in her mind how it felt when he had told her that she climbed well.

If she could do that, she could do this.

She stripped her clothes and tossed them down by Uldolf's. As she did so, it occurred to her how important they had seemed yesterday—real clothes, a sign of her master's approval. How was it that this boy's approval had become more important?

The breeze touched her bare skin, and she felt herself break into gooseflesh. She wanted to change, to grow fur against the chill up here—but it was exhilarating in a way she had never felt as a wolf.

She edged to the spot where Uldolf had jumped and she looked out over the water. It shimmered below her, reflecting green and blue. Uldolf floated off to the side, looking up at her and grinning.

She was actually going to do this.

Lilly jumped.

The air tore by her fast, sliding by her skin and whipping her hair up in a halo around her head. She fell feet first, the water's surface racing up at her faster than she expected.

Then the water sucked her into a frigid embrace that turned her skin into ice. She gasped and sucked in a mouthful of water. Her body suddenly wanted air, and she had no idea where the surface was. Panic raged through her, and she could feel her body start to react, the bones beginning to crack and lengthen, the muscles tightening and swelling across her back, through her arms, her thighs, the jaw growing, the teeth.

He fooled us. He has to die!

Even disoriented, body screaming for air in the frigid dark, she found the strength to scream, "No!"

The words were nothing in this fluid hell, just more bubbles. But her body listened to her, muscles loosening, bones retracting into their human shape. The effort resisting the change was exhausting, and she felt herself sinking.

Something grabbed her under the arms. In a second, her head broke the surface, and she choked and sputtered and tried to suck in mouthfuls of air all at the same time. Uldolf held her, and even in the water, she could smell his fear.

"Are you all right?"

Lilly blinked, realized that she *was* all right, and turned around, tears in her eyes. "That was supposed to be fun?" She pulled herself away from him, and suddenly felt herself sinking again.

"No!" She grabbed for the only support within reach, throwing her arms around Uldolf. They both went under briefly, but Uldolf somehow managed to pull them back to the surface.

"I'm afraid," Lilly whispered.

"I'm sorry," Uldolf said. "Why didn't you tell me you couldn't swim?"

"Swim?" Lilly asked.

☙

Uldolf spent a good part of the day teaching her to swim. By midafternoon, she gathered the courage to climb up and try jumping in again. This time she didn't panic, and managed to keep her bearings, kicking her way to the surface. She burst through the surface, laughing and shaking the water from her hair.

When Uldolf told her, "You learn fast, don't you?" her face burned with pride and she could barely whisper a "thank you."

Eventually, Uldolf looked at the sky and said, "I have to go home soon." He swam to the edge of the pool, where the floor was shallow enough for him to walk onto shore.

Lilly followed him, dripping, as he walked toward the boulder. "Do you have to go?"

He looked over his shoulder, saw her standing behind him, and his face flushed. "Yes." He looked away. "I'll be in trouble if I don't go back with the other kids. I have a way to walk to get to those stupid cows." He reached up and squeezed water out of his hair. "And it'll take me a while to dry off."

Even in the warm afternoon air, Lilly hugged herself and shivered a little. He sat down at the base of the boulder, drawing his knees up to his chin.

Lilly sat down next to him, imitating the way he sat.

"I wish you could stay," she whispered.

"You have no idea how my dad would beat me if he thought I was running off on my own."

Lilly nodded. "Yes, I do. My master . . ."

"Hey, you could come back with me . . ."

Lilly shook her head. "I would get in trouble if I did that."

"Oh." Uldolf paused a moment. "I'm not going to get you in trouble here, am I?"

Lilly looked over at him, and Uldolf stared at her with such concern that she almost cried. "No," she said. "If my master finds out, I think I can explain it so he'd understand."

"Good." He laughed. "I don't think I could manage that with my dad."

Lilly nodded, even though, deep down, she knew there was no adequate explanation for how she felt, or what she was doing. "Uldolf?" she whispered.

"What?"

"It *was* fun."

"I'm sorry I scared you. I didn't mean to."

"I know."

After a few minutes, Uldolf said, "Well, I'm dry." He stood up, gathered his clothes, shook them out, and began getting dressed. Lilly watched him, trying to memorize every part of him—every part of this day. She never wanted to lose a moment of it.

He turned around. When he saw that she was still sitting naked by the boulder, he turned his face away from her. "I might be able to come tomorrow."

"I'd like that."

"Do you live out here?"

"No. I'm just waiting."

"For what?"

"For my master to call on me."

Uldolf nodded. "You'll have to go away then, won't you?"

"Yes."

"I wish you could stay."

Lilly closed her eyes. "So do I."

"See you tomorrow." She listened as he splashed off along the creek bed. After his footsteps faded into the woods, Lilly sat naked, cold, and alone, trying not to cry.

None

Anno Domini 1239

Usquequo, Deus, improperabit inimicus?
Irritat adversarius nomen tuum in finem?

O God, how long shall the adversary reproach?
Shall the enemy blaspheme thy name forever?

—Psalms 74:10

XXI

The wagon with Gedim and his family arrived in Johannisburg a little after sundown. The Germans drove the wagon up to the castle where they were faced with a few hundred other Prûsan residents of Johannisburg and the surrounding area. Other than a large canvas shelter that extended over half the crowd, and a column of hastily erected privies, there were no other accommodations made for the Germans' "guests." Armed and armored men guarded the perimeter of the crowd, none wearing the characteristic black cross of the Order.

Gedim saw a graphic demonstration of the seriousness of these men when a local man broke from the Prûsan crowd as Gedim's wagon arrived. The man was dressed as a farrier and still wore the smock of his trade, as if he had come fresh from a stable. He was a fair distance from the noise of the wagon, so Gedim did not hear the words he spoke as he broke ranks from the mass of his fellows.

Whatever grievance the man had, it was answered by the butt end of a guard's ranseur. The guard brought the shaft of the polearm to connect with the side of the man's head. The farrier dropped as quickly as if the guard had used the bladed end of his weapon, and he did not move afterward. And as Gedim was unloaded with the rest of the wagon's occupants, a trio of guards came to carry the fallen man away.

"Mama," Hilde whispered from behind him. "They hurt that man."

"Shh," Burthe told her.

It's happening again, Gedim thought. *They're going to split us between the "good" Prûsans and the "bad" Prûsans.*

And somehow he got the sense that the dividing line this time was going to amount to more than a sprinkle of water and acceptance of a foreign god.

Gedim remembered how eight years ago the Order had gathered all the survivors of Mejdân. Those who had been baptized regained their homes—if they still stood—and their lands—if they had any. Those who refused . . .

The old priests had been burned in Perkûnas's own holy fire, before the perpetual flame was extinguished and the sacred oaks cut down to make crosses for the new god's church. Warriors like Gedim had been executed. Women and children had been taken away for slaves.

Eight years ago, knowing the consequences of refusal for him and his family, baptism had not been a hard decision for Gedim. He was not a particularly spiritual man, and it didn't matter to him whom he was supposed to pray to. The Christians won, in a bloody and final way, and Gedim accepted that his family would then pay homage to the winner's god. But as he led his family to a less crowded part of the bailey, he wondered what price the Christians would ask of him now.

Shortly after the call for Vespers, a trio of men entered the crowd wearing white linen surcoats bearing the black cross of the Order. They carried baskets, and methodically handed out bread. Gedim was insulted at being placed in the position of a beggar accepting alms from the Germans, but not enough to refuse when the knight held out half a loaf to him. He had a daughter, and that took precedence over his pride.

He passed the bread to Hilde after taking it from the knight. Something about the man looked vaguely familiar.

"Tell the man thank you, Hilde," Burthe told their daughter.

Hilde stepped up, looking at the ground, and said, "Thank you, sir."

"You are welcome, child," the man said. He looked around at Gedim and Burthe. There was an expression of contemplation on his face, and Gedim suddenly recognized the man. This was the same knight that had come to his farm earlier, looking for Lilly.

Of all the ill luck it was possible to have . . .

The knight looked at Burthe and asked, "How fares your sick daughter? I do not see her here."

"She passed away," Gedim said, before anyone else could respond.

Please, by Christ your god, take that answer and go your way.

"You have my condolence, I pray then she did not suffer, and she went to her Lord in peace."

"Thank you, sir."

"I recall you," the knight said, "but forgive me, I do not recall your names."

"I am Gedim, and this is my wife, Burthe."

The knight nodded but showed no sign of walking away. Also, when Gedim glanced around, he saw that the other knights seemed to have taken note of this one's pause.

"Well met." The knight lowered himself to one knee in front of Gedim's daughter. "And what's your name, child?"

She edged toward Burthe. "H-Hilde."

"That's a good name." He smiled. "Can you tell me your big sister's name?"

Hilde grabbed Burthe's arm and shook her head.

"Sir," Burthe said, "she's still upset over our loss."

"I understand. But it is a simple enough question." The knight reached out and cupped Hilde's chin. "You can tell me her name, can't you?"

"L-Lilly. Her name's Lilly."

The knight let go of Hilde and stood. "God loves children most of all, I think, because they are so free of guile."

The other knights were now approaching them, weaving through the crowd. The knight looked at all of them in turn. "Lilly is an unusual name, don't you think?"

Gedim stepped between the knight and Hilde. "Please," he whispered, "let nothing happen to my daughter."

The knight looked at Gedim. "She's been the most truthful among you. I would worry less for her than for yourself."

In a moment, four knights of the Order surrounded them.

hilde had never seen Papa scared before. She didn't understand what happened when Papa stepped between her and the big man with the bread, but she was suddenly afraid that she had said something wrong. When the man grabbed Papa's upper arm, Hilde cried, "Leave him alone."

She ran at the man. Behind her, she heard Mama call her name, but all she could think about was that Papa was scared of the man, and it was because of what she had said. "Leave him alone!" She struck the man's leg as hard as she could, hurting her fist.

The basket he carried fell to the ground, scattering crusts on the ground around her. She attacked the man, biting her lip, tears streaming down her cheeks. She heard Papa yell, "Hilde, no!"

A large hand grabbed her arm and yanked her away. She looked around and yelled, "Papa!" when she realized it wasn't Papa who had grabbed her. The man who held her hoisted her up off of the ground, wrapping his mail-covered arm around her chest so snugly it hurt. "You will respect your elders, child." The man was hard to understand. He spoke his words so thickly that Hilde would have thought him funny if she wasn't so scared.

The man turned and started carrying her away. Behind her she heard the other man yelling something at her parents. Papa yelled something back, but he was interrupted by a loud thump.

"I'm sorry," Hilde whispered as she cried. "Please don't take me away."

The man carrying her didn't listen.

Burthe tried to grab her, but Hilde moved too fast. Burthe watched in horror as her daughter attacked the knight who had taken hold of Gedim. Fortunately, for all its ferocity, Hilde's attack raised little more than an expression of bemusement on the knight's face. Burthe ran forward, hoping to end things before Hilde was hurt.

But one of the other knights scooped up Hilde before Burthe reached her.

"No!" Burthe yelled at the man as he muttered something in an incomprehensible German accent.

The knight with Hilde turned and walked away.

"Give me my daughter!" Burthe tried to follow the man, but another knight blocked her way. Behind her, the knight holding Gedim said something.

In response she heard Gedim yell, "You damned German bastards, give her back!" She turned to see Gedim striking at the knight holding him.

She gasped, her chest now so tight that her voice was completely gone.

Unlike Hilde's attack, Gedim's blow had some force and skill behind it, and it inspired more than bemusement from its target.

Burthe saw the knight's head turn aside slightly, a trail of blood on his cheek.

The knight drew his dagger, and Burthe found her voice. "No! Don't hurt him!" She dove at them, but mailed arms restrained her from behind.

The knight slammed the hilt of his dagger into the side of Gedim's head. The force of it dropped her husband to his knees.

"*Stop!*"

The knight's boot came up, striking Gedim in the face.

"*You bastards—*"

"Mind yourself, woman!" The knight leveled the blade of the dagger in her direction, pointing at her throat. "Do not compound your sins. Your daughter is unharmed, and your husband will live. Do not act or speak thoughtlessly now."

Burthe stared down at Gedim. His face was covered in blood, and one eye was already swollen shut. Bile rose in Burthe's throat, and she had trouble catching her breath.

The knight gestured to the keep with his dagger. "Take her to a cell." He pointed at one of the other soldiers who had been guarding the edges of the Prûsan crowd. "And you, help me with her husband."

As he woke up, Gedim thought, *That wasn't the smartest thing I've ever done.*

"Burthe? Hilde?" The words hurt. His lips were swollen, split, and partly clotted together. Moving his jaw ignited pains all across the right side of his face, and the sound of his own voice fed into a stabbing headache behind his temples.

Most painful, of course, was the fact that he didn't receive an answer.

He tried to open his eyes, but only his right eye responded. The light, dim as it was, fueled the throbbing in his head.

Above him, a stone vault reflected flickering orange light from a lantern.

He pushed himself into a sitting position, despite the protests from inside his skull. As he sat up, he heard chains rattling. He looked down and saw that his legs were manacled to a heavy chain at the ankle. He reached up and touched his face. The left side was swollen and crusted with blood.

He was on a straw mat on the floor of a small room. The light came from a lantern outside, shining through a small square window in the door.

He got the feeling that they were going to want more than baptism from him this time.

❖

Günter opened the door on a cell only a few hundred paces from where the beast had escaped seventeen days before. He still felt uneasy down here, even though he knew the man he was about to visit.

He stepped inside and Gedim turned to look at him. The man was a mess. His shirt was coated with blood, the left side of his face misshapen and swollen.

Günter sighed. "Why would you do something so stupid?"

"The bastards took my daughter." Gedim spat up a small bit of blood when he spoke. It rolled over a swollen lip and trailed down his chin. He reached up to wipe it off, but he only smeared it over his face before he winced and pulled his hand away.

"That isn't what I am talking about."

Gedim stared at him with the eye that wasn't swollen shut.

"You need to tell us where she is."

"Where who is?"

Günter rubbed his forehead. "Stop with the games, Gedim. Your own daughter told them her name. Do you even know what Lilly is?"

"Who's Lilly?"

"That's enough!" Günter reached down and grabbed Gedim by his shirt and dragged the man to his feet, slamming him against the wall of the cell. "You think this is just about you and your family? Bad enough that this . . . this thing you're protecting slaughtered sixteen of my men. You want me to describe it? How she tore Manfried's arm from its socket, or ripped Jacob apart, or tore Uli's jaw free from his skull?"

Gedim stared at him, his right eye wide.

"Any night, you understand, this thing could have feasted on your family's entrails. But that's not the worst you've done, sheltering this creature. Why do you think they've gathered all the Prûsans left from Mejdân?"

Gedim shook his head.

Günter let the man go and stepped back. Gedim slid to his knees.

"The Order is no longer in charge here. We have a bishop from Rome now—a bishop who believes that the Order was not thorough enough in Christianizing the pagans. A bishop who is already convinced that this monster, Lilly, was freed by a Prûsan insurrection."

Gedim shook his head. "No."

"You gave him just what he was looking for, you arrogant fool. Did you think they sent out knights of the Order to search for someone—some*thing*—trivial? You better start thinking of what you're going to say when the bishop's inquisitor questions you, because if you say the wrong thing, you will grant him an excuse to wipe out every last Prûsan in Johannisburg."

XXII

In the boarding room in Johannisburg, Uldolf sat on a chair next to the bed, watching Lilly sleep. There wasn't really room on the bed for two people, even if Uldolf could sleep.

"Don't you remember?" she had said.

"Remember what?" Uldolf whispered. He reached up and rubbed the hollow where his right shoulder ended. He remembered what she had said in the cave when he had asked her about her own past: *"It's bad to remember."*

He thought about that phrase, and how he had felt about her since she had said it. Her body might be whole, but he couldn't help imagining that their wounds were very similar. Maybe that was why his nightmares and the flashes of memory were becoming worse; maybe something in him knew that he couldn't help her if he still couldn't face his own past.

What he did know was that she faced demons as painful as his own, and from the way he had found her, they were much more recent. Thinking about it in those terms made her recovery, and her personality, all the more amazing. Less than a month from finding her mute and injured, and she was more talkative now than he had been a year after his own injury.

He balled a fist into his shoulder socket and moved his thoughts away from his own wounds.

Ulfie's not that brave. Not yet . . .

He needed to think of his family. That was his concern right now. The Germans had taken them. If Lankut was right, they were looking for signs of some sort of insurrection.

What if what all they really wanted was Radwen Seigson's son? Maybe if he offered himself, they would let his family go.

But what about Lilly?

He would have to get her out of Johannisburg, *then* try and parlay himself into a trade for his family. If he slipped her out the gate at dawn, he could lead her through the woods . . .

His thoughts were drifting too far toward desperation. He couldn't just lead her to the woods and leave her. He knew that his father would want him to make sure she was safe. She was their responsibility.

That could take days.

"What do I do?" He sat, clutching his shoulder, feeling nothing but a dark sense of despair that threatened to engulf him.

After too long like that, he thought he heard something. He lifted his face and looked around.

Singing?

The sound was soft, barely audible. The sound so faint that at first he thought it might be coming from outside.

Then he realized that it was Lilly.

He leaned forward and heard her softly singing a lullaby to herself. "Mother will protect her child. Should any nightmares come."

Uldolf shook his head. Where had he heard it before? The words ran a chill through his entire body. The voice, he had heard that voice, those words . . .

The girl, he remembered. *The girl right before . . .*

"Her name was Lilly," Uldolf whispered, staring at the curve of Lilly's face.

How could he have forgotten her? How could he have forgotten the strange girl he had played with in the woods? It was the best memory he had before his life had been torn apart.

Why would he have forgotten that?

He reached over and brushed the hair off her cheek. "Why did you come back?"

Lilly blinked and looked up at him. "Ulfie?"

"Lilly." He smiled down at her. "I remember you now."

Her eyes widened and she sat up.

"It was you, the girl in the woods."

Lilly's eyes glistened, and a single tear rolled down her cheek. She shook her head, as if she was denying it.

"Is that why you were at the pool? Were you looking for me?"

"I— I—" Her hands balled into fists, knotting into the bedding. She sucked in breaths, her back shaking.

Uldolf moved to sit on the bed next to her. He placed his arm around her shoulders. "What's wrong?"

"D-don't."

"What?"

She turned and wrapped her arms around him. "Don't remember. Please don't remember."

"Huh?" He reached down and lifted her face from where it was buried in his chest. "Why?"

She looked into his eyes and bit her lip.

"Why shouldn't I remember, Lilly?"

"I— I—" She hugged him, pressing her face back into his chest, shaking her head.

"Lilly?"

Gradually, she stopped shaking her head. She let go of him and settled back so that she faced him. She touched his cheek, looking at him, eyes clear.

"Lilly, what is it?"

"I love you, Uldolf." Something in her voice, her expression, had suddenly changed.

Uldolf stared at her a long time; the spill of black-dyed hair across her shoulders; the curve of her neck where it met her jaw; the spider lines of the barely healed scratches where she had cut herself; the swell of her lower lip, trembling slightly; the dampness on her cheeks; her glowing green eyes . . .

"Then why are you crying?"

She turned away. "Because you cannot love me."

Lilly started to stand up, but Uldolf grabbed her, pulling her back down to him. She gasped slightly and stared at him with wide eyes.

"In the name of all the gods, why not?"

"Your family, I—"

"I'll deal with that. It isn't your fault."

"No, you don't understand—"

"Do you want me?"

"What?"

"Do you want me?"

She shook her head. "This isn't right."

He grabbed her and said, "Answer the question!"

In response, she pushed him down on the bed, suddenly showing the strength he had seen in his family's field. The same strength he had seen, years before, when she had bounded up his oak tree like a giant squirrel.

Lying there, pinned with her hands on his shoulders, something flashed in his mind, the image of claw marks on the trunk of his tree, the fresh white scars bleeding sap—

"Yes!" she yelled down at him. "I want you. *We want you!*" Her face fell on his in a savage kiss, a starving animal digging into a fresh kill. Uldolf reached up and pulled her to him, opening his own mouth, giving in to her desperation.

When she pulled her face away, they were both out of breath.

"I want you, too," Uldolf whispered.

A sad smile crossed Lilly's mouth and she shook her head. "No, you don't."

He reached up and traced her lips with his fingers.

She shuddered. "Please, stop."

"Why?"

"Because I can't . . ."

Uldolf's hand moved, tracing her shoulder, down the side of her body.

She gasped, but she didn't pull away. And when he reached for her surcoat, she helped him—yanking her clothes off with the same desperate ferocity with which she had kissed him. Then she pulled at his clothes, igniting the same white-hot need within his body.

They attacked each other as if their lives depended on the outcome, as if each gasping breath was their last. He expected something slower, gentler, especially when he felt her maidenhead tear. He could feel her body tense, but in response, she became even more feral, tightening her grip and pulling him into something bloody, bestial, and abandoned, where there was no thought of anything but pushing hard, far, deep, falling into her until there was nothing left.

◈

What are we doing?

The thought hung there, in the back of her mind, even as she hungrily took all that Uldolf would give her. She tried to pretend that the desire, the need for him, was too much for her to control . . .

One part of her thought, *We want this.*

The other part responded, *We can't.*

Of anyone who had ever taken this from her, Uldolf was the only one who had ever deserved it. He was the only one she wanted to give it to. Lilly fought with herself to hang onto him, to hang onto this moment. She lost herself within herself, not knowing who held him, who pulled him to her.

At this moment, all that mattered was that Ulfie wanted her. Uldolf wanted her. Despite everything, he *wanted* her.

He doesn't know, he doesn't remember . . .

We can forget, too . . .

Part of her knew that this was wrong, that he still didn't understand what she was, what she had done. But she wasn't strong enough to stop it, she was too weak to deny what he asked when, deep in her heart, his asking was everything she ever wanted.

"*I want you, too,*" he said.

Both of her.

All of her.

Whatever he wanted, whatever came from this, she gave herself to him. And miraculously, he took her. And beyond all of that, beyond the emotional vortex that stripped her down to her soul, he showed her that this act could be about something other than submission, power, or brutality.

She gave herself to Uldolf, but Uldolf also gave himself to her.

She gasped and clutched at him as the first unexpected waves broke across her body. She shuddered, thoughts fragmenting in the force of her climax.

He gave himself to us.

We'll only hurt him again.

We'll never hurt him.

No!

Yes!

Lilly arched her back underneath him, wrapping her legs around his waist.

"*Ulfie!*"

❖

They didn't move for a long time after. Uldolf felt as if the gods had taken turns shaking his body until his bones had liquefied. He was quite certain that he would soon have a fair share of oddly shaped bruises down his back and legs. Lilly appeared nearly as drained, eyes closed, mouth half open, face glistening with sweat.

Uldolf rolled on his side, as much as the narrow bed would allow. He shook his head. "What were we thinking?"

Lilly blinked and turned to look at him. "I love you, Uldolf."

"You mentioned that," Uldolf said. He laid his head down next to hers. "I love you, too."

XXIII

Gedim didn't sleep. The pain in his head and the absence of his family merged with the weight of Günter's words to keep him from any thought of rest. The sense of helplessness tore at his gut. There was no way out of this for him or his family. This wasn't like the fall of Mejdân, when the victorious Germans were satisfied with fealty and professions of faith. The choices then were stark, but they were choices.

No choices faced him now. He could do nothing to change the horrid outcome. For all of Sergeant Günter's assertions, the man was blind. Gedim's words would not change anything. The sergeant's self-deception was probably necessary; the man worked for these pitiless Christian bastards. If the man had understood what Gedim did, he probably would be forced to slit his own throat.

This bishop from Rome wouldn't care for what Gedim said, under whatever duress he said it. Gedim had seen enough in his life to know that if this man had come to Johannisburg in search of a Prûsan conspiracy, he would find one.

He didn't know if what the sergeant had said about Lilly was true or not. But, in his despair, he was quite aware that the truth of the matter was beside the point.

In his heart, he unexpectedly found himself hoping that the story was true. If they were to slaughter him and kill his family, he would wish the full wrath of the old god Pikuolis upon them, his gray hand on their throats, dragging them into their graves. If Lilly was such a monster, such a servant of the Evil One, let her work his will upon them. Let them feel his pain.

The guards threw open the door to his cell sometime before daybreak. They hauled him to his feet and marched him out into the hallway. Neither man was familiar. Both had the paler skins and narrower faces of the Germans.

For all of the sergeant's words, this was no longer a Prûsan town ruled by Germans. It was a German town with an inconvenient Prûsan population.

The two Germans dragged him through the bowels of the keep, up to a room that was slightly bigger than the room where he had been held. The only light was from a pair of torches set in sconces by the far wall. There were at least three men in the room, but Gedim did not get a very good look at them as the guards pushed him across the floor to face the wall between the torches.

Someone spoke in thickly accented German. At best, Gedim's understanding of the language was elementary, but this speaker mangled the language too much for him to make out.

"I don't understand," he said, in his own butchered German.

One of the men holding him pushed his face into the wall, igniting a flare of pain from the side of his wounded face.

A familiar voice said, in Prûsan, "You are Gedim, son of Lothar, brother of Reiks Radwen Seigson of Mejdân?"

"Damn it, Günter," he spat in Prûsan, flecks of blood staining the wall in front of him. "You know who I am."

The men pressed him roughly into the wall.

"Answer yes or no."

"Yes!" His lips tore against the rough stone as he spoke.

Günter repeated Gedim's answer, in German.

Someone behind him pulled his arms back and bound his wrists together as the man with the bad German spoke some more. Günter translated, voice flat, as if he was dictating a letter. "You farm land to the west of Johannisburg, lands retained by you after Mejdân was Christianized?"

"Yes." The word was half a gasp as his arms were pulled straight back and upward behind him. He heard a rustle above him. He looked up to see anonymous hands pass a rope over a hook embedded in the ceiling.

More unintelligible German, and Günter translated. "You accepted baptism and our Lord Jesus Christ?"

"Yes."

"Do you not still pay homage to the pagan idols of Perkûnas, Patrimpas, or Pikuolis?"

"No."

The rope pulled taut and his whole body spasmed as his arms were pulled upward behind him, yanked by the rope binding his wrists. Agony tore through his shoulders, overwhelming the faint pains where the broken flesh of his face ground against the rough wall.

Bad German shouted in his ears, and Gedim almost felt the breath of the questioner on the back of his neck, despite the pain.

Distantly, he heard Günter speak. "Lies will not lessen your pains. Truth now. Do you worship these false gods? Do you sacrifice to their idols?"

Gedim could barely sputter. "No."

The rope pulled again, and his heels left the ground and his body slammed into the wall before him. He could feel with a searing clarity the point at which the bones of his shoulders separated.

Gedim's awareness faded until his whole universe was the sensation of bone twisting against flesh.

Then it faded slightly as the tension released. Feet flat on the
ground again, he slumped against the wall, gasping and sweating.
He couldn't move, because any shift in his weight fired agony in
his dislocated shoulders.

"Confess your idol worship," Günter translated, and this time
the sergeant added the word "Please."

Some errant part of Gedim's mind rebelled. *Why should I ease the
weight on your ass-licking soul?*

Then the tension returned, and Gedim blacked out.

❖

Cold water fell like ice across his back, snapping him awake
and igniting the fire in his arms.

"Confess your idolatry." Not Günter this time, but spoken in a
German slow and deliberate enough that Gedim could follow.

Gedim spat. "May Pikuolis come himself to drag your soul
screaming to Hell."

The room was silent for a time. Günter, still present, translated.
"He honors Pikuolis, lord of the dead."

Gedim hung his head. He pitied the poor sergeant. Somehow
Günter still thought he could improve on the situation. *Even with
pain and blood blurring my vision, I can see the only thing separating
you and me is time . . .*

More German, too quick to make out.

"The truth will end this sooner," Günter told him. "You will now
tell us of the creature named Lilly, and how you came by her."

They put tension on the rope, not enough to make him pass
out—but enough to remind him of what it *could* feel like.

He didn't want to tell them anything. The last thing he
wanted to say was how Uldolf had found this woman, or what

it seemed he meant to her. He would sooner kill himself than tell them how Burthe had conspired to hide the woman from the Order.

But they wouldn't let him kill himself, and when he thought his limits were reached, his feet left the ground. At that point, what he wanted didn't matter anymore.

XXIV

From the window of his room, Uldolf watched the first pre-dawn light reach the sliver of sky that was visible between the stable and the inn. The sky was deep violet, becoming lavender near the eastern end of the alley.

Soon the gates would open for the day.

He looked down at Lilly, asleep on the bed. She had wrapped the single blanket around herself, leaving only her head and her left leg exposed. He found himself splitting his time between watching the sky, looking at her face, and allowing his gaze to travel along the naked length between her ankle and where the curve of her thigh tucked under the blanket.

Strangely, or perhaps not so strangely, he wasn't looking at her in a particularly lustful manner. He stared at her more in fascina-tion, the way he would at a striking sunset, or at a field of wildflow-ers on a particularly clear blue day, or the way he did sometimes at the pool by the oak he had shown her so long ago. There was her beauty, but there was something else. It danced on the edges of his mind, as if he only saw the shimmering surface of the water. Underneath was something dark, cold, threatening . . .

"Nonsense," Uldolf whispered.

Lilly stirred, blinking. "Ulfie?"

Who was she? Was she the smiling, almost childlike person looking up at him now? Or was she the cold unhappy one . . .

They both said they loved him.

"Ulfie?" she repeated. He looked at her, and the smile she gave him now was anything but childlike. The way she let the blanket slide off her shoulder was very distracting.

"We have to leave soon," Uldolf told her. He gathered her clothes and handed them to her. Reaching for them, she let the blanket fall completely away from her upper body.

"You need to get dressed," he told her.

Her smile faded slightly, and she nodded.

Uldolf looked back out the window as she stood to put her clothes on. "We're going out the gate. Once we're outside the walls, I'm going to take you back to the farm. We'll stay in the woods, and when you're safe, I'll come back here."

He felt her hand on his shoulder.

He turned to look at her. "You know I have to do something for my parents, and Hilde."

Her hand tightened on his shoulder. "I— I— I know."

"You understand, don't you?"

"I understand."

She let go of him, and before she turned away, he took her wrist and drew her back to him. He kissed her and whispered, "Then you know I'm not going to forget about you, either."

She pulled away with an expression that made him think he had said the wrong thing.

"O f course," Uldolf whispered. "It is not going to be that easy."
The two of them stood in the same spot where Uldolf

had been standing the prior evening, watching the main gate from the dawn shadows. His plan had been to slip out at sunrise—but where last evening the only person really paying attention to the gate had been Lankut, this morning Uldolf saw two extra men at the gate. And the new men weren't Prûsan.

As he watched, a man wearing the cross of the Order came up to talk to one of the extra men.

Lilly placed a hand on his shoulder, and Uldolf reached up and held it with his own. "I'll think of something."

They could try and scale the village wall. But even if she still could climb like she had when she was a child, Uldolf couldn't. They could retreat back to his room, but that didn't get them out of danger, or get him any closer to rescuing his family. He thought of leaving her at the inn and going to try and get his family out by himself.

Uldolf shook his head. That wouldn't work, either.

He still had the dagger and the collar, though; the silver was worth something. Wagons came and went all day. He just needed to find someone who was willing to hide them. He patted her hand. "I think I know what to do, Lilly."

He turned and led her down a narrow street away from the main road. He was going to get her out of harm's way, one way or another. He'd talk to the innkeeper. The man was sympathetic enough that he might know someone willing to smuggle them out of Johannisburg.

He wove their way through the side streets, and right before the last turn back to the rooming house, Lilly frantically grabbed his arm.

Uldolf turned to face her. "What?"

Her eyes were wide, her nostrils flared, and she was violently shaking her head. "Ulfie, n-no!"

They stood between a building and the stables behind the boarding house. Uldolf could see the wall of the boarding house at the end of the alley.

Lilly tried to pull him back the way they had come, away from the boarding house. "They're c-c-coming," she said. "They're coming!"

Now he could hear boots up ahead, in the alley behind the boarding house.

He backed Lilly away from the intersection, but it was already too late. He had taken only a few steps when a quartet of men walked in front of the exit to their alley. One of them wore the black cross of the Order.

Uldolf pushed Lilly away from him and whispered harshly, "Run."

She staggered a few steps away from him, and Uldolf faced the men who had just turned in his direction. He took a step forward and bowed slightly at the knight and his entourage. "Greetings, sir."

Please, Lilly, get out of here while they are focused on me.

The knight stepped forward and looked him up and down. "What is your name?"

Uldolf swallowed. "My name is Uldolf."

"I see." The knight stood in front of him, the others walked into the narrow alley to join him. "And for what reason are you sneaking behind these stables at this early hour?"

"I have a room in the house over there." Uldolf gestured at the house, past the trio of Germans. One of them said something in German that Uldolf couldn't understand. The knight glanced back at the man, and then returned his gaze to Uldolf. "He wonders if you prefer to enter by the window."

Uldolf heard Lilly gasp, and he turned away from the Germans.

She had tried to retreat, but too late. Two more men had come upon them from the other direction. Lilly struggled between them; each of the pair had hold of one of her arms.

"Let her go!" Uldolf shouted. He moved toward them before he had a good chance to think about what he was doing.

The knight grabbed for his arm, but he was grabbing from Uldolf's right. He had no arm there to grab. Instead, the knight took hold of his cloak, and the strap of his bag underneath. Uldolf took another few steps before the knight pulled back on him, and the strap on his bag snapped taut across his neck.

Lilly screamed, "Ulfie, *no!*" as his head snapped back and he fell backward. Uldolf slammed back into the mud at the knight's feet, his cloak splayed beneath him, and the contents of his bag scattered on the ground around him. The breath had been knocked out of him, and it took a few moments to push himself upright.

When he did, he saw the knight picking something up out of the mud.

The silver dagger.

XXV

Things were going too fast for Lilly to make sense of them. Her mind was still reeling from Uldolf's—Ulfie's—embrace last night.

He had said he loved her.

Loved her.

Hope was an emotion that she couldn't understand—either of her. Her thoughts slid back and forth so often now that it became hard to figure out who was thinking them. So she followed Uldolf, barely paying attention to what was happening outside her own head.

She had to tell him. She couldn't tell him. No, she had to tell him everything, no matter how painful. But saying the words now, even if she could say them, would ruin everything. But if there was any small chance that he could understand—that he could know and still love her—how could she deny him the truth?

It was bad to remember.

But was it better to forget?

She sensed the Germans' approach much later than she should have. She shouted her pathetic, stammering warning too late.

Ulfie told her to run.

But she hesitated, not wanting to leave him. She had hesitated long enough for two rough Germans to catch up with her and grab her arms. Then the knight grabbed Ulfie and yanked him to the ground, tearing his cloak and his bag.

Now the knight had something in his hand, and Lilly froze.

A dagger.

The dagger.

The dagger she had used to . . .

She shook her head, tears welling up. *No! This isn't my fault. It isn't!*

The knight grabbed Uldolf by the shirt and pulled him from the ground with his left hand, dagger in his right. He slammed Uldolf into the wall of the building opposite the stable. Two of the other Germans ran to hold him there.

"Tell me how you came by this dagger."

"I found it."

The knight took the pommel of the dagger and slammed it across the side of Uldolf's face, tearing a savage gash across his cheek. Blood poured down the side of his face.

"*No!*" Lilly screamed.

The knight looked cruelly down at him and said, "Do not lie to me."

"I was . . ." Uldolf spat up a mixture of blood and saliva. It trailed from his mouth and down his chin. "T-trapping game. I found it in the woods."

The knight backhanded him again. Lilly felt the blows as if they were striking her. She wished they were. She knew that she would recover from the blows. Uldolf wouldn't.

She closed her eyes, her brain screaming, *Help me.*

Help us.

She looked for the other, frantically trying to pull her braver self out of the twisting chaos that was her mind. The other one could save Ulfie—save Uldolf.

Uldolf spat more blood, and it splattered the front of the knight's white surcoat. The knight slammed his fist into Uldolf's gut, dropping Uldolf to his knees—

Lilly's rage finally spilled over the fear and confusion, mixing and twisting and leaving someone who wasn't quite her, nor anyone else.

"*Stop it, now!*" she screamed.

Everyone stopped, even the knight beating Uldolf. They all turned to face Lilly, the sudden tenor of her voice commanding their attention.

She faced them all, no longer struggling. She stood, arms spread as if she didn't even notice the men holding her biceps. Her dyed black hair hung in strings across her face. She stared at them with eyes that were green, cold, and pitiless.

She stared especially hard at the knight, who was looking at her with a slowly growing realization.

"Leave now," Lilly said. "While you still can."

The fear in his face made her smile.

It didn't surprise her when he yelled at the others, "She's the beast! Use the silver, kill her!"

The two men holding her might have heard her laugh, right before she dropped to her knees in front of them. They held onto her upper arms, and the suddenness of her movement pulled them forward, bending them over her shoulders—shoulders that were already broader and more muscular. Her nose wrinkled in her lengthening muzzle as she smelled the sour musk of fear from the men beside her.

Her surcoat tore when she reached up and sank her claws into the necks of the men to either side. The Germans in front of her were still scrambling to draw weapons and form a line, the knight still yelling about the silver.

She ducked down, flipping the two men over her shoulders and into the line of Germans. The line split apart, one of the Germans falling to the mud under his thrashing, wheezing comrade.

Lilly stood, the bloody rags of her human clothes falling to the mud beneath her paws. Her muscles rippled under red fur marked by a streak of black dye that extended from her forehead down the length of her back. She flexed forepaws that still resembled hands, and bore claws longer and sharper than any wolf's had a right to be.

She snarled, breathing in the scents of blood, sweat, piss, and fear. She spread her arms, as if to embrace the quartet before her. She still smiled.

"Will you leave now?" she asked them in German.

Despite their surprise, the men were well disciplined, and prepared. They closed ranks before her, holding silvered blades in guarded positions before them. They left no openings in front of them, giving their fallen member time to get to his feet. Once all four closed ranks, they advanced on her deliberately.

She could retreat back down the alley, but there would be more soldiers that way, friends of the two now squirming in the mud.

Besides, Lilly didn't *want* to . . .

She growled and leapt—not directly at the men as they expected, but up and to the right, at the wall of the stable. In one bound she had grabbed the edge of the roof and pulled herself onto the thatched surface, above the Germans. She rolled a few times and dropped off of the edge, behind them.

They were too close together and too slow to follow her that quickly. She grabbed the man on the end nearest the stable. She wrapped one arm around his neck and hooked her other hand over his helmet, yanking his head back hard enough to shatter vertebrae.

As the man went limp, Lilly realized that she *felt* it happen. This wasn't some strange dream she would wake from. These were her own red-furred arms holding a once-living man.

Her master's training took over as the next man swung his silvered weapon at her. Without thinking, she turned to place the corpse's armored torso between her and the blade. She let the body drop with the blow so that the corpse folded over the second man's blade, dragging it down. She thrust her claws up, piercing the fleshy underside of the attacker's jaw.

I am doing this . . .

She tried to distance herself from the frenzied blood lust, but she couldn't. The rage she felt wasn't some cold outsider, it was her own. This is what it felt like, to be the other one . . .

But she *was* the other one.

Another man fell groaning to the ground, broken by her master's training. The last one standing was the knight, a brother of the Order. She wished he was her master.

Even so, she asked, "Why?"

"Return to Hell, you bitch!" he screamed at her, taking a wild swing at her head.

Lilly easily avoided the blow. She had trained for this all her life, and the motion of the swordsman was too familiar. One-on-one, she could see and read his movements, react to them before he knew himself what he intended to do.

She could have torn open his throat as he passed, or taken an arm, or landed a crippling blow on the back of his neck. Instead, she let him stumble by unscathed, spinning around to face him as he turned back around.

"Why don't you run?" she asked as he screamed something inarticulate, bringing his sword to bear. This time she ducked and grabbed his arms. The impact hurt her wrists, but she was more used to pain than he was. The sword tumbled out of his grip.

She slammed him into the wall of the stable. "Why is it so important to kill me?"

"You are a creature of Hell!" the knight spat back at her.

"What does that make my master?" she asked.

She held him there, pinned, his face a hair's breadth from her muzzle. She could smell the fear on him as his composure began cracking. He began chanting a prayer in Latin.

"What does that make my master?" she asked again, fighting the rage, fighting the desire to sink her teeth into his face and end his—

"Uldolf?" she whispered. The word felt alien in her lupine mouth.

No, please, no!

She slammed the knight into the wall and whipped her head around to look at where Uldolf had fallen.

He was gone. His satchel and cloak remained where they had fallen, now resting in a stew of blood and mud. He had seen it all.

No.

He had seen enough.

Lilly looked down at her gore-covered forearms pinning the knight to the wall and whispered again, "Ulfie . . ."

Blood and tears fell from her face onto the black cross of the knight's surcoat.

Interlude

Anno Domini 1231

A few days after Uldolf taught her to swim, Lilly heard the horn of her master, calling her to Mejdân. It came in the night before dawn. Three long blasts, followed by two short blasts.

Her first thought was that she would not see the boy Uldolf again.

Something inside her objected to the thought. *Is that how we serve our master?*

Guilty over thinking about something other than her master's will, she walked through the woods, circling the timber walls of the city and making her way toward the main road and the gate inside. The woods were strangely still, the creatures as silent as they were when Lilly used her real form to eat.

Something else inside her objected to that thought. *Is that body more real than the pink flesh we're wearing now?*

Until Uldolf, she had been trained to think little of her human body. It was nothing more than a shell, a disguise, a falsehood. It wasn't until Uldolf had treated her as another human, and she had learned that her human form was capable of more than receiving punishment, that she thought of her human form as real.

The wolf is the real one. That is the will of God.

Telling herself that made her calmer and less frightened.

As she pushed through the woods, the sky lightened through the branches above, turning purple, and then pale rose. As she moved west, she caught scents on the air. She smelled something acrid, as if something far away was burning. As she came closer to the main road through the woods to Mejdân, she smelled the stink of people and animals.

Before she came in sight of the road, she could hear them, feet and hooves slogging through mud, the breathing of men and horses, and the rattle of wheeled carts. She heard very little speech.

She stepped out of the woods at the edge of the road to face a column of people heading for Mejdân. The smoke smell was closer, as were the smells of blood and urine and burnt flesh. Whole families trudged in silence next to exhausted horses. Wagons carried wounded men and women, some whose stillness showed them past living.

Lilly stood and watched the procession. These were the people who troubled her master, godless ones fleeing before God's army. They would seek refuge within the stronghold of Mejdân.

False refuge.

"Hurry, child," someone called to her, "do not fall behind."

Lilly smiled to herself as she slipped into the moving column of Prûsans. She would make her master proud.

Lilly made it inside easily. In the chaos of refugees, no one paid any attention to a nine-year-old girl. The guards of Mejdân were more interested in getting all the farmers, animals, and wounded behind the defensive walls of the village as quickly as possible. It was simple enough for her to slip away and find an unobtrusive hiding place.

She made a nest in a stable loft above a dozen goats that were shoved into a stall meant for one or two. It was the perfect spot, because it was in the shadow of the central stronghold, which sat on a rise overlooking the rest of the village. There were no buildings between her and the stronghold.

She heard the Mejdân defenders shut the gates that evening.

A few hours later, she heard her master's army arrive. She heard the gallop of fresh mounts and the rustle of mail. Even padded, it had a metallic sound distinct from the Prûsans' leather armor.

It would be soon.

During the night, to build her strength, she took one of the goats. She did it carefully and as silently as possible—though no villager could have heard her movements through the terrified bleating.

She was cautious to snap the kid's neck without recourse to tooth or claw, and withdraw into the loft with her kill as quickly as possible. No blood splattered the stall below, and when a guard came to investigate the commotion, he was confronted only by eleven terrified goats that bolted for the gate as soon as he arrived.

In the human scramble to recapture the goats, no man looked up into the loft to see her dark-furred silhouette huddled against the straw. She remained motionless until the men left.

Only then, to the distress of the animals below her, did she begin to eat.

When her master's second trump sounded two nights later, calling her to attack, there was little left of the animal but greasy bones and bloody straw.

Three days into the siege of Mejdân, Uldolf woke to someone screaming.

His eyes opened as the sound abruptly cut off. He lay in his cot, half convinced it was a dream. His father had explained siege-craft to him. It was all waiting. All about who had more food, more will. The Christian invaders didn't have near enough men to throw an attack against the wall of the village—not a successful one, anyway.

Someone else screamed.

Uldolf sat up. This was no dream, and the screams came from inside the stronghold. The enemy was inside.

Uldolf crawled out of his bed and crept up on the narrow door to his room. When he reached the door, he felt his foot slide in something wet and sticky. He shuddered slightly and opened the latch.

The door swung into the room, pushed by the weight of the body leaning against it. He stared at it, uncomprehending. Even as he felt the fear drain into a small cold ball buried in his gut, his conscious mind could not make the image sensible.

Several long seconds passed before he was able to form the question in his mind.

Where is his head?

He took a step back, staring at the corpse in the lamplight that spilled from the hallway. Blood caused the dead man's leather armor to glisten in the firelight. The man had drawn his sword, and the blade rested next to his leg, as if he had never had the chance to use it.

Uldolf's father had been wrong. There would be no long siege. The enemy was attacking them now.

Almost as if in a dream, Uldolf watched himself step over the body and pick up the sword. It was heavier than the wooden ones his father's guards let him train with, and the hilt was slick with blood and sweat.

Uldolf stepped into the hallway and saw the dead man's head, upside-down, leaning against a wall. His name had been Oldan, and he had been one of the men who showed Uldolf how to wield that wooden sword—how to block, to cut, to thrust.

Uldolf tightened his grip on the sword and ran down the hallway.

He ran past more bodies and parts of bodies. He didn't spare the time to look at them closely, to see if he knew them—to see if they were friend or foe. His feet were coated with blood, sticking to the floor with every step. His breath burned like molten copper.

He turned the corner and saw the doorway to his parents' chamber. Just as he came in sight, something small flew out of the doorway, to slam into the wall. It bounced off, to roll nearly back to the threshold.

Uldolf stared for several seconds at it, before he understood what he saw.

Jawgede.

It was his sister, barely half his own age, and her torso had been torn open, legs to throat.

He screamed something that might not have even been words and ran through the doorway, past his sister's body.

It was the blood he felt first—so *much* blood. It splattered the walls and coated the floor, the ferric smell of it so heavy that his throat closed up, choking on the thick, humid air. Then he saw the bodies—pieces of bodies—strewn about with the broken furniture and shredded tapestries.

And in the midst of it all stood a monstrous red-furred, half-wolf *thing—*

It had its back to him, pulling apart a body it had pinned to the wall. Under the creature's clawed hand, Uldolf saw his father's face.

Uldolf moved without thinking, charging at the thing's back, forgetting what little training he had been given on the proper way to wield a sword. He used it as a spear, without thought of defense. He connected because the wolf thing was paying him no attention

at all. The blade only penetrated because he hit it in the soft part
of the torso, under the rib cage.

The creature howled, letting go of his father. But, to Uldolf's
horror, his attack was far too late. His father's body slid to the
ground, followed slightly later by his head.

The shock of the sight prevented Uldolf from reacting to the
creature as it turned on him, snarling. He felt its claws gripping his
right arm and twisting.

A blinding flare of pain, and he stumbled backward clutching
his shoulder with the surreal realization that his arm was no longer
there.

His breathing went quick and shallow, and he felt as if he was
falling away inside himself. He stepped back, and his foot slipped
on something. He saw it as he fell backward; he had tripped on his
own mother's hair.

Seeing his mother's mutilated face caused something to give
way inside him. He scrambled away, and he could dimly hear himself screaming, "Stop it! Please, stop it!" over and over, but he
wasn't completely there anymore.

His vision went gray, and the wolf thing bent over him. He could
feel its breath on his face, hot and stinking of blood. Somewhere
inside himself, he was prepared to die.

Then the creature's inhuman hand, matted with blood, lightly
touched Uldolf's cheek.

To Uldolf's deep horror, it spoke. "No. Not you."

"Stop it!" Uldolf shook his head. "Please, stop it!" The only
three words left he could say. Tears burned his cheeks, and the fire
in his shoulder throbbed to his pulse, overwhelming everything
else. His vision dimmed to black, with occasional flashes of white
and blood red.

"I wasn't supposed to hurt you, Uldolf."

Before he allowed his mind to slide into a dark, welcoming
abyss, he realized that the wolf's voice was familiar.

Vespers

Anno Domini 1239

Nam et si ambulavero in medio umbrae mortis,
non timebo mala, quoniam tu mecum es.
Virga tua, et baculus tuus,
ipsa me consolata sunt.

Yea, though I walk through the valley of the shadow of
   death,
I will fear no evil: for thou art with me;
thy rod and thy staff they comfort me.

—Psalms 23:4

XXVI

Uldolf ran.

He ran, trying to escape the images that had burnt themselves into his brain. It wasn't Lilly. It couldn't be Lilly.

But it was.

Heart racing, not looking where he was going, he dove into an open doorway, tripping and falling face-first to the ground. After a moment, he rolled onto his back, clutching his gut where the knight had punched him.

He closed his eyes. In the distance he heard the snarls and growls of the thing that had been the woman he—

Has your farm been troubled lately . . . by strange beasts? Men or animals killed or injured?

He sucked in ragged breaths, only feeling the pain in his face and in his stomach now that he had stopped running. His pulse hammered at him, screaming at him from inside—

Run!

His hand balled into a fist over his stomach, pulling his shirt tight. In his mind he kept replaying what had happened to Lilly, changing from the first woman he had made love to, to the beast that tore into the Germans like, like . . .

Like what had happened in the stronghold of Mejdân.

Uldolf folded over on himself, huddling against a wall. He didn't want to remember. He didn't want this image in his mind. He tried to will himself to forget, to push it away, to erase the vision.

He curled against the wall. His phantom right arm hurt worse now than it had since that same monster tore the living arm from his body.

"I don't want to remember this," Uldolf whispered.

But he remembered now.

He remembered the demonic red wolf leaning over him, breath sour with blood, muzzle streaked with gore. He remembered it speaking in Lilly's voice. *"I wasn't supposed to hurt you, Uldolf."*

He remembered everything.

❖

Lilly tossed aside the knight in her hands. He rolled over by one of his dead comrades, arms broken, eyes closed, still chanting his prayers.

She ignored him. She needed to find Uldolf.

She went to Uldolf's cloak. As she walked, muscles slid over creaking bone. Her body shrank and her joints moved as the wolf retreated inside her. She was long used to the changes it wrought in her balance.

She pulled the cloak out of the mud and draped it over her naked shoulders. The fur lining settled warmly against her skin, smelling of him—feeling like the moment by the pool when they faced each other, briefly innocent of their past.

She had no idea what she was supposed to do now—but overriding everything was the need to face him.

She retrieved his bag and followed his scent. It wasn't hard; the miasma of sweat, blood, and fear flowed like a river. And it didn't go far. After rounding only two corners of the long stable, she was ultimately unprepared when she found him.

He huddled in a doorway, back to the wall, clutching his right shoulder where she had ripped his arm out of its socket.

No, Ulfie. It wasn't supposed to be like this.

She stood, barely two paces from him, unable to move. Her mind twisted and fragmented under the weight of memories— taking his food, swimming with him, making love, tearing free his arm, slaughtering his family.

"Ulfie," she whispered.

His head snapped around. He scrambled to his feet. "No. Don't you dare!"

"Ulfie, please—"

Still backing away, he clutched his empty shoulder, face as pale as if the injury had just happened. "You have no right to call me that!"

She took a step back, chest tightening as if Uldolf had struck her. "Please. I am so sorry."

"You killed them! Jawgede was barely five! *Why?*"

Lilly shook her head, tears streamed down her cheeks, and she clutched Uldolf's cloak closer to herself. "I— I served my master."

Uldolf shook his head. "Then why let me live? Why not pull my head from my neck, like my father?"

"Don't—"

"Why not tear me open like you did my sister? Cut my face open like my mother?"

She stared into his face, and saw nothing but hate there.

"Why?" He kept backing away. "Why spare me? Does your master want to torment me that much?"

"No. I loved you." She sucked in a breath and repeated, "I love you."

Uldolf shook his head. "You monster! How dare you say that?" He shook his head and looked past her. "Oh, no."

"Uldolf?"

"They weren't taken, were they?" He shook his head. "My family. I left them alone . . . with you."

"No."

"Is that why you're here? *You've come to kill my family again!*"

He leapt at her, grabbing her neck. His attack was clumsy, but she was unprepared for it, and she fell backward under him.

"I didn't!"

His knees fell painfully on her chest as his hand clutched at her throat. "What did you do? *What did you do?*"

"I didn't. I—" She choked back the word *couldn't*, because she knew it was a lie. Of course she could have. It was what she was, wasn't it? She stared up into Uldolf's terrified face, and could see the ten-year-old boy she had left bleeding eight years ago. He was right; it would have been kinder if she had torn his heart out.

With the blackness filling her soul, she laid her head back, exposing her throat, allowing him to throttle her. Perhaps, if she gave in to it, it would all be over. Her life was all she had left to give him, the only compensation she could offer.

She gasped and wheezed, her lungs not nearly as resigned as her brain. It took all her effort not to struggle as her vision slowly went black.

I am sorry, Uldolf. You will never know how much.

XXVII

Lilly didn't know what she expected from death. Maybe her master's Lord Jesus Christ might make an appearance to explain why she wasn't worthy of his forgiveness or an afterlife. She was nothing but a soulless animal, after all. Or maybe she would fall into a deep dreamless sleep where she could lose herself so completely that it wouldn't matter what she was.

She did not expect to sneeze, or itch, and she did not expect to smell horses. Lilly opened her eyes and found herself staring up at the underside of a thatched roof.

From beside her, she heard Uldolf's voice. "You're awake?"

She turned her head and saw him standing over her. They were in an empty stall in a stable somewhere. From the blood smell that still hung in the air, she could tell it was behind the rooming house, where she had killed—

She shook her head and tried to sit up, but something tightly bound her arms and legs and she couldn't push herself upright. She glanced down at herself and saw she was naked, sawdust sticking to her skin. Her arms were tied behind her, and she saw that her legs were bound as well.

Uldolf had wrapped her legs together with a long leather strap that circled from her knees halfway down to her ankles. He'd done a better job of restraining her than the bastard who had raped her. She could probably break the leather, but only if she had some leverage or freedom of movement, and from what she could feel, he had done as good a job on her arms, strapping her forearms together behind her back.

"I don't think you're getting out of those," Uldolf said. He walked over and hooked his hand under her armpit and lifted her so that she was in a sitting position. Then he dragged her a couple of steps across the sawdust-covered floor of the stall so she could lean against the wall.

"Thank you," Lilly said quietly.

Uldolf shook his head and walked away.

"Why didn't you kill me?" Lilly asked.

He turned around and looked down at her. "I tried," he told her. He held up his hand, palm up. "You didn't leave me much to work with."

"Oh." She didn't realize until then that she had held out some hope that he might have had a change of heart, that he might still have a scrap of feeling for her.

He paced around the stall, and she saw that he had the silver dagger back, shoved into his belt.

If he has that . . .

"Why didn't *you* kill *me*?" Uldolf asked her.

I loved you. I've always loved you.

"I told you." Lilly shook her head. Then she realized that the silver torc was back on her neck.

Uldolf saw her notice and he smiled grimly. "I don't know very many German words, but I do know the word for silver." He pulled the dagger out of his belt and held it up before him. "I drove a sword through you once and you don't even have a scar, but the cuts you made yourself with this dagger are still trying to heal.

There's a reason the Germans are armed with silver weapons, isn't there?"

"Y-Yes."

"And there's a reason they put that around your neck."

"Yes."

"They know what you are."

Lilly nodded.

"Tell *me* what you are." He crouched down across the stall from her. She sucked in a shuddering breath, watching the dagger, wondering if he would use it. *Hoping* he would use it.

He gestured with the dagger. "Tell me."

"They say I'm an animal," Lilly told him. "A beast that can mimic a human being. They say my true form is the wolf thing you saw, the one that hurt you."

"Who are 'they'?"

"The monks of the Order," Lilly whispered. "I was raised in one of their monasteries."

"You're *their* creature?"

"I was."

Lilly told him of her life, such as it was. She told him her memories of the ruined monastery where she was raised, how she had served her masters in the Order. She told him of the villages she had attacked, preparing the way for the Order; how she would slip in with the surrounding villagers and farmers trying to escape the attack, and when the town was shut up for the siege; how she would slip into its heart and tear it out.

Uldolf shook his head.

"You let them use you like that?"

"It was what I was for."

"Because that is what they told you?"

Lilly nodded.

"If they abused you so, why didn't you just run away? Leave one of those villages before you started killing?"

"I had nowhere to go."

"Then where were you going when you escaped from them now?"

Lilly raised her head and looked up into Uldolf's eyes. He stared back for a long time before shaking his head.

"No, you're not telling me—"

"I tried to forget this place," Lilly said. "I tried to force myself not to remember what happened here. I thought it had killed every part of me that felt anything good . . . But I didn't forget—"

And I didn't kill that part of myself. It woke up when I saw you.

Uldolf turned away. "Stop it," he whispered.

"When my master abandoned me here, it all came back—so much I lost myself in it." She blinked back tears. "Uldolf, if we could have been together, without a past—"

"Even if I didn't remember, you aren't even *human*. How could you believe, even for a moment—"

Lilly shook her head. "We both did, for a moment."

Uldolf was silent for a long time. He finally said, "You are cruel."

"God is cruel," Lilly whispered.

"Were you telling the truth, that the Order took my family?"

"Yes, I was. I didn't hurt them—"

"No?" Uldolf whispered. "Why were they taken, Lilly? Why is any of this happening?"

"I didn't want any of this."

"But you caused it, didn't you?"

"I—"

"They want their pet monster back. What do you think they'll do to my family when they find out we sheltered you?"

"No, your family didn't know—"

Uldolf whipped around, striking her on the face with the back of his fist, the blade of the dagger he held coming perilously close to her eye. Her skin burned where he struck her, the sharp taste of blood filling the left side of her mouth. "These are the people responsible for the slaughter of my first family! You think they'll show mercy to my second one? Do you think innocence means anything to them? *You think you're the only monster here?*" Uldolf stood up. "You are right about one thing. Your God *is* cruel."

He is not my God.

"What are you going to do?" Lilly asked, surprised at the sound of fear in her voice.

"I'm going to offer them a trade."

Landkomtur Erhard von Stendal bent over his brother knight Gregor. The man was a wreck, arms broken, skin pale, barely conscious. Even so, he prayed as if his soul was in mortal danger. Gregor was the only one left conscious.

"What happened, Brother?" Erhard asked him.

Two of his fellows had never even had the opportunity to draw their swords. One was dead, neck horribly twisted; the other had bruises and deep wounds on his neck mirroring those on the corpse, but somehow still breathed.

Three other bodies still lay where they had fallen in the road, necks broken, windpipes crushed. The wounds showed the rending of claws that, combined with the position of the men, left no doubt that this was Lilly's doing.

I trained her too well.

She would have been a monstrous foe if she had been left ignorant in the woods of her birth. But that wasn't enough. He had taught her how to be a much more effective monster.

He didn't know what troubled him more—the fact that she was now back inside the walls of Johannisburg, or the strangely bloodless way she had overpowered six men. Until he had returned her to this place, he had never known her to leave a victim alive. When they let loose the creature on the pagans, it had torn through the enemy with pain and terror as much a goal as the death she left in her wake. By comparison, what he saw here was dispassionate, almost merciful.

What did it mean?

Why was Gregor alive?

"What happened here?" Erhard asked more forcefully than he should have of an injured man. Gregor blinked up at him, eyes focusing.

"Gregor?"

"Erhard . . ."

"What happened here?"

"We have sinned. Lord save us, but we are damned for what we have done."

"Gregor?" Erhard grabbed his surcoat and the injured knight winced.

"Pray with me, Erhard," he whispered. "May Christ have mercy on our souls." He closed his eyes and began praying again. Erhard let the fabric slide through his fingers, letting Gregor ease against the wall.

Erhard crossed himself and joined Gregor in prayer. *What have we done?*

The dozen men with Erhard now seemed inadequate.

"*Halt!*" one of the soldiers with Erhard called out in Prûsan, interrupting Erhard's prayer.

He turned toward the man. Sir Johann was a minor lord from south of Hamburg, from a family line so dilute that his inheritance consisted of only a title and a horse. Johann was one of many secular knights crusading with the Order who saw Prûsa, potentially, as the seat of a new family demesne. He was also the German in this company with the best command of Prûsan, outside of Erhard.

Johann's outburst had an urgency that pulled Erhard to his feet, prayer unfinished. Erhard turned toward the focus of Johann's attention, as did the eleven other men filling the crowded alley.

A young man, eighteen or nineteen years old, stood at the entrance of the alley, by the corner of the neighboring stable. He wore muddy breeches and a linen shirt that was splattered with brown stains that could have been blood. He was missing his right arm, and over his left shoulder he carried a burden wrapped in an oversized leather cloak.

God help us, another body?

The one-armed youth struggled with his burden, half walking, half staggering. A fresh wound cut across the right side of his face, black and purple with dried blood and the bruise underneath.

Günter pushed forward from behind the ranks to stand next to Erhard. "Uldolf?" Günter asked. "Is that you?"

Uldolf. Erhard knew that name. Uldolf was one of the Prûsan men that the bishop had ordered rounded up. Uldolf in particular, because he was the son of the last chieftain of Mejdân.

Uldolf stopped advancing. "Yes," he answered Günter and looked around at the mass of soldiers.

Judging by the complete indifference with which Uldolf regarded the dead, and the near emotionless character of his voice, Erhard suspected he had been present for the bloodletting.

He lost his arm during the fall of Mejdân. He has seen this before.

Erhard stepped forward. "The bishop would have a word with you."

"Am I your concern?" He swayed a little, and lowered himself onto one knee. When he did, Erhard saw that he held a dagger flat against the top of his burden. The other men, upon seeing the unsheathed weapon, drew their own blades. All except Günter.

"What do you mean, showing naked steel to a knight of the Order!" Johann barked at him. "Speak quickly if you mean to keep your head."

Uldolf looked up at all of them as he deftly unrolled the body from his shoulder. "Not steel," he said to Johann. He looked at Erhard. "But you know that." He stepped back from the body, keeping the dagger pointed at it.

Lord Jesus, please grant me strength . . .

Uldolf had not brought them another corpse. The cloak fell open as he backed away, revealing a naked seventeen-year-old girl, severely bound and quite conscious. She looked up at Erhard with familiar green eyes. Around her neck was a silver torc.

"Uldolf, my boy, how did you capture her?" Günter said.

"So, am I right? This is what you want? Not me, not my family?"

Erhard found it impossible to believe that he faced her again.

"Lilly?" he finally asked.

"Master," she answered quietly.

Ⅰn the stable, when Uldolf had draped his cloak around her and picked her up, Lilly had tried to retreat into herself. Things weren't supposed to happen like this. She had given up. It should have been over. But Uldolf didn't give her an escape into death, and the refuge she had in her own mind no longer existed.

She wanted to give control back to the other one, her other self, but felt a sick confusion when she couldn't remember who that was or who she was now. Memories mixed in her head refusing to retreat, ignoring her attempt to segregate them between one or the other.

Please, where are you? I don't want to be here anymore.

No answer.

She heard someone yell at Uldolf, and in a few moments, he rolled her off his shoulder onto the ground. And Lilly found herself staring up at the face of Brother Erhard.

"Master," she whispered.

He looked down at her, and she could read the betrayal written across his face. Seeing him, so soon after Uldolf's rejection, she reached a nadir of self-loathing. The Order had been the one thing that had given her purpose—a purpose for what she was, not something she could only pretend to be.

One of the knights attacked her, but her master stopped the man before the blade fell.

"Sir," the man said, "the bishop ordered her death. After all of this—"

"Too many questions remain unanswered," Erhard said.

How could she explain her betrayal? She had turned on everything the Order had given her. For what? A memory? To give herself to someone who had every reason to hate her?

Uldolf demanded to see his family, and her master promised he would. But her master's voice was flat and dead, leached of all the authority she remembered. It frightened her that her master seemed as near hopelessness as Uldolf did.

Please, she thought, *let my return mean freedom for Uldolf's family.*

Her master closed the cloak about her and picked her up. Several others objected, shouted warnings. But even if her master cared to heed them, the warnings were unnecessary now. Even if she had been unbound, she had no reason to try and escape. She had nothing left to fight for.

✦

Uldolf handed the silver dagger to Sergeant Günter and stood as the knight bent down to pick up Lilly. He wanted to feel something, but all he had left was a throbbing numbness—as if his emotions had been amputated like his arm, leaving only a phantom itch behind.

Sergeant Günter slapped him on the back. "I think you saved us all, son." The man smiled broadly at Uldolf.

"I just want my family," Uldolf said.

The sergeant chuckled. "You know, I'd hold out for some greater reward." He lowered his voice. "You have any idea how many Germans they had hunting this beast? Look at what it's done."

Uldolf nodded, and looked away from him and toward the other soldiers. Günter's cheer seemed blasphemous in the face of what had died here.

The leader cradled Lilly in his arms and called out orders to the others in German. Uldolf couldn't follow what the knight said, but it was fairly clear that he was separating out one group to accompany him to the keep, and another to take care of the dead and wounded.

Uldolf looked at Lilly's face but all he saw there was a blank resignation . . .

He turned away, rubbing his right shoulder. There was no question that this was the right thing to do. No question at all.

But—

The knight holding Lilly—Brother Erhard, her "master"—was as much the reason for the slaughter of Uldolf's first family as Lilly was. More so, since it was his hands that created her—if not the monster herself, then her mind.

If you didn't hold my family, I would see you both dead—but you, sir knight, most of all.

Günter babbled on about Uldolf's heroism as they walked back to the castle. To the sergeant's mind, Uldolf's capturing of the she-wolf was worthy of a saga in its own right. Günter asked a few questions about how such an event came about, but the man was so enthused that he had already started stringing together his own unique version of events.

Günter was too involved in his own half-fictitious drama to notice what Uldolf saw—that none of the Germans in this group of soldiers seemed to share his enthusiasm. Uldolf thought that they looked at him with the same ill regard with which they looked at Lilly. Disturbingly, it seemed as if that attitude extended to the sergeant as well.

Finally, Uldolf said, "Perhaps there may be a better time to discuss this."

Günter squeezed his shoulder. "We should regale these Germans with a tale or two of a true Prûsan hero."

That drew a few stares that even Günter couldn't completely ignore. He let go of Uldolf's shoulder and said, "But you're right. Not now."

The whole procession had taken on the aspect of a nightmare—a dream where he walked a fixed path toward some dread outcome and found himself powerless to stop or turn aside.

When the cluster of soldiers walked through the gates of the castle, Uldolf saw exactly how nightmarish the world had become.

People were massed under a canvas shelter in the bailey of the castle, as if escaping a siege. Men, women, children—Uldolf saw most of the free Prûsan population of Johannisburg crowded against the castle wall and under guard by frowning Germans. Uldolf saw garments ranging from barely utilitarian rags to finely woven and brightly dyed clothes of wealthy merchants.

They were quiet, and for the most part already looked like ghosts. But they weren't the only ghosts Uldolf saw here.

The stronghold of Mejdân had once stood upon the site of this castle. Somewhere beneath his feet, the blood and bones of his first parents had been buried with the ruins of what had been Uldolf's home for the first ten years of his life. Now the only sign that it ever existed was the mound upon which the keep stood. The new Christian rulers were very good at erasing the remnants of the old order.

Bringing the monster to account should have finally put that part of his past to rest. But his feelings were all wrong.

He had hidden from what happened, had refused to acknowledge it for years, and he began to realize that regaining the memory came at a deep cost. Every step he took into the Order's realm cut deeper, and every breath he took seemed more suffocating.

Confronting Lilly had been a reflexive, almost unthinking act. Far from relieving the pain he had just begun remembering, it brought the memories into sharper focus.

He could still *smell* the blood.

He could hear Radwen Seigson's ghost whispering, *"These are the enemy, the hands that cut these stones and placed them on my grave—as much as the hands that tore my head from my body."*

Inside him, he felt long-forgotten dams crumbling. The eight-year-old barrier leaked memory, anger, and grief; a maelstrom of blood and pain, the scope of which he was only beginning to perceive.

He was left to wait with a guard in a small chapel next to the keep. He sat down on a plain bench, alone before a large wooden cross, and slowly realized that there was nothing he could do.

It could not be fixed.

After eight years, in the chapel of his enemy's god, Uldolf finally wept for his family.

XXVIII

Sergeant Günter made a point of being the first one to bring the news to Bishop Cecilio. He made his way to the bishop's chambers as quickly as he could while still maintaining a measure of dignity. In some sense, this was still *his* castle—and now that the episode with the wolf creature was over, everything should return to some semblance of normalcy.

It couldn't be soon enough.

Günter had accepted Christ and served the Order, but he had the uncomfortable feeling that his superiors were forgetting on whose land they trod. It was one thing to treat unbaptized pagan idolaters like this, but the people the bishop had rounded up were Christian freemen whose only crime had been the ill luck of being Prûsan.

He reached the bishop's chambers, and for all his hurry, was made to wait by one of His Grace's personal guard.

No, definitely not soon enough.

As he waited outside the door, he imagined the bishop's expression when he told him that it was a *Prûsan* they had to thank for capturing the monster. It was an uncharitable thought, but unlike the brother knights of the Order, Günter didn't consider himself obliged to feel guilty for it.

When he was led in, the bishop was bent over a long sheet of paper. The bishop spent several moments writing what seemed to be a substantial order before glancing up in Günter's direction.

"What is it, Sergeant?" The bishop spoke in his mutilated German, pushing himself away from the table with some effort.

"The monster has been captured, Your Grace," Günter said, in better German than the bishop could manage. "The hunt is over."

"We are certain of this?"

"I witnessed it myself, and Brother Erhard was present to identify the creature."

"Is it dead?"

Günter shook his head. It was the one part of the whole episode that did not sit well with him. "No, Brother Erhard wanted to question the creature beforehand. He is restraining it now."

The bishop shook his head and muttered something in a language Günter didn't know. Then he returned to his laborious German. "I will have to talk to Brother Erhard. Questioning the devil's subject will only lead him into further deception. Thank you for your news." The bishop turned to regard his paperwork.

Günter remained where he was, wondering how to properly continue the conversation.

The bishop glanced back at him. "Is there something else?"

Günter nodded. "Yes, Your Grace. The man who captured the creature, his name is Uldolf—"

"That name . . . He is one of the Prûsans who hadn't been brought to the castle yet? Part of—" The bishop stared a moment, as if trying to remember the name. He shook his head. "Part of the old chieftain's family?"

"Yes, he is. He managed to subdue the monster and brought it to Brother Erhard, bound and—"

"He is here, then?"

"Yes."

"Good. Secure him in a cell."

"What?"

The bishop nodded. "He is part of the family that sheltered this creature and hid it from us. He is also the son of the last pagan chieftain here. It is clear that he is central to the secret pagan community here."

"Your Grace? I don't think you understand. Uldolf brought the creature to us."

"Indeed, you said he captured the thing. May I ask how?"

"I . . ." Günter felt a chill fall over the room, and began to sense that relating stories of Prûsan prowess would not be the best thing right now. "I was not present when he captured it."

"Considering how much harm this thing has inflicted on Christian soldiers, do you think that one pagan youth could subdue it with any natural methods?"

"Uldolf isn't a pagan. He was baptized, as you and I—"

"This youth must have had some diabolical sorcery on his side, or else he was in league with the thing to start with."

Günter could not comprehend the bishop's logic. "Your Grace, I don't understand what you're saying. If he was in league with it, why bind it and bring it to us?"

The bishop smiled. "Of course the forces of Satan are dismayed now that the Church has stepped in to compensate for the laxness of the Order. The devil's hand was free until now."

"Your Grace—"

"Sergeant, I see you still don't understand. This Uldolf brought the beast back to us explicitly to convince us of his righteousness— a mark of desperation."

Günter lacked the wit to form any response at all in the face of that assertion. The premise was so absurd, and voiced with such conviction, that it seemed an assault on the very basis of reason itself.

"Despite his motives, this turn of events is favorable. The search for this creature took men away from the investigation."

Günter resisted the urge to look back toward the door, to see if there was something to mark the threshold between the world of sense and the world he found himself in. "Investigation?"

The bishop nodded. "We will find every grove, every idol, and every helpmate of Satan. Do you understand, Sergeant?"

"Yes, Your Grace."

It was clear that the bishop would release no one—not until he was satisfied that they were Christian enough. Günter had the sick feeling that in the world that the bishop lived in, a Prûsan *couldn't* be Christian enough.

"May I ask a question?"

"Yes, Sergeant?"

"The spring planting. There are too many farms left unattended—"

The bishop picked up the letter he had been drafting. "Do not worry for that. There are plenty of lords in Christendom who can donate serfs to assist us with planting and harvest."

"I understand." He did. The bishop meant to appropriate what land remained in Prûsan hands. And if serfs and slaves tilled the land, not free men, it left little debate as to whose hands would then own that land.

This wasn't a hunt for a monster, or a battle with Satan. It was all a pretext. This man wanted Johannisburg for his own fief.

"Good, Sergeant. I will need the few good Prûsans to be clearheaded as we go about this. I think Uldolf and the rest will make a fair demonstration of the seriousness of these matters."

"Demonstration?"

The bishop nodded. "Their punishment should help encourage the true Christians to come forward and expose the remaining idolaters in their midst."

"I see."

The bishop waved a hand, dismissing him. "Please, go see to the youth. I need to finish this letter and see to Brother Erhard."

Günter spoke the three most difficult words he had ever uttered. "Yes, Your Grace."

He turned and left, before he could do something rash in the bishop's presence.

Good Prûsans?

Demonstration?

For once, Günter prayed to no gods at all. They were worse than deaf—they were actively hostile.

"But the question remains," he whispered to himself, "what do I *do* about it?"

❖

Things had come full circle. Erhard stood within a cell in the lowest level of the keep in Johannisburg Castle. When he had first left her here, Lilly had been clothed like a typical Prûsan peasant woman, with only the token restraint of a silver manacle on her ankle. She had been standing when he had left her.

Now she was at his feet, naked, curled on the floor, bound by thick leather straps that tightly wrapped her legs and arms together. Around her neck was the silver torc that prevented her from changing to her true form.

Lilly looked up at him in a way that almost begged him to correct her. She had always been distant and cold, and seeing a human emotion in her face was wrong.

"You are going to be punished," Erhard said.

"I am going to be killed," Lilly replied. It was the first time she had ever directly contradicted him, and it was almost as shocking as the fact that she had escaped. He reached down and backhanded her, splitting her lip open.

"You do not talk back to me!"

"Am I wrong?" she whispered.

Erhard raised his hand again, but stopped himself. *What is the point of this?* He lowered his hand. "Why did you do this?"

Lilly shook her head. "It doesn't matter anymore."

"It's the only thing that *does* matter!" He wanted to strike her again—not to discipline or correct her behavior, but simply to vent his own frustration. He turned away, because he was frightened of the anger that welled up inside him. He asked God for some semblance of composure. "For years, you worked in God's service. Why would you now turn on everything you've ever known?"

"I've turned on everything that ever loved me."

"What?"

"It's my purpose, isn't it? It is why you value me at all. I can kill." She looked up at Erhard, tears in her eyes. "My worth is measured in the blood I shed in your God's name."

"Why did you escape?"

"You abandoned me here. Of all places, *here*! I tried to forget what you made me do. For *years* I tried."

"Forget what?"

Lilly closed her eyes and shook her head.

"You need to tell me why you escaped."

"Your God will forgive you?"

"What?"

"Your God will forgive your sins?"

"If I truly repent and do penance."

Lilly looked up at him with shimmering green eyes. "You are the only God I have. Will you forgive me?"

Erhard took a step back from her. "Don't speak such blasphemy."

"I'm giving my life in penance for my sins. Are you so cruel to deny me absolution?"

"You cannot ask for absolution."

"Why?"

"Because animals have no souls."

Lilly looked down at the floor.

"Why?" Erhard repeated. "Why did you escape?"

"Because I am an animal," Lilly said. "Because I have no soul. Because I am beyond the forgiveness of even the men who raised me."

"Lilly—"

"Kill me and be done with it!" she screamed. And in that moment, Erhard didn't see the creature he had trained, the wolf thing that Brother Semyon had bequeathed to him. He couldn't see the emotionless thing he had taken from battle to battle.

What he saw was all too human.

No, the Church ruled on what they were. Just animals . . .

But the pope had changed that ruling. What basis did Erhard have now to say *what* she was? If she could *ask* to receive God—

"The bishop is right," he whispered. "You are born of the Father of Lies. You've twisted me against the Church, against God. You are the work of the devil."

Lilly shook her head. *"You* did this to *me!"*

"I have been misled." Erhard backed to the door, staring at the naked succubus, beating down every sympathetic impulse, every merciful thought.

"You told me I was serving your God!"

Erhard didn't trust himself to say anything more. He knocked on the door so the guard would let him out.

The confusion in Lilly's face was painful to see. Erhard turned away from her as the door opened. As he left, he heard her call out, "If I belong to the devil, it is because you gave me to him!"

Then the guard closed the door behind him and Erhard was able to breathe a sigh of relief. But only for a moment.

"Brother Erhard," spoke a painfully familiar voice.

Erhard looked up. "Your Grace."

The bishop stood in the hallway, his rich clothes and jewels giving him the appearance of a grotesque apparition in the plain stone corridor. He smiled at Erhard. "I see your Sergeant Günter spoke truth. The beast is again in your hands."

"Yes, Your Grace."

"I heard some of your conversation."

"I see."

"You've satisfied yourself of your error?"

"Your Grace has proved wiser than I in this matter."

The bishop chuckled to himself. Erhard couldn't help but think it unseemly.

"I am about to order her execution," Erhard said.

"You forget that I now dispense authority in Johannisburg. I shall direct the disposition of any prisoners."

Erhard bent his head. "Forgive my imposition. What would you have me do?"

"She will meet her fate with those who gave her succor. My inquisitor has identified the family that fed and clothed her, and they will all face the flames as one."

When the bishop said that the family belonged to the young man, Uldolf, Erhard found that he was not surprised.

Come with us."

In response to the broken Prûsan, Uldolf looked up from the floor and saw a quartet of armed men. The one speaking wore the black cross of the Order. Uldolf stared a moment at the unfamiliar knight and said, "I am supposed to see my family."

"You will see them, in time."

He looked at the four of them and realized that this was not going to go well. But since there was little else he could do, he stood and said, "Take me, then."

The four men arranged themselves on both sides of him, making sure he followed precisely where they led. Uldolf asked them where they were going, but the men were unresponsive.

He was only partly surprised when they took him outside, across the bailey, and toward the keep. He looked across at the mass of Prûsans still gathered here. Seeing the prisoners extinguished whatever small hope he had that giving the Germans their monster might have ended this nightmare. He saw a few faces he recognized—mostly farmers for whom he had done leatherwork.

More frightening was what was happening on the other side of the bailey, by the walls of the keep itself. A rough platform had been erected about waist height off the ground. In the middle of the platform, four stakes half again as tall as a man formed the outline of a diamond. Men piled wood around the base of the platform and the stakes. Uldolf looked from the stakes, back to the crowd, and saw in his countrymen's eyes all he needed to know.

For the briefest instant, as the stone pile of the keep towered over him, he considered trying to run for it. It was only the briefest of flashes. Even if there weren't four guards escorting him, there was nowhere to run to. Then they led him through the door to the keep, and he lost even the illusion of escape.

XXIX

*U*ldolf . . .
     Ulfie . . .
     The bishop's words, from beyond the cell door, burned into Lilly like acid dripping on her skin. They were going to kill Ulfie and his family for the crime of helping her. Because of her, Ulfie was going to be hurt again.

     She closed her eyes and wished she had the ability to simply will her heart to stop beating. She curled into a shaking ball, the stone floor cold against her skin.

     "Stop it."

     She surprised herself by speaking. She froze a few moments waiting for the other one to take over. It took a few seconds to realize that there wasn't another, not anymore. She sucked in a deep breath and thought back, remembering herself.

     Rarely did she try to think back on what she did. The killer was someone else, some*thing* else.

     But it wasn't.

     She was that bloodthirsty thing that killed without thought or remorse. And worse, the thing was here with her now—Lilly could tell because the thought of the guards she had beaten earlier made her smile.

Why was she so frightened of herself? The single greatest regret of her life, what she had done to Uldolf and his family, didn't happen because she was a monster. No, she might be a bloodthirsty animal, but she had hurt Uldolf because she had been weak. She had been too weak to say no to her master. If she had been stronger . . .

She realized that she was being weak now.

She had given up.

Uldolf deserved more.

She deserved more.

And dear master Erhard certainly deserved more.

She wiggled and brought herself up into a sitting position. Uldolf had done a very good job of restraining her, enough that the Order hadn't elaborated upon it. Thick leather straps wrapped her legs from the knees down, painfully tight. With a little leverage, she might have been able to pull apart one or two thicknesses of it, but not a dozen.

So she wouldn't force it.

She rolled on her back, lifting her legs up and folding them over. With her arms bound behind her back, it was difficult, and she had to rock back and forth several times, almost falling over twice. But eventually she got the top of her feet to touch her forehead, and she grabbed a length of the horse-flavored leather in her teeth.

Even her human jaws regularly chewed through bone, so gnawing through the leather was not terribly difficult. It was more difficult contorting herself to reach the straps with her mouth. But by the third one, the binds loosened, and she was able to scissor her legs apart, leaving the greater part of the leather to spiral off of her legs.

She panted from the exertion and lowered her legs to the

ground. Sweat covered her legs and torso, and she tasted blood and shreds of leather in her mouth.

Her arms were still tightly wrapped, bound behind her back, the leather tied too high up her forearms to allow her to pull her arms around in front of her.

Time was leaking away and she had committed herself. She couldn't be half free when the guards came for her.

She sat up, felt around, and found the massive staple in the floor that had once held the chains binding her leg. She backed up to it and grabbed the ring with both hands and thought of her options.

With a grip on the ring, she could force her arms the wrong way over her head. It would be painful, but she would heal from the damage. Only she didn't know how quickly. Losing a foot wasn't too critical, but severely dislocating both arms? Thinking of her foot made her aware of another option. If she lost one hand, wedging it in the ring and pulling her wrist free, that would give her some slack to pull her arms loose. But that had the same problem; her hand might not grow back before they came.

If she could only change. As strong as she was now, as the wolf she was stronger. It was the silver wrapping her neck that truly bound her. She could remember vainly stabbing at this torc with the dagger. The cuts the silver blade had made in her neck still stung with her sweat. It had taken Uldolf prying at the hinge to get it off.

But this was the same torc, wasn't it? It must have been weakened.

She felt the iron staple anchored into the stone floor of her cell. It was hard—harder than the silver she wore. She slid down, the grit on the floor digging into the skin of her legs and her backside. She stopped when she was on her back, the back of her neck resting on the staple as if it was some torturer's pillow.

The hinge was on the back of the torc, and she did her best to center it on the staple. She sucked in a breath and slowly sat up, stomach tensing as she pulled her torso up and bent forward as far as she could.

It would be bad to miss.

"But," she whispered to herself, "I am not going to miss."

She sucked in a deep breath, tucked her chin to her chest, tensed her muscles, and threw her torso back as hard and as fast as she could manage. The back of the torc slammed into the iron staple with a force that cracked her neck like a whip. The impact reverberated through her skull, throwing dancing lights across her vision.

She lay there, stunned, every muscle and tendon between her jaw and her shoulder blades locked in a blinding spasm of pain. Then the tension slowly released, allowing her head to sag backward. Several moments passed before she could manage to unclench her jaw, and several more before she could sit upright.

When she did, the torc slid off her neck and down across her chest, into her lap. It was too dark to see if the trail it left was sweat or blood.

Even though it hurt, she managed a small smile.

She tried to stand, but was still dizzy from the pain induced by the impact and fell over on her side, the torc rolling off into the darkness.

It's fine, as long as the metal is no longer touching me—

She closed her eyes and willed the wolf into her body.

In response to her desire, her heart hammered, every beat forcing more and more blood through her body, the pulse a pressure against tightening flesh. Her muscles tensed, pulling against lengthening and twisting bone, and began to slide under her flesh with an instinct of their own. Her skin itched as every hair on her body became alive, lengthening, thickening, rippling across her flesh. She felt her teeth grow and sharpen as her jaws pressed outward.

Her breath quickened, and she groaned even though she was trying to be quiet.

There was pain as her body tore at itself and knit itself back together—pain that vibrated through her skin and every fiber of every muscle. Pain that she felt deep in the core of her body. Pain that she welcomed. It tore her apart, but with it also came a blinding ecstasy that could only compare to the climax she'd felt with Uldolf.

The binding of her forearms heightened the pain. She could feel her growing bone, muscle, and flesh pushing against the straps. The leather held her arms against the movement of her joints, trying to tear her arms out of her broadening shoulders. She felt her skin begin to tear, and blood drip onto the fur of her wrists. She heard an anguished creaking sound, and didn't know if it was the leather holding her arms or her own body.

Lilly roughly exhaled as the transformation completed. She rested her muzzle against the floor of her cell, panting. Her forearms were still bound behind her, even more painfully now. She could smell her own blood. And her limbs were so tightly twisted that she had no motion in them at all. Her hands had gone numb.

It felt as if even the wolf in her didn't have the strength to break these bonds.

Lilly entertained a brief thought: attacking the guards as they entered, just as she was. She could do a lot of damage just with her teeth.

But as much as she despised her master now, he had trained her better than that. They would have a choke point at the door, and have five or six men, armed with silver. These men would be prepared, aware of what she was and what she could do. They would look in the cell before opening the door, and if she wasn't docile and bound as they'd left her, they would probably just shoot bolts at her through the door until she stopped moving.

If this was going to work, she couldn't just be stronger than they were. She had to be smarter.

She still heard faint creaking, and now she was sure it was the leather.

Maybe this was enough.

She pulled the wolf back inside herself. It was hard, firing a desperate hunger inside her. Even as her skin pulled back into its human shape, it felt as if she could keep deflating, falling into the burning cavity in her stomach. She realized that she hadn't eaten since yesterday. And now she had changed twice since . . .

Even in the dark, she could tell that she was thinner. She could feel the nubs of her spine against her wrists. It was inevitable. Her body had only so many resources. The next time she changed, she was going to be weakened by hunger.

She closed her eyes and told herself that it was just another thing she was going to take into account. It wouldn't matter if she couldn't free herself.

She sucked in a breath and tried to move her arms.

Her transformation didn't break the bonds, but the leather had stretched just enough to allow her now slightly thinner arms to worry themselves free.

She flexed them in front of her, then hugged herself. She only spared a few seconds to allow the freedom of motion. She didn't know how long it would be before they came for their monster, and when they did, she had to be ready.

She felt around the cell floor until she retrieved all the leather straps, and after a few uncomfortable minutes, the silver torc. As she did, she formed the basis of a plan . . .

◈

Erhard silently prayed as he led seven men back down into the dark halls underneath the keep. Despite a decade believing otherwise, he now knew that as Bishop Cecilio had said, they were about to retrieve an agent of Hell itself. The fact that Lilly had shredded Christian flesh as readily as she had pagan should be enough to show the devil's hand. Erhard knew that now.

"*You are the only God I have . . .*" she had said.

No, she wasn't an animal. An animal cannot blaspheme.

In his heart, Erhard wanted to finish this all now. One quick stroke separating head from shoulders would be enough to end this threat to body and soul. However, God and the bishop had decided to multiply his trials. He could not end things so simply now.

It was punishment for his pride. In his hubris, he had held some hope that if he could just talk to Lilly, she could give him an explanation. She could give him a reason that might acquit him of his role in raising her.

Not until she started uttering such evils did he realize how grave a sin he had been committing. Not simply ten years of nurturing her kind. For that sin, at least, he had the mitigation of his own deception—a deception that extended all the way to the pope. No, his sin, and what he now paid for, was the fact that he sought absolution, and forgiveness, in the eyes of Satan. Instead of looking to God, he had turned to Lilly.

Instead of praying for guidance, he had placed his faith in the words of a demon. He had wanted her to say something that would let him believe that the bishop was wrong, something that would let him believe that he hadn't spent the last decade in the service of the devil.

That arrogance, placing his own will before that of God, weighed now on his soul. A weight that might not be lifted even when he bore Lilly to the pyre, demonstrating the ultimate triumph of God to the Prûsans confined to the bailey.

Erhard was sick at the thought. Not for Lilly's sake, who in Erhard's mind was already consigned to the Lake of Fire, but because

Erhard believed the bishop was erring for the sake of spectacle. God commanded that praise and glory be given unto Him, and making such a public display smacked more of giving praise and glory unto Bishop Cecilio.

Perhaps there would be a point in forcefully correcting any errors of the Prûsan natives. However, the bishop wasn't confronting some unrepentant pagan village, recently conquered. These people had all pledged their fealty to the Lord and the Order.

But in the end, what grounds did he have to critique the righteousness of Bishop Cecilio? If they were on a road to Hell now, was Erhard not the one who laid it?

His procession stopped at the end of the corridor to Lilly's cell. Erhard stood and took a few deep breaths. He was not going to allow any more mistakes. Restrained or not, Erhard knew how deadly Lilly was.

The deference she had once shown him would be gone. Even with eight men, there was no room for any sort of complacency.

"You two"—he pointed at two crossbowmen—"take your aim."

The two men nodded and knelt, bracing one on either corner of the short corridor. The silver heads of their crossbows glinted in the lamplight. They were the best marksmen present at Johannisburg Castle, and Erhard didn't doubt that if they fired, each bolt would find its mark.

Halfway to the door, he told the other men, "Draw swords and hold here for a moment." He advanced on the door alone, carrying a lantern. He would be the only person in immediate reach when he opened the window and looked into the cell.

He felt his heart pulsing in his throat as he reached up and opened the iron shutter. Nothing emerged to menace him from the dark portal other than the smell of urine-soaked straw.

He raised the lantern to the opening and saw her.

She rested on her side on the floor, arms behind her. Leather straps wrapped her legs, and from her neck Erhard could still see a glint of silver that was not nearly as reassuring as it should have been. She made no threatening moves. All she did was blink up at the lantern.

He turned toward the other men and said, "Come here." He pointed at a spot of the corridor a step beyond the grooves the door had worn in the floor. They lined up—three in front, two behind—silver blades glinting in the lantern light.

With his men in position, Erhard opened the latch and pulled the heavy door open. It moved slowly, screeching in protest. When Erhard had pushed it all the way against the corridor wall, he shone the lantern back into the room.

She hadn't moved. She didn't even look at him. Her eyes were closed and she had turned her head down, tucking her chin against her chest. He wished that she had been clothed when that boy Uldolf had bound her. She was dressed in nothing but leather bindings. However, he had come prepared to protect his men's modesty, if not hers.

He walked into the room and pointed at two of the men in the hallway, waving them forward. One carried a bundle in addition to his sword.

"Cover her," Erhard ordered. The man nodded and sheathed his weapon. The other man stood guard as the first unrolled a long burlap sheet. He draped the rough cloth over Lilly's nakedness. She offered no resistance as the man rolled her up in it. She still refused to look at them—head bent, eyes closed.

Erhard waved another man forward and handed him the lantern.

This was his sin, and he would be the one to bear it to the surface. He thanked God for the fact that Lilly remained silent as he bent and picked her up. Only her head was exposed, and as he cradled her in his arms, she curled into a tight ball, burying her face in the burlap covering her body.

She's trying to keep from facing God, he thought, and accompanying that thought was the painfully blasphemous question: *My God, or hers?*

He looked at the three men in the cell with him. "You stay ready for attack. Should I call out, or if she drops from my arms, dispatch her without concern for me."

"Yes, sir," the trio said in unison.

He walked to the doorway and looked at the men ahead of him. Two swordsmen stood just outside the swing of the cell door, and the two crossbowmen at the end of the corridor.

His men arranged themselves as he had told them earlier, the swordsmen surrounding him a pace out of arm's reach. One crossbow moved ahead of him twenty paces, the other to the rear at twenty paces.

They knew that if they had to shoot, they would have no time to reload. He had warned them before the descent. "Shoot only when you see her head, and put the bolt in the brain if you can, the throat if you must, and try for the heart only if you have no other choice."

Not one showed a hint of a question in his face. He had picked each one of these men because they all had personal experience of what the girl in his arms was capable of, either from his decade of using her as a weapon for Christendom, or from knowing and working with the more recent victims of her bloodlust.

None of these men would be deceived by the image of a pathetic child wrapped in rough burlap. Each man was armed with a proper weapon against her. They would not panic if they were suddenly faced with fang or claw.

Should she somehow attack, escape the bonds of silver on her neck, she might take Erhard's life, but she would not live to take any more.

Fortunately, God was with them, and she made no hostile moves. In fact, she barely moved at all. As Erhard walked up out of the bowels of the keep, surrounded by guards bearing silver weapons, Lilly began to tremble.

However, when he carried her outside, Erhard swallowed a growing unease when he realized that she wasn't trembling.

Very quietly, almost inaudibly, Lilly was singing.

XXX

They came for Uldolf before he was ready.

Then again, he never would be ready for this.

Even though he had been living on borrowed time since his arm had been torn from its socket, he didn't want it to end this way. When the men came for him, he rushed the guards. It was a hopeless attempt. It only took one of them striking his already swollen face to drop him to the ground.

However, it would have been worse to go with them meekly, without at least trying.

The men roughly bound his arm to his side and yanked him upright. He screamed something obscene and one of them shoved a block of wood in his mouth, binding it fast with a strap of leather. Two more of them half dragged, half carried him through the stone corridors, up the stairs, and out into the bailey in front of the keep.

The sun had set, and the courtyard was lit by ranks of torches carried by narrow-faced German soldiers. The Prûsan prisoners formed an audience behind the torch-bearing soldiers.

The focus of the audience was the pyre.

In the torchlight, the wood structure loomed even larger than
Uldolf remembered. The space under the platform had been piled
high with wood and tinder. The quartet of closely grouped stakes
pointed at the sky, fingers of some giant sinking back into the
earth.

Even with so many people, the air was deathly still and quiet.
No one in the audience spoke above a whisper. The loudest sound
was the combined crackle of the burning torches.

Uldolf stared at the pyre, and it finally sank in.

Four stakes . . .

No. They can't be so brutal . . .

The soldiers dragged him up on the platform, throwing him up
against the stake nearest the keep's entrance. He struggled as they
pulled a rope around, binding his chest and upper body to the
stake. As he thrashed against the bonds he saw past the guards.

He tried to scream *"Mother,"* but the wooden gag in his mouth
prevented anything but a weak grunt.

Still, Burthe heard him and turned her head. Uldolf saw her
eyes widen, and if it weren't for the ropes binding him, he would
have fallen to his knees in shame.

Worse than seeing his mother bound and gagged, worse than
seeing her face bruised and bloody, was seeing the loss of hope in
her eyes and knowing it was his fault she would now see *both* her
children die.

The men who had bound him left to drag her up to the platform. They pulled her out of sight to the stake directly behind him.
He whipped around to try and see what they were doing, but he
could only turn his head enough to see the stakes on either side of
him, to the front and back of the platform.

Then they brought out his father. If he hadn't known it was
Gedim, he might not have recognized him, the beating was so se-
vere. Gedim's face was a swollen patchwork of red and purple.
Blood caked his mouth, which apparently was too swollen and

broken to fit a gag. His nose was a bloody mass of flesh, and there was a fist-sized lump where his left ear should be. The way the two soldiers carried him, he didn't appear conscious. His body flapped like a rag doll as they tied him to the stake to Uldolf's left, facing the wall of the keep.

Uldolf's hand balled into a fist. His heart raced. They were going to bring out Hilde and tie her to the stake facing the crowd. The sight would break him.

But pride of place wasn't going to go to his sister.

The entourage that emerged now from the keep was much larger than the one that had escorted Uldolf or his parents, and they moved as if they were in the midst of a military campaign. First came a man with a crossbow, who walked out past the pyre and took up a spot in front of the torch-wielding soldiers. He knelt and aimed back where he had come.

Next came two soldiers, swords drawn and glinting silver in the torchlight.

Following them walked a knight of the Hospital of St. Mary of the Germans in Jerusalem. He wore a white surcoat bearing the black cross of the Teutonic Order, and in his arms he carried a burlap-wrapped body.

Lilly had curled into a ball, her face buried in the filthy bindings. Her hair hung free, and much of the black had sweated away, so that her hair glinted red in the torchlight.

The knight bore his burden to the foremost stake, to tie her facing the crowd. As he mounted the platform, Uldolf heard something. Singing. An old lullaby that Uldolf recognized.

"Fear not the road before you . . ."

Uldolf swallowed, unprepared for the series of emotions slamming into his gut.

The first thought on seeing Lilly was that this was justice. She *should* burn in place of Hilde, payment for his first sister's death, the death of his whole first family.

But the singing . . .

Mother will protect her child.

No matter what the darkness brings.

The girl he had known in the woods as a child; the woman he found in the same woods, the one who called him Ulfie; the one he had made love to, who had warned him not to remember.

Were they *all* that monster?

He *wanted* to see her burn.

But he *didn't*.

❖

Lilly sang to calm herself.

It would have been so easy to snap, to reach up and taste the flesh of Erhard's throat, to punish her cold and unforgiving God. But what purpose would that serve? She knew she could take lives.

But could she *save* any?

Fear not the road before you,

The broken stones, the empty trees,

Mother will protect her child,

Wherever that road leads . . .

She knew that her master was afraid. She felt it in the tenseness of the arms bearing her. She heard it in the way he breathed and in the thudding of the pulse in his chest. She smelled it in his sweat, even over the scent of mildew in the burlap that wrapped her. The rough cloth itched, but it also covered her, hiding the way she gradually moved her legs and arms apart, keeping the now-loose leather bindings taut.

They had been waiting for her. During their ascent from her cell, she had been aware of all of them; the two crossbowmen, the five men with silvered swords. They had expected her to fight. They had been waiting for it. One or two, she sensed, might have even been eager for it.

How often had she relied on the ignorance or stupidity of her adversary? Surprise was more deadly than the wolf, as her rapist had discovered. But she had no surprise in the keep.

If, somehow, she could shed her bonds and stay unmolested for the few seconds it took for the wolf to come, she trusted in the wolf's ability to take anyone. But that couldn't happen while Erhard carried her, surrounded by swordsmen. Five swords would have pierced her body before Erhard's body hit the ground.

Fear not the bear, the troll, the wolf,

Or other evil things . . .

When they emerged into the night air, she saw the wooden structure of the pyre, she saw the soldiers carrying torches, and she saw the Prûsans who would be forced to watch.

It was a familiar scene—the Order demonstrating the wrath of their God.

I was that wrath . . .

Mother will protect her child,

No matter what the darkness brings . . .

She saw Uldolf, and Burthe, and Gedim, bound and held in place upon the pyre. Uldolf faced her. Bloody. Beaten. The sight ignited a coal of rage in her chest, and she could hear the muscles and bones in her body groan and creak—

Not. Yet.

Fear not the cloak of slumber,

When the sky has lost its sun . . .

Erhard carried her up to the last stake on the pyre, facing the crowd. She allowed three men to hold her up against the stake. She smelled the fear on all of them. They left the burlap in place around her body as they took a heavy rope and tied her to the stake. Through it all, she kept her head down, chin to her chest pressing against the torc, and she kept her limbs rigid against the pull of the rope.

The three men tightened the rope, but even though they knew what she was, and even though they expected her to try and

escape, they still—as everyone did—underestimated the strength
of her frail human body. As they pulled the rope tight against her,
they didn't realize that her arms were behind, pushing against
them, giving her space at least the width of her arm between the
small of her back and the stake.

Mother will protect her child,
Should any nightmares come . . .

❖

Uldolf watched as Lilly's master carried her up to the pyre. He
wanted to scream at him, at everyone. If Lilly was evil, she
was an evil created by them. An evil created in service to their
own cruel God. If she should burn, those in the Teutonic Order
should roast in the same fire.

He strained his neck to look out over the crowd beyond the
torches. All those people, many who knew him, knew his family.
Would they just stand there, watching them put to fire?

Whenever he met someone's eyes, they turned away.

This is really going to happen.

He turned to look at Lilly, and even she seemed to have given
up, face down, singing quietly.

Of course she's given up. She gave up when I attacked her . . . She
had been ready to die at his hand. Why would that change now?

He had only spared her out of the hope that he could exchange
her for his family. That's what he told himself.

He kept telling himself that.

Even if the Order had commanded her actions, that didn't absolve her from what she had done to him. Even if it did, how could
it excuse what she had done after, coming to him years later, taking
advantage of his fragile memory . . .

"It's bad to remember . . ."

She had been ready to die at his hand.

Why?

He wanted to scream at her. She was a monster, and a monster doesn't show remorse.

Once Lilly was secured, the soldiers left the platform. The swordsmen who had accompanied Lilly out of the keep stepped back to take their places in the line of other soldiers with torches. The men with the crossbows remained in the front line, kneeling, loaded bows aimed up at Lilly.

Uldolf watched Brother Erhard take a position with the other knights of the Order. Of all the soldiers here, only six men stood bearing the black cross. None of the Teutonic Knights bore torches. That duty seemed reserved for the secular knights, their squires, and the few guardsmen remaining from the original garrison here.

The pyre now was the sole focus of a large semicircle of armored Christians. The ground around the pyre was clear for twenty paces in every direction, lest the righteous be singed by the flames. The Prûsans gathered behind the soldiers, staring at the pyre, their faces painted with the same disbelief that Uldolf felt.

They were Christians, weren't they? They had pledged their fealty to the Order and the Order's God. They were supposed to have the rights of any Christian—to speak their defense, to face a trial, to only face punishment ordained by law. Summary execution, being burned on a pyre without even the offer to recant; not even unrepentant heretics were treated this way.

A wedge of guards wearing checked colors of green and gold parted the crowd around the pyre. In their midst walked a large man wearing crimson robes trimmed with fur. Next to him was Sergeant Günter. Günter's face was blank, unreadable, a stark contrast to the man's enthusiasm when Uldolf had handed Lilly over.

Where are your epic stories of Prûsan prowess now?

Günter and the fat man emerged into the cleared area around the pyre. The fat one strode the ground as a man with no challenge to his authority. He surveyed the audience and shouted something in German.

When he was finished, Günter repeated in Prûsan, "Eight years ago, this village was saved from pagan damnation."

The man spoke again in German.

Günter translated. "The sword of God struck down the wicked, and delivered the truly righteous to the bosom of Christ. All of you who have accepted Christ should rejoice in your hearts that you have escaped the eternal fate of your unrepentant countrymen—the lake of eternal fire that awaits the heretic, the infidel, and the pagan."

Günter did not match the animation of the fat man. When the large man spoke, it was with force, the guttural syllables hammering the listeners like physical blows, his arms waving, throwing his sleeves out like blood-soaked wings.

When Günter translated, it was emotionless and flat, as if he didn't understand the words.

"The fight against the Evil One, against damnation, is ever waging. It is fought not just with the swords of the Order, but within the soul of every man, woman, and child here. There are those who profess obedience to God, but speak falsely. There exist those who have not renounced their idolatry. There are those who worship Satan in his many guises. Satan himself can walk among us, taking into his service the false, the unwary, the wrathful, or the ignorant."

The robed man spun and pointed at Lilly, words hammering from his mouth as if his speech alone could kill.

Günter translated. "This woman is an agent of the devil, responsible for the deaths of many Christians. She holds inside her a soulless beast that exists only to feed on the blood of men. Those beside her are complicit in her crimes—harboring her, providing for her, and hiding her from the agents of God. As such, these idolaters will suffer her fate."

Didn't you harbor her, provide for her? Does she only now serve the devil because she refused to serve you?

The man turned toward the audience and said something low and threatening.

"As will," Günter continued, "any who are found to have raised their hands in opposition to God and the Church, or hinder those who wield the authority of the pope."

The robed man allowed the words to sink in. He continued, less forcefully, and waved toward the cluster of guards who had brought him and Günter forward. The men parted to reveal a young child.

Hilde! Uldolf wanted to scream, but the gag still blocked his mouth, and the ropes were so tight that he could barely breathe.

" . . . show that God is merciful as well as strict," Günter was in the midst of saying. If anything, his words were even flatter now, drained of every hint of humanity. "This child, while equally complicit in her family's actions, will be spared so she can be brought into the full grace and forgiveness of Christ."

This is mercy? Uldolf thought. *Forcing her to watch her family burn? To watch him die, as he watched his sister die?*

The man with the robes took Hilde's hands in his own, pulling her forward. Hilde looked up at the pyre, as if just seeing it for the first time. She called out, "Mama! Ulfie!" She tried to run, but the man held her too tightly. He shouted something in German that Günter didn't translate.

The soldiers threw the torches. Uldolf watched as they all cut burning arcs against the night sky trailing sparks. The torches struck the base of the pyre, landing in the tinder at its base, scattering across the platform.

Hilde screamed.

Flames spread around the base of the pyre, and Uldolf could already feel the heat licking his face, the smoke burning his eyes. He looked at his sister, and saw her staring wide-eyed, tears streaming down her cheeks.

Please, Hilde, close your eyes. Don't watch this.

The man holding Hilde spoke, and Günter translated, "Let us all pray now for this child's soul."

The man started chanting something in Latin, and all the Christians lowered their heads.

Lilly raised hers.

Interlude

Anno Domini 1231

Lilly wrote her master's will across the stronghold of Mejdân, scrawled in the blood of the wicked. She met the enemy in dark narrow hallways, rending limbs and flesh. They swung swords and knives and clubs, but in most cases, simply stepping out of the shadows to show her true form was enough to shock the heathens into ineffectiveness. The panicked blows that did land wouldn't have been mortal even if she had no gift of healing.

She slaughtered her way toward the center of the building, leaving no one alive behind her to raise a warning of God's approaching wrath.

Almost no one.

Even with blood on her lips and the scent of death filling her lungs, she paused at a door. Whatever was behind it had been important enough for a Prûsan guard to block her way, until she relieved him of his head. She could hear breathing behind it, slow and steady. Someone sleeping.

Her clawed hand rested against it, and she made a low growl in her chest that never emerged from her throat. Her claws left small trails of blood smeared across the wood, but before she pushed the door open, the room's occupant groaned in his sleep.

The voice was familiar.

Uldolf?

She snatched her hand away from the door as if it had burst into flame. She stepped back, over the body of the headless Prûsan slumped at the threshold.

No. The one word was all that her confused thoughts could muster. She would not allow her master's will to fall over this one boy. It mattered little, anyway. Her master wanted fear, and dead swordsmen. Both he would have in great measure without Uldolf's body.

"Sleep," she whispered to the door, turning to tear her way into the heart of the stronghold.

❖

It should have ended there.

It should have ended with her half-human, half-lupine palm resting on Uldolf's door. She should have stood there and realized the full measure of what she was, what her master was, and what it meant to serve his God.

Some part of her mind did realize it. Something in her recoiled at the thought that Uldolf was here, in the midst of the damned, condemned by her master's God. Inside her, there was a nine-year-old child named Lilly who understood.

However, there was another Lilly—hunched, red-furred, and snarling; a Lilly born to endure the attentions of her first master; a Lilly who was cold and cared little for pain, or sadness, or joy. This Lilly tasted the blood of man and in it she tasted her master's favor and a vent for her rage.

This was the Lilly who entered the chambers of Reiks Radwen Seigson of Mejdân.

◈

Five people were in the chamber when she slammed the door open. Two guards rushed her in a futile charge that ended with their torn limbs scattered in the midst of piles of broken furniture. It left three alive: a woman, a child, and Radwen Seigson himself.

The woman fought as Lilly reached for the child, but one blow tore free the intervening limb, and another tore the woman's face open and dropped her to the ground.

Radwen tried to hide the child behind himself, but Lilly tore the small body from his arms and threw it away, back toward the door.

She slammed the pagan chieftain against the wall and started to tear him apart.

As the warm blood splattered her muzzle, pain slammed through the small of her back, impaling her and causing her muscles to spasm. The pieces of Radwen's body fell to the ground as she spun in a fury, grabbing her attacker's sword arm.

The small limb was torn free from the attacker's body even as she realized who it was.

Everything inside her stopped as the world froze.

Nothing moved except Uldolf, stumbling away from her, blood pouring from his wrecked shoulder. His face shone a pasty white in the lamplight.

He took a step backward, feet tangling in the woman's corpse as he fell backward. He looked at the woman and his mouth opened in a terrible soundless scream as he pushed backward with his feet, smearing a new trail in the blood on the floor.

She stared at the gaping wound of his shoulder as if it had been torn in her own flesh. Her master forgotten, she took a step forward.

He stared at her with eyes wide and empty. He screamed at her, "Stop it! Please, stop it!"

Somewhere inside her, a voice said, *God wants this.*

"No," she whispered.

Uldolf stared through her, tears cascading over pasty skin. "Stop it. Please, stop it."

My master wants this.

She reached out and touched his cheek. Her inhuman fingers left a trail of blood across Uldolf's face. "No. Not you."

It is what I am.

Uldolf violently shook his head, escaping her touch. His voice was weaker. "Stop it. Please, stop it!"

"I wasn't supposed to hurt you, Uldolf."

It is what we are.

"No, it isn't."

You as much as I, child.

Lilly shook her head, her own tears mixing with the blood on her face. She turned and ran.

◈

When her master came for her, she had recovered from the shock. Her thoughts of the boy Uldolf were locked away safely, along with the feelings of the other Lilly—the one who remembered lullabies and who had learned to swim. The one who idly thought that the weak pink body she wore now was somehow "real."

Lilly told herself that she was no longer a child, and she would never cry again.

Over the following years, she served her master very well, the wrath of his God personified. She knew nothing of mercy or remorse, and told herself that she cared for nothing, much less the village of Mejdân and the boy who had lived there.

◆

Then, eight years later, Lilly sat in the rear of a wagon, the kind used by farmers and merchants, enclosed on three sides by unpainted wooden sides high enough to hide the contents in the flat bed. The inside was dim. A canvas sheet above her softened the dawn light and cast the interior into shadow.

She rested in one corner, wearing the plain surcoat, chemise, and skirts of a Prûsan peasant woman. Her hair was unbound, falling across her shoulders. She sat on the thick straw bedding with her legs drawn up so she could rest her cheek against her knees. Under her skirt was a silver manacle on her ankle, its chain leading to a hole in the wagon floor that was hidden under the straw.

She watched as her master unlatched the rear gate and lowered it. He stared a moment at her meal. Resting in the center of the floor, just within her arm's reach, was the leg of a hind the Christians had taken and gutted two days ago. The flesh was half eaten, the red-stained bone visible up to the first joint.

He looked at the leg of venison and asked her, "You haven't eaten very much. Do you feel ill?"

"No, I saved it for the journey." When he frowned, she asked, "Have I displeased you?"

"No, Lilly. If you wish to worry your meal, you may do so."

She turned her face away and looked up at the canvas above her. "Have we reached the pagans yet?" It was what little she had to look forward to.

"No, there's been a delay. I've been called away to Marienwerder. I can't bring you that deep into Christian lands, so I am going to place you in a nearby village, Johannisburg."

"They are not pagans?"

"No. It was one of the first towns you helped bring to God. Its pagan name was Mejdân."

She lowered her face until her chin touched her knees. Her hair obscured her face from Erhard. "Mejdân?" The word sent a chill through her body, a fear that she shouldn't be feeling.

"Do you remember it?"

After a long time, she lied. "No, I do not recall it."

Compline

Anno Domini 1239

Iudicabit in nationibus, implebit ruinas;
conquassabit capita in terra multorum.

He shall judge among the heathen, he shall fill the places
    with the dead bodies;
He shall wound the heads over many countries.

—Psalms 110:6

XXXI

O n the pyre, Lilly raised her head, releasing the broken torc she had been holding in place with her chin. The silver wrapping her neck separated and fell open in front of her, breaking into two half-circles when it struck the platform. Between the call to prayer and the obscuring flames, no one took notice.

She exhaled and let her muscles go limp as she flattened herself against the stake. The ropes binding her went slack, and she could feel the leather straps slide down her legs under the burlap. Behind her back, she slid her arm out of the leather bonds she had stretched out inside her cell.

The bishop's Latin continued.

No one outside the flames noticed her shift in position. The ropes still bound her, but loosely. She slid down slightly, placing her hips below her bonds, and moved her arms around in front so she could grab the top two lengths of rope.

She listened to the bishop's prayer and whispered, "Pray for your own sorry souls."

◈

Uldolf strained to watch as Lilly raised her head. Her silhouette against the flames had lost all trace of submission or fear. Her profile had turned to iron. Even before the torc tumbled off her neck to break in half at her feet, Uldolf realized that until now she had been acting.

She might have been ready to submit to Uldolf's judgment, but she wasn't about to accept the Order's. Something in him was glad for that. Should anyone be judged here, it was the armed men facing them, not her.

Was I wrong?

She moved slightly and seemed to collapse against the stake. He saw her feet move closer together, and the ropes wrapping her torso seemed to sag slightly. By her feet, Uldolf saw a few remnants of the leather straps he had used to bind her.

If she had freed herself from those bonds, why did she let them tie her to the stake? She could have escaped. What is she doing?

Uldolf looked toward the crowd, but sheets of flame, smoke, and heat obscured his view. Staring through the fire made his eyes water, and he couldn't tell if anyone had taken note of Lilly's movement. The crackling flames were so loud now that he could barely hear the Christian prayer spoken beyond them.

The four of them were isolated in their own tiny Hell—a shrinking bubble wrapped in fire.

"Pray for your own sorry souls," he heard Lilly whisper.

He turned to look in her direction.

Her head was bent forward again, but this time it was in the midst of effort, not resignation. The ropes were taut again, angled forward and down. Uldolf could see her legs bent under the burlap sheet, and he could see the cloth vibrate as the muscles underneath trembled.

She was leaning forward, against the stake.

What is she trying to do?

The whole wooden structure of the pyre groaned, the creaking wood louder than the crackling flames. Uldolf stared at her face in the firelight. Her eyes narrowed to slits, her jaw clenched, and a trickle of blood dripped from the corner of her mouth. Her nostrils flared, and the cords stood out on her neck, the veins so prominent that it seemed they might burst. Above her, the top of the stake leaned slightly. The creaking increased in volume.

He heard his mother's voice from what seemed an eternity ago, *"She's stronger than she looks."*

◈

Lilly had her forearms against the rope wrapping her as she strained forward. She pushed as hard as she could, every muscle in her body taut and trembling. She heard the rope groan, the wood creak, and felt her own muscles vibrate as if they might tear free from the bone. She tasted blood in her mouth.

She had forced her human body to the edge. Her breathing was so labored it felt as if she was already sucking flames down her throat. But the rope was way too heavy for her to break. She pushed against it with all she had—more than she had—and all she managed was to shift the wooden stake slightly forward.

But she had expected that.

When the groaning in the wood behind her reached its apex, she thought, *Now.*

◈

Uldolf watched, horrified, as the muscles in Lilly's neck suddenly began swelling and writhing. The pulsing veins grew, branching, and spidering under the darkening skin. Her cheeks lengthened and her nose flattened as her clenched teeth pushed forward, sharpening under snarling lips that thinned to invisibility.

Her shoulders broadened, and Uldolf saw claws poke through the burlap, between the ropes in front of her. Below her, the front of her feet splayed out into massive paws whose claws dug into the wood surface of the platform.

The groaning increased in volume, and Lilly jerked forward.

Someone beyond the fire shouted in German.

Two bolts erupted from the stake, near her head. One grazed her neck, the other tore through the flesh of her ear on the other side.

The whole platform shook with a massive snap, as if God himself was cracking a whip to scourge the heathens. Even the flames danced in response, rolling up with an eruption of smoke and embers. The top half of Lilly's stake toppled forward as more bolts thudded into the platform around her. Uldolf felt a pain in his shoulder and momentarily thought he had been hit by one of the bolts.

He looked down and saw that it wasn't a bolt, but a massive wood splinter, about the length of his hand, sticking out of his right shoulder. He glanced up and saw the bottom half of Lilly's stake, split and broken, with a pile of shredded burlap and leather at its base. For a few moments, he didn't see where Lilly had fallen.

Günter numbly watched the proceedings. He knew that what he felt right now was probably matched by all the Prûsan eyes focused on the flames in front of the keep. The Order had promised that a Prûsan who accepted the Christian God would be the same as any Christian; that the Church would respect a convert's life and property.

The bishop's pyre argued otherwise.

It was as if the last eight years had not happened. How many times would the Church insist on demonstrations of fealty?

Uldolf and his family weren't any less Christian than Günter was, any less than most of the Prûsans here. But the bishop was showing that baptism, and worship of the Christian God, wasn't enough.

How many of us still respect the old gods?

Uldolf himself had returned the creature to the Germans, and now he faced a horrid death for his efforts. Günter looked at the bishop next to him, who was holding Gedim's screaming daughter as he shouted a prayer in Latin. Günter, bishop, and child stood in the clearing between the pyre and the curved line of soldiers.

If this is your path to salvation, Günter thought, *then let me be damned.*

"The creature is moving!" someone shouted in German.

Günter turned to face the pyre. It was hard to see through the glare. The four stakes were rippling silhouettes behind heat and flame. But there was something happening in front, where the monster had been tied. He saw a shadow there, half crouching.

He also heard a creak underneath the crackling flames, as if a long-unused door was opening.

He heard the snap of crossbows firing from the line of soldiers behind him. He didn't see where the bolts went, but right after the first ones fired, he heard a sudden massive crash, as if the opening door had slammed shut.

The monster's stake collapsed to the platform, and the flames belched rolling smoke and embers toward the sky. Günter felt burning heat wash across his face and his eyes watered. As the flames died down, he saw that all that remained of the monster's stake was a splintered stump pointing crookedly at the sky.

The bishop stopped praying.

More bolts sailed into the flames, but Günter didn't see their target.

It's using the flames for cover. The crossbowmen can't see well enough to aim . . .

Suddenly a monstrous lupine shadow moved behind the flames. It raised a five-foot length of splintered wood above its head—the top half of the creature's stake.

The splintered log sailed out of the flames and arced over Günter, Hilde, and the bishop to slam into one of the crossbowmen, knocking him back into the crowd of Prûsans.

"Kill it!" the bishop screamed in German. "Shoot the thing."

More bolts sailed into the pyre, to what effect Günter couldn't tell.

The shadow moved behind the flames, too fast for him to follow. Günter had horrid visions of the fight in the keep. *This thing will not die . . .*

The bishop was wrong. This was not a tool of the Christian Satan, something subject to the wrath of the Christian God. This creature was serving the lord of the dead Pikuolis, come to punish the Prûsans for turning away from the old gods.

A flaming chunk of wood sailed from the pyre. It arced to Günter's right, striking another crossbowman in the side of the head. The man vanished under a shower of sparks, and his crossbow fired, the wild bolt striking another soldier in the thigh, taking him to his knees.

The Prûsan crowd swelled. German shouts came from the fringes of the mass of people. At the edge of the crowd, away from the pyre, a line of soldiers tried to keep order. They were too far away to immediately realize what was happening at the pyre. All they knew was that the mass of Prûsans were trying to escape. They didn't yet know why the Prûsans were trying to run from the pyre.

Günter stared in horror as he saw torchlight glinting off a raised German sword at that end of the crowd.

He heard Brother Erhard screaming "No!" at the Germans, but his order was already lost in the screams as the soldiers began cutting down Prûsan men, women, and children.

✦

Uldolf couldn't follow what was happening anymore. The fire was too close, the heat and smoke burning his eyes and making them water. He heard people yelling unintelligibly in German and Prûsan. He heard screams. But all he could think of now was the burning in his chest, and the heat on his skin, and the smell of burnt hair. He prayed that the smoke would asphyxiate him before the flames licked against his feet.

Then a nightmare image blocked his vision. A slavering muzzle appeared in front of his face, its breath even hotter than the air off the burning pyre. Its red fur was scorched, and the skin beneath cracked, blistered, and bloody. It looked at him with green eyes.

Lilly, if you kill me now, it would be a mercy.

The massive jaws opened and she bent down, burying her face in his chest. He felt teeth and saliva. He felt claws raking his chest. He felt the flex of her jaw muscles against his chest, and very briefly, the slither of her tongue against his stomach.

Then the ropes supporting his body gave way.

He fell forward, toward the fire, stopped only by a massive arm covered in scorched fur. She bent over him and her muzzle descended to meet his face. He felt the thing's lips against his as its teeth bit through the leather holding the wooden gag in his mouth. When the wolf's face lifted from his own, he spat out the wood. "What—"

Her face descended again, and he felt a pain in his shoulder as she bit the large splinter and pulled it free from his flesh.

Then she hugged him to her chest, smothering his face in scorched fur, and jumped. He felt the heat of the flames as they passed through. He tried to scream at her not to leave his parents, but he could barely breathe.

She let him go and he fell back against a cold stone wall, facing the pyre. The flames now reached higher than the tops of the stakes. He looked into the flames, eyes watering, trying to see his parents.

"Uldolf!" his mother called to him.

Uldolf turned and saw her sitting against the wall. His father's head rested unmoving in her lap.

"Mother?" Uldolf shook his head. Too much had happened too fast. "Is he . . ."

"His wounds are bad, but he breathes." She looked up past him, face pale.

Uldolf turned to see the wolf thing standing there. She was little more than a shadow against the pyre, half wolf and half human. He wondered where the soldiers were. He could hear swords clashing and men shouting, but it was all on the other side of the pyre from him.

"Why?" Uldolf whispered.

The monster spoke in Lilly's voice. "See to your parents."

Then she leapt away, and he lost sight of her in the glare from the pyre.

XXXII

Something sailed out of the crowd and struck Günter in the side of the head. The impact rang against his helmet and knocked him to his knees, the fire towering up ten or fifteen paces in front of him. It took a few moments for his vision to clear, and in those moments, chaos had come to reign. The mob had become a living thing, a monster worse than the wolf—a mass of peasant rags and panicked faces, pulsing and swelling. The soldiers tried to raise their weapons against it, but it was like attacking the sea.

It had only been moments since the riot started, but that had been long enough for panic to turn to rage. The space in front of the towering pyre was a shrinking circle held by the Germans. Every armed man, aside from the bishop's personal guard, faced out, trying to keep the mass of humanity back.

As Günter watched, one of the soldiers took a misstep, and dozens of hands grabbed him, dragging him into the mass. He heard the man scream as he fell into the crowd. Seconds later, Günter saw a Prûsan man raise the soldier's sword above his head and scream, *"Death to the Germans!"*

Günter looked into the face of the screaming man. Günter

knew him. A farmer with three children who Günter had never known to even raise his voice in an argument—but there he was, wild-eyed, face smeared with stripes of Christian blood, screaming like a saga warrior.

Günter looked around for the bishop and his entourage, and saw them backing through the entrance to the keep next to the towering pyre. It was the only escape route left. He heard Erhard call out, "To the keep."

Günter scrambled to his feet and ran for the doors the bishop and his men had just gone through. By the time he reached them, he was pressing through with a half-dozen other men.

"Ready the doors!" Erhard called out. He stood with his fellow knights, slowly backing toward them. Günter saw sword-waving Prûsans converging toward the small knot of knights, but the men of the Order were more disciplined than their secular comrades. They didn't falter, or allow a man to fall out of their ranks. When a hand reached to strike them, it was met with a sword.

Then Günter realized that only five men backed toward him. On the ground, somewhere in the bailey beyond the line of Prûsans, the knights had lost one of their own.

And Günter saw that the mob was growing more disciplined as well. Instead of madly rushing the knights, the way the crowd had the other soldiers, the armed Prûsans formed a ragged line in front of the knights, meeting them step for step. They knew the Christians were backing into a place with no retreat.

As the last of the soldiers fell back into the keep behind the knights, the men inside—Günter included—began pushing the doors shut. The knights stood in front of the closing doors, only slipping through one by one when the gap was barely man size. Erhard was the last through the gap, and then it became a shoving match—Günter and two dozen Christians against the mass of Prûsans outside.

The Christians had the advantage briefly because they were already braced and in position to push the siege doors shut. The gap was closed before the Prûsans were in position. The men inside held the doors while the knights dropped the massive oak timbers to bar the entrance.

They were safe.

But they were also trapped.

For a few moments after Lilly disappeared, Uldolf was convinced that guards would converge on them. But the first armed men he saw were panicked soldiers running toward the doors of the keep, about ten paces away from him. They didn't spare Uldolf a second glance; they didn't even look in the direction of the pyre.

In their midst he saw Sergeant Günter, blood streaming down the side of his face.

What's happening?

Something inside the pyre collapsed, and a hot wind blew across Uldolf. There wasn't much room between the keep and the pyre, and it wasn't safe anymore. He turned to his mother and said, "We have to get him away from here."

She nodded and helped him as he bent to pick up his father's limp body. He draped Gedim's dead weight across his shoulders. His mother tried to help him bear it, walking next to him and trying to support him, but she wasn't much better off than his father, so he didn't lean on her as much as he needed to.

A crowd had massed by the entrance to the keep. Uldolf headed in the other direction.

When they emerged from behind the towering pyre, he heard his mother gasp. It took him a few more seconds for his eyes to adjust so he could see what had shocked her.

First he saw the mass of Prûsans shouting and running toward the entrance of the keep. Many of them seemed to be armed now, and for a moment he was confused about where the weapons came from. Then he noticed that the people were jumping over obstacles that littered the ground.

Bodies.

Bodies lay on the ground, Prûsan and German, in near equal measure as far as Uldolf could tell—so many that the earth had turned muddy with blood.

Uldolf saw a familiar face in the surging crowd and called out, "Lankut!"

Lankut turned to see him, and Uldolf saw his eyes widen in shock.

"Over here!" Uldolf called, groaning under the weight.

Lankut stopped, causing another man in the crowd to slam into him broadside. Lankut dropped to one knee, and the other man kept running toward the keep.

Lankut got to his feet and held up a warning hand as he dodged through the press of his countrymen. Fortunately, the crowd was thinning and he made it over to them without any more collisions. "You're alive."

"We need help," Uldolf said. "I can't carry him myself."

Lankut nodded and lifted Gedim off of Uldolf's shoulders. He hooked his arms under Gedim's shoulders and told Uldolf, "Take his feet—" Then he glanced at Uldolf's one arm and elaborated, "Each of you, take a foot."

Once they did so they started making better time, moving Gedim away from the riot.

"What happened?" Uldolf asked. "What's happening?"

"The bastards started swinging their swords into the crowd," Lankut said. "Once that happened—"

"They just attacked?"

"God only knows what they were thinking." He shook his head. "No, I know *exactly* what they were thinking. They were looking for an insurrection. Well, they found it."

Sir Johann backed away from the door, appalled at how quickly the situation had degenerated. He had seen the damned creature moving on the pyre, and in minutes he had been fighting for his life. The Prûsans had nearly overtaken him and, worse, he had seen his squire fall into their grasp. The boy was barely old enough to grip his sword, and had panicked before the sudden raging crowd, swinging his weapon wildly before Johann could command him otherwise.

He could still hear the boy's screams as he was pulled into the mob.

Then Johann had been fighting a retreat with the knights of the Order, pressed back into the keep. Only now that the door was barred and the immediate danger had passed did Johann feel the pain in his thigh. Whatever had stabbed him had pierced the mail enough to leave a hole that drained blood down his leg to pool in his boot. He could feel it slide between his toes every time he took a step.

However, aside from a slight limp, it was nothing important.

"There are more crossbows in the armory!" Erhard called out, and he pointed at Johann. "You. Take six men to the armory. I want every embrasure on the east side of the keep manned by archers. Fire on every Prûsan holding a weapon, and anyone who appears to be in command."

"Yes, sir."

Johann surveyed the soldiers in front of him. He saw twenty-three men.

Did we lose that many?

Four of the men were knights of the Order, and those were congregated about Erhard. They would remain in command here. Another four were Prûsans who had been part of the original garrison here. Johann was not about to take them. He ran down the line, pulling men out from the remaining fifteen.

Beyond them, he heard the mob pounding outside the door. Johann smiled. Unlike those few hundred farmers, he had participated in sieges before. He knew what it took to break one, and that rabble outside didn't have it. Without supplies, command, or a plan, the mob wouldn't be able to hold out an hour—especially when crossbow bolts began raining down on them. Seven men, taking care to aim, could take out thirty or forty men in five minutes.

He led his six men up the curving staircase, toward the armory. Once on that level, they moved through a stone corridor. Torches had been taken from their sconces, leaving most of the hall in darkness. The pyre, still burning outside, cast light through the arrow slits in the embrasures along the outside wall, the light making flickering yellow crosses against the ceiling.

Johann raised his hand, halting the advance.

Ahead of them, opposite another embrasure, the armory door hung open, the light from inside casting moving shadows on the opposite wall.

Did some of the Prûsans make it in here?

Or the creature?

He gestured for silence and drew his sword. The six other men followed suit. He led them down the corridor, and ahead he could hear the movement of men and the clatter of metal.

He edged along the inside wall, toward the armory door, his men following suit behind him. He reached the edge of the door and peeked around briefly—just long enough to see two men rummaging through the armory and note their positions.

He looked back at his men, pointed at three of them, and waved them forward. Then he rushed into the room.

"In the name of God," he yelled at them in Prûsan, "lay down your arms and yield!"

The man nearest him made the mistake of turning on him with a sword raised. Johann blocked him and followed through with a blow to the neck. The blade glanced off the man's gorget, but hit with enough impact to knock him back.

The man stumbled back, coughing.

"No. Please!" the other man shouted in broken German, holding his hands spread. "We are the bishop's men."

Johann lowered his sword and looked at the two men. They still wore the bishop's colors, gold and green. "Why in the name of all that's holy would you swing a blade at me?" he yelled at the other one in German, who still clutched his neck.

"You talk the pagan tongue," the man said.

Wonderful. The Italian bastard probably didn't even understand what I said.

"Get the crossbows," he told the three who'd stormed the armory with him. The trio sheathed their swords and began gathering the weapons.

Johann looked at the bishop's men. "What do you think you're doing, raiding the armory?"

"We protect the bishop."

Johann shook his head. "Your swords are not enough?"

"The . . . creature . . ."

"I've seen what that thing can do. If it was here, you would already be dead."

"Sir Johann!" one of his men shouted.

Johann turned around to face the man. He had already grabbed three crossbows, but as Johann turned, the man dropped them and reached for his sword. The man's eyes were wide, his skin pale, and he faced the door to the armory.

Johann turned to face the doorway himself.

At first he didn't see anything but the light cast across the corridor by the lanterns in the armory. Then he glanced at the floor. In the hall, in front of the door, a slick of blood was slowly edging into the light.

XXXIII

Lilly had been following the bishop's men up the stairway in the keep. She had paused when two men ahead broke off from the others to go into a room by themselves. She waited for the other men to disappear higher into the keep, leaving the two stragglers alone.

She did not want to leave two armed men behind her as she went after Hilde. She would have to deal with them. Just when she was about to charge the room, she heard more men ascending the curved stairs behind her.

Instead of ambushing the two men, she backed herself into an embrasure between the top of the stairs and the door. She flattened herself, fur against stone, in the alcove alongside the arrow slit, in the deepest shadow next to the light shining from the pyre outside.

She watched as a knight led six men down the corridor past her.

She recognized the man. He was the man Erhard had kept from beheading her. He held a silver weapon. She looked at the other six, and saw only two other silver swords. But the others might have silver daggers and she couldn't allow them the time to use them.

They passed by her, oblivious.

She watched as four of the men rushed the room where the bishop's men had gone. The three men remaining in the hallway had swords drawn, all their attention focused on the open doorway.

She silently padded from the embrasure and behind the rearmost soldier. She grabbed his face, covering his mouth, and snapped his neck before he could even suck a breath in surprise. The man in the middle noticed something and turned toward Lilly as his comrade slid to the ground. She silenced him with her claws, gently lowering the bleeding corpse to the floor of the corridor.

The last man made the mistake of paying all his attention to what was happening inside the room. His body slid to her feet as she licked her muzzle. In a moment, her prey would realize something was wrong.

She waited in ambush, three bodies by her feet.

Lilly quietly panted, thinking, *This is what I do. This is what I've been trained for.*

Why does it feel wrong now?

From inside the room, she heard someone call out in German, "Sir Johann." She heard people move, and something crash to the ground, and she could smell fear.

A shadow moved in front of the doorway, and from inside she heard a voice call out, "No, don't—"

A man stepped out of the doorway, bearing one of the silver swords in his hand. He faced Lilly, and she snarled.

Even stinking of fear, he brought the sword to bear for an attack, stepping toward Lilly. But he was too focused on her, and didn't watch his footing. His left foot came down on the hand of his fallen comrade, throwing his stance off and giving her an opening.

She leapt, taking him down by his left shoulder. The impact carried them down the corridor, past the doorway. Her jaws clamped down and she tasted metal, leather, and smoke. He tried to bring his sword back up to ward her off, but the flat bounced off her forearm.

His back slammed into the floor and she landed with her full weight on his chest. He only managed one more weak swing in her direction before the weapon clattered to the ground and he stopped moving.

She sensed three more men advancing on her from behind, almost on her. She whipped around and jumped, not at the trio, but over them.

She was too quick for them to bring a blow to bear. They held their swords defensively, protecting their bodies, not the space above their heads. Even the knight with the silver sword moved too slowly.

They all spun to defend against an attack from the rear, but it had not been Lilly's intent to attack the three of them.

Erhard had taught her that surprise was more deadly than the wolf.

❖

It leapt directly at Johann, and he brought his sword to bear to cut into its belly as it attacked him, but he had misjudged the height. It didn't leap on him, it leapt over him. He could feel the heat of its breath on his face the moment it was above him. He smelled blood and scorched fur.

He pivoted around with his remaining two men, expecting to be attacked from behind. Instead, the beast took a bound and dove away, into the armory.

What?

A green-and-yellow-clad form sailed out of the doorway,

slamming into the opposite wall. Inside he heard the other man scream.

Then the lanterns went out, plunging the corridor into complete darkness except for the flickering crosses shining through the arrow slits.

"It's trying to blind us!" Johann called out too late. A massive shadow erupted from the darkness, passing to his right. He tried to bring his sword down on it, but it was already gone, as was the man on his right.

"Back to the wall," he called out to the other man. He fell back, and heard something strangled and wet to his left. "Do you hear me? Fall back!" He heard no answer from either man.

Something growled in the darkness. "They can't hear you anymore."

Johann's heart raced. He looked around, but all he saw were vague shadows in the darkness and the pyre burning behind the crosses of the arrow slits. He held up his sword, its silver the only ward against this thing. He pressed his back against the corridor wall and pleaded, "Get thee behind me, Satan."

"I am not Satan," whispered the thing in the darkness. A feral snarl seemed to come from every direction at once. Then, abruptly, a massive shadow eclipsed the sight of the arrow slit in front of him.

"And I am not behind you."

Johann screamed.

◈

When the screaming started, the first thing Erhard thought was, *Lilly is in here with us.*

Everyone looked toward the curving stairway, and for the moment the riot on the other side of the main door was forgotten. For close to a minute, the noise continued from up the stairs. The last voice, Erhard recognized as Sir Johann . . .

Five more men near the stairway had swords drawn and were already climbing. Erhard called to them, "Hold! Do not go up there."

"Sir?" One of them turned toward Erhard. "The bishop is up there!"

Erhard nodded. "You will stay here. I will take my brothers to rescue the bishop."

"Sir, there are only five of you—"

"Meaning there's only twelve of you to guard against a breach." Erhard looked at his brother knights. They smiled at him grimly. "And, unlike you, we know how to fight this thing."

He drew his sword and led his men up the stairs.

❖

Lilly followed the bishop's men up to a large storeroom at the top of the keep's tower. Here the stairs ended. Ahead of her was a torchlit room stacked with boxes and barrels. Large iron cauldrons sat next to large murder holes set in the floor by the exterior wall. Massive pillars supported squat vaults bearing the weight of the ceiling. About a third of the sconces along one wall held lit torches, as if the bishop's men had been in the midst of lighting them.

None of the bishop's men were in sight, but their smell was mixed with the scent of dust, dry wood, and the stench of tar and pitch.

She stayed low to the floor, slinking along behind a row of wooden crates that smelled of old canvas.

"Give me the girl," she called out to them in German, "and I will let you live."

The edge of the crate in front of her splintered as a crossbow bolt blew through to embed itself in the stones of the floor. She reached over and pulled the bolt out.

It wasn't silver.

She licked the blood off her muzzle and bared her teeth.

rhard and his brother knights gazed at the carnage outside the armory. He looked at the bodies, barely visible in the light coming through the arrow slits from the dying pyre outside. The bodies were twisted, broken, echoing every battlefield he had ever seen.

Perhaps it was the press of time, but again Lilly's violence was uncharacteristically restrained. The two men with the bishop's livery still breathed, and Johann's men had fallen with their bodies intact.

That was a bad sign. For him, Lilly had always fought like an animal, tearing her victims apart, leaving a horrid display for the survivors to reflect upon. Since her escape, she seemed to fight more and more like a soldier, attacking not for the slaughter, but to take her opponent out of the fight.

I have done this, he thought. *I taught her. I showed an animal how to fight like a man. Better than a man.*

"Gather crossbows for us," he told his men. "And silvered bolts."

One of his men carried a hooded lantern and edged the shutter open just enough to illuminate the armory itself, slightly better than the corridor.

"You know what we face," he whispered. "If you're within arm's reach, she can kill you. She's heading up after the bishop, so she will be cornered." He hefted a crossbow, pointed it down, put his foot in the stirrup, and drew back the tension. "If you see a shot, take it. Kill or disable. Keep the walls to your back so that you see her coming."

He loaded a silver-tipped bolt.

"Don't let her surprise you."

The men of the bishop's entourage were little effort. The first had been crouching to fire ineffective crossbow bolts at her. She leapt on his chest and pulled his upper torso up until she broke his spine in half.

The second swung a sword at her while standing too close to a murder hole. She dove low, biting his calf, hamstringing him, sending him screaming backward through the hole, falling five stories to the bailey below.

While she was crouched before the murder hole, the third one cut deep into her shoulder with his sword. She sensed the man approach her, but the fact these men were not armed with silver allowed her to concentrate solely on attack. And even though the blow was only about a hand's breadth from being mortal, decapitating a moving target with one stroke of a sword was a near impossible task.

He didn't get the second stroke. His head collided with one of the tar-filled cauldrons, hard enough to crack the iron and knock the lid askew with a massive clang. The lid released noxious odors from the viscous black contents. The man dropped his sword and went slack.

She heard the fourth man running toward her and raised her limp burden up between herself and the attacker. The attacker's sword glanced off the unconscious man's mail. The attacker shifted to thrust around Lilly's improvised shield, and Lilly threw the unconscious man at him.

The attacker fell backward under the deadweight and she could sense that he was the last soldier in here.

Where's the bishop? Where's Hilde?

As the man scrambled to push his comrade off of him, Lilly leapt on his sword arm, biting through his wrist. He yelled curses as he dropped his sword. Lilly didn't understand the language.

She grabbed him by the neck one-handed, and dragged him upright.

"Where is she?" she growled at him in German.

The man closed his eyes and prayed.

She held him for a moment, muzzle wrinkled in an angry snarl, shoulder itching where the latest wound knit together. She felt a horrible ache in her stomach, the smell of blood igniting a fierce hunger in her gut. The wolf was pure bloodlust now. All it wanted was to taste more of this man's warm pulsing flesh.

But the wolf was not the only part of her present.

"You think death is the worst I can give you?"

The man continued praying, and Lilly dragged him to the open cauldron. She slammed his back to the wall. His eyes flew wide and his prayer stopped with a gasp.

"Tell me!"

The man shook his head.

She hooked her claws into his belt and upended him, shoving him headfirst into the cauldron. The tar was barely liquid; the brazier heating the contents had just begun its work. Even so, she managed to shove his body in all the way to the upper torso. His legs kicked wildly, his arms flailing.

Pulling him out was more difficult. His belt pulled free and she had to take her grip on his thigh.

He came free with a sucking sound, his helmet lost somewhere in the cauldron. His body was featureless black from the chest upward. Fist-size clumps of warm tar dropped from his face. It took him several seconds of effort to even open his mouth.

She righted his body and slammed him back against the wall, his face a blank lumpy mass, his mouth a ragged hole opening in a gasping wheeze.

She stepped to the side as he choked and started raising him toward a blazing sconce set in the wall.

"Do you feel the fire yet?"

The man started screaming in Latin, Italian, and German. "No . . . Don't . . ." were the only words she could make out.

"Tell me!"

Lilly's world was focused on this one man, who knew where Hilde and the bishop had gone. Her ears filled with the man's polyglot pleading and cursing. Her nose filled with the scents of tar, pitch, and blood.

That was why she was unaware that her master had followed her here until a silver-tipped crossbow bolt tore through the left side of her back.

XXXIV

Lankut helped Uldolf and Burthe carry Gedim clear of the riot, over to the outer wall. Here they were just one of a dozen small groups tending to injured. Uldolf looked at the blocky form of the keep, solid and impenetrable.

"It's going to be a slaughter," he whispered.

Lankut brought a bucket of water and asked, "Whose?"

"All they have to do is wait everyone out. I'm surprised more of the guard hasn't come to finish us off."

"Uldolf, do you know how many guardsmen are Prûsan?" He reached down and wiped blood off Gedim's face. "There's a reason they guarded their prisoners with foreigners."

"What about Sergeant Günter?" Uldolf asked.

"Oh, him and his bootlicking—"

"Please." Burthe's voice cracked. "Have you seen Hilde? Do you know where my daughter is?"

Lankut shook his head. "I'm sorry. I was manning the gate when—"

Uldolf stood. "What is that?"

The top of the keep tower was wider than the base, the floor extending out over the tower walls supported by closely spaced wedges of stone. Between every third pair of those wedge-shaped supports there was now a square opening flickering with torch-light.

"Someone opened the murder holes," Lankut said.

"What?" Burthe asked.

"The siege defenses," Lankut explained. "So the defenders can throw stones and pour burning tar on attackers."

Uldolf shook his head. "Why aren't they just firing crossbows into the crowd?"

"I was wondering—" Lankut began.

Someone screamed by the tower. Uldolf turned his attention back up to the top of the tower. A body fell through one of the murder holes, plummeting, flailing and screaming, to slam into the bailey just behind the thickest mass of the Prûsan crowd. Before the crowd enveloped the body, Uldolf could see the tattered colors of gold and green.

"That was one of the bishop's men," Lankut said.

"The bishop had Hilde," Burthe whispered. Uldolf looked up at the top of the keep.

His sister was somewhere up there.

Did Lilly go in there?

For Hilde?

❖

Erhard led his men slowly up the cylindrical staircase. They treaded softly and slowly, twisting rightward toward the top of the keep. The route was narrow, and the stairs uneven, to give the advantage to the defenders against attackers coming from below. Even in the confined space, the five knights carried cross-bows nocked and ready to fire.

The stairwell would be a bad place for a fight. Just spacing out enough to wield their weapons meant that Erhard wasn't even in sight of the last two men following.

He led his men while leaning forward and looking up, extending his sight line as far as the slit in the hooded lantern would allow. As they reached the last few spirals of the stairway, he noticed light from above.

He waved back so the man behind him shut the lantern. The darkness closed in, but not completely. Above them he heard a massive clanging noise, followed shortly by a familiar growling voice.

"Where is she?"

By the position of the voice and the subsequent crashing and screaming, they had their opportunity. He waved the knights after him, running as quickly as they could manage up to the highest level of the keep.

"You think death is the worst I can give you?"

The few seconds it took him to run up the last two circuits of the stairway gave him time to realize why the bishop had retreated up here. He came up here to ready the siege defenses. In Erhard's opinion, the impulse was terribly premature.

"Tell me!"

They emerged from the stairs, spreading along the walls to prevent an attack from the rear. However, God was with them. Lilly was in the open, by the one section of the wall where the bishop's men had lit the sconces. She stood with her back to the knights, in all her lupine fury.

Muscles rippled in her back, her fur streaked by blood, soot, and tar. She had a man pinned, his upper body covered by black ooze, and her muzzle was wrinkled in a horrid snarl as she slammed him into the wall close to a flaming sconce.

"Do you feel the fire yet?"

Her tar-coated victim screamed a babble of languages at her.

Tell me!

His men had taken the few distracted seconds to take cover and aim. The first shot buried a bolt in Lilly's back, just above her left hip. The next was a split second later, just as she started reacting, burying itself in her back just below her right shoulder. The third and fourth bolts missed as she dodged, dropping the tar-covered man, who fell against the sconce, releasing a shower of embers. Erhard fired, and buried a bolt in her left thigh as she disappeared behind a thick stone pillar.

For a moment the only sound was the creak of the bows as the five knights recocked their weapons.

Then the bishop's man started screaming. Erhard looked away from Lilly's hiding place, and saw the tar-covered man staggering away from the wall, toward the knights. Flames licked at his head, and toxic black smoke rolled from his shoulders. He tried to beat at the fire with his hands and only succeeded in spreading the burning tar.

Erhard shook his head and leveled his crossbow at the man's head, which was already an orb of orange flame. Erhard fired, ending the man's agonized screams. The body fell over flat on the stone floor, rolling flames covering its back.

He gestured to the others, pointing along the walls of the stone room. They nodded, two going the short way toward Lilly's refuge, the other two going the long way. Then Erhard bent, putting a foot in the crossbow's stirrup to recock his weapon.

"Brother Erhard?" The familiar voice was labored, wheezing.

Erhard ignored her as he placed a bolt in his crossbow. The silver tip glittered, reflecting flames from the burning corpse in the room. Oily black smoke spread across the ceiling.

"Is your God just?"

Bolt cocked, he leveled it at the storeroom in front of him. There were piles of boxes and barrels between the stone pillars, offering some cover around the edges of the room. However, standing here by the stairs, he could cover the central area of the large room. With the others circling to flank her, the injured monster couldn't move without entering a field of fire.

He heard her cough, and he aimed the crossbow toward the sound.

His eyes watered and he wanted to cough himself. The flames from the burning corpse filled the room with the stench of tar smoke and charring flesh.

One of the pair of knights circling around the dark side of the storeroom fired at something. Erhard couldn't see them anymore. He had lost both men in the dark and the haze. He heard something crash and splinter, then everything was quiet for a moment.

He heard her cough again. "Would a just God forgive you?"

He heard one of his men in that direction cry out.

God, don't let me lose focus.

Erhard reined in his own sense of panic and braced himself to cover the open area should Lilly reveal herself.

Across the room, on the other side of the burning body, Erhard saw the other two knights moving, crossbows raised. Then he lost sight of them behind the rolling black smoke.

Erhard heard the sounds of a struggle, someone uttering a startled "Huh?" Then he heard a crossbow fire. A few seconds later, a second one fired.

Erhard thought he heard a body thudding to the ground.

They got her!

Erhard coughed. They had to find the bishop and get out. The smoke was thickening, and the flames had spread to some of the storage crates. There were barrels of tar among the stores, and when those caught it would become Hell itself up here.

He ran around to the knights. He had to follow along the wall because the fire made the central part of the room impassible. "Do you see where the bishop—"

Erhard stopped, because one of the knights lay crumpled on the ground, a crossbow bolt sticking out of his right eye. His own crossbow rested on the ground between his legs, bolt still nocked.

Erhard spun around, too late.

Ahead of him, just visible through the smoky haze, stood a naked, blood-soaked seventeen-year-old girl. She stood over another body, this one with a bolt buried deep in his throat.

"Would a just God let you live?" she said.

She held a loaded crossbow braced against a crate.

Don't let her surprise you, he thought as a bolt ripped through his chest. He dropped his crossbow as his whole body spasmed with the pain of the impact. He wheezed and his mouth filled with blood.

Erhard looked up and saw her limping toward him. She was hemorrhaging from the two massive wounds in her torso. Half her body shone slick with her own blood. She dropped the spent crossbow as she approached, kneeling unsteadily in front of him.

He tried to speak, but his throat filled with blood.

"We both serve cruel masters," she whispered, placing a hand on his cheek. "But, at least I can punish mine."

She grabbed the other side of his head and twisted until his neck snapped.

❖

Master . . .

She stared at Erhard's face as it went slack between her hands. She stared into his eyes until she felt the light go out of them, then she let him go, allowing his body to crumple on the floor.

She coughed, sending pain shooting out from the wounds in her torso. Her leg shook, and she felt light-headed. She didn't know if it was from blood loss or from the toxic black smoke rolling from the center of the storeroom.

She clutched the wound above her left hip. The bolt had passed clean through, leaving a crater in her gut next to her navel. That one was the worst. She could feel her life pulsing out through the hole. In seconds, her clenched fist was coated with her own blood.

That would be the wound that killed her, and she wondered idly if Erhard had fired the bolt that caused it. Somehow, it would be fitting if he had.

But she couldn't die yet.

"Hilde!" she yelled, tasting her own blood on her lips.

She heard nothing but crackling and hissing flames.

"Hilde!"

She could feel the skin peeling off her throat and started coughing.

Then, when her own wheezing subsided, she heard someone crying. She looked around, moving her head, trying to focus on the sound. It took her a few moments before she realized where it was coming from.

The sound came from above her.

Lilly looked around and saw it dimly through the smoke, leaning against a pillar.

A *ladder.*

❖

Mama. Papa. Ulfie. Lilly.
The four names repeated through Hilde's head over and over. Even with her eyes screwed shut, she still saw the men tossing the torches. And it was all her fault. If she hadn't talked to the man, hadn't told them Lilly's name . . .

She had been crying and screaming when the fat man grabbed her and dragged her into the castle, so she wasn't sure what was going on. When he shouted at the other men, he spoke words she didn't recognize.

The fat man half carried, and half dragged her up one twisting stairway.

"Why did you hurt Mama?" she yelled, beating at his pudgy arm with her fists. "Papa, Ulfie! Why?"

But by now she had run out of breath and her screams were mere wheezes. She was so tired that she couldn't even make him notice her fists.

They passed through a room of boxes and the other men started doing soldierly things by the walls, lighting the torches. The fat man spoke with one of the soldiers, and pointed to a ladder leading to a small hole in the ceiling. He gave Hilde to the soldier and climbed up the ladder.

When the soldier pushed her up the ladder after the fat man, she was too tired to resist. She climbed up, the soldier's rough hands pushing on her backside, until she tumbled out under the sky on top of the tower.

Once she was clear of the trapdoor, the fat man slammed a wooden door in place. He barred it, sighed, and smiled. Hilde hated that expression and, anger surging, ran up to pound on the fat man's back.

"I hate you! I hate you! I hate you!"

The man reached up and placed a hand on her chest, pushing her away from him. He said something she didn't understand. She sobbed, swinging and kicking, but he easily held her out of reach.

"Child. Stop," he finally said in real words.

She shook her head violently and managed to bite his thumb.

He shouted and pushed her away. She tumbled down on the roof and lay there sobbing. What was the use? There was nothing left of her family. "Mama," she wheezed. "Papa. Ulfie. Lilly . . ."

The man walked up to her and placed a hand gently on her head. She shrunk away, but he spoke softly. "Keep. Safe," he said.

She shook her head. The fat man was an awful creature. Why would he care about her?

He pulled a chain from around his neck, made a gesture across his chest, and kissed it. Then he dropped it around her neck. The chain was gold and heavy, and long enough that the cross on it fell onto her lap.

"Keep. Safe," he repeated, and then he took her hands and held them together in his. "Save. You."

Then he began muttering in a language she didn't understand.

She tried to back away, but the man held her too tightly. He wasn't even speaking to her anymore, he was almost chanting. His hands were clammy on hers, and sweat dripped from his brow.

He was afraid, and that scared Hilde.

She began hearing things from below. People talking, people yelling, and then people screaming. The fat man stopped chanting, scooped her up, and dragged her away from the trapdoor. She screamed, but he clamped a fat, smelly hand over her mouth. His rings bit into her lips.

She heard shouts in German, clanging, wood breaking. After a few moments someone screamed in agony. Then the screaming abruptly stopped.

Under the smell of sweat from the fat man's hand, she could smell smoke. Nasty, sticky, burning meat mixed with something evil.

She watched, wide-eyed, as wisps of smoke trailed up from the trapdoor.

They were going to burn her, too.

She renewed struggling, trying to get away from the fat man.

Then, below her, she heard someone yelling, "Hilde?"

It was Lilly's voice, but different—harsher, deeper. In her mind, Hilde could picture Lilly walking from the pyre, following her, still burning.

"Hilde?"

Hilde screamed against the fat man's hand, but all that came out were muffled sobs. She tried to bite him, but his hand was too big and he was able to hold her jaw shut.

She didn't hear Lilly's voice again and, for a few moments, Hilde thought that she had left. Then something slammed into the trapdoor.

The fat man scrambled back, all the way to the wall marking the edge of the roof.

The trapdoor vibrated with another impact, and Hilde saw splinters break from the top of the thin wooden bar holding the door shut. The fat man was chanting again.

Then the bar splintered, and the trapdoor flew open, releasing a rolling cloud of smoke.

The fat man sucked in a breath and Hilde stared, terrified, as a monster climbed out of the smoke. It had matted fur covered with blood and soot. It walked on wolf legs thicker than a man's. It had a sunken belly and a broad chest. Hilde could almost count its ribs. Its forelimbs ended in long-clawed hands, and it had the head of a starved she-wolf.

But it had Lilly's green eyes.

◈

Lilly pulled herself out of the hole. She had nothing left; she could barely hold her cadaverous wolf form upright. The only thing that kept her pulling forward was the sight of Hilde in the bishop's arms.

The man shouted something at her.

"Give her to me," she snarled at him in German.

"No!" The bishop held up a golden cross that dangled from Hilde's neck. "You can't have this child's soul."

Hilde stared at her with terrified eyes, and in her face Lilly saw Uldolf, eight years ago. She looked down at Hilde and said in Prûsan, "Don't be afraid."

Hilde shook her head violently.

"Your mother, your father, Uldolf. They're alive, waiting for you."

Lilly continued walking while the bishop shouted things in Latin, backing up until he was on top of the wall itself. When she was within reach, she took both his wrists and slowly, painfully, peeled his hands off of Hilde.

When Hilde fell from his grasp, she screamed at Lilly, jumped off the wall, and ran away across the tower roof.

The bishop spat at Lilly. "The child sees you for what you are, fiend!"

Lilly snarled.

The bishop stiffened. "I am not afraid to see God."

"Are you sure that's who's waiting for you?" She turned toward Hilde, and the bishop grabbed for her uninjured arm. She pushed him away from her, and he stumbled, falling backward over the wall.

He screamed something unintelligible on the way down.

A column of flame erupted from the trapdoor. She could feel the floor warming under her feet. It was only a matter of time before the heat from the fire cracked the stone supports and the roof caved in.

If it was only her up here, that wouldn't matter . . .

"Hilde."

"No," Hilde sobbed. "Go away."

"Please, I won't hurt you." Lilly heard a crack, and something shifted enough to make the floor vibrate. She limped around to where Hilde huddled against the wall. She reached down and stroked her back.

"No." Hilde shook. "I'm frightened."

"Shh," Lilly said as gently as the wolf could manage. "Close your eyes and listen to my voice."

"Lilly?"

"Yes."

Hilde curled into a tight little ball under Lilly's clawed half-human hand. "W-why are you so scary now?"

Another cracking and a few stones by the trapdoor caved in, blowing out sparks and flame.

"It's the only way I could save you." Lilly reached down and picked Hilde up, firing severe pain in her shoulder. She hugged the child to her chest.

"You're bleeding."

"Don't worry."

Lilly stepped up on the wall, above the bailey. Wind whipped by her, and trails of smoke bit at her eyes and nose. Hilde curled tighter as Lilly turned her back toward the drop. "I'm frightened," Hilde sobbed.

So am I.

Lilly bent her legs, tucking her chin down over Hilde's body. She started singing softly.

> *Fear not the cloak of slumber,*
> *When the sky has lost its sun,*
> *Mother will protect her child*
> *Should any nightmares come.*

Slowly, under her arms, she felt Hilde's body relax as the fear drained away.

When the roof started collapsing in front of her, she wrapped herself tightly around Hilde's body and pushed back, falling backward into the night.

XXXV

First Günter saw Sir Johann take seven men up the stairs toward the armory. Then he heard the screams, and Erhard took the last four knights of the Order upstairs.

Twelve men were left to guard the door against a breach, however improbable—four Prûsans and seven Germans. Günter stood by his countrymen, because he could feel the situation crumbling.

The collapse began sooner than he expected. The knights had barely vanished up the stairwell when one of the Germans walked up to Günter and the three men with him.

"Why didn't you come to defend the bishop?" He was one of the men who had run to the stairs as the screaming started. Blood ran down his face from a cut above his eye, and crusted the left side of his beard and mustache.

"This is the Order's castle. I follow *their* commands."

"How convenient." The knight placed a hand on the pommel of his sword.

You bastards have no idea what that thing is. What it can do.

"Nothing to say, Sergeant?"

"I don't answer to you," Günter said.

The man looked back at the mass of men behind him. The others started stepping up to face the quartet of Prûsans.

"From what I've seen here, the Prûsans don't answer to anyone."

Günter shook his head. "You don't want to do this."

"Was that a threat?" The man slid his weapon out of its sheath. Suddenly the air rang with the sound of liberated steel as everyone, German and Prûsan, drew his weapon.

The man smiled at the four Prûsans who faced him. "Sergeant, you should back down. We outnumber you two to one."

"That's almost even," Günter said.

The air resonated with a crash as their blades met.

❖

Smoke!" someone yelled. Uldolf looked up from his father. Wisps were trailing from the arrow slits at the top of the tower, the smoke gray-black against a deep purple sky, underlit by the diminishing pyre. Under the walls, where the murder holes were still open, the light was different—redder, fiercer, more unstable.

Lankut muttered, "The stores are burning."

Uldolf nodded.

"What's happening up there?" Lankut asked.

Uldolf suspected what was happening. He had seen it before. Lilly, or the monstrous thing Lilly became, was loose in the keep with the Germans. She was doing to them what she had done to the stronghold of Mejdân, rending her former masters the way she had destroyed the pagans.

The way she had destroyed his family.

Uldolf felt his shoulder and stared at the keep. It was too easy for him to picture what was happening in there. He had seen it, and the freshly returned memory festered in his mind's eye as if it had just happened.

She had killed everything he had ever loved.

But now . . .

Suddenly, a pillar of smoke curled up from the roof of the tower. The base of the column was bright, as if the fire had found its way out. Then a shadow moved on top of the wall, in front of the column of smoke.

"The bishop!" Lankut whispered.

The shadow tipped over the wall and tumbled out into space. Uldolf watched the long fur-lined robes flap in the wind like ineffective wings. The man slammed solidly into the ground.

Back above the tower, the smoke column was now rooted in a plainly visible tongue of flame. The whole keep now had the appearance of a gigantic candle.

On the edge of the roof, a figure climbed onto the top of the wall.

Lilly.

The *thing* that was Lilly.

Even from this distance, the silhouette was obviously inhuman, with wolf legs, a tail, and a lupine profile. In its semihuman arms it carried a small bundle . . .

Oh, no . . .

"Hilde!" his mother shouted before he could think it. "*It has Hilde!*" His mother's voice sliced through him. Uldolf was running for the tower before it became clear what Lilly was doing.

More sparks and flame erupted from the top of the tower as he ran, and Lilly turned around to face the conflagration.

Just as Uldolf reached the edge of the keep below them, the top of the tower belched a crashing roar of smoke and fire. Stone crumbled above with such force that Uldolf could feel the impact in the ground beneath him.

And, above him, Lilly fell backward.

Uldolf stared straight up and saw the monster's fur-covered back topple toward him. He screamed up at them. "Hilde! Lilly!"

Then Lankut was pushing him aside, barely in time. Lilly's back slammed into the ground right where he had been standing. Uldolf felt something warm and wet splash his face.

He shoved Lankut away and ran up to Lilly's body.

Blood poured from her ears, nose, and mouth. Her legs and neck were horribly twisted, and as he watched, her body seemed to shrivel in on itself, face collapsing inward, limbs shortening, fur fading. In seconds, the body was human.

Her bony arms fell away, revealing a form curled on her chest in a fetal position. Uldolf reached for Hilde and heard her sobbing.

"You're alive!" He pulled Hilde off Lilly's body and held her.

Hilde buried her face in his neck. "Ulfie!"

Uldolf looked down at the broken body at his feet. "She saved you," he whispered.

You killed everything I loved . . .

You saved everything I love . . .

"Lilly's hurt," Hilde said into his neck.

He patted her back and whispered, "I know."

A cheer went up in the crowd about a hundred paces away. Uldolf looked in that direction and saw the doors of the keep opening. Standing in the entry, Uldolf thought he saw Sergeant Günter.

"I guess he took sides," Lankut said.

Uldolf nodded and looked down at Lilly's unmoving body. *So did she.*

Coda

Anno Domini 1239

Six months later, during the fall harvest, Uldolf returned to the newly renamed town of Mejdân, carrying elk hides from a tannery outside town. The tannery's stink still hung on the hides, in Uldolf's nose, and probably his clothes as well. The putrid combination of urine, dung, and rotting flesh was the primary reason retrieving the freshly tanned skins was work for the leatherworker's apprentice.

The old man he was apprenticed to was a Prûsan who claimed to have known his father, Radwen. It was an increasingly common claim. As more Prûsans moved in, retreating from more recently Christianized areas, it was becoming fashionable to acknowledge the past.

Uldolf reached the city gate and Lankut called from his post, "So, Uldolf, what do you have there?"

One thing hasn't changed . . .

"Fresh tanned hides for Master Ryliko." Uldolf hefted his bundle. "Care to inspect them?"

Lankut walked over, coughed, and shook his head. "I doubt Chief Sejod cares for tribute from you, of all people." He wrinkled his nose. "And you stink to high heaven."

"If you think that, you should meet the tanners themselves."

"Thank you, no."

"And what do you mean, 'you of all people'?"

"You're still Radwen Seigson's son."

Uldolf sighed.

"Look, don't forget that. There are plenty of people, old-timers, who think you should be running things."

"Günter is doing a fine job without Radwen Seigson's son."

Ever since the Germans were driven out of the town, once-Sergeant Günter Sejod had managed to hold things together, largely based on the fact that he was the highest ranking Prûsan under the Christian occupation. The chain of command among the Prûsan soldiers remained intact.

The old-timers Lankut talked about were dissatisfied by the fact that someone who, in their view, had been a German puppet was now chief of Mejdân. Ever since Uldolf had begun working in town, barely a week passed without one of these men approaching him and talking about the grand days of Reiks Radwen Seigson, mentioning the current opportunity to reclaim them. Of course, these old men often saw themselves as having some important role supporting Uldolf, should he make any claims to his rightful position. Uldolf thanked gods both Christian and Prûsan that those old men had no power base of their own to be more forceful in their suggestions.

"If ever you change your mind," Lankut said, "remember your friends."

"I will." Uldolf walked through the gate wondering if Lankut was just teasing him.

"Gedim's waiting for you," Lankut called after him.

Uldolf paused. Master Ryliko's shop squatted just inside the city gate. And when Uldolf stopped, he had already walked in far enough to see the front of the old man's shop.

His father stood outside the shop, leaning on his cane, and waved at Uldolf. "There you are."

Uldolf walked over and set down his burden inside the doorway. "Here I am."

"You look well."

Uldolf nodded. "How is the farm?"

"The harvest goes well."

"Good."

"We miss you there."

Uldolf nodded. "You know why."

"Yes. I understand." He put a hand on Uldolf's shoulder. "And you had to make your way sooner or later."

Uldolf looked down at the leather bundle, feeling a wave of guilt. "I didn't want to force you to—"

"Look at me."

Uldolf looked up.

"I told you, this had to happen sooner or later. I only had an independent farm because I was tied to the past, a little sliver of an estate the Order let me keep. After everything, the land doesn't seem that important anymore."

Uldolf shook his head. Because he left—because he *had* to leave—Gedim had to negotiate with three neighboring farms. The three families now farmed all the land in common, sharing the crop and the labor. "It was everything you had."

"You, Hilde, my wife—*that's* everything I had. Still have. The land . . ." Gedim shrugged. "I know why you couldn't stay."

Uldolf sighed. "You're not here to ask me back?"

"No. But I'm asking you to talk to her."

"I can't do that." Uldolf bent to pick up his bundle, and Gedim grabbed his arm.

"Yes, you can."

"Please, don't."

"I'm the one who carried you out of that slaughterhouse when Mejdân fell. My brother, his wife, my niece. I saw. I understand."

"Father—"

"If you don't do it for yourself, then do it for me."

Uldolf looked into his father's face, and realized that it was more deeply lined than he remembered. He saw a pleading look in Gedim's eyes.

Uldolf asked him, "You brought her here, didn't you?"

Gedim nodded.

"Why?"

"Because I asked him to." Her voice came from the shadows inside the shop. Uldolf straightened up and watched as a young woman stepped out into the light. Her hair was red, except for a single white streak emerging from her temple, and she looked at him with deep green eyes.

"Would you please walk with me?" Lilly asked.

◈

Uldolf followed her down the road, out the gate, and into the woods. "You seem well."

"Your mother took good care of me," Lilly said. She shook her head. "I didn't expect to live."

No one expected you to, Uldolf thought. He remembered his shock when Lankut announced that she was still breathing. Even as his mother organized a wagon to move the injured away from the chaos that was the fall of Johannisburg, Uldolf kept expecting that life had fled Lilly's broken body.

But she had hung on.

She had hung on, and Burthe had insisted on taking her back home. Even though they knew what she was, and what she had done. Not only was this someone they had already taken into their home, but all of them owed their lives to her. Uldolf was silent for weeks afterward, as she lay unconscious and healing in his family's home.

When Gedim told him that he was considering easing the harvest by joining his land with the two neighboring farms, Uldolf decided to find his apprenticeship in town. He had left before Lilly had recovered enough strength to speak.

He didn't know if he left because he couldn't face her, or because he couldn't face his father. Uldolf still had trouble understanding how Gedim could reconcile her nature, and her past, more easily than he could. Gedim's loss at her hands was as deep as Uldolf's own. He had lost his brother . . .

Why was it so hard to accept when Gedim said, "She was a warrior." Was it because Uldolf could see Radwen Seigson saying the same thing? *She was a warrior, son. In war, people die.*

"I didn't want to drive you from your home," she told him as they walked through the woods.

Uldolf shook his head. "My father must have told you. It was going to happen eventually."

"But it was because of me."

Because I didn't want to face you, or because I didn't want to face my feelings for you?

"My mother was right to take you in."

"Even if it hurt you?"

Uldolf walked off ahead, staring up at the orange-red leaves. A chill was already in the air, and he could feel the first bite of winter when he took a deep breath. After several moments of silence, he said, "Why are you here?"

"I wanted to see this place with you, one last time."

Uldolf lowered his gaze. He had been so wrapped up in his own discomfort that he hadn't realized where she had been leading him. There was the pool, reflecting the blazing orange canopy. There was the mossy boulder next to the creek, and there was the oak, the claw marks dried and healing.

He stared at the wounds on the oak. The marks were permanent, but the tree itself lived on, scars covered by new bark. The canopy was as broad as ever, the leaves as vibrant, the branches just as inviting for a child who wanted to climb.

"You came here to find me, didn't you?"

"I was so confused, Uldolf. I don't even know if I can put it into words. The girl you found here, she was a part of myself I had locked away. For a long time I thought she had died."

Uldolf felt the socket where his arm used to be. For the first time he thought back to Mejdân, his first parents, and he remembered clearly without the gasping panic that had plagued him for years. Instead, his thoughts were colored only by a deep sadness.

"I fell in love with you here," she whispered.

"I—"

"I know you can never forgive me," Lilly said. "You gave me the happiest moments of my life, and all I've ever given you is pain."

He placed his hand on her shoulder. "Don't, please—"

She sniffed and turned to look at Uldolf. Tears streamed down her cheeks. "I don't want you to hurt anymore. I brought you this."

In her hand she held a silver dagger by the blade, hilt toward him. He stared at it, and for a moment the only sound was the leaves rustling above them.

"Take it," she whispered.

❖

She held the handle of the dagger toward him, her pulse thundering in her ears. She could still see the anger in his face, the grief and loss etched there.

He took the dagger from her, holding the handle so the blade glittered between them. She steeled herself, drawing herself upright and facing him. Uldolf deserved this, and she deserved to atone for what she had done—for what she had done to everyone, but to him most of all.

Besides, she no longer wanted a life that didn't include him.

The blade shook in his hand, and she stared at the wicked edge. She wanted to close her eyes as he drew back the weapon, but she had spent the last eight years turning away from her life, turning away from what she had done to him. She would not do that now. She refused to allow herself to flinch from her fate as Uldolf thrust with the dagger.

He is not a brutal man, she thought as the blade slashed forward. *He will make it quick.*

But he didn't swing it anywhere near her, he swung it over his head and, to her astonishment, he let it go. It tumbled through the air in a lopsided spin over the lake. She watched it twist in the air, arc downward, and finally cut into the water with a splash.

Ripples tore through the mirror surface of the water, breaking everything into fragments. She stared at the ripples, not daring to breathe.

She felt his hand on her shoulder, spinning her around to face him.

"You think I want that?" he shouted at her.

"U-Ulfie?"

"I thought you were dead! Because of me! For a month, I woke every day afraid that Mother would tell me you had slipped away during the night." He shook her. "I don't want to lose anyone else!"

Lilly stared at him dumbstruck.

"It has been eight years, and I can only now think about what happened without crumbling under the grief— I keep asking myself how could I forgive anyone that?"

"I am so sorry, Ulfie." She reached up and touched his cheek.

"And . . ." his voice lowered to almost a whisper, "how can I repay you? For Gedim, Burthe, Hilde?" He reached up and took her hand in his own. "It's as if the gods, in their cruelty, decided to settle accounts with equal measure of flesh and bone."

He bent down and, very tenderly, kissed her.

Lilly embraced him, pulling her to him, her heart racing.

He stroked her hair and whispered, "I still love you."

"B-but you left," Lilly whispered.

He pulled away from her and shook his head. "I didn't want to lose you."

Lilly opened her mouth and Uldolf laid a finger on it.

"You survived. I convinced myself that was enough. But I didn't think I could look at you and not see past the thing that tore my life apart. I didn't believe I was strong enough to love you, as wounded as I was."

As we both were, Lilly thought.

Uldolf lowered his hand and walked over to the edge of the water. The ripples had finally ebbed, and the surface was as smooth and as motionless as a stone. Lilly walked up next to him and saw their reflections in the water.

Uldolf muttered something and Lilly felt as if her heart had fallen out of her chest. Her legs suddenly felt weak, and it was hard for her to breathe. She wasn't sure if she had heard him correctly.

"What did you say?" she asked him.

When he had looked into her eyes as she handed him the dagger, he had found the strength. She had punished herself enough. She had nearly perished to save his present family, and she had still stood before him offering her life.

Standing next to her, staring into the still water, Uldolf spoke the three hardest words he had ever had to say.

"I forgive you."

She grabbed him, turning him to face her. She was shaking her head, her intense green eyes shiny and wide with disbelief. "What did you say?"

"I forgive you." The second time, it was easier to say, especially when he saw the weight lift off of her face. With it, he felt a weight lift off his own heart.

He pulled her close and said it again.

"I forgive you."

◈

For so long she had run away from the past, run away from what she was, what she had been, that it was inconceivable that anyone could care for her, love her. Even her master had turned from her in the end.

But Uldolf held her now. After everything, he accepted her. After everything, he loved her.

He gave her something she could never have asked him for.

Hope.

ABOUT THE AUTHOR

According to the author, "I went to college at Cleveland State University to study mechanical engineering, but I dropped out when I sold my first novel. Since then, I've had a variety of day jobs including working as a lab assistant, doing cost accounting, managing health benefits for retired steelworkers, and most recently managing a database at a large child welfare agency. In the same time I've written almost twenty novels under various names, of which I think *Wolfbreed* is my best work."

S. A. Swann grew up and still lives in northeastern Ohio, along with three cats, two dogs, a pair of goats, a horse, and one overworked spouse.

Lilly lived a life of lies,
hiding her wolfbreed nature from those she loved.

But what if you were wolfbreed
and didn't even know it. . . .

In 1343, Poland is a newly reunited kingdom enjoying a tenuously brokered peace with the monastic state in conquered Prussia. Maria, a young woman of low station, lives a quiet life, except for the unwanted advances of a crude soldier and her father's frantic insistence that she never remove the silver cross that hangs around her neck.

But Maria's blood holds a terrible secret, one that will leave her torn between the injured Teutonic knight she's caring for and the savage male wolfbreed who is the cause of the knight's wounds.

A secret that will change her life forever.

Make sure to read the next WOLFBREED novel

WOLF'S CROSS

from S. A. Swann

A BALLANTINE SPECTRA BOOK

FALL 2010